Praise

"Mr. Lovegrove is one of the best writers out there... Highly, highly recommended."
– *The Fantasy Book Critic* on *The Age of Ra*

"Lovegrove's bluntness about the gods' Jerry Springer-like repugnance refreshingly reflects the myths as they must appear to modern eyes."
– *Strange Horizons Magazine* on *The Age of Ra*

"One of the UK SF scene's most interesting, challenging and adventurous authors."
– Saxon Bullock, *SFX* on *The Age of Ra*

"A compulsive, breakneck read by a master of the craft, with stunning action sequences and acute character observations. This is the kind of complex, action-oriented SF Dan Brown would write if Dan Brown could write."
– Eric Brown, *The Guardian* on *The Age of Zeus*

"The action is just unbelievably good."
– *The Fantasy Book Critic* on *The Age of Zeus*

"The reader feels as if they are right there accomplishing something along with our heroes... You definitely feel like you got your money's worth."
– *Sci-Fi & Fantasy Review* on *The Age of Zeus*

AGE OF VOODOO

AGE OF VOODOO

JAMES LOVEGROVE

SOLARIS

Peterborough City Council	
60000 0000 97138	
Askews & Holts	Mar-2013
SF	£7.99

www.solarisbooks.com

ISBN: 978 1 78108 085 6

10 9 8 7 6 5 4 3 2 1

A CIP catalogue record for this book is available from the
British Library.

Designed & typeset by Rebellion Publishing

Printed in the UK by CPI Group (UK) Croydon, CR0 4YY

PROLOGUE

"Holy. Fucking. Christ."

The Secretary of Defence rubbed his eyes, as though he might be able to wipe them clean. On the monitor in front of him was an image, paused, blurred, a pale figure in motion like a phantom in mid-flight. He had just finished watching the harrowing footage for a fourth time.

His office in the outermost of the Pentagon's concentric layers, the E-ring, had a view looking across the river and the greenery of West Potomac Park all the way to the Washington Monument, which lanced upward, a white dagger stabbing the heavens. It was a beautiful summer's afternoon in DC. Out there, on the other side of the tempered blast-resistant glass, the world was sunlit, bright, normal. In here, not so much.

Grimly, the Secretary of Defence reached for the phone and pressed for an internal extension.

"Sir."

"General."

"Let me take a wild guess what this is about." The Chairman of the Joint Chiefs of Staff had a grizzled voice, as raspy as the bristles of his razored haircut. "Anger Reef."

"Precisely."

"What a goddamn fiasco. Those were good men. What happened to them... Well, I'm not sure what happened to them. But I think we can safely assume the worst."

"Agreed," said the Secretary of Defence.

"That damn Seidelmann creep. I'll say it now, for the record. I never did trust him. What the hell was he up to anyway?"

"You read the same briefings I did."

"Yes, but what I meant was, how did we let it get so far? So out of control? Why wasn't there greater oversight?"

"We gave him free rein. We trusted him."

"And look where it's got us. Those poor bastards killed. The whole project FUBAR. Someone's head should roll over this."

"Now's not the time for the blame game. We need to consider options. Airstrike?"

"Conventional bombardment won't work," said the Chairman of the Joint Chiefs. "Even a MOAB hasn't got the penetrating power. Way that place was built, so far underground, all that concrete, nothing short of a tactical nuke would make a dent. I don't suppose...?" His tone was faintly, disquietingly hopeful.

"We'll table that one for the moment, general. In case of need. Although, given Anger Reef's history, it may prove to be a moot point. Can I tell you what I think?"

"Of course."

"As a matter of fact, it's not just me. Langley's had its analysts going over the footage with a fine-tooth comb. Consensus is, this is a grey-ops scenario."

"In other words, Team Thirteen territory. Yeah. Yeah, I can see that. There's a problem, though. Those guys have just run a half-dozen missions straight, back-to-back. Right now they're somewhere over the Bering Sea, inbound from Siberia, where, by all accounts, they did not have a fun time. They're exhausted and they deserve a furlough. They've been flat-out since May. World seems to have gone nuts this summer. More nuts than usual."

"Still, the CIA figure they're our best bet," said the Secretary of Defence. "This is their kind of situation. And seeing as the matter is time-sensitive and of the highest priority..."

"No rest for the wicked," sighed the Chairman of the Joint Chiefs. "I'll make the call to the Special Activities Division, confirming Thirteen are available."

"The Agency has one other recommendation."

"And that is?"

"We bring in some sort of local liaison. Someone who knows the lie of the land and might be able to provide relevant intel."

"Okay. Yeah."

"Do you know of anyone?"

The Chairman of the Joint Chiefs hummed in thought. "There is one guy I can think of, off the top of my head. A Brit. One-time covert wetwork operative."

"Ugh."

"Retired now. Inactive. He seems to have made contacts in the region. Well embedded."

"You know him personally?"

"He's worked with the military on a couple of occasions."

"So he could be persuaded to participate?"

"It's worth a shot. He has dual US/UK nationality, so technically he's one of us. Under the circumstances, he's the right man for the job. Certainly the best we can hope for at such short notice."

"All right then. Get a hold of him. Thank you, general."

The Secretary of Defence replaced the phone handset and returned his attention to the monitor on his desk. He rewound the footage part of the way, his hand trembling ever so slightly as it manipulated the mouse. Once again he watched the final hellish three minutes, the death throes of a mission gone badly wrong.

Men running. Men screaming. Semi-naked figures lurching at them in the shimmering green phosphorescence of image intensification. Gunshots rippling near and far.

One commando yelling, "What the fuck—what the Jesus fuck are they? They're taking hits; they just won't fucking go down!"

Another: "They're coming from all sides. God help us, they're everywhere!"

A third, to his commanding officer: "Sir! Sir! What are our orders? What do we do?"

Distantly, a man sobbing, crying for his mother, and another man intoning the Lord's Prayer.

And then a figure lumbers towards the commando whose helmet camera is recording the chaos, and there is a final, shrill, hideous scream, abruptly cut short.

In the silence that ensues, a voice can be heard, elated, triumphal.

"Bondye! Bondye! Hear me, Bondye. I am coming for you."

The clip vaporised into a hissing burst of screen static and white noise, and the Secretary of Defence spun his chair away from the desk. An American Airlines 747 was coasting in to land at Ronald Reagan airport. The sky was boundless and blue. A city of half a million people—hell, a planet of seven billion people—and none of them had a clue what was going on down in the Caribbean, a thousand miles due south. Not a fucking clue.

It was up to Team Thirteen to ensure things stayed that way.

ONE
POSH BOYS

TROUBLE DIDN'T COME knocking often at Wilberforce's Rum Shack, and when it did, it was never anything Lex Dove couldn't handle. Usually it could be dealt with using just stern words and a bit of eyeballing; sometimes, however, more was called for.

Case in point on this Friday evening: a trio of drunk posh boys. On holiday from England. Probably their first time abroad without mater and pater. Nobody to keep an eye on them and keep them in line.

They were big and brawny, in that well-fed, upper-class way. Shoulders broadened by rugby and rowing. And they thought they were something special, with all that paid-for education filling their heads and that trust fund money filling their pockets.

At first they just behaved rowdily, and it was safe to ignore them and hope they'd eventually leave of their own accord.

But after downing several of Wilberforce's patented rum roundhouses—'stronger than just any old rum punch,' as the drinks menu put it—the three posh boys became lairy and obnoxious. They began braying crude personal insults at the tops of their voices, at one another and at the other customers.

They made disparaging remarks about the state of Wilberforce's shack, which admittedly was in need of some upkeep but wasn't nearly as much of a health hazard as they made out.

One of them then started hitting on an islander girl, trying to chat her up by bragging about his parents' ski chalet in Val d'Isère and the job his father was going to get him in September with a hedge fund firm. The girl kept shying away from him, but she was too polite and well brought up to do what she needed to, which was tell him to fuck off and leave her alone.

That was when Lex intervened. He looked to Wilberforce for consent first, and got a nod. Wilberforce, behind the bar, made an air-patting gesture: *take it easy, man, don't go too far.*

Lex moved between the posh boy and the islander girl.

"Listen," he said to the boy. "I think you've had enough to drink. And I know the lady here has had enough of you. How about you and your mates call it a night, eh? Go back to your hotel, get some sleep, start over tomorrow. Okay?"

Posh Boy fixed him with a bleary, malevolent glare. "And just who the fuck are you?"

"Does it matter?" said Lex. "A bystander. Someone who wants a quiet Friday-night drink and no trouble." He laid a light but distinct emphasis on the last two words.

"Oh, yeah?" slurred Posh Boy. "Well, Mr Bystander, stop sticking your nose into other people's business. This has nothing to do with you. This is between me and her." He pointed at the girl with the hand that was holding his drink; rum roundhouse slopped onto her skirt, but he didn't notice. "She happens to be very interested in me, and later tonight she's going to give me the best blowjob ever. You can tell by looking at her. She's got that kind of mouth."

The girl gasped in dismay.

"So," Posh Boy went on, "I'd be very much obliged if you'd fuck off out of it."

"Yah," said one of his friends, taking up position behind him. "You tell him, Timbo." To Lex: "Timbo does martial arts. Karate and a bit of, whatchemacall, june keet do. Is that right?"

"Jeet kune do," said Timbo.

"Yah," said Posh Boy #2. "So you'd better not mess with him. He can kick your scrawny arse."

Conversation at the rum shack had trickled almost to a halt. Only the reggae on the stereo was continuing as loudly as before—Bob Marley and The Wailers, 'Fussing And Fighting.' Everyone was monitoring the confrontation, keen to see how it played out.

"I said I don't want trouble," said Lex, keeping his voice low and calm. "I'd like it if you—all three of you—would simply go elsewhere and stop bothering us. This is my favourite drinking place on the whole island, I come here most evenings. Is it too much to ask that I and all the other customers here are able to enjoy our cocktails and the beach and the night air in peace?"

Timbo balled a fist.

Posh Boy #2 encouraged him with a clap on the shoulder. "Right behind you, Timbo. You show the little fucker what's what."

"Don't do this," Lex said. Not a plea. Just sound advice.

Which Timbo didn't take.

He swung a punch, and to his credit it wasn't a bad punch. There was some bodyweight behind it, and he kept his forearm straight, wrist solidly locked. If it had connected with Lex's nose, as it was intended to, the blow would have done some damage.

Lex, however, ducked under it as though Timbo was delivering it in slow motion. At the same time his hand came up, fingers rigid, and chopped like a knife into the side of Timbo's neck, just below the jaw. The blow struck the mastoid process, the rounded projection of bone at the base of the skull. Had it been delivered at full strength, it would have killed Timbo outright, but Lex gauged it so that the boy was merely stunned. Timbo's brain went into shock, and he reeled and sank to the sand.

Posh Boy #2 looked astonished for a moment—outraged—and then he smashed his glass against the edge of a table and stabbed the jagged remains at Lex's face.

He was even more astonished to find himself on his knees with the broken glass crushed in his hand, shards embedded in his palm and fingers. He started howling in pain.

Posh Boy #3 now joined in, incensed that his two friends had been so easily bested by this ghastly jumped-up little prole. It was not the natural order of things. Status and breeding triumphed every time. That was what he'd been brought up to believe. That was the proper way.

He lunged at Lex, rugby-tackling him round the waist. Together they crashed into a table, a flimsy trestle-type affair; it collapsed under them and they sprawled on the ground.

Lex was irritated by this. Sand got down the collar of his shirt. He hated sand getting down his shirt.

He threw Posh Boy #3 off him, almost without effort even though the lad weighed a good thirteen stone, rolled over and straddled him, and swiftly rendered him insensible with a rapid one-two-three to the temples. He stood up and shook his shirt out.

Timbo was just this side of conscious. Posh Boy #2 keened and wailed over his injured hand. Posh Boy #3 was silent, out cold.

Wilberforce shook his head sadly. "My table, Lex. You wrecked it. Those things cost money."

"Not that much," said Lex. "Besides, *I* didn't wreck it. He did." He indicated Posh Boy #3. "So he can pay for it."

A quick search of the boy's pockets unearthed a wallet stuffed with currency—dollars, both US and Manzanillan. Lex fished out enough of the latter to buy a new table and also a round of drinks for everyone, which seemed only fair.

THE POSH BOYS slunk off along the beach, sheepish and sobered. Timbo had recovered enough that he and Posh Boy #2 were able to drag Posh Boy #3 between them, although he was clearly in a great deal of pain and Lex predicted he would have a dire headache for the next couple of days. Over his shoulder Posh Boy #2 muttered about calling the police and getting Daddy's lawyers to sue, but Lex brushed aside the threats. The three of them knew they'd been lucky to get off as lightly as they had. They wouldn't stir things up any further. It was a humiliating incident they would rather forget than have to explain to others and account for.

"One thing's for sure," said Wilberforce. "They won't be coming back to Manzanilla any time soon. And good riddance, I say. We're better off without them."

"No argument here," said Lex, settling himself back on his usual stool at the bar. "If you ask me, this island started going to the dogs the day they started letting tourists in."

"Not just tourists, white folk." Wilberforce looked pointedly at Lex.

Lex frowned, then tapped his chest. "Ohhh," he said disingenuously. "Oh, I see. That's a dig at me, is it?"

"Been downhill all the way since you came, Lex," Wilberforce said with a grin. "Used to be this was a respectable country. Law-abiding. Then you turn up, and..." He sucked his teeth in disapproval.

"Respectable? Law-abiding?" Lex snorted. "Manzanilla was a shithole. It's been a shithole as long as anyone can remember. In the olden days it was teeming with pirates, whores and runaway slaves, and you could get your throat slit in any dockside tavern just for looking the wrong way at someone's pint of grog. Nobody wanted it for a colony. The Spanish gave it to the French—didn't surrender it or anything, *gave* it like an unwanted Christmas sweater—and the French passed it on to the British with barely a murmur, and when you finally asked for independence from us in 1968, did you have to fight for it? No. We let you have it. Couldn't have been happier about it. The Wilson government virtually begged to be shot of the place. I think the governor at the time said something like, 'If the Manzanillans want to run their country themselves, they're welcome to. I certainly can't.'"

"And now," said Wilberforce, his grin widening, "now it's a damn paradise."

It wasn't, not really. Manzanilla remained a speck in the middle of the ocean, more or less equidistant between Cuba and Haiti. It had a few beaches, but none that could compare with the sweeping white strands of Barbados or Antigua. It had mountains and rainforest, but not on the scale of Martinique or Tobago. It grew sugarcane and pineapples, but was too small and remote to compete as an agricultural exporter.

Up until five years ago, in fact, Manzanilla had been the forgotten Caribbean island, the one few people had ever heard of. Tourists seldom came, and if they did, the conditions at the island's only hotel, the inaptly named Grand, deterred them from ever returning.

Added to that, most of the coastline was a no-go zone back then, thanks to a combination of dense mangrove swamp and, worse, thick outcrops of manchineel tree. The manchineel, with its poisonous fruit and toxic sap, formed a shaggy defensive ring around the island's perimeter. The tree was so hazardous to human health that it was unwise even to stand under one for shelter during a storm. Drops of rainwater made caustic by contact with the bark and leaves could burn your skin. Manzanilla took its name from the Spanish for manchineel— *manzanilla de la muerte*, 'little apple of death'—and seemed destined to be forever defined by this noisome arboreal guardian, until the government instituted a programme of felling and burning and cleared the entire island of manchineels in under a year.

At a stroke, Manzanilla was open for business.

Hotels and an airport were built. Tourists flocked in their droves. Jet-ski, windsurfer and scuba hire companies sprang up. The local economy boomed. From pariah destination, Manzanilla was suddenly 'the undiscovered gem of the West

Indies,' 'the new hot place to go,' 'the island everyone's talking about,'"and tour operators were doing a roaring trade in package deals for people who liked to think they were both hip and not entirely without a sense of adventure.

Manzanilla today was not the Manzanilla that Lex had adopted as his homeland seven years ago, nor the Manzanilla on which Wilberforce had been born thirty-two years ago. And if anything, incomer Lex was less pleased about the change than native Wilberforce was.

"Yes, paradise," Wilberforce repeated, and he wasn't being ironic. Wilberforce was doing okay out of Manzanilla's rise in the world. Holidaymakers liked to drink, and Wilberforce's Rum Shack prospered.

And he had dreams. Ambitions.

The photo of a forty-two-foot Sealine F-series flybridge sports cruiser tacked up behind the bar was testament to that.

Fishing expeditions. Wealthy white westerners keen on catching marlin and tarpon out at sea.

There was big money to be made there. And one day soon, when he had saved up enough for a down payment on the boat, Wilberforce would be making it.

Wilberforce blew the picture a kiss, as was his wont, and ambled off to take an order from a newly arrived couple.

Lex, meanwhile, hunched over his rum sour, stirring the swizzle stick aimlessly round and round. At times like this, in the aftermath of violence, he tried not to think about anything. His life now. His former life. The man he had once been and the man he was striving his hardest to become. He tried not to think at all.

Then his phone went off in his pocket.

The caller's voice was one he hadn't heard in years.

One he had hoped never to hear again.

TWO

SERAPHINA

"Lex."

"Jesus Christ."

"Lex, Dove."

"Yeah."

"That's what you're calling yourself these days, right?"

Those soft, husky tones. Those neutral, accentless cadences. That beguiling touch of primness.

"Seraphina," he said.

It wasn't her real name, any more than Lex Dove was his. He had never known her real name, or cared to know. Seraphina had been his link to his former paymasters, the sole point of contact between them and him, nothing more than that, nothing less.

But, oh, hearing her speak, it was as though the years hadn't passed. As though Lex had never quit the dark, clandestine world he used to inhabit. As though he hadn't managed to put a wedge of time and distance between past and present.

He stood up and strode away from the rum shack, away from the music and the glow of the overhanging fairy lights and Chinese lanterns. He went to where the surf ruffled the shore, surging and effervescing like champagne. The moon was a shaving of gold. The stars bristled. His legs were trembling. Phone to ear, he exhaled heavily to steady himself.

"How did you find me?"

"Wasn't hard," said Seraphina. "We've known where you are for some time now."

"Been keeping tabs?"

"Why would we? You made it very clear you were out of the game. We were willing to respect your wishes."

"But still..."

"But still, we'd be remiss in our duties if we didn't have some idea of the whereabouts of our erstwhile operatives. Think of it as a mother keeping an eye on her grown-up children after they've left home. We were aware you'd holed up somewhere in the Caribbean. Narrowing your location down wasn't difficult. Satellite data, voice analysis, facial recognition... No one's ever truly anonymous these days. No one can ever truly hide. Not even if they get their nose done."

"It was broken anyway," said Lex. "Needed fixing and neatening."

"Software doesn't just map facial features any more. Gait, posture, the speed at which you walk, your range of common gestures. The whole head-to-toe biometric package. There's one ATM in Port Sebastian that you frequent, at the Banque de Caribbée on Palm Boulevard. We've got numerous shots of you taking cash out from it. Baseball cap and Aviators don't do enough to disguise you, darling. Don't suit you much, either."

"What's the use in keeping track of us once we're retired?" Lex asked, although he thought he knew the answer to the question.

"One can never tell what you might get up to," said Seraphina. "Or who might approach you. The things you lot know—the secrets in your heads—could be very valuable to the right people, or the wrong people. You can't blame us for wanting to be sure that our ex-assets don't become someone else's new assets, can you?"

"I suppose not."

"Well?"

"Well what?"

"Aren't you going to ask me why I'm calling, Lex?"

"No."

"Why not?"

"Because you're bound to tell me anyway, so why bother?"

"How are you, Lex dear?" Seraphina's voice dipped to a solicitous purr. He had had fantasies about this woman—what she looked like, what she wore while she was at work, what she wore when she wasn't working. He had built up a mental image of her. She was blonde, but not naturally. She had voluptuous lips and a crooked smile. She had a penchant for pencil skirts and stiletto heels. Her bra and panties were always black and always matched.

In reality she was probably nothing like that. But the Seraphina he imagined, the Seraphina her voice conjured up in his mind's eye, was a seductive, sultry creature with a hint of the dominatrix about her. Predatory and irresistible, a modern-day Veronica Lake.

"I'm okay," he said. "Life's treating me well."

"Retirement agreeing with you?"

"I saved up enough money to be comfortable. I'm frugal, and the interest on my nest egg goes a whole lot further here than it would back in England. The weather's great, the girls are pretty, the booze is cheap. Can't complain."

"What could make it even better for you?"

"Nothing."

"Not even a hundred grand?"

Lex hesitated briefly—but not briefly enough—before replying. "Not interested. No deal. I'm out. You know I'm out. I can't be brought back in, not for any amount."

"It's a tidy sum," said Seraphina. "And it's not for a Code Crimson, either."

"I don't care."

"I think you do. We're talking sterling here, not US dollars, definitely not Manzanillan dollars. For a couple of days' work. Nothing that'll demand your old skills. Friends of ours need a little help, that's all."

"Friends with stars on their shoulders and stripes on their chests?"

"Well put. Yes. They asked for you specifically. I think you impressed them, way back when. Left a lasting impression, at any rate."

"Is it local, the job?"

"Very. They need a man on the ground, someone who knows the game, someone they can trust. A hundred K, Lex. Not to be sneezed at. Even if you yourself don't need the money, you might know someone who does. Your chum Wilberforce Allen, for instance."

"You have done your homework, haven't you?"

Seraphina let out a crackly laugh. He pictured her holding a long, thin, lavender-coloured cigarette in her free hand, throwing her head back in amusement.

"We're thorough when it's required," she said. "Mr Allen has his heart set on opening up a deep-sea sports fishing business, does he not? He's talked to you about going into partnership with him. For the sort of money that's lying on the table, you and he could buy that boat, along with all the equipment you need—get the ball rolling so that Wilberforce doesn't have to spend his evenings slinging rum cocktails at sunburned holiday rabble and you don't have to spend yours being his unpaid, unofficial bouncer. How does that sound, Lex, my love? To me it sounds like the future, a departure, a way forward. Or would you rather stay as you are—bored, a little bit lonely, drinking more than is good for you and trying to live down all you've done? Up to you."

With a wrench, Lex said, "The answer's still no. I made a promise to myself. I've—I've put all that behind me. I can't go back, not for any reason."

"Lex…"

"No, listen to me, Seraphina. I have blood on my hands, so much blood, and I've only just begun to believe that they're clean again. You, you of all people, know what I've done, the acts I was ordered to commit. It leaves a stain. Inside. However I try to justify or compartmentalise, it's always with me, always. I'm not returning there. I'm not even going close. You understand? I'm not dredging all that up again. Thank you, it's a generous offer, but—and please don't take this the wrong way—you can shove it up your arse."

If Seraphina was affronted, it didn't come through in her voice. "Well, Lex, it's been a pleasure talking to you regardless. Lovely to hear you again. I always liked collaborating with you. Of all my operatives, you were easily my favourite. A shame we couldn't make it work this time."

"Yeah, a real pity."

"Should you reconsider…"

"I won't."

"But should you, feel free to call me back. There's a window of about fourteen hours. This number's fine for me, any time of day or night. If anything comes along that helps you change your mind, I'll be right here. The next fourteen hours. That's noon tomorrow your time, the deadline. Midday Saturday. I do hope you'll be in touch before then."

"Unlikely," Lex said, and jabbed the disconnect button.

He trudged back up the beach to the rum shack and resumed his seat.

"Freshen that for you?" Wilberforce had studied Hollywood movies and picked up some bar-service-speak from them, in order to ingratiate himself with his American clientele.

"Go on, then."

"You look out of sorts, my friend, if I may say. Your expression—like you've had bad news. Who was it just phoned?"

"Double glazing company. I told them I live in a cave."

"Ha ha. No, really."

"Ghost from the past."

"No wonder you're so spooked. Want to talk about it?" Wilberforce was being sincere now. "A problem shared is a problem halved."

Lex stared at his drink.

"Come on. We're pals," Wilberforce said. "You've been a regular for three years. We have those long chats after closing time, just two guys bullshitting, you know? I tell you everything about me and about the women in my life who drive me crazy and about my plans, and you... Well, you listen. You don't give much in return, but I figure that's just your way. So now I'm prepared to do the listening for a change. It's only fair. I've never seen you like this. What's going on in that rainy grey English heart of yours?"

"It's..."

Lex glanced up at the picture of the Sealine F-series. Somewhere, Wilberforce had a sales brochure about the boat, so well thumbed it was falling apart.

All at once he felt inexpressibly guilty.

"It's nothing," he said. He stood. "I'm tired. I'm going to head home. Goodnight, Wilb."

Wilberforce held out a hand to him. They shook, Wilberforce a little ruefully.

"See you tomorrow," he said.

"Yeah."

"And thanks for earlier." The posh boys. "I could have dealt with them, you know."

"Of course. But I'm here to do the nasty stuff, so no one else has to."

THREE

CROSSROADS

IT WAS A three-mile walk from the rum shack to his house. Streetlights were few and far between in Manzanilla, but on most nights under the bright stars, Lex had no difficulty seeing. Palms whispered on either side of the road, swayed by a humid onshore breeze. Now and then a taxi or a pickup truck swept past, very occasionally one of the puttering minibuses that were the island's sole form of public transport and were as reliable as a horoscope.

He came to the crossroads where he would turn off the coastal highway and head inland, uphill, to his house.

As usual, the old beggar was there, sitting cross-legged beside the junction. With him were his dogs, a pair of mongrels of the type known locally as *cane dogs*—all breeds and none, the end-products of a dozen generations of casual back-alley couplings. They panted in the night heat, heads on forepaws, tongues lolling.

Lex lofted a hand as he went past. "Hey there, Gable."

"Mr Dove," replied Gable. He puffed on his corncob pipe, releasing a cloud of aromatic fumes. It wasn't just tobacco he was smoking. "Gorgeous night, huh?"

"Yeah."

One of the cane dogs wagged a listless tail while the other, wishing to add something to the conversation, *woofed* softly.

"Same to you, you lazy mutt," said Lex.

Gable rose clumsily, supporting himself on a rusty hospital crutch. There was something wrong with his feet, though Lex had never been able to ascertain what. Some kind of birth defect, perhaps. Polio?

"Me don' suppose...?"

Lex halted and fished in his pocket for some spare change. He handed over a wad of Manzanillan dollars, about M$70 in all, the equivalent of a fiver.

"Much obliged, boss." Gable tucked the money away under his battered straw hat. "You a good fellow, Mr Dove. Don' let anyone tell you otherwise, 'specially not you'self."

"You have a nice evening, Gable." Lex made to walk on, but the beggar reached out and grabbed his elbow with a bony but startlingly strong hand.

Lex tensed, old instincts readying him to retaliate.

He told himself to relax. Stand down. Gable was just a harmless tramp who lived at the crossroads, panhandling most of the day and sleeping in a camp he had made for himself in a nearby thicket, just out of sight of the highway. He wasn't by any stretch of the imagination a threat. Neither were his dogs, both of them too scrawny and nondescript to be intimidating.

"Mr Dove," Gable said. All of a sudden his wizened, weatherbeaten face, normally genial, had turned deadly serious. His eyes no longer twinkled, but instead reflected the starlight in a pale, unnerving fashion. There was a sharpness in them that hadn't been there previously, an *intelligence*. "You need to lissen up now an' lissen good."

"Gable..."

"No." The grip on Lex's elbow tightened. Both the dogs stood erect, ears up, and one of them bared its fangs and started growling. "Me said lissen. T'ings are rollin', boss. Me ain't jokin'. Bad t'ings for you. Sumtin's started that has to be stopped, and you is the man to do it. But you ain't goin' to manage it alone. Help'll be offered you, and when it come, you don' turn it away, you knowum sayin'? Whatever your finer feelin's, you don' say no."

"I have no idea what you're—"

"Can't you feel it?" Gable pressed his face closer to Lex's. Lex smelled rum and ganja on the man's breath, along with the musk of his body odour. The breeze from the sea intensified, pummelling the palm fronds overhead, and then dropped abruptly, leaving a profound hush. The second dog joined the first in growling, and their two deep rumbling vibratos rose and fell in eerie counterpoint. "Change on the wind. The end of a beginnin' an' the beginnin' of an end. You'll need to make the right choices, boss. What's best for you, what's best for others, though the two mayn't necessarily be the same. You here for a reason, even if you don' realise it. But you goin' to learn, oh, yes. You goin' to learn the hard way."

Then Gable let out an enormous gale of laughter, howling with hilarity at some magnificent jest which only he understood. He let go of Lex and waved him onward with the crutch.

"You go now, Mr Dove," he said, still chuckling. "Dismissed. On your way. An' don' say me didn't warn you. No, sir, don' never say that."

At the same time, both of the dogs relaxed, prone on the ground, as though obeying some silent command.

Lex peered at Gable for several heartbeats, nonplussed. He debated whether to remonstrate with him, force him to explain further what he'd been talking about. But what would be the point? A tramp, befuddled with booze and cannabis, could hardly be expected to make sense. The man had had a sudden brain-fart that had caused him to grab hold of a passerby and spout a stream of non-sequitur banalities. Maybe he was schizophrenic. Not beyond the realms of possibility, given his lifestyle.

Whatever the reason, it wasn't worth getting worked up about. The sooner Lex ignored it, the sooner he could forget about it.

BUT HE HADN'T quite succeeded in doing that by the time he reached home. Gable's odd outburst continued to prey on his mind. The right choices? Learn the hard way? It had the ring of prophecy about it. What did it all mean?

Nothing, he told himself. Nothing whatsoever.

Lex's house was built along Spanish colonial lines, adobe-plastered, capped with rounded roof tiles, and laid out in the indoor-outdoor style. It had a central courtyard, wide open to the elements on one side, the other three sides surrounded by rooms without a dividing wall, just a waist-high partition. These constituted the main living area—kitchen, lounge, study. There were other, fully enclosed rooms in a wing that ran off perpendicular to the courtyard, plus a garage and storage space. The garden was lush with hibiscus and bougainvillaea, and the coarse lawn was studded with acacia trees and a tall tamarind whose fruit was an irresistible lure to the vervet monkeys. High in the hills here, where the trade winds blew harder, it was always a couple of degrees cooler than at sea level. The daytime views over rolling jungled slopes to the ocean were spectacular.

Lex poured himself a couple of fingers of neat rum and went out onto the verandah to sit and listen to the nocturnal chorus of chirruping insects and whistling tree frogs. It had been an unsettling evening. First Seraphina, the proverbial blast from the past. Then Gable with his peculiar rant. All Lex wanted was a quiet life. He thought he had found it, and he was determined to hang on to it as hard as he could.

A rustle in the shrubbery, and out onto the verandah popped Rikki. First a sharp, conical snout poking between two posts of the balustrade, then a lithe, cylindrical body with a striped back. The mongoose scuttered a few steps across the floorboards, then paused and peeked up at Lex with his tiny, fierce black eyes.

Lex tipped his tumbler at the creature in greeting. "Wondered if you might be putting in an appearance tonight."

The mongoose moved a fraction closer, cautious, not timid. Finally he halted beside Lex's chair and settled down to grooming his whiskers and fur.

He wasn't a pet, but over the past year Rikki—named after the Kipling story—had become a kind of companion for Lex, a silent little familiar. In the late 1800s mongooses had been introduced to Manzanilla by the Spanish in order to tackle the island's chronic snake problem. The place had been infested with cascabel, fer-de-lance and bushmaster, so much so that death by snakebite accounted for at least twenty per cent of fatalities among the population. A hundred mongoose breeding pairs had been released in the interior, and by the turn of the twentieth century snakes were all but a thing of the past. Enough survived to give the mongooses something to hunt and eat, but they were no longer the omnipresent danger they had been.

Lex welcomed Rikki's presence on his property. It meant he never had to worry about where he set foot. He could walk around house and garden with no shoes on and be perfectly safe.

Also, he felt an affinity with the mongoose. A ruthless, efficient killer. Specialty: getting rid of creatures no one wanted, the ugly ones with venom and fangs and a bad temper. Lex could identify with that.

He finished his rum and drowsed for a while. The tumbler slipped from his grasp and clunked to the floor, rousing him briefly and sending Rikki racing for the shadows of the garden. He thought about going to bed, but the drowsiness overtook him again and he fell asleep right there on the verandah.

His dreams were never peaceful. They were always about restless things. Beings that should be dead but weren't. The faces of victims. Mouths that yawned at him, sometimes soundlessly, sometimes uttering words in languages he only half understood. Accusing. Insisting. Demanding to be remembered, to be taken into account.

A few he recognised. The rest looked like strangers, even though he ought to know them.

A roll-call of evil. Dictators. Tyrants. Terrorists. Mass-murderers.

The deservedly dead. The righteous dead. Code Crimsons.

Yet they would not leave him alone.

Lex awoke, startled.

His phone was ringing.

If it was that bloody Seraphina again, already...

But the caller ID said Wilberforce.

"Wilb?"

"Lex. Thank God. You got to come. I'm in deep shit. For real."

"Wilb, where are you?" Lex's watch said 1.10AM.

"Outside home, in my car. I just pulled up. There's these men waiting for me out front. I wouldn't have stopped if I'd seen them in time. Now they've spotted me, and I'm screwed. Please. Help. Quick."

"I'm on my way."

"Great. Just hurry, because—"

There was the sound of voices other than Wilberforce's, shouting, angry. A car door opening. A scuffle.

Then the line went dead.

Lex was on his feet, sprinting for the garage.

FOUR
THE GARFISH

Wilberforce lived on the outskirts of Port Sebastian, Manzanilla's capital, in an area that was only one step up from a shanty town. His house was a wooden cabin painted bright green, yellow and red, with a tin roof that groaned under the weight of a satellite dish and a solar-heated water tank.

As Lex pulled up in his Subaru 4x4, he saw Wilberforce's battered Mazda saloon parked outside. The driver's door stood wide open. There was a car blocking Wilberforce's driveway, a hulking Jeep Grand Cherokee tricked out with bull bars, running boards, chrome trim, rally headlamps and blacked-out windows. Few Manzanillans could afford a pimp ride like that, fewer still who weren't involved in some kind of shady dealings.

What the hell was Wilberforce mixed up in? How had he got on the wrong side of a gang of criminals?

Contain the questions for now. Focus on the matter at hand.

There was nobody about on the street, but lights shone in Wilberforce's house. Lex left the Subaru, vaulted a low chainlink fence and padded across the front lawn. He listened out. From indoors came the sound of a raised voice. Lex couldn't make out the words. Then the unmistakable *smack* of fist striking flesh, and a cry of pain—Wilberforce.

Lex stiffened. His pulse rate increased. He felt a surge of adrenaline. His senses sharpened and his awareness of his environment intensified. An old familiar calmness suffused him.

It was strangely glorious to have it again.

He began a stealthy circuit of the house. The bad guys, whoever they were, were confident. Overconfident. They hadn't posted anyone on guard duty outside. They must not have seen Wilberforce making a phone call from his car. They had no idea he had summoned reinforcements. They thought they had him entirely at their mercy and no one would interrupt them while they worked on him.

Lex arrived at the back door. Wilberforce never locked it, but the hinges needed oiling and the door always squealed like a banshee when opened.

But the window next to it, giving onto the bathroom, slid up as silently as you please.

Lex slithered through, easing himself via the toilet onto the tiled floor. He had a gun, a SIG Sauer P228, tucked into the waistband of his trousers, hidden under his shirttails. It was loaded with Speer Gold Dot 9mm parabellum rounds, the kind of bullet that put two holes in the human body, a neat entry wound and a massive crater of an exit wound. He had no intention of using the SIG except as a last resort. Luckily, Wilberforce shaved with a cutthroat razor. Lex plucked the razor from the basin and levered it open, exposing the blade which Wilberforce stropped religiously and kept wickedly sharp. Then he stole over to the bathroom door, nudged it ajar, and peeked into the living room.

Wilberforce was fastened to a chair by plastic zip restraints. Three men surrounded him, and one was clutching Wilberforce's head by the jaw, tilting it up so that they could see eye to eye.

"The boss has been waitin'," he said to Wilberforce. "Waitin' real patiently. He's a kind man, a generous man, but even he can't wait forever. He makes a loan, he expects it to be paid off as and when the instalments come due. How come you ain't done that?"

"I—I missed one repayment, that's all," Wilberforce stammered. "I didn't mean to. I got my books messed up. It was insurance premium renewal time on the rum shack. I had enough for that, but not for anything extra."

"So the lousy fuckin' insurance company comes first, not the boss?"

"I thought he wouldn't mind. I will pay up, honest. Double the usual at the end of this month."

"Yeah, you will," said the thug. He wore a blue and gold football shirt, Manzanilla United's home strip. The Other Man U, as it was known. "Of course you will. But you're wrong about the boss not mindin'. He minds plenty. It's the principle of the thing, see. One person lets an obligation slide, then everyone else thinks they can. Which is why you need to be taught a lesson. Not for your sake, for everyone else's."

Lex glimpsed brass knuckledusters. Wilberforce's head snapped to the side. Spatters of blood flew.

Football Shirt drew back his fist for yet another punch.

Lex was on him faster than a cheetah. He whirled Football Shirt round, yanking his arm up between his shoulderblades. The cutthroat razor hovered at his Adam's apple.

"Pay attention," Lex told Football Shirt's two comrades. "I will slice from carotid to carotid if you do not do precisely as I say. You have to the count of five to leave.

"One.

"Two."

Neither of the other men budged. Football Shirt whimpered deep in his throat.

"Three. I'm not kidding. In a couple of seconds' time this man could be aspirating his own blood.

"Four."

Football Shirt nodded urgently to the other two.

The two edged towards the front door. Lex followed, pushing Football Shirt before him.

"That's it," he said. "Out you go. Nice and easy."

Outside, Football Shirt murmured, "You're makin' a serious mistake, man."

"Says the dickhead with a razor blade at his throat."

"You fuckin' with the wrong guy."

"I think you'll find it's you who've fucked with the wrong guy."

They approached the Jeep.

"Get in and go," Lex ordered. "You come back here, any time, and I'll know. And then I will seriously mess your shit up. Understand?"

The front passenger door of the Jeep swung open and out stepped a giant in a seersucker suit. He was holding a pistol, a long-barrelled Desert Eagle .44 Magnum which, though a sizeable weapon, was dwarfed by his massive hand. A pair of Calvin Klein sunglasses perched atop his smooth-shaven head.

"Tell me again," the giant said in a bassy booming voice. He levelled the Desert Eagle at Lex, and diamond cufflinks sparkled at his wrists. "Who goin' to mess whose shit up?"

LEX KNEW EXACTLY who this was. He had never seen him in person before, but everyone in Manzanilla had heard of Garfield 'the Garfish' Finisterre. Seven foot tall, skinny as a whip, he was the island's premier drug lord and loan shark. Garfish were pencil-thin, electric-blue fish that darted through the beach shallows and among the reefs, but there was nothing pretty or innocuous about this character. He had everyone who mattered in his pocket, from government bureaucrats to police officers. He was a master of top-down corruption and, it could be argued, Manzanilla's true head of state.

Wilberforce had really screwed up if he was in hock to the Garfish. But then, that put him on an equal footing with fully a fifth of the island's population. Maybe as much as a third, if some reports were to be believed. When you wanted to borrow a lump sum of money, but didn't have the kind of equity or capital a bank demanded, Finisterre was the man you went to.

"Saw you creepin' round the back," Finisterre said to Lex. "Reckoned you'd try and save my friend Wilberforce in there, but I didn't think you were anything my boys couldn't cope with. Runty white punk like you. Seems like I guessed wrong."

"Seems like I should have checked that car first before I went in." Lex was making light of it, but he could have kicked himself. Rookie blunder. He'd been on civvy street too long. Rusty.

"Told you you were makin' a mistake," gloated Football Shirt.

"Shut up, you." Lex pressed the razor hard enough against the man's neck to break the skin. Blood trickled from an inch-long incision. Football Shirt let out an anguished hiss.

"Yes, shut up, Maurice," said Finisterre to his henchman. "You haven't exactly covered yourself in glory tonight, lettin' yourself get sneaked up on and caught. Amateurish, that's what it is. Not what I expect from an employee of the Garfish.

"So," he said, returning his attention to Lex, "we appear to find ourselves at an impasse."

"We do."

"You got my guy at your mercy, I got you covered with this." He jerked his head at the Desert Eagle. "How we goin' to resolve this?"

"Simple. You back off, or Maurice here gets it in the neck. The three of you climb into the Jeep and drive away. Then I let Maurice go free and he can make his own way home. How about that?"

Finisterre rebalanced his sunglasses on the dome of his head, pretending to consider Lex's proposal. "Maybe."

"You don't have a clear shot," said Lex, careful to keep Maurice angled between him and Finisterre. "Miss me, even wing me, I'll still be able to give him a new breathing hole. And don't doubt that I'll do it."

"Oh, no." Finisterre looked deep into Lex's eyes. "I can see that. You got it in you, all right. You have the look. I know who you are now. The Englishman who lives on the hill. What's your name? Goose? Pigeon? Somethin' birdy like that. You sort out troublemakers at Wilberforce's shack, but always real polite, askin' them to leave if you can rather than makin' them. Placid on the outside. Don't look like you'd harm a fly. But below, deep down—somethin' dark in there, I can tell. Somethin' dangerous. People've wondered what you used to be before you came here. Now I think I know. Yeah, you'd kill Maurice in a heartbeat, no question. Only trouble is..."

"What?"

"I don't care. Don't care at all if he gets hurt. The stupid incompetent asshole."

Finisterre angled the Desert Eagle downward.

Maurice managed to yelp, "Boss! No!" before Finisterre shot him in the kneecap.

Maurice shrieked and sagged in Lex's arms, suddenly dead weight. Lex, thrown off-balance, stumbled. He went crashing to the ground with Maurice on top.

That saved him, because when Finisterre fired again, Maurice took the bullet, right in the chest. In the same instant, Lex dropped the razor and reached behind him for the SIG.

His return shots had, perforce, to be quick and desperate. There was no time for luxuries like sighting, lining up, aiming for centre of body mass, any of that. He snapped off three quick rounds, scattering Finisterre and his men, none of whom had had any idea that Lex was packing a gun. He clipped one of the henchmen on the arm and managed to take out one of the Jeep's side windows.

Finisterre and his two men took refuge behind the car while

Lex pedalled himself backwards with his heels, keeping Maurice on top of him. He was making for the house, using the now very dead bruiser as a shield.

Finisterre's Desert Eagle barked twice across the Jeep's bonnet. Lex answered with the SIG, firing low under the car. The ricochets made the crooks dance and skip in panic. With a huge effort he hauled himself and the corpse across the threshold, then rolled Maurice aside and took up a kneeling position behind the front door. He squeezed off two more shots, destroying one of the Jeep's wing mirrors and putting a hole in the rear nearside door.

The Desert Eagle blasted the house, punching through windowpane and weatherboard. Finisterre emptied the magazine, and as he was reloading, Lex leaned out from cover and almost casually selected a target: a hand that was visible at the rear of the Jeep, supporting its owner in a crouch.

The henchman screamed as two fingers were obliterated. A string of patois curses filled the air.

Then, distantly, another sound filled the air. The *whoop* of a police siren.

A neighbour, hearing the gunfire, had called the cops, and by some miracle a squad car had been close by.

Finisterre swore. "We got to run, boys."

"But boss..."

"I know. It's only the Babylon. Nothin' cash can't solve. But I don't need to be caught in the middle of a fuckin' shoot-up. There'll be paperwork an' lawyers an' maybe some prick of a reporter wantin' to write a story. I don't need that bullshit. Englishman!"

"Yes?" Lex called out from behind the door.

"This isn't over, you know that? It's far from over."

"I'm quaking in my boots."

"Don't be so smug. Nobody crosses the Garfish an' gets away with it."

"As threats go, that'd be far more effective if you didn't have such a stupid nickname," Lex said. "The Barracuda—now that's a scary fish name. The Tiger Shark, that's another good one. But the Garfish?"

The three crooks were climbing into the Jeep. "I know where you live," said Finisterre. "Sleep with one eye open from now on, because you won't know where, you won't know when, but I'm comin' for you."

"You just told me, you daft git. My house, at night. I'll be waiting for you."

"You goin' to die. Slow an' horrible."

"Oh, give it a rest."

The Jeep started up and roared away. Moments later, the police car came into view, siren blaring, lightbar flashing. Lights flicked on in windows up and down the street. Heads poked nervously out from behind window blinds and front doors.

Lex sighed. What a monumental fuck-up. The perfect end to a shitty night.

FIVE
FOUR HUNDRED PER CENT

Lᴇx ɢᴀᴠᴇ ᴛʜᴇ police a selective and largely inaccurate version of events. He omitted to mention that he had been carrying a weapon. He maintained that he had turned up at Wilberforce's house for a visit, surprised some men who were hurting his friend, and scared them off. They had shot at him—an unarmed man!—as they were fleeing, and had accidentally killed one of their own.

The detective constable who took his statement was sceptical, to say the least.

"How do you account for the broken glass on the ground outside, Mr Dove?" he asked. "The bits of a car mirror? You're saying, in all the confusion, the intruders not only shot one of their own men but their car too?"

"That's exactly what I'm saying, officer. It was chaos. Bullets flying everywhere. Frankly, I was lucky to survive."

"And did you happen to recognise any of these men?"

"Complete strangers to me. Never seen them before in my life."

Wilberforce claimed much the same. Taking his cue from Lex, he said it had obviously been a random home invasion.

The burglars had tied him up and started hitting him in order to get him to tell them where he kept his valuables.

"Don't take this the wrong way, Mr Allen," said the detective constable, "but it isn't what you'd call a high-class neighbourhood. What sort of valuables do you think they were after?"

"Who knows?" replied Wilberforce. "I'm no robber. I've no idea what goes on inside these people's heads. Maybe they thought I got some secret stash of gold bullion or something."

"And do you?"

Wilberforce laughed, then winced, because laughing was painful. "Yeah, right. I'm sitting on a fortune. That's why I live in this palace."

The detective constable left with a parting shot. "Your stories don't add up. Neither of you gentlemen is telling me the whole truth. You'll be hearing from us again, sooner than you think. Maybe by then you'll have decided to come clean."

"Or worked out some better lies," Lex muttered to Wilberforce as he closed the front door.

He retrieved his SIG from the bathroom. He had dumped the gun in the toilet cistern as the police arrived, and taken the precaution of scrubbing the telltale gunpowder residue off his hands before going out to meet them.

As he dried off the SIG with a towel, he said, "All right, Wilb. Out with it. What's going on?"

Wilberforce looked rueful. He had a swollen eye and significant facial bruising, and was shaken after his ordeal, but basically okay.

"It's no big thing really," he said. "Just business."

"No big thing? How much do you owe the Garfish?"

"Not much. Couple of hundred."

"Seriously? A couple of hundred Manzanillan? That's nothing."

"Couple of hundred thousand."

"Ah. Well, still, not a huge amount." Lex did some quick mental arithmetic. At the current exchange rate, roughly £15,000. "I can lend you that, no problem. Clear the debt at a stroke."

"Yeah, thanks, but you see, it's not quite that simple. I'm paying it off at a pretty high rate of interest."

"How high?"

"Works out at around four hundred per cent."

"You what!"

Wilberforce fetched two bottled beers from the fridge, handing one to Lex. "What you don't appreciate, my friend, is this is Manzanilla. Things aren't as straightforward here as they are in a country like the UK. In the UK, you want a start-up loan, you go to a bank, show them a business plan, they either like it or they don't, and they maybe cough up the money, maybe not. All above board. Here, the banks don't lend, period. Too much risk. Plus, you got payoffs to make, councillors and planning officials to be bribed, all that sort of thing, which adds to your initial outlay. So you go to a guy like Garfield Finisterre. It's the only realistic option for a lot of folk."

"But four hundred per cent? That's taking the piss."

"Of course it is. But without it I'd never have had my rum shack. And with my rum shack I earn an income, enough to eat, cover the bills, pay the Garfish what he asks, and still have a little to put aside each month towards my boat—my beautiful boat. So it's all good."

"It's not all good." Lex took a swig of his beer. It was island-made, strong and sweet. "Now you've pissed Finisterre off."

"To be strictly accurate, you did that, Lex."

"Only to prevent you having the shit kicked out of you."

"Fair point. So we're both responsible. Question is, what do we do about it? Because the Garfish, he isn't about to forgive and forget."

There was a solution, Lex thought. Seraphina and her hundred grand.

He shook his head. No way. There had to be something else, an alternative to that. Anything but that.

"Let me sleep on it," he said. "Maybe I'll figure out something in the morning."

"How's your spare room?" Wilberforce asked. "Bed all made up?"

"You want to come for a sleepover?"

Wilberforce tried not to look pathetically grateful. "If it's okay. Kind of not feeling so safe under my own roof tonight."

LEX WAS AWAKE at seven. It had rained during the night, as it often did. The air was muggy, the garden hung with wreaths of ground mist. He ate breakfast in the courtyard—toast, fresh fruit, coffee. Rikki joined him at the table and feasted on a raw egg he gave him.

"Don't come to rely on me for your food," Lex warned the mongoose. "You'll get complacent. Lose your edge."

Rikki stared blankly at him, then resumed lapping yolk and albumen from the broken shell.

Lex's mobile lay beside the espresso pot. He half expected it to ring. Seraphina calling. Somehow she would know that he was reconsidering her offer. He kind of wished it would happen that way, sparing him the hassle and humiliation of having to make the call himself.

All of Wilberforce's problems solved. And the sports cruiser secured outright. Lex wasn't much of a sailor, but he quite fancied the idea of escorting tourists out to sea and helping them fish. How hard could it be? Wilberforce, having spent a year crewing on a glass-bottomed boat on the reefs, already knew a bit about seamanship, and Lex could pick it up as he went along. He was a quick study. It would be something to do with his days. A change from sitting and brooding and drinking.

He located Seraphina's number in the call log. His thumb hovered over the green phone icon, and finally came down on it.

It took nearly twenty seconds for the connection to be established. The signal had to be rerouted through several British government exchanges, hopping from one to the next and being scrambled and encrypted along the way. It would be next to impossible for any third party to trace either its point of origin or its destination, or indeed to eavesdrop.

"Lex," Seraphina crooned. "It still feels strange calling you that. Lex. Rather sexy, too. Like this is some sort of secret assignation."

"Isn't it?"

"When you put it like that, I suppose it is. How's tricks, anyway? I gather there was a bit of a wild rumpus in Port Sebastian last night. Gunplay in the streets. Nothing to do with you, of course."

"People are shooting each other all the time in Manzanilla." Sadly, this was true. The rise in tourism and the prosperity it brought had seen a concomitant decline in lawlessness, but armed robbery and gang violence were still far from unusual. Away from the coast and the hotel developments, crime remained a daily fact of life for many islanders. "Why assume I was involved?"

"I don't assume anything," said Seraphina. "I know."

"Naturally."

"Names get taken down at such incidents, reports get filed on police databases..."

"And dedicated search engines flag them up whenever they occur," Lex finished. "Bloody hell, it's almost as if you're stalking me."

"A run-in with local law enforcement, Lex. That's not like you at all. Hardly what one would call keeping a low profile."

"It wasn't intentional, believe me."

"I can make it all go away, if you like. Just say the word, I can get the investigation dropped. All it'll take is the foreign secretary to get in touch with the Manzanillan prime minister, him to lean on the chief constable, and hey presto, you're in the clear, like it never happened."

"The job," said Lex, almost wearily.

"Ah, yes. The job. 'Enough of the niceties, Seraphina. Cut to the chase.'"

"What can you tell me about it?"

"As a matter of fact, very little."

"You're not allowed to, or you don't have the information?"

"The latter. Our allies across the Atlantic are playing this one very close to their chests. What I do know, via back channels—and I shouldn't really be divulging this before the deal's sealed—is that a US special ops team of some sort is en route to Manzanilla and they're going to be staging there in order to carry out a mission nearby. They want somebody resident and amenable—that would be you—to be their local guide, arrange transport, and maybe one or two other things."

"Amenable? Me?"

"Well, you're American. At least on paper."

Lex's birth certificate stated place of birth as Miami, Florida. His parents had lived there for a couple of years in the late 1970s while his father had been attempting, and failing, to make it as a property developer. Lex's father's life had been one long parade of abortive get-rich-quick schemes and collapsed businesses, grand ambitions repeatedly foundering on the rocks of impracticality and lack of commercial acumen.

"And," Seraphina continued, "you're a known quantity. The Yanks would rather deal with someone they've already met and collaborated with than a complete stranger."

"So conservative."

"Or cautious. The vibe I'm getting, Lex, is that this is super-sensitive stuff. Discretion is the watchword here."

"Two hundred K."

"Beg pardon?"

"You heard."

"Lex, you naughty boy, you're being greedy."

"No, I'm not. They want me, they should be prepared to pay a decent rate. Besides, it's extremely short notice. Who else are they going to find in the time available?"

He was hoping she would say no. He was hoping he had priced himself out of the market, in which case it wouldn't be his fault if the job didn't happen. He wouldn't be to blame. He had made himself available, tendered his services, and if the Americans weren't willing to meet his demands, well, tough. Their loss.

"I think," said Seraphina, "that that could be arranged."

So much for *that* plan. Lex was crestfallen.

"I understand there's a contingency fund," she said. "Very deep pockets our American cousins have, especially when it comes to ultra-covert shenanigans. I would be very surprised if they baulk at going that high. As you say, there's really no one else of the same calibre and skill set available."

"Why don't you check, before making any rash promises?"

"Lex, I *am* checking. I have my laptop in front of me and I'm emailing my contact in the States even as we speak. It's called multitasking, something we women excel at. There. Sent. I don't think we'll have long to wait for the reply. In the meantime... Any lady friends out there, dare I ask? Anyone I should be jealous of?"

"Never you mind."

"That's a no, then. You really mean to say some lovely voluptuous Caribbean girl hasn't caught your eye? I'd have thought you'd be making hay. Handsome, unattached boy like yourself. Do you miss that from the old days?"

"What, the travelling?" He hated this, the bogus small talk they were indulging in. Yet it had been their habit to chat like this during the years when Seraphina would give him his Code Crimson commissions and he would go off and perform them. Their phone conversations had been long and informal, often flirtatious, sometimes quite intimate. Perhaps the intention was to anchor him in reality and make what he did seem normal, even mundane. Just as if theirs was any ordinary employer-employee relationship. "I don't miss the jet lag."

"But staying in one place, after roving far and wide across the planet..."

"Yeah, with stop-offs in every known strife-torn, bombshelled, poverty-stricken hellhole along the way."

"It wasn't all Third World dictatorships and civil war zones. I distinctly recall trips to Monaco, Singapore, Rome, even the Maldives. You did pretty well out of the Queen's shilling."

"Funny. All I remember is flea-ridden hotel rooms, dusty tents in deserts, lying in hides made of twigs and canvas for days on end, and freezing my arse off on rooftops."

"You're such a glass-half-empty person."

"Glass? I never even had a glass. I used to dream of having a glass, never mind something to fill it with."

Seraphina chortled throatily. "That's more like it. That's the man I used to know. Ever ready with a deadpan wisecrack. If you don't mind my saying so, you've lost sight of who you are, Lex. That's your trouble. You should never have jacked it all in. The soft life's eaten away at you."

"No, the job ate away at me," said Lex. "Retirement's allowing me to rediscover myself."

"If that were really true, we wouldn't be having this conversation." Before Lex could respond, Seraphina said, "Oh, look. Ping! A reply in the inbox. Told you it wouldn't take long. Just let me open it. Click. There. Yes. Thought so. 'Dear Seraphina...' Blah blah blah. 'Terms are acceptable... funds can be remitted as soon as required... kindly await further instructions.' There you go, Lex, you lucky sausage. Two hundred grand. I have your bank details. You certainly know how to drive a hard bargain. Remind me never to buy a used car from you. Now then, happy?"

Lex grunted.

"Delirious, I can tell," said Seraphina. "Keep your phone fully charged and at your side from this moment on. I'll text you your orders as they come in. It's just like old times, isn't it?" She gave a girlish giggle. "You and me, doing our thing.

The dynamic duo. You know, one day I might just fly out there to see you, Lex. Wouldn't that be nice? We could finally meet in person, there in your tropical paradise. You could show me the sights, I could show you myself in a bikini. How about that, eh, my darling?"

Lex could think of a number of comebacks, all of them snarky. He felt railroaded, exploited, a victim of circumstance and undue pressure. Seraphina had manipulated him, and that rankled. But worse—he had let her.

Finally he said, "One or other of us would be bitterly disappointed, and I'd rather it wasn't me," and he cut the connection.

At that moment, Wilberforce emerged from the spare room, stretching and yawning loudly. Rikki took fright and scarpered off into the garden, leaving a mess of sticky eggshell behind on the table.

"I see you're still hanging out with vermin," said Wilberforce.

"I am now the mongoose has gone," Lex shot back. "Sleep well?"

"Like a log."

"I know. I could hear you snoring through two solid walls."

"Man, I do not snore."

Lex laughed scoffingly. "There are pilot whales beached at Plantation Cove right now; they heard you in the night and thought it was one of their own in distress."

"Oh, ha ha." Wilberforce helped himself to coffee. The swelling around his eye had begun to diminish. Lex had made him ice it last night, and had dabbed antiseptic on his other contusions and applied adhesive surgical strips where the knuckleduster had split skin. "Someone's in a grouchy mood this morning."

"Being shot at by gangster goons will do that to a person," Lex said.

"Yeah, about that..."

"Don't apologise. Not necessary."

"I wasn't going to. What I was going to say was: you have a gun."

"Yes. I do."

"And you know how to use it."

"So?"

Wilberforce drew a deep breath. "So, we've known each other a while, and I think I've been pretty good at not asking you about your past and stuff."

"You've tried."

"And you've stonewalled, so I've given up. Judging by the way you deal with the rowdies at the rum shack, it's a safe bet you used to be a soldier or some such. You aren't scared of anyone. You know how to handle yourself in a fight. But you're so secretive, I don't reckon you were *just* a soldier. Know what I'm saying? Plus, you seem to live pretty well"—he waved a hand, indicating the house—"and I haven't heard of a military service pension that pays out like this." An anxious expression came over his bruised face. "I don't really want to pry, but I have to ask. Who are you, Lex? No. Scratch that. Who *were* you?"

The question hung in the air, as good questions tended to.

Lex was tempted to come clean. He could trust Wilberforce, and the man was already pretty close to the truth. Why not give him the rest?

Wilb, I'm a former professional murderer. The British government used to pay me handsomely for eliminating people whose activities or politics were inimical to the interests of the Crown. I worked freelance, meaning I was off the books, not employed by any security agency or Whitehall department, utterly deniable. I carried out covert executions sanctioned by the highest authority in the land, and some of those killings were arranged to look like accidents and others were public and splashy and very obviously assassinations—stiletto or hammer, depending on the offender's circumstances and the message I was supposed to be sending. I was a high-value asset, ex-SAS,

*trained in the art of homicide, and I served my paymasters
with distinction, indeed honour, for the best part of a decade.
I have fifty-one confirmed kills to my name, for which I have
received neither official recognition nor medals, and I believe
my actions have made the world a safer place... albeit at the
price of my own peace of mind.*

All this he so nearly said. The words were accumulating on
his tongue, ready to pour forth, when Wilberforce's phone
rang.

"Hold on. Just let me take this."

Saved by the bell.

Wilberforce strolled off into the garden, coffee cup in one
hand, phone in the other. Lex tried not to listen in, but he
gathered that Wilberforce was talking to a relative of his. The
conversation—this side of it, at any rate—became animated
and forceful. When Wilberforce returned to the table, he
looked flustered and peeved.

"Who was that?"

"My cousin."

"Which cousin?" said Lex. "Oh wait, *that* cousin. The one
you don't want me to meet. What's her name—Alberta?"

"Albertine."

"I've never been able to work out why you insist on keeping
her and me apart. Is there something wrong with me? Do you
not approve of me? If that's it, I'm hurt. Really offended."

"No, no, nothing like that."

"So why so protective?"

"I'm not," said Wilberforce. "I'm embarrassed, is what it is.
Albertine, see, she got this thing—this mad thing. I'm really not
sure about her. I mean, don't get me wrong, I love her. We were
close, growing up. More like brother and sister than cousins.
Now, though..."

"Not an evangelical Christian, is she?" Lex cajoled. "Bible in
one hand, tambourine in the other?"

"Hell, no. You couldn't be more wrong."

"Then what's the problem?"

Wilberforce puffed out his lips and glanced up at the sky. "Probably best you find out for yourself."

"Okay. When?"

"Not long. She's on her way over."

"Here?"

"Yeah. She was insistent. She gets that way sometimes, and there's no arguing with her."

"She's coming here?" Lex repeated. "Why?"

"Couldn't talk her out of it," said Wilberforce. "She knows I'm in trouble, and she says she knows about you, and you're in trouble too."

"But I've never met the woman. How can she—?"

"Lex, enough with the questions. Let Albertine explain it herself when she arrives. Believe me, the shit she's going to come out with, it'll be the craziest shit you ever heard. Just listen and keep smiling and try not to blame me."

SIX

ALBERTINE

WILBERFORCE WOULDN'T BE drawn any further on the subject. He seemed ashamed, as though whatever was wrong with his cousin reflected poorly on him somehow.

At last a car came up the drive, a Suzuki soft-top off-roader faulty engine timing and a screeching fan belt. Out of it stepped a smartly dressed woman with the crisp, efficient air of a highly-placed, well-respected executive. She carried a large leather Mulberry shoulder bag and her hair was a mass of braided extensions, interwoven strands of gold, copper and bronze arranged in a neat bun at the back of her head. Lex watched her smooth her skirt down, and thought she was just about one of the most elegant and poised women he had ever seen. From the picture Wilberforce had painted, he had been expecting a frumpy wild-haired fruitcake in flip-flops and a kaftan. Not this. The only thing that detracted from her smartness were the trainers she wore on her feet, but they did at least look box fresh and were, on Manzanilla, far more sensible than heels.

As Albertine Montase climbed the front steps, Wilberforce opened the screen door to greet her.

"Albie."

"Wilberforce. Long time no see, cuz."

They embraced and pecked cheeks—warmly on Albertine's part, not quite so on Wilberforce's.

"How have you been keeping?" Albertine asked. A trace of an American accent was folded into her islander lilt, like cream into coffee.

"Fine."

"Those bruises say otherwise."

"Tripped and fell."

"Onto somebody's fists."

"No. No. Nothing like that."

"Yes. Yes. Exactly like that. And this is him." She turned velvet-brown eyes on Lex. "Your rum shack peace enforcer."

"Lex Dove." Lex extended a hand. "Pleasure to finally meet you. Wilberforce has told me a lot about you."

"I bet he hasn't." Her hand was dry and firm in Lex's. "Wilberforce prefers not to acknowledge my existence."

"I do not!"

"You do."

"I can't see why he would," said Lex.

"That's because you don't know me," said Albertine. "And also because you don't know how people like Wilberforce think. Wilberforce is all up-to-date and twenty-first century, the very model of a modern West Indian. There are certain deep-seated cultural factors he simply won't accept. Our racial heritage is an enemy to him, something he fears would hold him back. He rejects it, denies it..."

"I reject it because it's bullshit," said Wilberforce.

"No, because you're scared of it."

"I'm not scared of booga-booga tribal mumbo-jumbo."

"Calling it names only shows how scared you are."

"Scornful, maybe. Not scared."

"If you're not scared, say its name," said Albertine. "Call it for what it is. Go on, I dare you."

"Don't be silly, woman."

"You can't, can you?"

"Of course I can. I'm—I'm just not indulging you in this nonsense of yours."

"Ahem," said Lex pointedly. "I hate to butt in on a family row."

"Then don't," Wilberforce and Albertine both said in unison.

"But," Lex went on, "as this is my home, and I'm the host, may I offer you a drink, Albertine? Something hot? Cold? Alcoholic? Not?"

Albertine grinned. Her teeth were huge, even and brilliant. "Sure you can. Sorry about me and Wilberforce going off like that. We always did like to squabble. And he can be such a dope at times."

"I may be a dope," said Wilberforce, "but at least I'm an enlightened one."

"Shut up, Wilberforce."

"No, you shut up."

"Tea would be nice, Lex," said Albertine. "Earl Grey if you've got it. Milk and two sugars."

THE SUN HAD burned off the mist. They sat at a parasol-shaded picnic table in the garden.

"So you know nothing about me," Albertine said to Lex.

"Beyond your name, no."

"Black sheep of the family, huh, Wilberforce?"

Wilberforce huffed. "Just because some of us have standards..."

"What can you tell about me, Lex, just by appearances?"

"Aside from the obvious, you mean?"

"The obvious?"

"You're stunning."

She laughed. Wilberforce, by contrast, scowled.

"Lex," he growled.

"Just a statement of fact," Lex said. "You've spent some time in the States. College?"

"Not bad," said Albertine. "I did my master's degree at Cornell. What else?"

"You have a decent job. Accountant?"

"IT consultant. I help run and maintain the government systems. The servers, the websites, the software for the power grid."

"High flyer."

"I do okay."

"But you're careful with your money. You couldn't have splashed out much on that Suzuki."

"What's the point? Manzanilla roads are so atrocious, only a fool would have a decent car. Better an old banger, something that's easy to fix when it goes wrong and doesn't matter if it picks up a few extra scrapes and dents."

"You're conscious about your appearance."

"Show me the islander woman who isn't. Is that all you've got?"

Lex shrugged. "I could go back to telling you how gorgeous you are, if you like."

"Feel free," said Albertine.

"Don't," said Wilberforce.

"You'll have to forgive my cousin, Lex. He still thinks I'm the little girl in bunches and spectacles who he had to keep the bullies away from in school."

"It's very sweet, the way he looks out for you," Lex said.

Wilberforce gave him a glare that would have curdled milk.

"It's very sweet, the way *you* look out for *him*," said Albertine. "Especially last night. I warned Wilberforce not to get into bed with the Garfish. But oh, no, big fat smartypants, he knew better. He thought it would never come round to bite him on the backside. Thank God he has you for a friend. His own guardian angel."

Lex was only too happy to take the praise.

"So you have the measure of me, yes?" Albertine said.

Lex nodded. "I think so. Unless there's something I'm missing."

"What if I told you I'm into *vodou*?"

"*Vodou*? Is that the same as...?"

"...what you would call voodoo? Yes."

Lex frowned. "What, so it's a hobby of yours? Something you study for fun?"

"No. Oh, no. Lex, I'm a mambo. A *vodou* priestess. I worship the *loa*—the spirits. I talk to them and they talk to me. And they are telling me that you, Lex Dove, are in the greatest danger of your life."

SEVEN
A MESSAGE FROM THE LOA

"Run that by me again," said Lex.

"A little context first," said Albertine. "My—and Wilberforce's—family hail from Haiti originally. Our mothers came over here in nineteen seventy-seven with our grandparents, fleeing the reign of Jean-Claude Duvalier, Baby Doc as he was known."

"A lovely chap, by all accounts."

"Not a patch on his father, Papa Doc, but a monster all the same. Baby Doc inherited one of the most corrupt regimes on the planet at the time, his position reinforced by the private militia his father created, the Milice de Volontaires de la Sécurité Nationale."

"Better known as the *Tontons Macoutes*."

"You know your Caribbean history."

That, and one of Lex's fields of expertise was dictatorships. "The Tontons Macoutes were some of the biggest bastards ever to walk the earth. They made the Stasi and Pinochet's DINA look like girl scouts. Twenty thousand Haitians dead at their hands, is that right?"

"Some estimates put it as high as fifty thousand. Dissidents and opponents of the regime, slaughtered in their droves. People would disappear in the night and be found the next morning, or rather their mutilated corpses would. Anyone who was believed to be an anti-Duvalier agitator, they and their entire family would be killed, utterly wiped out. Rape and extortion were commonplace. All this while Duvalier *père et fils* helped themselves to Haiti's sovereign wealth, lining their pockets and becoming obscenely rich while honest citizens scrabbled to make a living and went hungry."

"Haiti's still a shitbox," Wilberforce opined, "only now it's at least a democratic shitbox."

"Yes, thank you for that, cuz," said Albertine tartly. "The land of our ancestors, dismissed in a single sentence."

"And the earthquake a couple of years back?" Wilberforce added. "That was Mother Nature commenting on the place. She was trying to finish the job Papa Doc started."

"You're sick."

"Just saying."

"The Tontons Macoutes," Albertine resumed, glowering at her cousin, "sowed terror among the population not only by their actions but by their appearance. They wore denim like Azaka, the loa of agriculture, and used machetes like Ogun, the loa of iron and war. Even their name was designed to prey on people's fears. Tonton Macoute is a bogeyman from Haitian folklore who kidnaps children and carries them off in a sack. Essentially, they were a perversion of *vodou* beliefs, just as Papa Doc himself was, with his black undertaker's suit, hat and heavy sunglasses."

"I don't get it," said Lex.

"Papa Doc styled himself after Baron Samedi, the loa of death and cemeteries. His look said, 'I have power over life and death, and don't you forget it.' Although actual practitioners of *vodou* were not held in high regard by him and his bullyboys."

"Because they might point out that he wasn't all he claimed to be."

"Just so. To them, he was a blasphemer. The braver ones said as much, not that it helped. The Tontons Macoutes dealt with them the same way they dealt with all troublemakers. When Papa Doc died in 'seventy-one and Baby Doc took over, things got even worse. More chaotic. Baby Doc didn't have his father's charisma or ruthlessness. He fell out with the Tontons Macoutes and was finally forced into exile in 'eighty-six, by which time Haiti was all but ruined. Most of the middle classes and the wealth creators had quit the country long beforehand—the Haitian Diaspora, which took them to places like Cuba, the Dominican Republic, the United States. My grandparents were among them. They came to Manzanilla with my mother and her little sister, Wilberforce's mother, to seek a better life, but not only for that reason. Also to escape execution. Specifically the execution of my mother."

"Why?"

"Because she, though only in her teens, was showing signs of becoming a powerful *vodou* adept. And, being in her teens, she was naturally outspoken and rebellious. The two things in Haiti during those years were not a good combination. Things got hot for my family. My grandparents bought passage on a little fishing boat, leaving everything they had behind, and made their way here to begin again. My mother, Hélène, kept up her *vodou* training and studies, and within a decade had become a mambo to be reckoned with. Truly one of the greats."

"A big woman in every way," said Wilberforce. He whistled and shook his head. "You should see her, Lex. A metre and a half tall and about a hundred kilos. She's like a ball, almost perfectly round."

"Hey, that's my mama you're insulting," said Albertine.

"Who's insulting? She is big. You can't deny it. You could shove Aunt Hélène down a hill and she wouldn't stop rolling 'til she reached the sea."

"Do you want her to put a *wanga* on you, Wilberforce?" Albertine said. "I can ask her to. A quick phone call is all it'll take. Steal a washcloth from your house, tie seven knots in it, drop it in a river, and you won't be able to get hard again, not until you beg her forgiveness. How about that, eh? Your limp little *zozo* dangling between your legs, no use for satisfying any of those dozens of girlfriends you're forever boasting about."

Wilberforce blanched, then tried to brazen it out. "It wouldn't work. You can't cast a hex on someone who doesn't believe."

"But don't you believe? If you believe even a little tiny bit, it'll happen. Trust me."

Wilberforce seemed about to argue further, but Lex intervened. "I'd leave it there if I were you, mate. Don't want to go messing around with that sort of thing, especially when it involves a part of you you're so very fond of."

"Wisely spoken, Lex," said Albertine.

"I take it the role of mambo is hereditary, then," Lex said.

"It can be. In my case it is. My sister Giselle and I grew up watching our mother hold her ceremonies, give gifts to the loa, ask them for help on her own behalf and on others', be ridden by them during the rituals. Giselle pooh-poohed it as peasant superstition, but I knew it wasn't. It was more than that. It brought tangible results. It was *truth*. So when I was old enough, I asked Mama to start teaching me the ways, and soon I was a *vodouisante* myself, familiar with the loa *nachons*, the songs, the dances, the drumbeats. I now have my own peristyle—a sacred space, kind of a temple—at home, and in my spare time I offer people consultations and advice. I make candles for them to purify their homes with, cast spells to ward off evil or bring luck, heal them if they have some sickness of the soul..."

"It's a nice little sideline," said Wilberforce. "They give her money, expensive gifts, free meals. Fleecing the gullible, I call it."

"Oh, yes?" Albertine said. "And the inflated prices you charge at your rum shack—what's that if it isn't fleecing?"

"It's a legitimate mark-up."

"But having a two-tier system, one set of prices for locals, another for tourists?"

"That's just simple economics."

"And what about when you flew your seaplane, before

the airport was built? You used to charge outrageous prices for ferrying passengers and packages between islands. And sometimes you'd claim a parcel had got lost, but for twenty dollars you could 'find' it again."

"The price of aviation fuel—"

"You're as bad as the Garfish," Albertine said hotly. "You and he deserve each other. What annoys me is that you wouldn't even have to owe the man anything if you'd only sold that damn plane of yours."

"I'm not selling *Puddle Jumper* for anyone or anything," Wilberforce shot back. "She's my pride and joy. Besides, I don't think I'd get that much for her."

"Not even as spare parts?"

"Cruel. That'd be like selling your own children's organs."

"So you'd rather borrow from a crook instead?" Albertine sucked her teeth so viciously it sounded like swearing.

Lex was loath to intrude again, but neither could he take much more of it.

"We've gone a bit off-topic," he said diplomatically. "Albertine, I'm happy to accept that you're a mambo. Each to their own. Whatever floats your boat. But you say I'm in danger. Do you mean from the Garfish? Because if so, not exactly a newsflash."

"Not just him. Not him at all, I don't think."

"Then who?"

"The loa were not able to specify. Here's what happened. Last night, I was making an offering to my three husbands."

Lex raised an eyebrow.

"My three loa husbands," Albertine clarified. "Every mambo or houngan—that's a *vodou* priest—is 'married' to at least one loa, more usually three. They are the ones who favour us the most and watch over us. Mine are Damballah, Loko and Erzulie Freda, who's actually female and also Damballah's wife, but don't let that confuse you."

"Not confused at all," Lex said wryly.

"As I was serving Damballah a saucer of white flour with a white egg on top, all of a sudden he took control of me. I became his 'horse,' as we say. His *chwal*. An image of him appeared in my mind. Damballah has many forms, but most often he manifests as a serpent, a white python. He slithered inside me and I in turn fell to the floor and started slithering too, and as I did so he spoke. He told me that the balance of life is at risk of being upset. Cosmic equilibrium is threatened. He gave me your name, saying you were at the centre of it all somehow, and he informed me that you are a friend of my cousin's, which I knew already as Wilberforce has talked about you now and then. He speaks highly of you, by the way."

"So I should hope."

"Damballah was very alarmed, and it is not comforting to see a spirit, an aspect of the godhead, alarmed. He said I must go to you and offer my aid, and must not take no for an answer." She spread out her hands. Her nails were long, beautifully manicured, lacquered in the richest of reds. "And here I am."

"Ah," said Lex. "Interesting."

Gable at the crossroads last night: *Help'll be offered you, and when it come, you don' turn it away, you knowum sayin'? Whatever your finer feelin's, you don' say no.*

Lex felt an unaccountable shiver run through him. What the fuck was going on here? He felt as though he had been thrown into the middle of some bizarre conspiracy, tides of coincidence swirling heavily around him. This time yesterday morning he'd been contemplating nothing more arduous than going for a run before the sun got too hot, then heading down to the beach afterwards for a spot of snorkelling. Now: a job from Seraphina, a gun battle with gangsters, voodoo, or *vodou* if you preferred...

"All right," he said to Albertine. "I have no inkling what this danger you're talking about could be, and you don't either, so what we're going to do is back-burner it for now. No point stressing over unknowns. When and if an adverse situation presents itself, then we'll take action. In the meantime—"

His phone bleeped. A text. From Seraphina.

Rendezvous with Caribair flight CBC301 from Washington via Bermuda, arriving 12:20 local. Five friends disembarking. They will brief you further. xxx Seraphina

He glanced at the phone's clock. A couple of hours to go. But Nestor Philippe Airport was all the way over on the windward side of the island, and there were no decent roads between here and there save the six-mile stretch of the René Smithson Highway. Being late would not look good.

"Tell you what," he said. "If neither of you's got anything else on, I could do with a hand on the transportation front. Got some people I'm meeting off a plane, and we'll need two cars."

"Not a problem," said Albertine. "I'm sticking with you until my skills are needed, whenever that is."

"And I'm sticking with her," said Wilberforce. "Because if there's going to be some sort of aggravation…"

"I'm perfectly capable of looking after myself," Albertine protested.

"But if Aunt Hélène found out I'd let you go off on your own, without some muscle to back you up, God knows what she'd do to me. Worse than giving me the droop, that's for certain."

"Muscle? I'll have Lex for that."

"Stringy streak of piss like him?" Wilberforce snorted.

"Cheers, Wilb," said Lex.

"No offence."

"None taken, I'm sure."

"I mean, I'm not saying you're not good in a pinch, but…"

"No, I understand. Albertine is family."

"Yeah."

"Honestly, Wilberforce," Albertine said. "I'll be fine."

"No arguing, cuz."

"*Please*, no more arguing," Lex implored. "Wilb can tag along if he wants. The more the merrier."

EIGHT

TEAM THIRTEEN

THE CONVOY OF two, Subaru and Suzuki, reached the airport with quarter of an hour to spare, despite being held up on the way by an achingly slow tractor and a broken-down farm truck with a flatbed full of anxiously bleating goats. Lex requested that Albertine and Wilberforce stay with the cars while he went inside.

The terminal building was a draughty concrete structure, built more with diligence than panache. Bright, gaudy posters occupied the walls of the arrivals lounge, showing sun-seekers at play in the sand and surf and advertising day-trips to Manzanilla's modest natural wonders: the waterfall at Cannon Rock and the caves in the King Alfonso Hills with their three-metre-tall stalagmites of bat guano.

Flight CBC301 was on time, but the customs and immigration process was invariably slow, so Lex had leisure to peruse the racks at the news kiosk. A two-day-old copy of the *Daily Mail*, from back home, had a headline deploring the latest tax hike from Westminster, which the paper dubbed 'fiscal lunacy' and 'an insult to the hard-working, hard-pressed middle classes.' As a rule, Lex tried to avoid keeping up with events in the UK.

It always filled him with a disquieting mixture of nostalgia and disdain. He wondered if anything would ever tempt him back to his homeland. Probably not. After seven years away it seemed a remote place, drab in his memory, and while he had been living there he had been something of a nomad anyway, seldom occupying his London flat for any significant length of time. Britain had been a base he returned to between forays abroad, a convenient foxhole, nothing more. He felt little affinity for the country, and whatever allegiance he owed it he had more than discharged.

At last CaribAir passengers began filtering through from the luggage carousels. Lex had no idea who he had come to meet, but he was confident he would know them when he saw them.

Sure enough, a group of five—four men, one woman— appeared through the doors, and one glance told Lex these were his people. They were dressed like tourists: shorts, sandals, eye-watering Hawaiian shirts, here and there an item of ostentatious jewellery such as a Rolex. Two of the men had stubbly chins and another sported collar-length hair.

They didn't move like tourists, though. They didn't gaze around themselves wide-eyed, or fan themselves in the stifling, inadequately air-conditioned atmosphere of the terminal, or check their phones to see if they had network coverage yet. They didn't grapple with overloaded baggage trolleys—they had travelled with personal carry-on only. They walked as a unit, calm but purposeful, subtly aware of their surroundings.

US military, no question. Lex wasn't fooled by the 'relaxed grooming standards.' Lean, efficient killers. Special forces.

He drew away from the news kiosk, making himself obvious. He had decided he would downplay his own talents until he got to know these people better. It was preferable for them to underestimate him, not perceive him as an equal or a rival. It would give him something in reserve if he needed it.

"Afternoon," he said to the frontmost man in the group, a rangy, grizzled figure, mid-forties, athletic build, moustachioed like a porn actor. Instinct told him this was the leader.

Grey eyes peered at him from beneath bushy brows. "You Dove?"

"I am."

"Tom Buckler. Put her there, sport." His grip was strong, and Lex resisted the temptation to match it, pound-pressure for pound-pressure. "These here are my associates. That's Bob Tartaglione."

A glossy-haired Italian-American gave Lex a nod.

"Corey Sampson."

A tall African-American touched finger to forehead. "Pleased to meetcha."

"Madison Morgenstern."

The woman's short blonde bob offset a firm jawline. "Hi."

"And him back there's Pearce."

This one looked like a farmhand or a cowboy, trim and permanently sunburned.

"He doesn't go in for first names," said Buckler.

Pearce grunted something barely audible.

"Or talk much," Buckler added.

"Lex Dove," said Lex, meeting everyone's gaze in turn. "Welcome to Manzanilla. I'll be your tour guide throughout your stay. Anything you need, don't hesitate to ask."

"What we need right now," said Buckler, "is to go retrieve our gear. It's come through under diplomatic seal and I guess it's being held somewhere private off to the side. Maybe you can assist with that...?"

IT WAS A test, of sorts. A way of establishing Lex's bona fides and level of competence. He'd anticipated something like this, however, and had already identified a senior member of airport staff in the arrivals lounge. Within minutes he and the Americans were in a private room whose tinted windows afforded a good view of the runway and the mid-sized passenger jets parked in a row alongside the terminal building like piglets at the teat. Paperwork was checked and approved, dotted lines were signed on, and shortly each of the five Americans was in possession of a large canvas duffel bag whose contents clanked dully and heavily.

"We're booked in at the Cape Azure Hotel," said Buckler to Lex. "Any good?"

"Don't expect Radisson standards and you'll be fine."

"Website says it's got five stars."

"Deduct one for exaggeration and another for this being Manzanilla."

Two of the Americans went in the Suzuki with Albertine and Wilberforce. The rest rode with Lex in the Subaru.

"Guess I should introduce us properly," said Buckler as Lex pulled out of the airport car park. "Lieutenant Buckler's my full title, and they call us Team Thirteen. We're a Navy SEAL platoon, only not quite."

"Not quite?"

"Well, for one thing, there's five of us in this boat crew. The average SEAL platoon's sixteen strong—two officers, fourteen shooters. And for another thing..."

"We do the jobs other SEAL teams don't do," Tartaglione chimed in.

"Don't or won't?" said Lex.

"Don't, 'cause they wouldn't know how to handle 'em."

"Right. Meaning dirty work."

"Hell, no. SEALs do dirty work all of the time. It's what they're there for."

"We do... stuff," said Sampson. "It's kinda hard to classify. 'Grey ops' is the official name for it."

Lex shrugged. "Still none the wiser. Is that black ops but a few shades paler?"

"Put it this way, hoss," said Buckler. "There's shit out there in the world, and then there's freaky shit. Me and my shooters get parachuted in to deal with the freaky shit."

"Oh. Okay," said Lex.

"More than that is need-to-know only. I'm told you have top-level clearance."

"I do." Lex certainly used to, and it seemed it hadn't yet been rescinded.

"But unless or until you're actually operational with us, you're better off staying in the dark. Speaking of which. Those two civilians back there..." Buckler jerked a thumb in the direction of the Suzuki, behind them. "Pearce won't say a word to 'em as a matter of course, and Hospitalman Morgenstern knows to keep her trap shut. But they can be relied upon to be discreet, yeah?"

"I guarantee it."

"Good. Good for their sake, and for yours."

Lex was forming an impression of Lieutenant Buckler, and it was not a wholly positive one. He understood that the man had a job to do and wasn't a Navy SEAL officer because of his impeccable social skills. Nonetheless, there was no excuse to go around treating people you'd only just met with a brusqueness bordering on contempt.

Under normal circumstances Lex wouldn't have stomached such an attitude from anyone. But two hundred grand bought a great deal of leeway. If Buckler wanted a dogsbody to boss around for a couple of days, at that price he could have one. Lex could swallow his pride.

The René Smithson Highway, Manzanilla's most impressive infrastructure project, petered out to become a narrow, badly asphalted road. Thirty bumpy, swerving minutes later, the two cars pulled in at the turning circle outside the Cape Azure. The hotel was a set of low buildings laid out haphazardly on a promontory—two-storey oblong blocks with seaward-facing balconies and picture windows.

As the SEALs checked in at the reception desk, Wilberforce and Albertine kept shooting quizzical looks at Lex: *Who are these people? What's your connection to them?* Lex responded with an expression which he hoped said, *I'll explain later.*

"My guys are going to grab some sack time," Buckler told Lex once the formalities at reception were through. "We've been in transit for the best part of thirty-six hours and our body clocks barely know what time of day it is. You and me, though, we should have words. Somewhere private."

"Of course," said Lex. "I'll just tell my friends they're free to go."

"As a matter of fact, sport," said Buckler, drawing Lex aside, "your friends might want to hang around. Morgenstern got chatting with them on the way over, and she figures at least one of them could be useful to us, more likely both."

"What? No."

"Morgenstern has a way of getting people to open up. Seems like there's some talent there we might tap into."

"They're civilians; your word. Whatever you're here to do, it surely can't involve noncombatants."

"It surely can if I deem it necessary."

"I won't allow it." Lex was incensed. This was outrageous. Buckler was overstepping the mark. He couldn't go dragooning Wilberforce and Albertine into service just because they happened to be present and available. "If there are people with specialist skills you need, I can find them for you on the island, no problem. But I'm not having you exploit these two simply because they fit the bill. I don't even see what good they'll be to you. Wilberforce runs a bar. Albertine's an IT expert. Unless you're hankering for a cocktail or your laptop's on the blink..."

Buckler bent his head even closer to Lex's, speaking quietly but with force. "Listen, Mr Dove. You are the hired help here. You know nothing. I have certain operational requirements which you cannot possibly understand, and I will employ any and all measures to ensure that they are met. You can either do what you're being paid to do and comply with my wishes, or you can back off and get the fuck out of my way. Capiche?"

"And you, Mr Buckler," Lex replied, not the least bit cowed, "can get your face out of mine, or I will gladly rearrange your features, starting with that gleaming American dentistry of yours. Capiche?"

Buckler didn't blink. There was calculation in those snowy-grey eyes, a steady reassessment of the Englishman in front of him. Everyone else was looking on with curiosity and concern. The tension between Lex and Buckler crackled outwards, filling the space around them with an uneasy charge.

"Let's us take this outside," Buckler said. "Discuss it where there's no audience."

"Fine by me."

"You two." This to Wilberforce and Albertine. "Mind waiting here a while?" Buckler thrust a fistful of Manzanillan dollars at them. "Have lunch on me. Mr Dove and I are heading out for a nice friendly stroll."

NINE

A REASONED, GENTLEMANLY EXCHANGE OF VIEWS

LEX WAS SIZING Buckler up physically as they exited the lobby, debating how easy—or not—it would be to take the American down. A Navy SEAL was the hardest of the hard in the US military, the soldier's soldier. The training programme was second to none in its brutality and attrition rate. On average, four fifths of candidates flunked the initial eight gruelling weeks of instruction and exercise, which was designed to break a man down to the core and show him the true measure of himself. The rest were left with the belief that they were nigh on indestructible. Further training turned these graduates into killing machines with exceptional tactical and strategic sensibilities and an uncompromising, never-say-die ethic. Buckler would be a fearsome opponent in any form of combat, armed or hand-to-hand.

That was all right, though. Lex was no slouch in the fighting department either.

They passed sunbathers who were lounging beside a crisp blue swimming pool, sipping drinks, fiddling with their smartphones, scrolling through books on their e-readers, plugged into music on their MP3 players, yelling at their children—all blissfully oblivious to the hostility simmering between Lex and Buckler, the potential for bone-crunching violence.

Then the two men were on the beach, striding across sand like muscovado sugar, fine-grained and fawn. They walked until they reached the beach's end, where coconut palms grew thick and tourists were few and far between. They were well out of earshot of the hotel, distant specks to the unaided eye.

"I'd prefer this not to come down to a smackdown between us," Buckler said. "We're meant to be co-operating. Special relationship and such."

"I'm happy to co-operate," said Lex. "What I will not accept is some bloke who thinks he's hot shit waltzing in and taking advantage. Whatever your mission is, Wilberforce Allen and Albertine Montase have no part in it. I draw the line there, and you do not cross it."

"You, Mr Dove, if I may say, are arguing from a position of total ignorance. You wouldn't be so quick to make blanket statements like that if you had the first clue what we're up against and how urgent it is that we see the matter resolved."

"Ignorant I may be, but some things are non-negotiable, and this is one of them."

"Has it occurred to you that your friends might volunteer their services, willingly, if asked?"

"Whether that's the case or not, I'm not prepared to let you ask them or put undue pressure on them in any way. Because you will, and they're good people—innocents—and I won't have them placed in harm's way, even if it is with their consent."

Wearily Buckler shook his head. "You know, it's a shame. I was hoping you and I would be able to settle this with a reasoned, gentlemanly exchange of views."

"Then, lieutenant, back down. Simple as that."

"No can do, ace. Let me just say that in eight seconds I could have you on the ground, in a chokehold, unconscious. And all's I'd have to do is maintain the pressure for a few seconds more, starve your brain of blood and oxygen, and that'd be that. Lights out. Permanently."

"Of course you could," said Lex. "And by the same token, I could grab you, spin your round, take hold of you from behind by the jaw with both hands, and kick your legs out from under you. You'd fall, and your own bodyweight would separate your skull from your spinal column at the Atlas bone."

"It could happen," said Buckler nonchalantly. "Or I could slam your head backwards against that there palm tree trunk—shatter the back of your skull. What'd kill you, though, is your brain getting hurled forward, tearing against the inside of its case."

"Funny you should mention palm trees," Lex replied. "My speciality is making it look as though someone has died through mishap rather than design. I use what's around me. I often improvise. See these coconuts lying around?" There were several on the beach, smooth green seed pods the size of rugby balls. "People get killed by those all the time. They can fall from the tree right down onto your cranium, from a height of thirty feet or more, and each is a solid thing weighing up to five pounds when fresh. Wham! Instant fatality. A body gets discovered here, at this very spot, with a bloodstained coconut nearby, and the coroner will draw only one conclusion. It won't occur to him that someone might have slammed the coconut down on the deceased's head."

"Cute. How about this? I pull you forwards and down into a headlock. I grab your pants belt, haul you up upside-down, and fall backwards, landing on your head. Our combined weight crushes it like an egg."

"It would work better on firmer ground than this. Tarmac or concrete, or a tiled floor. But I take your point."

"It's called the Brain Buster," said Buckler. "There's also the Russian Omelette."

"That's the one where you cross the fellow's legs, fold him over with his shoulders to the ground, pull his legs up on top, sit on them, and snap his spine at the base."

"Yep. Those psychos in the Spetsnaz love that one."

"Hmm. It's always struck me as a bit elaborate. Besides, the subject has to be out cold at first, or at least stunned."

"Easily arranged. A jab to the summit of the nose or the upper lip—that'll have the guy reeling, not knowing what the hell's going on. You can do pretty much what you want with him after that."

"I agree that everything goes much more smoothly if your opponent is too dazed to resist or put up a fight," said Lex. "So imagine that that's happened here. My next move—this is me taking the 'accident' route again—would be to drag the person out into the shallows. This lovely flat beach sand extends only so far. There are rocks and reefs out there below the surface. Just last year a youngish man, only in his late twenties, was larking about with his wife in the surf not a hundred yards from where we're standing. They were newlyweds. Honeymooners. He plunged under, whacked his forehead on a hidden rock, end of story. A terrible tragedy. So it's not unprecedented that someone could die in that way just here."

"It would surely be a pity if history repeated itself."

"It would, Lieutenant Buckler."

Lex and Buckler continued to face each other, gazes locked. A breeze stirred the tips of Buckler's silver-flecked moustache. Waves crested and plunged, blazing in the sun.

"I believe we have arrived at a stalemate," Buckler said.

Lex nodded. Stalemate was a good word for it. They had just played a game of verbal chess, each of them gauging the measure not only of the other's abilities but also of his willingness to follow through on his threats. Each now knew that he was facing a serious proposition. It wasn't only in what they said, it was in the calm conviction with which they said it. Each was left in no doubt that the other was prepared to do whatever it took to get his own way.

"Compromise," suggested Lex.

"I'm all ears."

"Let *me* talk to Wilberforce and Albertine, not you."

"Sounds doable."

"That way they'll be getting it from somebody familiar, somebody they trust, rather than some random American they don't know from a hole in the ground. And I'll phrase the request however I see fit. No arm-twisting, no guilt-tripping."

"I can probably go along with that."

"But," Lex added, "first, before anything else, I'll need a full mission briefing."

"Fair enough."

"And if I don't like the sound of it..."

"Mr Dove," said Buckler with something like a sigh, "let me be frank about this. A Team Thirteen op is never going to be tea and crumpets on the lawn, or whatever it is you Brits like to do of an afternoon. I can guarantee you it's going to be grim and insane and nightmarish. A total bitch. I wish it weren't, but it always is. That said, my unit are the best there is at this job. They do what no one else could or would dare to, and they do it with the utmost courage and professionalism. You *won't* like the sound of it, I can assure you of that, but if anyone's got a chance of pulling this thing off successfully, meeting the mission aims, surviving—then it's me and my shooters."

"Am I supposed to feel all fired up and happy now?" Lex said.

Buckler very nearly cracked a smile. "That was my best pre-game pep talk. Sure you are."

TEN

JANITORS OF THE UNCANNY

BUCKLER TURNED THE air con in his suite up to full. The vent rumbled into life, scaring a tiny brown lizard clinging to the wall nearby. The reptile scurried for safety into a crack in the skirting board.

Coolness sifted slowly into the sweltering room.

The American removed a ruggedized laptop from his carry-on bag and set it on a small round table by the window. While the computer booted up, he pulled a couple of beers from the mini-bar fridge and passed one to Lex.

"Hotel'll charge you an arm and a leg for those," Lex warned.

"Uncle Sam's picking up the tab. He can definitely afford a couple of beers."

Lex twisted off the bottle cap. "So tell me. A grey op. What is that? You said 'freaky shit.' How freaky? Freaky in what way?"

Buckler pondered how to put it. "Okay. Take our most recent assignment. Day and a half ago we were in Siberia, can you believe it. Roughly six hundred klicks north of Krasnoyarsk, wading through swampland and taiga west of the Yenisey river. Worst fucking terrain imaginable."

"I know. I've been."

"Swarms of horseflies and deerflies so thick you can scarcely see through them, biting worse than any mosquitoes. Nothing but pine forest and sodden ground for mile upon shitty mile. Guess what we were hunting there?"

"I'm going to hazard it wasn't pheasant. Men?"

"A man," said Buckler. "One lone man. But like no man you've ever known. A man who was also an animal."

"I've met a few of those in my time."

"No, you don't understand. Literally an animal. A bear."

"A man who was also a bear?"

"A werebear. As they call it in Russia, *medvyedchik*."

Lex laugh-snorted. "You're kidding me."

"I look like a kidder to you?" said Buckler. "This guy was a shape-shifter. An indigene from one of the Samoyed tribes. Some of the locals thought he might be a shaman—medicine men round those parts are supposed to be able to transform themselves into animals—but a couple of the shamans we spoke to denied it. Said no true shaman would be so destructive. He'd been roaming the area for a while, this werebear, preying on reindeer herds, scaring the hell out of villagers. Then, come winter, when the reindeer were moved south to warmer pastures, he started snatching children. The smallest of kids, sometimes even babies. Got a taste for them. He'd take them from their cribs in the middle of the night."

"He did this in the guise of a bear?"

"Looking like a bear. Behaving like a bear. But a bear with human ingenuity and cunning. He could open gates and doors. Undo window latches. Sneak in and out of houses without a sound. Avoid traps laid for him."

"And you're certain it wasn't just an especially smart bear?"

"Shut up and listen," said Buckler. "We got to hear about what was happening thanks to a Russian air force base up in that region. Used to be, back in Soviet times, they'd send up Tupolev Falcons and Swifts from there to fly reconnaissance missions over the Arctic Circle. Tribesmen went to the base and asked the airmen for help. The airmen couldn't do squat. Basically they're a maintenance unit, a skeleton crew keeping the runway in useable condition and a bunch of rusting planes just about airworthy in case some big new conflict suddenly blows up. Not much in the way of weaponry. Or guts. Mostly men bored out of their minds, drinking vodka all day long and jerking off over internet porn. But the officer in charge, veteran pilot by the name of Captain Zhdanov, he'd made friends in the USAF during the post-*glasnost* period when Americans and Russians started doing manoeuvres together, before his booze problem got the better of him and he was packed off to this nursemaid job in the middle of nowhere. Zhdanov phoned a guy he knew at Nellis in Nevada, asked a favour, the Nellis guy passed the info on to our CIA controllers in the Special Activities Division—bingo, it's a job for Team Thirteen."

"So you went in, chased down the werebear, presumably killed it..."

"No mean feat. Fucker wasn't only cunning, he was huge. Fifteen feet tall on his hindlegs. Strong as three grizzlies put together. Near invulnerable, too. Our first run-in with him, he got wind of us coming and went on the offensive. Caught us on the hop. We poured dozens of bullets into him, and it barely made a dent. That's the trouble with mystical beasts, we've found. Conventional arms don't always work. Sometimes you've got to upgrade, think laterally."

"How?" Lex was struggling to believe he was even having this conversation. Buckler really expected him to take this nonsense seriously? A *werebear*?

"Well," said Buckler, "we went back to the shamans and said, 'We followed the *medvyedchik*'s trail, met him, shot him, frightened him off, but we know now we're not going to kill him with just plain rifle rounds. Any suggestions?' See, this is how we roll. We use local support whenever and wherever we can. And the shamans told us they'd tried warding charms and prayers to the sky gods and what-all-else in hopes of getting rid of the werebear, and no joy, but one of them said maybe there was a medicine that could help. He disappeared off into the woods to gather ingredients and soon he was back with armfuls of herbs and tree bark and such, and he cooked it all up in a pot, chanted over it, and what it was was a potion, a kind of gluey liquid that we were to smear over ourselves and it would make us undetectable to the *medvyedchik* so's we could get close enough up to him to inflict some serious damage. Stank to high heaven, that gunk, but we stripped down to our skivvies and slapped it on all over like sunscreen and went out again into the forest to track our target."

"Did it work?"

"Sure as shit did. We snuck up on old Barney the Mega-Bear like we were ninjas. He didn't hear us coming, definitely didn't smell us coming. The medicine disguised us like Harry Potter's cloak of fucking invisibility. The reek confused the werebear's senses, disoriented him. A couple of RPGs landing by him disoriented him a whole lot further, and then, when we had him on the ropes, Petty Officer Sampson went in to deliver the coop dee grace—an M67 fragmentation grenade. Sampson tossed that grenade straight into the werebear's gaping mouth. Guy's got a hell of a pitching arm on him. Could have played baseball in the major leagues, I reckon. Now, a mystical beast can withstand a lot of punishment, as we've already established, but the monster hasn't been found yet that can argue with six-and-a-half ounces of Composition B explosive and a shitload of steel fragments erupting inside its head. Werebear was damn near decapitated. And as it fell..."

"What?"

"It became just a man again," said Buckler. "Morphed, shrank, until it was this naked, puny little stringbean, kind of like you. Headless, of course. No longer a terrifying red-eyed creature. Just a dead human body with a ragged stump of neck, lying sprawled in the undergrowth. Kind of anticlimactic, that." He looked rueful. "After so much spooky supernatural hoo-hah, to see that all you've done is eliminate a person, nothing more. Some guy who had the bad luck to get cursed by a gypsy or bitten by another werebear or something, as much a victim as a villain. Sort of sours the victory for you, know what I mean?"

"I imagine it does." Lex examined his half-empty beer bottle. "Can I ask, Lieutenant Buckler—how long have you been a functioning alcoholic?"

"Oh, ha ha. Wiseguy."

"Must be me, then. I must have hallucinated the past few minutes while you've been telling me about hunting Winnie-the-Pooh's mutant monster cousin in the wilds of Siberia. I vow never to touch another drop."

"Now you hold it right there, sport." Buckler leaned across, thrusting his face directly in front of Lex's, so close his moustache almost brushed Lex's nose. "You stow that snarky bullshit. I've been running this boat crew for five years now, and in that time I've seen things. Things you'd never credit. Things that'd leave someone like you gibbering in the corner in a puddle of your own piss, just at the sight of them. Me and my shooters have confronted some of the goddamnest awful and inexplicable crap the world has to offer, and we haven't done that simply so that assholes like you can come along and mock. Look into my eyes. Look deep. Are these the eyes of a madman? Of someone who'd make shit like this up?"

Lex had to concede that there was nothing but sincerity in Buckler's eyes. Sincerity of the most alarming kind. Sincerity that bordered on blazing zeal.

"You think there aren't monsters in the world?" Buckler went on. "I've seen 'em. Seen 'em all. Vampires? Believe you me, I've killed vampires. More of them than Buffy and Van Helsing put together. They're nothing like Count Dracula, I can assure you, and nothing like those twinkly *Twilight* douchebags either. Then there's devils. You reckon devils are just something made up by the church fathers to frighten folks into being good and not straying from the righteous path? Devils are real, pal, and what's more, they're slippery, twisty, lethal motherfuckers. Djinns? Lake serpents? Gigantic burrowing worms in the Mongolian desert that can swallow a horse whole? All fictitious, right? Straight out of legend, or books, or bad sci-fi movies, right? Wrong! They're as real, as tangible, as you and me. Know how I know? Because I have beheld them with my own two eyes, *these* eyes, and not only that but I have blown shit out of them, too. Any idea what I was doing Christmas before last, while everyone else was tucking into turkey and knocking back the eggnog and trying on the godawful sweater their Aunt Mabel just gave them? I'll tell you. I was with Team Thirteen in Moldova—which is barely even a country, more a stain on the map—in the foothills of the Carpathian Mountains, in a cavern, destroying a clutch of dragon's eggs with flamethrowers. And that's no word of a lie."

"Dragon's...?"

"You heard correctly. My life is spent leading a group of people who hunt down freaks of nature and eradicate them. Name me something you think is fantasy, something you reckon can only be found in myth and folklore. I'll tell you if I've come across it."

"All right," said Lex, bemused. "Werewolf."

"Huh. I've given you a werebear. A werewolf's nothing. My squad dealt with one in Germany, the Black Forest, about three months back. Try again."

"Vampire."

"I already said about vampires."

"Oh yes. Troll."

"Sjunkhatten National Park, Norway. Living beneath a road bridge over a fjord, snatching hikers who went trip-trapping across. Try harder."

"Okay, then. Chupacabras."

"We've fragged the odd South American goat-sucker."

"Ghoul."

"Bahrain, two years ago."

"Abominable Snowman."

"Well now, he's not exactly what you'd call a clear and present danger to anyone, stuck way up in the remote Himalayas like that, all by his lonesome."

"But you've seen him?"

"I've seen some pretty convincing spy-satellite footage of him," said Buckler. "Is that it? The best you can do?"

"Honest politician," said Lex.

Buckler couldn't help but chuckle. "Now you're being ridiculous. Everybody knows there's no such thing."

Lex sat back. He didn't like to admit it, but he was halfway to thinking that Buckler was telling the truth. If not, then the man was delusional or a phenomenally good liar, and the impression Lex had so far formed of him suggested he was neither.

"But it would be front-page news, wouldn't it?" he said, scrabbling for a rebuttal. "Trolls in Norway, werewolves in Germany..."

"Would be if the CIA and the Pentagon ever allowed it to be," Buckler replied. "We got people, Langley data analysts, employed full-time covering up any and all reports of Team Thirteen activity. We do covert like no one else does covert. You'd know a thing or two about that yourself, career history like yours. Tell me if there's one journalist who even got close to publishing a story about your involvement in a high-profile assassination."

"We have ways of making them not talk," Lex said. "And that's assuming I was ever careless enough to leave a trail of evidence in the first place."

"Precisely. Same here. Folks want safe, orderly lives, don't they? They want to know their jobs are secure, their kids are getting taught properly at school, the bills are paid, the car works, they can go fishing at the weekends or catch a movie or have a burger at McDonalds or whatever. They *don't* want to know that there's people like you who go around offing the bad guys so that those safe, orderly lives can continue for them."

"'People sleep peaceably in their beds at night only because rough men stand ready to do violence on their behalf.'"

"Yeah, I like that quote. Orwell, right?"

"Attributed to him. There's some dispute. It could be Kipling, or Churchill. But it's been a mantra of mine since as long as I can remember."

"The principle applies equally to Team Thirteen," Buckler said. "You think the world would stay calmly spinning on its axis if suddenly there was absolute, definitive proof of, say, the existence of vampires? Scrawny, slimy bloodsucking motherfuckers with the blackest tongues and worst breath imaginable? We're here to tidy them away without the general population finding out, sweep them under the carpet so that global sanity can continue. We're the janitors of the uncanny. It's a thankless task, but someone's got to do it."

"Okay," said Lex. "Let's say, for argument's sake, that I accept everything you've just told me." He couldn't, not quite, but he was getting there. "I suppose the next logical question is, what's going on around these parts that demands the attention of Team Thirteen? What sort of 'freaky shit' have you come to our shores to shovel up?"

BUCKLER TYPED SOME commands into the laptop, then spun it round so that the screen faced Lex.

"What you're about to see is classified 'Sensitive Compartmented Information'—above top secret," he said. "It's footage streamed from the helmet camera of a member of a unit of US Marines who were inserted into a location not far from here some thirty-six hours ago. The location is a US military research installation, and the leathernecks were sent in because there'd been a sudden and catastrophic loss of communications. All radio traffic and satellite uplinks went dark two days ago, and SOP in response to such a turn of events is to launch a recon-and-rescue party. The Marine commandos were helo'ed over from Hurlburt Field in Florida, and all's they expected to find on entry was that there'd been a power outage, uplink on the fritz, something of that sort. Nothing to get your panties in a bunch about. The research scientists and their military supervisor would all be fine and dandy, and everyone could go back home and have a drink and laugh about it."

"I'm guessing that wasn't how it turned out."

"Watch and see." Buckler clicked on the Play icon, and a video clip started up onscreen. It was night-vision footage, flickery and ambiguous. Vague green figures were running and yelling. Guns rattled. Hot white lines of tracer round flashed. Tight echoes suggested the firefight was taking place in close confines, indoors. The image jerked this way and that. Lex found it difficult to follow, or fathom.

"It's chaos," he said. "Who are they shooting at?" He kept glimpsing figures in the background, pale and elusive. "And why's there no return fire?"

"Hah. Spotted that, did you? The answer is, they appear to be shooting at an unarmed enemy. Which is not the Marine corps way, not normally. What's also anomalous is that the enemy seem to have the upper hand. Marines are dying. You can hear it on the soundtrack."

Lex could. Screams interspersed the gunfire, and they were screams of mortal terror—and mortal pain.

Finally there came a lull, and then a lone, hoarse voice calling from a distance: "Bondye! Bondye! Hear me, Bondye. I am coming for you."

Buckler pressed Stop.

Lex let out a breath he hadn't realised he'd been holding.

"Makes no sense," he said. "Enlisted men with automatic weapons, an elite force, coming off worst against... unarmed civilians? And who, or what, is a 'Bondye'?"

"Can't account for the first part of that, although I have my suspicions," said Buckler. "As for the second part, I can tell you that Bondye is a term used in voodoo practices."

"Voodoo..." Lex felt the ground underneath him begin to shift, solidity giving way to quivering uncertainty, as though he had stepped onto quicksand. Voodoo. Fucking voodoo again.

"It's pidgin French. Breaks down as '*bon dieu.*' Basically, it's the voodoo term for God."

"'God! God! I am coming for you.'"

"That's what the guy's saying."

"Shit. So what does it mean?"

"That," said Buckler grimly, "is the big damn honking question, isn't it?"

ELEVEN

PUDDLE JUMPER

Lex found Wilberforce and Albertine at the Cape Azure's main outdoor restaurant. It was set on a terrace overlooking the bay, wicker tables and chairs sheltering beneath a rattan-covered pergola.

Wilberforce's plate bore the remnants of an immense dressed lobster and he was licking sauce off his fingertips with relish. Albertine had plumped for beef curry with a side order of roti flatbread and fried plantain, which she was eating with far more delicacy of manners than her cousin.

"Hey! Lex, my man!" Wilberforce, to judge by his wild, expansive gesturing, was on at least his third rum and Coke. Perhaps he was self-anesthetising the ache from his bruises. "Come sit. You hungry? Food here's amazing, and there's plenty in your American friend's kitty to go round."

"He's not my friend," Lex said, pulling up a chair.

"What, then? Business associate? Someone you met on Facebook?"

"Colleague, sort of. We're working together, that's all."

Wilberforce narrowed his eyes. "This has something to do with the old days, isn't it? Your soldiering past."

Lex gave the merest of nods. "It's connected with that, yes. Tenuously. Now listen. Both of you. Mr Buckler—that's the American's name—has a proposition for you."

"There money in it?" Wilberforce said, quick as a flash.

"It'll be to your advantage, I'm sure." Lex hadn't discussed terms of hire with Buckler, but he was prepared to part with some of his own fee in the unlikely event that the American didn't stump up any cash himself for Albertine's and Wilberforce's services. "You still keep that seaplane of yours in flyable condition, don't you?"

"More or less. Haven't been up in *Puddle Jumper* for months, but as far as I'm aware there's nothing wrong with her. Why? Those guys want transporting somewhere?"

"They do."

"Then I'm your man. Mind you, I'll need to go check up on her first. Haven't seen her in a while."

"Let's do that in a minute. As for you, Albertine..."

"Yes, Lex?" Her deep brown, long-lashed eyes studied him with inquisitiveness and appraisal. He was struck, once again, by her beauty. He hadn't been so bowled over by a woman's looks since... he couldn't remember when. Those sharp, high cheekbones. Those full, lustrous lips.

"Buckler would like to draw on your expertise too," he said.

"What expertise is that?" she asked with a wry, languid smile.

"You know."

"You're going to have to spell it out for me."

"Your"—Lex lowered his voice—"voodoo."

"Oh, come now! You don't have to whisper it like it's a dirty word."

"I don't want people overhearing."

Albertine glanced round the restaurant. "Who's overhearing? Nobody here's listening. Nobody cares. They're all too busy chatting and eating and being on vacation. Lot of them don't even speak English."

"Still," said Lex. "Shouldn't we be discreet about it?"

"You can if you want to. Me, I'm not bothered. *Vodou* is core to who I am. It's my life. I'm never going to deny it or downplay it. Why does Mr Buckler need a mambo?"

"I don't know yet. Nor does he, exactly."

"It's got something to do with that danger Damballah told me you're in."

"Conceivably."

"No, darling, I wasn't asking a question. I'm telling you. I know it has. Papa Damballah sent me to you with good reason. He doesn't mess about. If Mr Buckler needs me, it's because you need me. I'm not going to ask how he found out what I do. That blonde woman in my car, Madison, she was being pretty nosy. Oh, she sounded like she was just making polite conversation, but I could tell she was probing. I mentioned my being a *vodouisante* to her because I had a good idea it was something she wanted to hear, a nugget she could pass on to her boss. Wilberforce, being Wilberforce, couldn't stop himself. He told her he was a pilot and most everything else he could think of to say about himself. Short of giving her his phone number..."

"I was getting round to that," Wilberforce said. "She turned from me to you before I could work it naturally into the conversation."

"She's too skinny for you, cuz," Albertine said.

"Says you. How come you're all of a sudden the expert on my taste in women?"

"You like them rounded. That Madison, she's got a flat butt and no boobs to speak of. I've met enough of your girlfriends to know you prefer something to grab onto."

"Maybe I'm expanding my range."

"No, you were trying it on with her because that's what you do. You can't help it. She's got a pulse and a pussy, so as far as Wilberforce Allen is concerned she's fair game. Besides, I'm pretty sure you were barking up the wrong tree there. I think she's a *madivin*."

"Yeah, not all of us speak Creole, cuz."

"A lady who loves ladies."

"You think?" A doggish grin. "Well, to me that just makes it more of a challenge. Like I said, I'm expanding my range."

Albertine rolled her eyes. "You really ought to think about doing the opposite for once. Discriminating. Looking for a wife, not just the next bed partner. Committing to someone. Your mama despairs of you, you know that? Every other day she's on the phone to my mama. 'When's my boy going to settle down, Hélène? When's he going to give me grandbabies?'"

"You first, Albie. You're the one in our family should be finding a spouse and having kids soon. You can't put it off forever. Biological clock must be ticking like crazy for you."

"I have three 'husbands' already. What would I want with a fourth? Besides, he'd have to be quite a man to hold his own against them. Lex? Would you have a problem being married to someone who has two men and a woman already in her life?"

"I'm staying out of this."

"I'm not asking you to audition, just to comment."

"Seriously." Lex felt like burying his head in his hands. "I have bigger things to worry about than your marital status, Albertine, or Wilberforce's inability to keep his pecker in his pants for more than five minutes. And I'm not here to play referee between you two. Seems to me the solution to both your problems would be to get married to each other."

Wilberforce's jaw dropped. "That isn't even funny. That's the most disgusting thing I ever heard. Man, you should be ashamed of yourself."

"Why not? Cousins can marry. It's allowed."

"Me? Marry a waster like him?" Albertine snorted. "Never in a million years."

"You already argue like husband and wife. Might as well tie the knot and make it official."

Both the cousins were so appalled by Lex's suggestion, they forget their squabbling.

Which was pretty much what Lex had intended.

* * *

THEY DROVE IN just the one car, Lex's, to where Wilberforce's seaplane was berthed, and during the journey nobody spoke, apart from Wilberforce making the occasional aside about how Lex was a sick man, a sick, sick man, and should go and see a therapist to get his depraved brain fixed.

Lex grinned to himself, enjoying the blissful reprieve from the cousins' seemingly constant antagonism. He watched the island's verdant scenery pass by, and even hummed a tune under his breath.

Wilberforce's De Havilland Canada DHC-2T Turbo Beaver had been elderly when he'd bought it, and during his years of regular flying he had done little in the way of maintenance beyond the bare minimum necessary to keep the plane from plummeting out of the sky. It now resided at a boatyard situated a few hundred metres inland on a broad river inlet. The boatyard owner was a mechanic, Virgil Johnson, to whom Wilberforce paid a peppercorn berthing rent, supplemented by free drinks at the rum shack every Monday. This wasn't an absolute bargain, since Virgil could consume his own bodyweight in booze on any given night, but it still worked out cheaper than the fees for a slip at the marina at Port Sebastian.

"There she is, the old girl," Wilberforce said, springing from the Subaru. "Looking lovely as ever."

In fact, to anyone not as fond of it as Wilberforce was, the Turbo Beaver looked dilapidated and forlorn. The paintwork on the fuselage and tailfin was peeling, the wing struts bore an alarming amount of rust at the welds, and there was even the odd barnacle clinging to the floats. The plane bobbed at its mooring, riding up and down on the gentle river wavelets with the air of a retiree in a rest home dozing off in a rocking chair while musing on the good old days. Alongside it, a handful of motorboats and small fishing vessels sat in various states of disrepair and decay.

At one time, the Turbo Beaver had shuttled back and forth as industriously as its namesake between Manzanilla and Haiti, Manzanilla and the Turks and Caicos, Manzanilla and Jamaica, even Manzanilla and Cuba. Propelled by its single Pratt and

Whitney PT6A-27 turboprop engine, the seaplane had lunged through clear air and the occasional thunderstorm, transporting passengers, delivering parcels, and picking up luxury items for resale. Havana cigars had been a nice little earner for Wilberforce, and fresh spices even more so. The mail boat to Manzanilla would put in only once a week, whereas Wilberforce had been able to get certain items of perishable produce to your kitchen table almost on the day they were picked. Bundles of marijuana had found their way into his cargo hold from time to time, but the vast majority of his trade had been legitimate.

Then had come the boom time for the island, and with it the construction of the airport. Virtually overnight Wilberforce's business had evaporated, as commercial air haulage carriers began freighting goods and people in and out of Manzanilla, offering a much cheaper and more reliable service. *Puddle Jumper* had had to be put out to pasture and Wilberforce had been obliged to seek a new revenue stream. The seaplane could still be chartered for sightseeing tours if anyone was so inclined, but there was a company in Port Sebastian offering helicopter rides around the island, and its Eurocopter AS350 Ecureuil was faster, more exciting, and in considerably better shape than *Puddle Jumper*.

Virgil Johnson emerged from the corrugated-iron shed that doubled as both workshop and office. He was a tubby, froglike man with greying dreadlocks and a faded Evinrude T-shirt stretched tight as a drum skin over his pot belly. He was simultaneously wiping his grease-covered hands on a rag and talking into a mobile phone crooked between shoulder and ear.

"...yeah, better go now," he said. "That's right. So we're cool? Yeah, same here. It's good, man. It's all good."

He terminated the call with one thumb, raising his arm at the same time in greeting.

"Wilberforce! My brother!"

The two of them embraced and did a two-part handshake— clasp then finger-grip.

"Man, you look like you've been in the wars," Virgil said.

"My face isn't as pretty as it used to be, but it'll get better. Wish I could say the same for yours."

"Thought you'd abandoned *Puddle Jumper* for good. Left me to look after the old lady all on my own."

"You know I wouldn't do that, Virge. I love her too much."

Virgil chortled. "Well, I've been turning the engine over once a fortnight, regular as clockwork, you know that. And only last Tuesday I cleaned out the compressor and put in some new gaskets. She purred like a happy cat when I fired her up after that. You going for a flight right now?"

"Not exactly. Just checking up on her. Chances are she'll be airborne in the near future, though."

"Oh, okay. Hey, Lex. How's it going?" Virgil shook Lex's hand briefly, then Albertine's at much greater length and with much greater vigour. "Very nice to meet *you*, pretty girl. I'm Virgil. That's Virgil as in the famous Roman poet. The love poet."

It was a chat-up line Lex had heard the mechanic use more than once at the rum shack. Corny, but it sometimes did the trick.

"Really?" said Albertine.

"No doubt. Actually, I've got a bit of love poet in me myself. You want to see? I can show you."

"No, I mean was Virgil really a love poet? Because, as I recall, he wrote epic poetry. You know, the *Aeneid*?"

Virgil looked so crestfallen, it was all Lex could do to suppress a smile.

"Yeah, I knew that," he said, recovering. "Epic love poetry. And epic love is what I'm all about."

"Well, if I want some of that, I'll be sure to give you a call," said Albertine.

"You do." Virgil turned back to Wilberforce. "She's a sharp one, brother. Where'd you find her?"

"Nowhere. We're related. That's my cousin Albertine."

"Your cousin? Oh. Ohhh. The one who...?"

"The same," said Wilberforce, nodding. "Now, come on. Show me how well *Puddle Jumper*'s doing. Let me see what I'm getting in return for you draining my bar dry every Monday night."

The two of them talked fluent engineering for a while, leaving Lex and Albertine with little to do but stand in the sun, watching. Virgil raised *Puddle Jumper*'s engine cowl to allow Wilberforce to inspect the plane's inner workings, after which Wilberforce climbed aboard, sat in the pilot's seat and started the motor up. There was a metallic cough, a puff of bluish smoke from the exhaust manifold, and the propeller began to turn jerkily. More smoke blurted into the air, and then the propeller settled into a spinning blur while the engine droned smoothly and comfortably. Virgil gave Wilberforce a thumbs-up through the windscreen, and Wilberforce returned it.

"Say what you like about my cousin," said Albertine, "but it was always his dream to fly, and he worked his backside off getting his pilot licence. Look at him sitting there. Like a little kid. It's his passion. Shame he had to give it up, mostly. Lex? Don't you think?"

"Hmm?"

"Lex. What's that look on your face?"

"Look?"

"That scowl. Like something's bugging you."

"Something is," Lex confessed.

"What?"

"Virgil. He's behaving strangely."

"Is he? I don't know him, but he seems normal enough to me."

"Normal, yes. Almost too normal. Something's off. It's as if he's trying too hard."

"Are you usually this suspicious of people?"

"Until lately I've had no reason to be, not since I started living here. Now, suddenly, I'm having to be a mite more cautious again. See the way Virgil's hand keeps going to his pocket?"

"I hadn't noticed," said Albertine, "but now that you mention it..."

Virgil was doing it right now, touching the right-hand pocket of his cut-off jeans, almost unconsciously. It was the ninth time the gesture had occurred since he started talking to Wilberforce. Lex was keeping count.

"It's where he put his mobile," he said.

"Maybe he's patting to check it's still there."

"Yes, but why? It's not likely to fall out. It's more as though he's worried about it—or about what he was just discussing on it."

"A guilty conscience about something?"

"Yes. And he's being extra friendly towards Wilb, and that's not how he ordinarily is at the rum shack. I mean, they get on well enough, but now he's acting like they're best mates."

"Could be he's different here. This is his boatyard, home turf. He's more at ease."

"Even allowing for that, it's uncharacteristic," said Lex. "The way he's carrying on...Call me paranoid, but all that chitchat—makes me think he's stalling. Delaying us on purpose."

"You *are* paranoid," Albertine said. "Except..." Her expression clouded. "I'm getting these whispers. From the loa. Loko, my husband, is concerned with justice. He has a strong sense of right and wrong, and he doesn't like cheats and frauds. If he spots one, he often tells me."

"So you feel it too? Instinctively?"

"Starting to. And it's the loa, not my instincts."

Before Lex could respond to that, Virgil's phone trilled. He took it out and put it to his ear, at the same time holding up an apologetic finger to Wilberforce.

"Yes?" Lex heard him say above the burble of the Turbo Beaver's turbines. "Yeah, man. Okay. I hear you."

Virgil began to move away from the seaplane along the dock, as though seeking somewhere quieter to hold the conversation. He shot a furtive glance in the direction of Lex and Albertine.

"Yeah, three," he said. "That's right. Three."

"Albertine," Lex said out of the corner of his mouth. "I want you to go to the car. Get in."

"What for?"

"Go. Don't argue." Lex grabbed her by the elbow and steered her towards the Subaru. He opened the passenger-side door, reached in to undo the glove box latch and retrieved his SIG Sauer from inside. Albertine's eyes widened in shock at the sight of the gun.

"Lex, what on earth—?"

"Do as I say. Get in. Lock the doors. Stay low."

"You can't order me around like that without—"

Lex's attention was caught by the sound of another engine, not that far off, getting louder. Without further ado he bundled Albertine into the 4x4 and slammed the door.

"Lock it," he barked. "And keep your head right down."

He turned. Virgil was hurrying for the shed now, barely making a pretence of casualness any more. His saunter had become an anxious hop-and-skip. Lex sprinted for the dock. A car appeared on the approach road, heading for the boatyard's open gates: a Jeep Grand Cherokee, missing a wing mirror and sporting several bullet holes in its bodywork.

The Garfish. Or some of his henchmen, at any rate.

Virgil had ratted. It was obvious. Garfield Finisterre must have contacted him earlier and bribed him to provide a tipoff, should Wilberforce visit the boatyard. The Garfish knew Wilberforce kept his plane here. It was no secret.

That was the conversation Virgil had been having when they arrived—alerting the Garfish that a car had turned up with Wilberforce inside. The second phone call, one which Virgil had been nervously anticipating, was the Garfish's men getting to the scene, time for him to take cover, get out of the line of fire.

"Wilberforce!" Lex yelled, but his friend was oblivious. He was busy examining the cockpit dashboard, inspecting the readings on the dials.

The Jeep crunched to a halt on the gravel parking apron, just behind the Subaru. The doors opened, and four men leapt out.

Lex could see Albertine cowering in the front of the Subaru, trying to make herself small in the seat.

The four men all had guns. No Garfish with them, but perhaps last night had deterred him from wanting to take a direct hand. What were henchmen for, anyway?

Lex sighted carefully along the barrel of the SIG and dropped the frontmost of the four with a single shot. The other three scattered. One hurried back to the Jeep and took shelter behind an opened door. The other two made for a stack of 55-gallon oil drums, shooting wildly as they ran. Lex went down on one knee in order to steady his aim and present a smaller target. He returned the pair's fire, but failed to hit either of them; they were moving too fast and the range was at the SIG's limit of reliable accuracy.

Wilberforce leaned out of the Turbo Beaver. "Lex? What's happening?"

"Get back inside the plane," Lex told him.

"Those men..."

"Virgil sold you out to the Garfish. Now for God's sake, stay in that fucking plane."

Wilberforce did as bidden. Lex crab-scuttled along the dock until he was behind a small bowrider sport boat with a Mercruiser outboard. He crouched with the gunwales at eye level and put a round into one of the oil drums. The drum was empty, alas. Ah, well, worth a try.

Bullets came his way, thwacking into the bowrider's fibreglass hull. The boat shuddered with each impact. Lex huddled down. He could hear shouting, someone giving instructions, but the words were indecipherable above the ruckus from the Turbo Beaver's engine. More shots, doing great harm to the bowrider's structural integrity. Maybe the plan was to sink it, thus exposing Lex. There wasn't much hope of that, though. At this angle the henchmen would never be able to hole the boat below the waterline. But if nothing else, they were keeping him pinned. He daren't raise his head or venture out from his hiding place.

That was when it dawned on him that they were trying to trick him. Sinking the bowrider wasn't their goal at all. The bullets punching into the hull were a diversion, a way of keeping him in one spot and busy while...

Lex peered out past the boat's stern. A henchman was sneaking along the dock towards him, squatting low, gun held out. His colleague behind the oil drums kept up suppressing fire.

The henchman was drawing level with *Puddle Jumper*. Lex did not have a clear shot at him. If he leaned out far enough to draw a bead, he would present himself fully to the henchman. Then it would be a case of who pulled the trigger first. Odds were it would be Lex, but it was far from a foregone conclusion. The risk seemed too great.

The only alternative was to slip into the water, swim under the bowrider, come up the other side, and try and take the henchman by surprise that way. But again, this scheme carried an unacceptably high level of risk. If the man spotted him emerging from the water, he would have the advantage.

As he debated his options, Lex noticed that *Puddle Jumper* was starting to swing out from the dockside. Wilberforce.

Lex felt a surge of admiration at his friend's ingenuity. At the very least it would startle the henchman, throw him off his stride. Lex could then make use of that.

The Garfish's man glanced up as *Puddle Jumper*'s wing passed over him, casting him briefly into shadow. He didn't seem to understand what was happening. Why was the plane moving?

That was his fatal mistake. In his confusion, he failed to appreciate that the wing going overhead meant the front end of the seaplane was closing in on him from behind.

And at the tip of the plane was a whirling propeller, a trio of four-foot aluminium-alloy blades rotating at two thousand revolutions per minute.

At the last instant, the henchman looked round.

He managed to get out a single strained syllable that sounded very much like "No!"

Then the propeller sliced into him, opening up his torso and unzipping his gun arm from his body cleanly at the shoulder. His entire frame juddered as the propeller hacked into him, and then he fell. Most of him landed on the boards of the dock. His arm was hurled high into the air and spiralled into the sea with a splash. The hand was still clutching the pistol as it plunged beneath the waves.

"Desmond!" came a despairing cry from the oil drums. "Des! No!"

Lex seized his moment. He sprinted along the dock, past the body of Desmond the henchman, which was still twitching, gushing blood everywhere. He ran for the oil drums in a zigzagging line, pumping out parabellum rounds from the SIG. The drums boomed resoundingly as the bullets smacked home.

He collided sidelong with the drums, toppling the stack like a bowling ball striking the pins; the drums tumbled onto the shrieking henchman.

Lex didn't pause. He grabbed the drum covering most of the henchman and thrust it aside. The man flailed his arms in shock and distress as Lex planted a bullet in his eye, point blank.

"Hold it right there!"

Lex looked up. His heart sank.

The fourth and final henchman was standing by the Subaru. The car door nearest to him stood open, window smashed. The henchman had Albertine by the throat. He was holding her in front of him, his pistol at her temple.

"Make another move, you ghost bastard," he snarled, "and I blow her fuckin' brains out. You get me? Lay down the gun and put your hands in the air, or the bitch dies."

TWELVE
WANGA FETISH

LEX HAD NO choice but to comply. The SIG was down to the last round in its clip. A single bullet left no margin for error; if his shot didn't find its mark in the henchman's head, he wouldn't get a second chance. Albertine would be done for.

"Okay, okay," he said. He showed the man the SIG, with his index finger arched ostentatiously clear of the trigger guard. Then he bent, placing the gun on the dead henchman's chest. He straightened again, both arms aloft. "I'm doing exactly as you say. The gun's down. I'm no threat to you any more. Now please, let her go."

"Lace your fingers behind your head." The henchman had evidently watched a cop show or two in his time. That or he had been arrested himself and knew the drill. Probably both. "Go on, do it."

Lex again complied. His mind was racing. There were ways out of this situation, various means by which he would turn the tables on the henchman and survive. But he was having a hard time thinking of one that didn't end with Albertine dead.

"Albie!"

Wilberforce had powered down the engine, and now came clambering out of the Turbo Beaver. His panic-stricken cry echoed across the boatyard.

"Wilb, back off," said Lex, without turning round. "I've got this."

"You!" Wilberforce yelled at the henchman. He was hyped up, with anger and from the shock of watching his plane's propeller slicing the other henchman apart. "Let her go. Let my cousin go."

"I've got this," Lex repeated.

"Cousin, huh?" said the henchman. A grin smeared itself across his face. Lex recognised him as one of the three goons who'd been at Wilberforce's house last night. He had a gold hoop earring in one ear that lent him a vaguely piratical air.

"How much she worth to you, boy?" the man went on. "Plenty, I reckon. Maybe I should take her back to the Garfish's place so's he can keep hold of her for the time being. She can be—what's the word? Collateral."

"She's got nothing to do with this," Wilberforce pleaded. "Leave her be."

"Mr Finisterre would enjoy having a fine woman like this as a house guest. He'd be sure to look after her, entertain her properly. I imagine him and her'll have plenty of fun together while he's waitin' for you to pay him what you owe."

"You—" Wilberforce began hotly.

Lex interrupted. "Let's not let this thing escalate, all right?" he said with all the calmness he could muster. "Let's no one lose their temper. Otherwise someone could get hurt. You." He nodded at the pirate-like henchman. "I see you have a bandage there."

The hand with which Pirate gripped Albertine's throat, his left, was wrapped in surgical gauze and wadding. The thumb, index finger and middle finger were fine. The other two fingers appeared to be absent.

"Am I right in thinking you lost a couple of fingers last night?"

"Yeah," Pirate growled. "And we know who's to blame for that."

"Yes. Me. Bet it hurts, eh?"

"Not so bad. I got given good drugs at the hospital."

"Still, you'll be feeling a nasty throbbing ache that no amount of painkillers can quite touch. Not to mention an aggravating itch. And even when it's healed your hand won't ever be the same again. It'll never work properly again. Every time you use it, every time you look at it, you'll be reminded. You're deformed now."

Pirate looked daggers at Lex. "Too damn right I am."

"Bet you hate me."

"That's puttin' it mildly."

"Bet you'd like to punish me. So come on. Why not? Go ahead. Get your own back. Come and give me the retribution I deserve."

The gun wavered beside Albertine's head. Pirate was definitely tempted.

But then, "Uh-uh," he said, with a firm head-shake. "No, I'm not fallin' for that. This here's my bargainin' chip, this girl. I'm not lettin' go of her."

Lex tried not to look disappointed.

At that moment, he saw something.

The flap of Albertine's shoulder bag was unclipped and slightly open, and she was dipping a hand inside.

She saw that he saw, and her eyes told him not to let on.

She had some strategy in mind. She was up to something.

Lex's role now was to play for time so that Albertine could pull off whatever move she intended to make.

"So," he said to Pirate, "what next? You're going to make for your car, I suppose."

"That's the general idea."

"Report back to your boss. Tell him how three of his lieutenants are dead. How will he take the news, I wonder?"

"He'll be angry," replied Pirate. "But maybe not so angry when he sees the peach of a gift I brought him."

He gave Albertine a shake. Her hand was deep inside the bag, surreptitiously rummaging. So far, Pirate was wholly unaware of it. Lex had to continue to make himself the main focus of the henchman's attention. He had no idea what Albertine was preparing to do, but if it distracted Pirate for even a couple of seconds, it would provide Lex with an opportunity to take action.

"Might even give me a raise," Pirate went on. "Not as though I don't deserve one, seein' as how I've lost two fingers workin' for him."

"I'm surprised you don't take him to an industrial tribunal," Lex said. "Claim compensation."

"Lex, what are you doing, making jokes?" hissed Wilberforce. "This isn't the time for being funny."

"I'm quite serious. The man has been badly injured while discharging his duties. There's a case for prosecuting the Garfish for neglect, if not downright dereliction of care."

"He's a shotta!" Wilberforce exclaimed. "A fucking paid thug. Not a window washer who's fallen off a ladder. And he's holding my cousin hostage, in case you've forgotten. Stop messing about."

"I'm just saying everyone, whatever their occupation, is entitled to safe, hazard-free working conditions."

Albertine's hand slid clear of the shoulder bag. She was clasping a small object that seemed to be made mostly of feathers, black and red ones. Gripping it tightly, she began murmuring under her breath.

"Huh?" Pirate said to her. "What's that you sayin'?"

Albertine didn't reply, just carried on murmuring. Her eyes were closed. Her speech had a rhythm to it, somewhere between a song and a chant.

The tip of the pistol ground into the side of her head. "Shut up now, woman. I said shut up!"

Albertine's voice rose until individual words and phrases were audible. Lex caught a mention of a name he didn't recognise, Maman Brigitte, and another, Erzulie Dantor. Albertine was apparently asking the voodoo spirits for aid and protection.

"Stop that jabber right now, or I shoot!" Pirate yelled. "I will!"

Albertine's eyelids parted. Her eyes had rolled up inside her head. Only the whites showed. Her whole body was shuddering, as though in the throes of some kind of seizure.

She lifted the object in her hand up high.

It was a tiny figurine, a gaudy little wooden doll festooned with feathers and brightly coloured beads, and even a couple of small bones that must once have belonged to a bird or a mouse.

Very deliberately, Albertine took hold of one of the doll's legs.

No less deliberately, she snapped it in two.

Pirate let out a screech as his left leg collapsed backwards under him, bending like a liquorice whip. He crashed to the ground in a sitting position with his leg doubled beneath his bottom, shin folded against front of thigh, foot pressed to crotch. It was as though his knee had disintegrated—been struck by a blow from some powerful unseen hammer and utterly destroyed. He gibbered and writhed, near incoherent in his agony.

The man was incapacitated and clearly no longer a threat, but Lex nonetheless sprang over to him and snatched the gun from his grasp.

"Albie! You all right?" Wilberforce was at her side, cradling her, desperately concerned.

Albertine, emerging from her trance, nodded wanly. She looked like someone recovering from a severe hangover, brittle and delicate.

"I'm sorry, I'm so sorry," said her cousin. "This is all my fault."

"I'm fine, Wilberforce. Really I am. No need to worry."

"If anything had happened to you, I'd never forgive myself. Aunt Hélène wouldn't either. She'd kill me."

"She'd do a whole lot worse than that, cuz. Seriously, though, I'm okay. No harm done. You can stop smothering me now."

Wilberforce rounded on the thug. "Bastard! Holding a gun on a defenceless woman." He lobbed a wad of spit onto Pirate's contorted face. The man was in too much pain to notice or care.

"Defenceless?" said Lex, arching an eyebrow. "Apparently not. What did you do to him, Albertine? What is that thing?"

"This?" She held out the doll for him to examine. "What does it look like?"

"A voodoo doll."

"The correct term is '*wanga* fetish,'" she said. "But essentially yes, it's what you know as a voodoo doll. This one's consecrated to Maman Brigitte, who rights wrongs, and also to bitch-devil Erzulie Dantor, who safeguards women, especially when they're in danger from men."

"And you just happened to be carrying it in your bag?"

"I have it with me at all times," Albertine said. "A girl can never be too careful. Rapes and muggings aren't unheard of on this island. I got the idea for keeping an emergency fetish on me when I was at Cornell. A couple of coeds were assaulted in Ithaca one night, not that far off-campus. The dean of the faculty advised the female students to buy personal alarms and pepper spray, just in case. I thought I could go one better."

"So you break its leg"—Lex pointed to the fetish's snapped wooden limb—"and *his* leg breaks too?"

"That's more or less it. The fetish has to be primed with power first. You must 'baptise' it, giving it a name, and perform various other rituals and incantations over it. You must also offer it food and drink on a regular basis and talk to it like a friend. Otherwise the protective energies inside it will fade and it may not work when you need it to. Now and then it's good to fumigate it with frankincense and herbs as well, keeping it sweet in more ways than one."

"A name?" said Lex. "So what's yours called? Psycho Barbie?"

"It has a secret name, which I can never reveal. But its public name is Woman Scorned."

"As in 'Hell hath no fury like...'"

"Precisely."

Lex looked at the stricken Pirate, who was grey-faced and on the verge of passing out. He could scarcely fathom what had gone on here. Was he expected to believe that some sort of magic had just taken place? That the damage Albertine had inflicted on the fetish had somehow transferred itself onto Pirate?

He couldn't deny the evidence of his own eyes. The man's leg had been forced backwards at the knee without any visible physical cause. Was it possible that Pirate suffered from some underlying medical condition that would account for the knee giving way spontaneously? Some disease of the bones or joints? Extreme osteoporosis? Hyper-elastic tendons?

But even if that were so, it didn't explain why the injury had occurred at the exact same moment that Albertine broke the doll's pencil-thin leg, and so abruptly too. The power of suggestion, maybe. Or else an astonishing coincidence.

Lex was aware that he was clutching at straws. Unfortunately, the simplest solution here was also the one that was hardest to swallow.

Voodoo.

Voodoo existed. It was real. It worked.

That, on top of Lieutenant Buckler's revelation of the shadowy supernatural demimonde which he and Team Thirteen operated in... It was all too much. Too many absurdities to take in at once.

This was turning into one monumental head-fuck of a day.

THIRTEEN
EXTREMELY UNCIVIL

VIRGIL JOHNSON CRINGED in his office, hunched against the wall between a filing cabinet and a steel desk bearing a vintage computer and a litter of motor parts. He couldn't tear his eyes off Lex's SIG, not knowing that Lex had no intention of using it on him.

"Please don't shoot me, please don't." He looked beseechingly from Lex to Wilberforce to Albertine. "I didn't want to do it. The Garfish made me."

"Made you?" said Lex. "How? By offering you more cash than you could refuse?"

"No." And more vehemently: "*No*. Never. I'm not that kind of person. But he said if Wilberforce dropped by and I didn't let him know immediately, he'd do things to me. Awful things. And he'd torch this place, too. My whole livelihood would go up in smoke, he said, and I'd spend the rest of my days in a wheelchair, pissing through a tube. I didn't know what else to do, man. I mean, it's the Garfish. You don't say no to him."

Lex turned to Wilberforce. "What do you reckon? You believe him?"

"Can't see why he'd be lying." To Virgil, Wilberforce said, "I suppose you thought if I was stupid enough to get into the Garfish's bad books, then I deserved whatever was coming to me."

"No, no," the mechanic whimpered. "It never crossed my mind. I was more concerned about not getting into his bad books myself. I did wrong, Wilberforce, I realise that. But it was me or you. If you'd been in my position, under the pressure I was under, you'd have done the same."

Wilberforce pondered on this, then nodded. "Okay. Maybe so. But you know what? I reckon from now on I don't pay to keep *Puddle Jumper* here any more. She stays for free. And your drinks at the rum shack are no longer on the house."

"Yeah." Virgil sniffed mucus back up his nose. "Sure."

"We're square. After what you did to me, to us, I owe you nothing."

"I said yeah. It's a deal."

"One more thing," said Lex. He held out a hand. "Your phone."

Hesitantly, frowning, Virgil passed his mobile over.

Lex redialled the last number Virgil had called.

"Virgil," said a deep, rumbling voice on the other end. "I hope this is you tellin' me my men have Wilberforce Allen in custody an' they're bringin' him to me."

"Afraid not, Mr Finisterre," said Lex. "This is Lex Dove telling you that three of your men are no longer among the living and the fourth requires urgent medical treatment."

The pause that followed was surprisingly brief. "That is a pity," Finisterre said. "For you I mean. What you don't seem to appreciate, my friend, is that I own this island. I *am* Manzanilla. Everyone an' everything on this hunk of rock belongs to me, Garfield Finisterre. The Garfish is king here, an' if the Garfish decides he wants somebody dead—an' he most definitely does in your case, Mr Dove—then the Garfish will get his way."

"And if the Garfish insists on referring to himself in the third person, then the Garfish is clearly suffering from delusions of grandeur."

The already low voice dropped a further octave, until it was almost subsonic. "I will gut you like a pig, you white spook batty-boy. I will pull your entrails out an' eat them in front of you while you scream."

"A charming prospect," said Lex. "Me, I don't make threats. It's not really my way. I act. So you should listen to me, Mr Finisterre, and listen well. I'm advising you to leave me alone from here on. Wilberforce Allen too, and anyone who's connected with Wilberforce. That includes Virgil Johnson. Steer well clear. Because I can come for you any time. You will never see me, you will never hear me. I repeat, I don't make threats. I'm laying out the facts, that's all. I will be there when you least expect it, and no matter how many gunmen you have around you or what kind of security system you have in place, it won't be enough. I will be in your home, your bedroom, your inner sanctum, and you will have no clue as to my presence until the moment you turn round and I am behind you. It won't be you discovering me, it'll be me revealing myself to you. That's how it works. And then you will die. It will be as quick or as slow a death as I care to make it. It might be instantaneous, fast as a snake strike, oblivion in a flash. It might equally be long and lingering, so excruciating that you will pray for it to be over and you will feel as though your prayer will never be answered. Hear it in my voice. I am not bluffing. I am not lying. I am simply stating how it is going to be. Do you understand?"

"I understand that you're hammerin' even more nails into your own coff—"

"I repeat: do you understand, Mr Finisterre? I am not just some 'white spook batty-boy,' as you so charmingly put it. I am the very last person on God's earth that you want to have pissed off at you. You told me last night that you saw something dark in me, something dangerous. Here it is, speaking to you right now. Do not provoke it any further, Mr Finisterre. Do not let it out of its cage. It will be greatly to your cost if you do."

"You think I'm just goin' to cancel Wilberforce's debts, or forget that three more of my boys are dead thanks to you? That's four in total, countin' Maurice last night. Because if you think that, mister, you're the one with delusions, not me."

"I am recommending that you do exactly as I say, or I shall stop being polite and start being extremely uncivil. You really do not want me being extremely uncivil to you."

Lex ended the call.

"That ought to hold him for a while," he said.

"You don't reckon you've scared him off for good?" said Wilberforce. "Because, man, if that was me, I'd be on the next boat to Jamaica. I got chills up my spine just listening to you."

"Someone like the Garfish isn't easily put off. He's too arrogant, too assured of his own power. But I've at least given him pause for thought. He won't be hounding us quite so hard for the moment."

He returned Virgil's phone to him.

"Listen to me now," he said to the mechanic. "There are beach houses reasonably close by, witnesses who'll have heard gunfire. We can't cover this up, but the last thing I want right now is more hassle with the cops. You should call the police, and also an ambulance. You have to, otherwise it'll look suspicious. But no matter what anyone asks, we weren't here. You were indoors all the time and didn't see anything that went on outside. You just heard the shots, that's all. Got it?"

The mechanic nodded, more eager to please than ever now that his life wasn't in imminent danger.

"Give us a head start," Lex added. "Wait until a couple of minutes after we've gone."

Again, a nod.

"And we'll be back for *Puddle Jumper*. Not sure how soon, but the plane needs to be fuelled and ready to fly at a moment's notice."

"You got it, boss," said Virgil. "And thank you."

"Don't thank me," said Lex. "Just don't fuck up."

"He means don't fuck up again," Wilberforce put in.

FOURTEEN
ANGER REEF

BACK AT THE Cape Azure Hotel, Lex reported to Buckler in Buckler's room. Transportation by seaplane had been secured for Team Thirteen.

"Any difficulties with that?" Buckler enquired. He leaned a little closer to Lex and squited, ever so briefly, as though curious.

"Nothing insurmountable," Lex replied, slightly puzzled. The American had some odd mannerisms. "Wilberforce is glad for the excuse to be Captain Wilberforce of Wilberforce Airlines again."

Buckler leaned back, straightening up. "What about your lady friend? Albertine. She up for helping us?"

"She seems to be."

"But...?"

"It all depends on what capacity you want her to act in," said Lex. "If it's advice, technical assistance, background intel, I can't see a problem. Anything more hands-on..." He left it implicit: *not going to happen.*

Buckler stroked one frond of his moustache. "This her talking, or you? You're being kind of overprotective of her."

"I said it before—she's a civilian."

"She's also an asset. You can't tell me Mr Shit-hot British Wetwork Guy never used civilian assets when he was out in the field doing his stuff, and I'll bet he never gave a damn what happened to them during or afterwards. They were pawns on the chessboard, disposable. You know as well as I do, the end justifies the means. *Any* means."

"My life's different now. *I'm* different."

"You've gone soft, is what you're saying."

"You're not going to get a rise out of me that way, lieutenant."

"Not trying to, sport. Just stating facts."

"Tell me exactly what the mission is," Lex demanded. "We've reached that point. I'm not making any further commitment, on my own behalf or anyone else's, until I have a clearer picture of what I'm involved with. I need details."

"Hey, simmer down." Buckler made a placatory gesture. "I was just about to fill you in anyway. You don't have to get all 'Fetch my blunderbuss, Jeeves' on me. Truth is, what you already know isn't much more than I know myself. Shit's gone down at a US military site not far from here. Marines are compromised, likely dead. Team Thirteen's picking up the baton."

"Where is this site?"

"Well, now..." Buckler opened up the magnesium alloy case housing his laptop. He typed in some commands, fingers thudding on the rubber keys. A map appeared onscreen. "The north Caribbean. There's Hispaniola, to the right. There's Castro's Communist nirvana, very much to the left. And tucked between those two, the meatball in the sandwich, is the delightful sun-soaked resort destination that we call Manzanilla." He stroked the touchpad. "And if we track two hundred or so klicks north-northeast, and zoom in, and even further in, what do we find?"

A tiny green speck grew amid the blue of the ocean, an outcrop of land shaped like a stranded starfish.

"That, my friend, is Anger Reef," said Buckler.

"Anger Reef?" Lex racked his brains. "Can't say I've ever heard of it."

"Can't say I'm surprised. It was a bit of the Bahamas that got broken off and left behind while the continents were drifting apart. Used to be an atoll, a ring of islets surrounding a lagoon, but the lagoon silted up and dried out, making it an island proper now. Technically it's American soil, though it's so pissant small we never got round to officially claiming it as such."

Lex compared the island's longest axis against the scale at the corner of the map. Anger Reef measured barely a kilometre across at its widest point. Pissant small indeed.

"Rumour has it that Captain Edward Teach, better known as Blackbeard, buried treasure there in the early seventeen-hundreds," said Buckler. "But I'd discount that, on account of the island's almost impossible to approach by sea. Anger Reef. Clue's in the name. It's surrounded by banks of coral that rise to just below the water's surface. Those and hidden sandbars, treacherous currents and a perpetual heavy swell mean it's not safe to make landfall there even in a rowboat. You're going to get smashed to splinters if you try."

"Obviously you Yanks managed it somehow."

"Only recently. Back in the late 'fifties, it was decided to outfit Anger Reef as a listening post and early warning station."

"Because of its proximity to Cuba."

"Bingo. Give the man a clap."

"What, no prize?"

"Wasn't that big of a deductive leap, now was it?" said Buckler. "After the Batista regime fell and Castro seized power, someone somewhere in the Department of Defence realised Cuba needed keeping an eye on. The USSR's little puppet state right in our own backyard. So Anger Reef was chosen to be our tumbler against the wall. An installation was built there in record time, the majority of it underground. All the workmen, equipment and materials were either flown in by Hueys or landed aboard hovercraft. Radar arrays were set up to track ships and planes, sonar arrays to track submarines. Radio masts tuned to all broadcasts going in and coming out. Basically, Fidel couldn't fart in the bath without us knowing."

"Why not situate it at Guantanamo Bay instead? Much closer to the action."

"This was thought to be a whole lot more discreet. There's something to be said for not rubbing your enemies' noses in the fact that you're surveilling them. Besides, the government was worried that Cuba would be just the first in a series of dominoes to fall in the Caribbean. They wanted a generic, centrally placed lookout point in the region. Anger Reef ticked all the boxes. As it happened, the building work finished just in time for the Missile Crisis."

"That's handy."

"You don't know the half of it. Anger Reef is credited with picking up signals traffic that the Soviets were secretly constructing missile bases in Cuba capable of launching an intermediate-range nuclear attack. Thereafter the place was used to monitor the US Navy's blockade of the island, backing up the photoreconnaissance data that spy planes were providing on the approach of supply ships from Russia and other Warsaw Pact nations, as well as pinpointing the whereabouts of Soviet subs. When the supply ships turned back, Anger Reef was the first to report it."

"Khrushchev blinked, and Anger Reef saw his eyelids move."

"Neat turn of phrase. I'll be sure to use that myself sometime."

"Feel free."

"Come Reagan and the end of the Cold War," Buckler said, resuming his thread, "the installation was decommissioned. It wasn't required any more. The Russkies were on our side, the world had moved on, and Cuba had become an irrelevance, an anachronism, the land that time forgot. By the early 'nineties, Anger Reef was a relic, an empty shell. The listening equipment had been dismantled and taken away, and the installation itself left to rot. Miles of underground concrete bunker, three deep-buried levels of workspace, recreation and dormitory, home to a staff of nearly a hundred, now abandoned. No use to anyone."

"Except..."

"Except nothing the military owns ever goes to waste. Not if it can be repurposed and refitted and resurrected at a later date. See, there's this research scientist, goes by the name of Gulliver Seidelmann, and he had a bright idea."

"Don't they always?" said Lex.

"Yeah. Scientists, right? Full of inspiration. One day they'll be so inspired, we'll all vanish in a puff of smoke. But Professor Seidelmann's this special brainiac genius, beloved by the Pentagon, forever persuading the Joint Chiefs to dig deep and fork over serious bank for some supposedly amazing breakthrough or other. Now, if you ask me, more powerful guns, more effective body armour, more efficient and sensitive electronic gear, anything that makes a grunt's job safer and easier to do, I'm all for it. Long as our weaponry keeps outperforming the opposition's, that's fine by me. But the prof, that isn't his game at all. He's a biochemist interested in enhancing the human physiology."

"You mean giving us all bigger dicks."

"No."

"Pity."

"Sorry to get your hopes up," said Buckler.

"Actually I was thinking of you."

"Of course you were. No, Seidelmann's goal isn't better equipped soldiers, it's better soldiers period."

"Super-soldiers?"

"That's it. Faster, stronger, more durable, less vulnerable—all that Captain America crapola. Men who are more than men. Unbeatable battlefield paladins." Buckler gave a smile that was as much a sneer as anything. "Once again, I'm getting that 'you're shitting me' vibe off you, Dove. I can only say I wish I was. Welcome to my world."

Before Lex could come back with a smart retort, there was a rap at the door. Two members of Team Thirteen, Tartaglione and Sampson, entered the room.

"LT?" said Tartaglione. "We were just coming to check up on you, make sure you were getting some shuteye too. Wouldn't have knocked but we heard voices, not snoring."

"Aw, that's sweet of you guys," said Buckler. "I'll catch forty winks later. Right now I'm busy bringing Mr Dove up to speed on our situation. You stay. I could do with some moral support. Mr Dove doesn't seem to believe half what I tell him."

"Having a Whisky Tango Foxtrot moment, huh?" said Sampson, elongating himself out on the bed. "I still get those myself every now and again. Been a Thirteener for three years, nine months, and even I have trouble with some of the shit we run up against. Planet's crazier than you can imagine, underneath it all. Normal on top, insane below. Like a cookie jar with a nest of wasps hidden at the bottom"

"A nest of mutant wasps," said Tartaglione.

"Mutant flesh-eating wasps."

"Mutant flesh-eating wasps with lethal neurotoxin stings."

"I take it that's something else you've had to deal with," said Lex. "Killer wasps."

"Hell, no," said Sampson.

"Not yet," said Tartaglione.

"But it's probably only a matter of time."

"Yeah. Give it a week." Tartaglione leaned against the wardrobe. The SEALs now formed a triangle with Lex as its central locus. He was conscious of being surrounded, outnumbered, in a confined space. He swiftly worked out trajectories, lines of attack, a sequence of target elimination, should the three of them decide to rush him. They were allies, he had no reason not to trust them, but old habits died hard.

"Now where was I?" said Buckler. "Oh, yeah. Super-soldiers.

Prof Seidelmann seems to think he's created something that can turn ordinary enlisted men into unstoppable fighting machines. I've got a clip of him pitching his case to the Joint Chiefs arms procurement committee. It's grabbed from a teleconference call between him at home in Maryland and the committee in Washington. Here we go."

Professor Gulliver Seidelmann was a weak-chinned man in his early fifties with thin rimless spectacles and a greying widow's peak. He had sharp, beady eyes and a habit of gesticulating with both hands at once, in symmetry, like a college lecturer or a TV presenter. He was in what appeared to be his private study, a shelf full of scholarly-looking books behind him, at his elbow a Newton's cradle and an opened bag of mixed nuts and seeds. Framed diplomas were visible on the wall, along with a photo of Seidelmann shaking hands with the previous incumbent of the White House.

"Gentlemen," he said, "what I'm offering is a fusion of two biotechnologies, one cutting-edge, the other old, possibly ancient. It's something that to my knowledge has never been tried before—taking pharmacological knowhow that has existed for generations and bringing it bang up to date. I'm convinced that the results will be more than to your liking. You'll have read my preliminary paper, in which I set out the experiments I have already performed privately under laboratory conditions and the successes I have achieved with them so far. Mice treated with my process have shown themselves to be impervious to pain and to exhibit a level of durability that's increased by a factor of at least ten. Their need for sleep or any kind of rest is profoundly reduced and they are capable of withstanding stress situations—extreme heat or cold, wind turbulence, high-decibel sonic assault—for approximately seven times longer than the control subjects. That's just mice. Imagine the same level of augmentation applied to human beings."

There was a pause as the professor listened to a question, inaudible on the clip soundtrack.

"In case you're wondering, the voices of the committee members have been redacted," said Buckler.

"Heaven forfend that I might recognise one of them," said Lex.

"Quite."

Seidelmann resumed his side of the conversation. "In addition to various hand-picked lab technicians, I would be working in collaboration with one other person," he said. "I have yet to determine whom, but I have a shortlist of candidates, all experts in their chosen practice—or perhaps I should call it 'craft.' With that person's aid I'm sure I will be able to refine the process to the stage where tests on human subjects would be viable. In the meantime, however, I will require isolation and seclusion. This is sensitive work, and there is the matter of a certain delicacy of feeling amongst my peers."

Another question or comment from the procurement committee.

"Precisely that," said Professor Seidelmann, with a slight wince. "I think 'laughing-stock' is overstating it somewhat, but I undoubtedly would prefer not to be open to scrutiny, not until the work is complete. There are some very closed-minded individuals in the world of scientific research, and I'm sure you can easily imagine what the reaction would be if it got out that I was delving into this, rather... esoteric area of research. I'd be accused of dabbling in witchcraft, abandoning empirical rigour in favour of superstition, almost literally consorting with the devil. Just as it was heresy in Galileo's day to say that the earth orbited around the sun, so it is heresy these days, of a different kind, to stray from the narrow paths of scientific orthodoxy. At best I'd be shunned; at worst, I would be publicly ridiculed in all the important journals and online forums. My career might never recover. My reputation definitely would not. Hence absolute discretion is called for, at least until I have proven my theories in practical terms beyond a shadow of a doubt. After that, no stigma will attach to me: my accomplishments will speak for themselves."

There was a lengthy interlude before the professor's next statement.

"That," he said, "sounds highly satisfactory. A tad remote, I would submit, but I did ask for isolation and seclusion, and where better to find that than an island a hundred kilometres from the nearest major landmass? If the existing infrastructure can be brought up to an acceptable working standard, then I can foresee no problem establishing a facility there. Perhaps I shall even manage to obtain a suntan. We scientists are usually such a pasty, indoorsy lot, aren't we?"

With this rather feeble stab at witty repartee, the clip ended.

"That was last December," said Buckler. "In the months since, Prof Seidelmann has been nose to the grindstone at Anger Reef, in close collusion with this man."

He pulled up a police mugshot of a West Indian of similar age to Seidelmann, perhaps a shade younger, with a plethora of piercings, a smattering of tattoos, and a Mohawk stripe of bleached-blonde hair. The sclera of his eyes was yellow and full of broken capillaries, and one pupil was clouded by what appeared to be a cataract or optic scarring. He glowered at the camera, or at whoever was taking the photo, and from the resentful set of his jaw there was no question that this was an angry, unpredictable individual, someone who harboured a severe grudge against the world.

"Nice," said Lex. "Just the type of bloke you'd like your daughter to bring home."

Sampson chuckled. "Yeah, a regular contributor to society."

"He was christened François Deslorges," said Buckler. "A native of Haiti, mid-thirties, with a spotty employment record and a rap sheet as long as your arm. Busted mostly for drug dealing—marijuana, the odd class-A substance—but he doesn't appear to have spent a single day in jail. Either the Haitian cops can't make the charges stick or he knows whose palms to grease to keep him out of the courts—and I know which of those I'd lay money on. His principal source of income, outside of peddling dope, is voodoo."

"*Vodou*," said Lex.

"Sorry?"

"It's *vodou*, not voodoo. Apparently. So I've been told."

"Tom*ay*to, tom*ah*to," said Buckler dismissively. "This guy, anyway, he's a professional *houngan*, a male voodoo priest." The emphasis on the word *voodoo* was light but pointed. "He runs a temple at his house in downtown Port-au-Prince and it's said his regular worshippers, or *clients* maybe, number in the hundreds. An influential figure. There are also rumours that Deslorges is a *bokor*, which is a houngan who leans towards the dark side of voodoo."

"You'd never think it to look at him," said Lex.

"He's your go-to guy if you want to turn your neighbour into a frog or have your ex-wife fall down a well—like I wish mine would. I jest," Buckler added. "But a bokor isn't someone you want to mess with. Voodoo is serious shit. If used incorrectly or with harmful intent, it can cause real damage."

Lex flashbacked to the Garfish's henchman and his suddenly shattered leg. Had that been an incorrect use of voodoo on Albertine's part? He didn't think so. It had been a prime example of justified self-defence if ever there was one. But assuming that was 'good' voodoo, he shuddered to imagine what *dark* voodoo could do.

"I'll second that," said Sampson. "I'm from New Orleans, born and raised. We got voodoo there in the Big Easy—sometimes call it hoodoo—and man, you don't want to get on the wrong side of some of the motherfuckers who play around with that stuff. One time I remember, this guy I knew, friend of a friend, he started going out with this chick, a voodoo priestess with her own store on North Rampart Street, right across from Louis Armstrong Park. Some piece of tail she was, and she claimed she could trace her lineage all the way back to the Witch Queen of New Orleans herself, Marie Laveau. Anyways, the guy made the mistake of cheating on her with another girl. She found out and put a curse on him. Next thing you know, his dog gets run over by a car, he loses his job, and his house burns down in an unexplained fire. I mean, it'd be funny if it wasn't so tragic."

"Maybe she did it herself, the priestess," Lex said. "Drove the car that killed the dog, set the fire, somehow fixed it so her man got the sack."

"Maybe, or maybe she got the spirits to arrange it all for her, or maybe the guy just had a run of bad luck. Either way, there's a connection. He got her mad, she hexed him, bad shit happened. You can't prove that voodoo played a part, but neither can you disprove it. So it's safer to assume that voodoo works than that it doesn't."

An hour ago, Lex would have argued the point. That was before he'd seen a *wanga* fetish used offensively.

"So this bokor, Deslorges..." he began.

"Papa Couleuvre, as he prefers to be known," said Buckler. "It's his official title, or stage name, alter ego, whatever."

"Yeah, him. How are he and Seidelmann collaborating? What can a voodoo priest bring to a project to create super-soldiers?"

"The answer is, no one's sure, not even the Pentagon. Seidelmann's notes are vague on the subject. What we do know is that Seidelmann's own area of expertise is pharmaceuticals and their use in boosting the human metabolism in order to improve performance. Up until recently he was developing drugs tailored to enable soldiers to function for extended periods under duress. Now, air force pilots have been known to pop amphetamines from time to time to counteract fatigue during long flights, and infantrymen on watch shifts too. But we're talking something far more sophisticated—cocktails of steroid, stimulant, analgesic and sedative, balanced just right so you're operating at peak efficiency and not hampered by fear or pain."

"To me that sounds plain crazy," said Sampson. "Fear is the soldier's friend. It kicks your ass when you're under fire and keeps you frosty when you're out on patrol. Cut out fear and you're cutting out part of our basic survival mechanism."

"Agreed," said Buckler. "But the brass don't think that way. They like the idea of human robots who can go for hours, even days on end, without stopping, unemotional, unflappable. Men who are half GI, half Terminator. That's why they've been chucking money at Seidelmann by the fistful. This super-soldier project of his is just the latest in a long line of schemes he's come up with, and is probably the most ambitious and looniest yet."

"But what is it?" said Lex. "What have he and—Papa Couleuvre, yes?—what have they been cooking up together?"

"If you want my opinion," said Buckler, "based on the evidence to hand... it's zombies."

FIFTEEN
ZUVEMBIE

"YEAH, RIGHT," SAID Lex.

"I'm totally serious," said Buckler.

"I know, and I'm totally sceptical."

"Still?" Buckler adopted a patient expression. "Okay, so what is it you think of when you think of zombies?"

"Hordes of the undead roaming the land. Eating people. Groaning a lot. Looking all green and decayed. I've seen the movies."

"And it's fair to say that such creatures do crop up from time to time. We had to put a bunch of them down in Pátzcuaro in the Mexican Western Central Highlands, year before last."

"Fuck, yeah," said Tartaglione. "It was October thirty-first, Halloween, el Dia de los Muertos. There was an outbreak at a smalltown cemetery, corpses busting out of their graves and lurching through the streets. Nearby pesticide factory had been polluting the groundwater for over a decade, dumping raw waste product in the aquifers rather than processing it properly, organophosphates and some other genetically engineered shit. It seeped into the cemetery soil, somehow brought the dead back to life, and man, were they in a feisty mood. All these

Mexicans in costumes chowing down on candy skulls, and a bunch of reanimated corpses in their midst trying to chow down on *their* skulls."

"Head shot," said Sampson, making a pistol out of his fingers and aiming at the bridge of Lex's nose. "*Ka-pow*. Destroy the brain stem. It's the only way."

"Local media reported it as a Halloween stunt gone wrong," said Tartaglione. "Some of the revellers got drunk and took the role-playing a little too far."

"Plausible, too," said Sampson. "Nobody does Halloween like Mexicans do Halloween. Everyone downing tequila until they could hardly see straight, let alone tell the difference between a real zombie and a guy in a suit. Firecrackers going off everywhere, so many that our gunshots were barely noticed. We could have done the op wearing pink tutus and carrying a sign saying ZOMBIES THIS WAY, and probably no one would've turned a hair."

"That's one kind of zombie," said Buckler. "But there's another. The old-school kind. Which is what I think may be on the loose at Anger Reef."

"The old-school kind," said Lex, making a connection. "The voodoo kind."

"Indeed. The zuvembie. The living dead man raised from the grave by a voodoo priest to do his bidding."

"Oh."

"That's all? 'Oh'?" Buckler was surprised. "You're not going to call me on that one? You can accept zombies in a voodoo context?"

"As we've just been discussing, voodoo can rely on all sorts of psychological effects," said Lex. "It's a belief system, and its power can be put down, at least in part, to expectation and cultural conditioning. Sampson's friend's friend got hit by misfortune after misfortune and naturally blamed it on his woman placing a curse on him, because it seemed conceivable, if not the only plausible explanation. By the same token, couldn't someone with influence in voodoo circles promote the idea that creating a zombie—sorry, a zuvembie—is possible?"

"Go on."

"Well, I'm just saying that if a voodoo practitioner can persuade people he's able to raise the dead, they'll accept it as fact forever after. He could fake it with the aid of an accomplice pretending to be a reanimated corpse, or he could dupe someone suggestible, an easily swayed acolyte, into believing they're a reanimated corpse. Both achieve much the same result, making him look scary and powerful and cementing his reputation."

"Nice logic," said Buckler, "and there's some truth in it. Ethnologists have shown that people have been deceived into thinking they're zombified through the use of hallucinogens and ritual. A bokor—and this is the sort of thing a bokor will do, as opposed to a houngan—plies his victim with a drug that causes partial paralysis, amnesia and loss of will. It'll be a powder or a potion consisting of substances like tetrodotoxin, the venom from the puffer fish, and datura, a poisonous plant commonly known as angel's trumpet or moonflower, all brewed together with crushed-up dead baby skull and other equally delicious ingredients like toad and lizard parts. He makes the guy undergo a symbolic burial, sticking him in a coffin for days, maybe underground with a limited air supply, until this poor sap—bewildered, drug-addled, half-suffocated, possibly even brain-damaged—is convinced he must be dead. Then the bokor digs him up, 'revives' him, and now he's got someone who assumes he's nothing more than a soulless shell and will therefore do whatever he's told. Long as the bokor keeps him doped up and stupefied, he has himself a loyal, dull-witted slave. That's a zuvembie, or at least that's one way of accounting for the zuvembie lore that exists in the voodoo tradition. It's said that this was how they used to keep slaves on Haitian sugar plantations docile and obedient—they zombified them. And yes, I have been doing my homework."

"And this is what Seidelmann and Papa Couleuvre have been up to? Making their own form of zuvembie?"

"It's a working hypothesis, one that fits the data. Remember the head-cam footage? Those figures taking bullets and still coming? Seidelmann's process, whatever it is, has advanced to the human guinea pig phase. Only the experiment hasn't perhaps worked out quite the way he and Papa Couleuvre were hoping."

Lex said, "The mission, then, is to infiltrate the installation at Anger Reef, take down any and all of these zuvembies, if that's what they are, ascertain whether there are staff members and marines still alive, extract them, exfiltrate, go home."

"In a nutshell."

"Well..." Lex slapped his thighs with finality. "Consider me briefed and in full possession of the facts. Unless there's anything else I should know?"

"No," Buckler said. "That's it. Everything."

"Then when do we start?"

"'We'? You want in on the op itself?"

"Here's how I see it," said Lex. "You've already got Wilberforce flying you to and from Anger Reef. That's one civilian asset you're exploiting who's also a friend of mine. Now, I'm betting you're going to insist on dragging Albertine along with you too, since there's a mad, bad bokor waiting for you at the other end and probably zuvembies too. Am I wrong?"

Buckler's expression told him he was not.

"You want someone with practical voodoo skills, on the ground, immediately accessible," Lex went on, "in case the zuvembies prove hard to handle using conventional means. You want someone to fulfil the same role as that shaman in Siberia who enabled you to get close to the werebear."

"Goddamn werebear," muttered Sampson, with a disgruntled shake of the head.

Tartaglione gave his hand a sniff and wrinkled his nose. "I've had three showers since and I can still smell that rancid crap that guy made us put on. Don't know if it's ever going to wash off."

"You're going to coerce Albertine into coming with you whether I like it or not," Lex continued, speaking solely to Buckler. "It's even occurred to you that you might have to remove me from the equation somehow, if I object too strenuously. Don't worry, I don't take it personally. A leader has to think through all the variables in order to ensure mission success. There's a chance I could make life awkward for you, so disposing of me has to be at least somewhere on the to-do list. Now, right here in this room, would be as good a time and place as any. Three of you, one of me, a discreet, unarmed takedown. I'm not saying it would work, but you could try."

"You always this mistrustful, ace?" said Buckler.

"It's served me well in the past. It's certainly a little *convenient* that your two shooters happened to turn up when they did. You knew I was coming back here. You knew I was unhappy about your plans for my friend and his cousin. Sampson and Tartaglione aren't just 'moral support,' are they? They're backup, an insurance policy in the event that I don't play along. But, really, truly, I don't want to get into a fight. Whatever the outcome, even if you people win, at least one of you is going to end up hospitalised or worse, I can promise that. And then you'd be short-handed and the mission would be compromised and might even have to be scratched, which would be a pity. So this is what I'm offering—and it's not up for discussion. I come with you too. You take Albertine and Wilberforce, you get me as well. Think of it as a bargain package, like at the supermarket. Buy two, get a third for free."

"Dove, listen..."

Lex rose to his feet. "What part of 'not up for discussion' do you not understand, Lieutenant Buckler? Wilberforce's plane is an eight-seater, so there's room for me on board. You must be aware that I can handle myself in a firefight and have worked alongside American combat units before. You're heading into a hostile environment with two complete amateurs in tow, and chances are you'll be so busy watching your own backs you won't be able to watch theirs. Civilians are a liability, as we all know. That's where I come in. You may have a problem with it, but if you do, tough. It's a done deal."

Tartaglione and Sampson looked to their team leader to see how he would respond. Buckler pensively fingered his moustache, gaze fixed on Lex. Here was a man who appeared to wear his authority lightly but preferred not to have it challenged.

For a moment—just a moment—Buckler's eyes hardened.

Then he relented. A grin came, one that was a fraction too broad.

"All right, buddy," he said. "Fine. You're in. Guess it won't hurt to have an extra warm body. And you're right, someone looking out for your pals is a good idea. We might not have the leisure to do that ourselves. Welcome to Team Thirteen, Lex Dove."

Lex shook Buckler's proffered hand, and Buckler squeezed, crushing knuckles. Sampson clapped Lex on the back hard. Tartaglione ruffled his hair with a scrubbing motion.

These actions were not unpainful, and Lex was under no illusion that that was deliberate.

SIXTEEN
CROWD OF THE DEAD

THEY CAME OUT of the dark, singly at first, then in a horde.

Leading the pack was a despot from sub-Saharan Africa, massively overweight, his face grey as clay. Sticking out of the rolls of blubber at his neck was the hypodermic syringe Lex had used to inject him with a lethal dose of potassium chloride, the British government's answer to the man's repeated attempts to blame all his country's contemporary ills on its former colonial ruler. The UK did not take kindly to being made a scapegoat. Cause of death had been listed as heart attack, according to a coroner who didn't wish to enquire into the matter too deeply. Like most of his countrymen, he was just glad the psychotic fat bastard was gone.

Next was a Thai plutocrat who had been attempting to sell phials of weaponised hantavirus to some very shady characters on the Pacific Rim. While cruising around the Phi Phi Islands in the Andaman Sea in his luxury yacht, he had slipped on deck, fallen over the rail and drowned. Or so it was generally assumed. His bloated corpse showed signs of having been nibbled by small fish and gnawed by sharks. Water poured in a continuous stream from his mouth, nose and ears.

Following him came the Montenegran arms dealer who had moonlighted as a trader in state secrets, selling information he gleaned from his contacts in various defence departments to terrorists and religious fanatics, whoever would pay his exorbitant prices. His Lamborghini had left the road while negotiating the St Gotthard Pass in the Swiss Alps, plunging off the Teufelsbrücke bridge into the Schöllenen Gorge. The car had been so badly wrecked that accident investigators failed to find evidence of the remote-detonated packets of explosive that burst the two nearside tyres simultaneously and caused the driver's fatal loss of control.

Then there was the Ukrainian people-trafficker flooding London with abducted underage prostitutes, who had been found hanging in a wardrobe in what looked to all intents and purposes like an act of autoerotic asphyxiation gone disastrously wrong.

And the sheik with connections to al-Qaeda, apparently slain by one of his own bodyguards who had then immediately turned his gun on himself.

And the rabble-rousing neo-Nazi Russian demagogue, forever exhorting his country to unleash its nuclear arsenal on the decadent, racially-impure West, who had been shot in the back while on a moose hunting expedition in the Urals, killed by the same calibre of rifle bullet his fellow hunters were using even though every one of them swore blind that they had not fired at or even near him.

They all lurched towards Lex, charred, mangled, broken, dismembered, riddled with bullet holes, sporting gory wounds, eyes cloudy, mouths agape in silent screams of indignation. They converged on him from in front, behind, all around, encircling him, a dozen, a score, twice that number, more. Cold, clammy hands clutched at him. The crowd of the dead pressed in on him, threatening to overwhelm him with their weight and their putrid stink. Lex struggled, but he seemed to lack all strength. He couldn't escape. He was helpless. The dead surged over him like a tide, all the many people he had killed, all risen from their final resting places to claim their assassin and drag him down to whichever dark hells they now called home.

And now Lex heard laughter—derisive, crowing laughter. He scanned frantically to see where it was coming from. Maybe it was someone who could help him.

Beyond the throng of shambling corpses, somewhere on high as though on a podium, stood a man in a black tailcoat. He wore sunglasses with the right-hand lens missing and a crooked top hat on his head, a crow's feather protruding jauntily from the sash. His face was painted to resemble a skull, the white of the makeup contrasting starkly with the deep brown of his skin.

He brandished a cane in one hand, a spindly twist of wood with a carved ivory skull as its knob. He was using it like a conductor's baton, waving it to and fro in time to a rhythm only he could hear, and Lex could see that the crowd of the dead were under this frightful figure's command. He was urging them on, orchestrating their assault, and laughing heartily all the while, as if it was the finest entertainment imaginable.

The dead were now crawling over one another to get to Lex, their wretched bodies forming a dome over him, engulfing him. He was at the heart of a pile of soft putrefying flesh and writhing rotten limbs. He could barely breathe. He was going to suffocate.

And still that laughter pealed in the background, immense delighted guffaws from the cavorting, skull-faced man in black...

OF COURSE IT was a dream. Lex knew that even while he was in the thick of it, being buried under those corpses. Only a dream, and he fought his way out, thrashing up to the surface of consciousness to find himself, yes, in bed, at home, in darkness, lying tangled in the sheets with cicadas trilling outside the window and the ceiling fan whirling lazily overhead.

And then, to his horror, he realised that he was still pinned down. A body lay half on him, one arm across his throat. It had been no dream. The nightmare was real. The dead were here—*his* dead—and one of them had him in a tight embrace and was about to throttle him.

He threw the arm off and scrambled sideways, desperate to get away, desperate to flee the postmortem vengeance of his victims.

He tumbled off the bed onto the floor, thumping hard, backside first. He was slick with sweat, heart pounding. He thrust himself backwards with his heels until he struck the wall. He could hear a mewling coming from his throat, an abject sound, a wordless plea for mercy.

Then, from the bed, someone spoke.

"Lex?"

And a lamp flicked on.

"Lex, what's going on?"

It was Albertine, with the sheet clasped to her chest, leaning over him, beautiful, solicitous.

"What are you doing on the floor there? You look terrible. What on earth's the matter?"

Lex gasped, gulped, finally found his voice. "I... Shit. I had this... I was... Bad dream. Yeah. Really fucking bad dream."

Albertine looked him up and down. "Yes, I'd say so. Come on." She beckoned.

Reluctantly, unsteadily, Lex clambered back onto the bed. He was shivering, despite the heat.

"It was... Bloody hell. So vivid."

"Shhh. It's all right. Lie down."

He settled down against her. She was naked, as was he. How had this come about? How had they ended up like this?

It came back to him, gradually, piecemeal. He had rendezvoused with Wilberforce and Albertine at his house. They had been waiting for him here when he returned from the Cape Azure. There'd been dinner, during which Lex had laid bare the facts about Anger Reef and explained what Lieutenant Buckler required from each of the cousins. Then Albertine had retired to the spare room for the night while Lex made up the couch for Wilberforce.

Later, Lex's bedroom door had opened. Albertine had stepped through, shutting it softly behind her.

Not much was said. She was in a borrowed bathrobe. She let it slip to her ankles, revealing an ample shelf of bosom and wide, sinuously incurving hips. She slid in under the covers beside him. The warmth coming off her was tremendous. The musk too, the earthy female scent. Lex was erect almost before he knew it, and he didn't question her presence, didn't ask why she was there or why she wanted him. Didn't care. He threw himself at her, and there was sweat, and saliva, and pawing, and straddling, an inelegant ballet of lust, and it was over quickly, for both of them, an urgent, exultant coming together, and afterwards a precipitous rush into sleep, like falling off a cliff, oblivion chasing the heels of orgasm and exhaustion.

"You get nightmares often?" Albertine asked.

"Occasionally. Not like this one, though."

"Want to talk about it? Sometimes helps."

"No. Want to tell me why you... you know. Why we..."

"Got carnal?"

"If you have to put it like that."

Albertine gave a wry, slightly pitying chuckle. "One thing you should know about islander women. We're very passionate. Prim and proper on the surface, but underneath... Look out!"

"Not that I'm complaining, I hasten to add."

"I know you're not. I surprised you, that's all. I understand that. You weren't sure I was interested. But I can be very impulsive. Sometimes Erzulie Freda, she gets the better of me. She's a fine lady, fond of all the nice things in life, dainty in her way, and you'd think she'd be above getting all down-and-dirty, but she's not, trust me. She's got a wicked streak, and now and then, even when I haven't summoned her, she mounts me..."

"And you mounted me," Lex finished.

This time Albertine didn't so much chuckle as cackle—quite the lewdest laugh Lex had ever heard.

"And it was nice," she said.

"That's all? 'Nice'?"

"Very nice, then. You may not be the tallest man I've ever been with, but in other respects you're far from being the smallest."

"Thanks. I'll take that as a compliment."

"Do."

"What time is it?" Lex consulted his alarm clock. "Christ," he groaned. "Gone three. We're 'wheels up' at six, according to Buckler. Albertine, I know I've asked this a hundred times already, but now it seems more pertinent than ever. Are you sure you—?"

She placed a finger on his lips. "Don't even think about saying it. A bokor has been committing heinous acts, perverting *vodou* for his own ends. As a practising mambo, a true *serviteur* of the loa, I can't stand idly by and allow it to happen. And you've seen what I can do. I've got my bag of tricks with me, packed with all I need, and I'm not afraid to use it. I'm going into this with eyes wide open, Lex. It's kind of you to worry, but don't."

"I'm just saying..."

"Things are the way they are. You must understand, *vodou* is a very fatalistic religion. Accepting one's destiny is part of the deal. The loa know what's best for each of us, and it would be foolish to attempt to defy their will. It would only displease them, and make them more determined than ever to force you down the road they want you to take. And this, this mission, is the road for me. I know it. I have no doubts."

"Okay," said Lex. "Well, you can't say I didn't try. Shit." He pressed the back of a forearm to his forehead. All at once, in his mind's eye, came a vision of the figure in the funereal black suit, the cockeyed hat perched on his head, the cane carving patterns in the air. "The thing about the dream I just had... I've had similar dreams before. A recurring nightmare. But this time, it was worse than it's ever been. I suppose I'm just anxious about what's ahead."

"Who wouldn't be?" said Albertine. "If Lieutenant Buckler is right and we're going to be facing zuvembies, or something like zuvembies, anxiety is the only sensible response." Her tone shifted from sympathetic to inquisitive. "Was there somebody in this dream, by any chance? Somebody you've not seen before?"

"Yes," Lex said, a little too quickly. He backpedalled, not sure he wanted to give away too much about himself, about the workings of his subconscious mind. He had met this woman less than twenty-four hours ago. They had had sex, but he still hardly knew her. "Sort of. You know how, in dreams, someone can seem familiar even though they're a complete stranger? There was a bloke like that in this one."

"Describe him."

Lex supplied a brief verbal sketch of the top-hatted man.

"Baron Samedi," said Albertine. She didn't seem all that surprised.

"Oh yes. The one you said Papa Doc Duvalier cribbed his look from. I remember. That'll be why I recognised him. You see pictures of him all over the place, don't you?"

"The Baron? Nine out of ten tattoo parlours here have him in the window as one of their design samples. He's a popular choice of body art, particularly among young men. Decals on motorbikes, airbrushed pictures on surfboards, murals on the side of houses—you can find images of him just about everywhere you look. He's the loa even people who know nothing about *vodou* know about. Everyone thinks he's hot stuff, and that makes the Baron happy. He thinks he's pretty hot stuff too."

"And I suppose I was dreaming about him because you mentioned him yesterday." To Lex, this was comforting. Dreams were the mind's clearing-house, a way of sifting through, sorting and storing the jumbled data of the day. Albertine had talked about Papa Doc and Baron Samedi, and Lex's hindbrain had conflated the two and then invited the Haitian dictator to put in an appearance among the parade of human monsters whose shades haunted Lex while he slept. Duvalier may not have been one of Lex's Code Crimsons but he certainly fitted right in with the rest. The Baron Samedi get-up conferred a kind of star status on him, as though he were a veteran actor wheeled out of retirement to spruce up the cast of a long-running show.

"Maybe," said Albertine. "Or it could be that the Baron wished to take a look at you."

Lex could not help but feel a chill at her words. "Don't be daft."

"It would be just like him to drop by and introduce himself. If there's trouble ahead, and especially if it involves a bokor, then the Baron is likely to have a stake in the proceedings. Black magic and the Baron are never far apart. He wanted to get the measure of you, that's what I think. See what he's up against. Did he say anything?"

"No, just laughed. A lot."

"Was there anyone else with him?"

How to account for the presence of so many dead men in his dream? It was impossible without also cracking open a door onto his former life, one he had kept firmly shut since his move to Manzanilla, and inviting another person to peek through. He didn't know Albertine well enough for that—not by a long shot. "No. Nobody else. Only him."

"I just wondered if perhaps Legba showed his face too."

"Legba?"

"Loa of the crossroads. He's always there at the outset, when there are decisions to be taken, choices to be made, a journey to be embarked on. Looks like a beggar, usually has a dog or two with him, smokes a corncob pipe, walks with a limp..."

"You could be describing Gable," said Lex with an ironic laugh.

"Gable?"

"This old tramp, lives down by the intersection between the hill road and the coastal highway. You must have seen him, surely. I pass him almost every evening on my way to and from the rum shack."

"I don't venture out to this corner of the island much. I stick to Port Sebastian and the windward side. The civilised areas."

"Well, he's a fixture round these parts. I bung him the odd dollar now and then. He's harmless. Most of the time."

"But not all of the time?"

It was a leading question. Perhaps Lex wanted to be led.

"Well, not last night, that's for sure," he said. "He collared me as I was walking home. Had a bit of a funny turn. Grabbed hold of me and started banging on about beginnings, and me having a job to do, and not turning away help. I just thought he'd been hitting the hooch a little too hard."

Albertine sat up. "What was his name again?"

"Gable."

"G-A-B-L-E?"

"I presume that's how it's spelled."

"Saints preserve us." She swivelled round, sprang out of bed, gathered up the bathrobe.

"What's up? Why the sudden flurry of activity? Was it something I said?"

"We have to go out. You and me. We don't have much time, not if we're going to fit it in before picking up with Lieutenant Buckler and friends."

"Fit what in? You're not making any sense."

"Lex." She fastened the cord of the bathrobe, depriving him of a far from unpleasant view. "You have met Papa Legba, face to face. And if we're not too late, we should be able to get his personal blessing for what we're about to do at Anger Reef."

SEVENTEEN
NACHONS

GET DRESSED. I'll see you outside in ten minutes.

Those were Albertine's last words to him before she left the bedroom in a hurry. Ten minutes later, Lex was stationed beside the Subaru, waiting. Rikki poked his head out from the bushes and ambled over, looking more than a little bemused. His attitude seemed to be: *What are you doing up and about at this ungodly hour? This is when I prowl, not you.*

"Believe me," Lex said to the mongoose, "if I had the first clue what any of this was about, I'd tell you."

"Talking to animals, Lex?" Albertine had just emerged from the house.

Rikki took one look at the stranger, turned tail and fled.

"That doesn't seem like you at all," she continued. "Far too sentimental."

"The mongoose doesn't answer back," Lex said. "He's the perfect conversationalist."

He held the passenger door open for her, then climbed in the driver's side. Within moments the 4x4 was bouncing down the driveway, headlights peering into the mist-tendrilled dark.

"You probably think this is crazy," Albertine said, "haring off in the middle of the night to go see a tramp."

"Crazy isn't the first adjective that springs to mind. Not quite."

"It's typical Legba, though. He's such a cheeky one. Loves games and mischief, hide-and-seek and peekaboo. If there's a chance he can pull a trick on you, such as revealing himself to you without you realising, then he'll take it. He can't resist a bit of duplicity."

"You're saying Legba is... Gable? Gable is a voodoo loa in disguise?"

"No. I'm saying Legba elected to ride this Gable person in order to speak to you. Gable is the ideal candidate for being Legba's *chwal*. He's a beggar, like Legba. He has dogs, like Legba. He lives at a crossroads, and Legba is all about the crossroads. Did you say he's lame?"

"There's something wrong with his feet. He gets around using a metal crutch."

"Yes. Legba has difficulty walking because he has one foot in heaven and the other on earth. He's the intersection, you see, the gateway between the two realms. For that reason he's the first loa we salute in any ceremony. He opens the channels of communication in both directions."

"Like a sort of spirit walkie-talkie."

"You mock, but yes. And sometimes the reception is poor, and that's no accident. Legba enjoys baffling as much as he enjoys enabling. If he sends you a message, it's seldom direct and unambiguous. It can be interpreted several different ways, just as you can head several different ways at a crossroads. He has a penchant for riddles, anagrams, paradoxes..."

"Gable is an anagram of Legba."

"Exactly, and that'll be one more reason why Legba chose him as his mouthpiece," Albertine said. "So many similarities between the two of them. The name is merely the clincher, the icing on the cake."

"What if we get there, wake Gable up, and Legba chooses not to pick up the phone and call?"

"Then we'll have wasted our time. But we'll have lost nothing by trying."

"Nothing except a couple of hours' extra sleep," Lex muttered.

"Don't whinge. It doesn't suit you," said Albertine. "Besides, from what I can gather, you're used to this sort of thing. Functioning on little sleep. Being awake at strange hours of the night. Your job, military life, demanded it."

"That was then, when I was younger. I have a more relaxed work ethic these days."

"You mean doing as little of it as you can get away with."

"None at all, if possible."

"You're turning into an islander man. Shame on you."

"Can't be helped. I blame the humidity." Lex guided the Subaru down the snaking turns of the hill road, past smallholdings each consisting of a concrete house, usually unfinished, and an acre or two of crops—maize, cassava, sometimes pineapples—plus a goat for milk. Farming that was one notch above subsistence level. "So the loa, they're like gods, are they?"

"You're after a lecture on *vodou*?"

"Now seems as good a time as any. It'll help pass the journey, and since I appear to be bumping into loa on a regular basis, I suppose I should find out as much about them as I can. Forewarned is forearmed."

"Well, you asked for it," said Albertine. "*Vodou* is what's called a syncretic religion. That's to say, a fusion of religious traditions, one hiding under the other. You have the original belief system that was brought over to the West Indies from Africa with the slave trade. Overlaid on that is Roman Catholicism, which was imposed on the slaves by their masters, who Christianised them in the hope of 'civilising' them and wiping out their 'savage' tendencies. The two iconographies mixed and matched, swapped addresses, Facebook-friended each other, and *vodou* is the result. I wrote my degree thesis on this subject as part of my major in religious studies."

"Scholarship girl?"

"God, yes. I could never have afforded Cornell otherwise. Luckily for me, there are federal grants for students in the so-called developing world."

"America reaching out and doing its bit to foster US global hegemony."

"Cynic."

Lex took his hands off the wheel in a brief shrug.

"It was a serious culture shock," Albertine said, "going from Manzanilla to an Ivy League college. The first winter in upstate New York nearly killed me. You have no idea how strange it seemed to experience rain that was freezing cold—let alone snow. But I'm digressing."

"You are."

"*Vodou* originated in a number of regions of Africa, principally the Congo, Dahomey, which is now Benin, and Yorubaland, which is now part of Nigeria. It also has roots in the traditions of the indigenous tribes of the West Indies, the Arawak and Taino. It's a stew of different influences, but to me that's a plus, not a minus."

"Good sturdy mongrel stock. No inbreeding."

"Yes. That's it. Slaves, of course, were forbidden from practising their faith openly. They were regarded as infidels and would be punished severely for any overt expression of non-Christian belief. So they devised a cunning way of maintaining their ancestral customs without being seen to do so. They adopted the Catholic saints as stand-ins for the spirits and gods of their own religions, worshipping them by name but secretly worshipping the equivalent loa all the while. So St Patrick, for instance, was used as a substitute for Damballah, since both of them carry staffs and are linked to snakes. The Blessed Virgin Mary was used for Erzulie Freda, crippled St Lazarus for Legba, St George for Ogun... The list goes on. Their masters never twigged. The slaves also chose to acknowledge the supremacy of a single deity above all others, whom they named Bondye."

Lex recalled the footage from Anger Reef, the cry of "Bondye! Bondye! Hear me, Bondye. I am coming for you." Who had that been, shouting? Logic dictated that it was François Deslorges, a.k.a. Papa Couleuvre. And what did the words signify? He couldn't tell, but he was convinced they meant nothing good.

"The loa act as Bondye's intercessors," Albertine continued. "They represent Him to us and vice versa. They're spirits, saints, even angels, all rolled into one. Bondye is aloof and unknowable, while the loa are earthy, capricious, contrary, argumentative, benevolent, malevolent—just like us, in other words. They like to be honoured and flattered, sacrificed to, and if you treat them kindly they'll reciprocate, but if you annoy them or insult them, well, they'll let you know about it in no uncertain terms. There are three *nachons* of loa—three categories, three families. First you have the Rada *nachon*. They were brought over by the Fon and Ewe peoples of Dahomey. The Rada are wise, mostly, and tend to think things through before acting, although that isn't to say you can always trust them. All three of my husbands are Rada. My peristyle is entirely dedicated to them. They're 'cool' loa."

"They hang out behind the bike sheds smoking."

Albertine gave his remark all the respect she felt it deserved, which was none. "It's not a value judgement. 'Cool' means slow-working but reliable, easy to deal with. Then you have the Petro loa, a more forceful *nachon*, born in the swelter of the Congo. They're a lot more elemental and aggressive than the Rada. Finally you have the Guédé *nachon*. They're lords and ladies of the underworld, kings and queens of death, but they're not as gloomy and morbid as that makes them sound. They're incredibly lively, vibrant, not to mention violent. Death inevitably entails rebirth, a new start, the chance to begin again, one door closing, another one opening. And proximity to death sharpens the appetite for life, doesn't it? So the Guédé loa love to party, and intoxicate themselves, and even indulge in orgies. They're 'hot' loa in every respect, fiery and sensual."

"Okay," said Lex. "So they're the ones to get to organise your stag or hen do."

"And also the wake at your funeral," said Albertine. "So there it is, a very basic outline of the *nachons*. The system is somewhat more complicated than I'm making out. The divisions aren't necessarily so clear-cut."

"That's all right. I'm fine with the simplified version."

"I thought you would be. Would you like me to list which loa belong to which *nachon*?"

"Not right now."

"I understand. Informational overload. Lex Dove's memory cache has reached capacity."

"No." Lex pointed ahead. "It's because we're nearly there."

The crossroads was in sight.

Albertine's grip on the shoulder bag in her lap tightened. She struck Lex as excited, but also apprehensive.

He felt apprehension too, and tried to fathom the reason for it. They were just going to have a chat with a homeless hobo, weren't they?

No, not necessarily.

It could be a great deal more than that.

EIGHTEEN
LEGBA BY CANDLELIGHT

GABLE WAS NOT to be seen at the crossroads. The patch of roadside grass where he and his dogs liked to sit lay empty, an oval of flattened stems shining in the moonlight.

"He has a camp." Lex indicated the thickets of acacia and cabbage palmetto beyond. "Somewhere in there."

"You can see where he's trampled a path going to and from," said Albertine. "Let's follow it."

"Me first."

"My hero."

Lex carefully pushed through the fans of palmetto leaf, holding them aside so that they didn't slap back on Albertine. Twenty metres in they came to a clearing. There was a crude makeshift tent fashioned out of wooden stakes and a tarpaulin, and a small cooking fire which had long since gone out. The ground was littered with empty bottles, tin cans and packets of tobacco, chocolate wrappers, chipped crockery, pages from ancient editions of the *Manzanilla Times*, assorted grubby items of clothing, some damp-swollen paperbacks, and a few household electrical items, such as a broken transistor radio and a pocket calculator which Gable must have scavenged from a tip or somebody's dustbin. Of Gable himself, or his cane dogs, there was no sign.

"He can't have left," Lex murmured, mostly to himself. "He never leaves. He's always hanging around here. This is his home."

"He wouldn't have abandoned all his belongings, either," Albertine said. "No, he's nearby."

"Probably we scared him off, coming through the undergrowth like that. Gable," he called out softly. "It's Lex. The Englishman. I know it's stupid o'clock in the morning, but there's nothing to be alarmed about. I just want to talk. I've brought a friend. Very nice lady. You'll like her."

Past the camp lay nothing but dark forest. The trees— pine, seagrape, copperwood—whispered and hissed. Unseen creatures croaked and shrilled. Lex used his peripheral vision to scan the shadows, hoping to discern the silhouette of the tramp peeking nervously round a trunk, his canine companions at his heels. Nothing. Nothing but branches and leaves fluttering and swaying in the breeze.

Gable was out there, though. Lex sensed it. Instinct told him the tramp had not gone far. With those lame feet, how could he have?

"Gable, honestly, we mean you no harm."

"It's Legba," Albertine said to Lex. "He's playing hard to get. Sometimes he's like this, pretending to be coy. You have to make an effort with him, so that he feels appreciated."

"How do we do that?"

"First, a *vévé*."

"A what?"

Instead of replying, Albertine opened her bag and took out a jam jar filled with some kind of pale powder. Unscrewing the lid, she knelt and began tapping the powder out onto the ground in a pattern. First she sketched out a pair of bisecting lines of identical length to form a cross. This she ornamented with smaller crosses in all four corners where the lines met, followed by notches at intervals along the lines themselves, like increments on a ruler. Finally she added a design to the tip of each arm of the cross. At the north tip she put a circle divided into quadrants, and at the east an asterisk and beside this a fish shape and what appeared to be a shepherd's crook. At the south tip she drew what looked like a feather, or perhaps a fisherman's lure, and at the west another asterisk and something resembling a curly letter E.

"A *vévé* is a cosmogram," she told Lex. "Every loa has one—a sacred glyph embodying his or her essential nature. It's important to keep it as symmetrical and unbroken as possible. Drawing a *vévé* looks easy, but believe me, it takes practice to get it just right."

"What's the powder? Ground-up human bone?"

She shot him a look. "Cornmeal, as a matter of fact. Now the doorway to Legba is open. But a libation is needed."

She produced a miniature of rum and sprinkled some drops onto the *vévé*.

"And some illumination."

She set a small, stubby black candle down in the centre of the *vévé*, screwing the base into the dirt. A match flared. A flame guttered and grew at the candle's wick. The smoke coiling up from it was scented—floral and faintly earthy.

As the candle flame strengthened, shedding its glow over the campsite and Gable's meagre scatter of possessions, the surrounding forest seemed to quieten. The calls and songs of animals became muted, dwindling to a quick chirrup here, a piping squeak there. A stillness descended, and Lex, for no appreciable reason, felt the hairs on the nape of his neck stand on end. The air seemed charged, as though a distant storm was brewing, its power building in the atmosphere. He itched to have a gun in his hand. The SIG Sauer was back in the Subaru's glove compartment. He wished he'd brought it with him. He would feel safer then, more in control.

"And finally some rhythm," said Albertine.

Her shoulder bag, a seemingly inexhaustible fund of voodoo paraphernalia, yielded a rattle. It was made out of a gourd and adorned with multicoloured glass beads. The vertebrae of some creature—a snake was Lex's guess—dangled from it, strung on leather thongs.

"My *asson*," she said, and Lex was tempted to make an amusing pun on the word but resisted. It didn't seem appropriate. Or wise.

Albertine began to shake the rattle, initially beating out a simple four-four time but adding new quavers and semiquavers every few bars, increasing the complexity. Turning to face each of the cardinal points of the compass one after another, starting with west, she said, "*D'abord. À table*. Adonai. Olandé."

Next came some rapid chanting in French Creole, the words tumbling out too thick and fast for Lex to catch more than one in ten. The rhythm from the asson gathered pace. Seeds inside the rattle chittered drily while the snake vertebrae whirled on their thongs and clicked insistently against the gourd's thick mottled skin.

Albertine stirred her body into a gentle, swaying dance. She led with her hips, her feet moving to set positions, the rest of her following. The chant continued unabated, and the asson flickered in her hand, describing neat, wavy patterns in the air as it clattered and thrummed.

"Money."

Lex was so mesmerised by her actions, so transfixed by the spectacle of this woman conducting her one-person ceremony in the steam of a tropical night, that he didn't realise she was addressing him.

"Money." She barked out the demand again in a gap between the fluid sentences of her chant. "Put some money down on the *vévé*. An offering. A gift for Legba, to invite him to join us."

"Okay. Yes. Right."

Lex delved into his pocket and scattered some loose change onto the *vévé*.

"More," said Albertine. "That's nothing."

He extracted one of the M$100 bills in his wallet and added that to the coins.

"Good. Use this, Legba," she said in English, "to buy some of the sweet things that you love. Molasses, cane syrup, candied peanuts. Whatever will make your tongue drool and your belly happy."

Then she resumed her Creole chant once more, and her dance intensified, growing wilder and more abandoned. Her brow was knitted in concentration. Perspiration stippled her face. She seemed utterly lost in herself, the ritual evidently as hypnotic to perform as it was to watch. She was now another Albertine altogether, not the cool, self-possessed power dresser who fixed computers and wrote code for the government, rather an elemental being, the maenad who had entered Lex's bedroom just a few hours ago and seized him, gripped him, *devoured* him, slaking her lust with his. She vibrated with the frenzy of the dance, quivering like a twanged guitar string.

And then a voice sounded from the darkness of the forest.

"I hear your call, chile. I hear it an' I heed."

And out into the candlelight hobbled Gable, his two dogs beside him.

ONLY IT WASN'T Gable. Looked like him, limped like him, but it was not simply Gable. In his gaze was that unaccustomed clarity which Lex had seen the night before last, that deep mysterious intelligence, as though someone else's eyes had replaced Gable's, someone else was staring from his head, someone sharper, someone *other*.

The cane dogs, likewise, were more alert than normal. Still flea-bitten mutts, but with none of the languid happy-go-lucky look of a tramp's dogs, content with their humble lot. These were fierce animals, ear-pricked and watchful, as though the Alsatian or the Rhodesian ridgeback buried in their hodgepodge heritage had come to the fore, a single vital strand of canine DNA asserting itself over the rest. They weren't just with Gable—they flanked him, guarding him. Outriders in a pack.

"You've summoned your Papa Legba," said Gable to Albertine. "You've hauled me out of heaven, an' me accept your gifts, an' likewise your submission."

In response, Albertine sank to her knees, head bowed. Lex didn't know whether to do the same. A glance and a gesture from Albertine, a downward waft of the hand, put paid to his dithering. He joined her, circumspectly, in genuflection.

"We come as supplicants, Legba," Albertine said. "A journey lies ahead for us, one that may contain many dangers, and we crave your blessing and your counsel."

"Oh, me know 'bout your journey, baby girl," said Gable. "An' let me tell you, it's a hard road you goin' to be travellin'. Stony an' full of turns. Me wish you luck with it."

"Luck?" said Lex, unable to suppress a snort. "Is that all?"

Gable rounded on him, eyes ablaze. "You were maybe hopin' for somet'ing more? Lex Dove, me don' know what you think me is—me don' know if you yourself know—but one thing me do know is that me don' have the power to make life easy for you, no, sir. Me can't be wavin' no magic wand and makin' everyt'ing go zackly how you'd like. Loa don' work that way."

"He meant no disrespect, Legba," Albertine said. "He's a newcomer to the *dogwe*. He hasn't yet learned the right attitude."

"Too true, he ain't," said Gable. "An' me make allowances for that. That's why me still talkin' to you. Any *vodou serviteur* spoke to me like he just did, me would have upped and gone and probably wouldn't return for a month or more. My back would be well an' truly turned."

"Didn't mean to offend," Lex mumbled, more for Albertine's sake than Gable's.

"Yeah, an' you keep it that way," said Gable sternly. "Because, mister, you're already treadin' a fine line, and you don' want any more bad trouble comin' your way than you already got. Right now, it's friends you're in need of, not more foes, an' certainly not more woes. Foes and woes you got aplenty. Me see the dead that are all around you. Oh, yes, me see 'em all right. You been the Baron's right-hand man most of your adult life, whether you realise it or not. You been busy pilin' up the bodies, fillin' the grave holes."

Gable bent over Lex, staring hard into his eyes. Lex stared back, refusing to flinch or even blink. He would not let on how unnerving Gable's words were. They seemed to reach inside him like claws and scrape at his innermost self, his tenderest places, his most zealously guarded depths of conscience. He would not let that show.

"The dead won't leave you alone, Lex Dove. Change your home, change your name, change your face, don' matter, they always there with you."

A grubby index finger poked Lex in the chest.

"In here," Gable hissed. "Inside."

Lex fought the urge to swat the hand aside, maybe snap Gable's wrist in the process. That would teach him not to prod, not to provoke.

"The dead live," Gable went on. "The dead never die. They bound to you. You create 'em, you responsible for 'em, so they follow you forever after, like fledglings after the mama bird. You can fix that, but it's hard to do, so hard. You want to be free of the undying dead, you first got to face 'em. Confront 'em. Beat 'em down. You can destroy the dead, but you need to be careful not to destroy yourself while you're at it. That's my advice to you, Lex. That, an' this."

He leaned even closer and whispered in Lex's ear, a couple of short sentences, a handful of words.

"Got that?" he said, pulling back.

Lex nodded numbly.

"Good. Hee hee!" It was a wheezy laugh, a touch of bronchial wetness to it, as though all was not completely well with Gable's lungs, some underlying ailment, the consequence of open-air nights and a pipe-smoking habit. "An' you, my beautiful girl." He swivelled to face Albertine again, pivoting on his crutch. "Your husbands say to say hello. Erzulie Freda, she worried 'bout you. She don' like the idea of you headin' into that deep dirty pit of damnation you headin' into."

"Tell her I appreciate the concern," said Albertine. "I'll try to stay safe. Lex has vowed not to leave my side."

"There are some threats even he can't shield you from. Who'll be protectin' who, eh? That's the question. Who can you count on when hell's risin' up around you and the devil's knockin' at the door?"

"I can call on Damballah too. Damballah with his staff, to smite my enemies."

"An' he'll fight for you, for sure. But what you're goin' up against, even with Lex with you, even with him and those servants of Ogun, those warriors from America, even with all of them and loa swingin' for you too—it mayn't be enough. Bondye. Someone's arousin' Bondye's wrath. Someone's pokin' the biggest, baddest nest of hornets there is. You don' want to be there if Bondye comes screamin' out at you, all fire and fury. You ain't goin' to survive that, no, sir, not at all."

Gable's eyes dulled a fraction. His face slackened, losing animation.

"Legba," said Albertine. "Stay. Explain further. I beg you."

"Baby girl, me is..." Gable looked confused. Something was being withdrawn from him, like a hand pulling out of a glove. Legba was dismounting. "Me is goin'. Can't remain. This ain't a strong body. It won't hold me any longer. A weak *chwal*. Don' want to ride it death."

"Then I thank you, Papa Legba, for honouring us with your presence. I salute you, governor of destiny, guardian of the crossroads, and holder of the *poteau-mitan*, the ladder between heaven and earth. I and my friend Lex are your humble servants, undeserving of your grace."

A vacant expression came over Gable's face. He blinked uncomprehendingly at Albertine.

"Who—who are you?" he managed to blurt out, and then his head lolled back and he collapsed in a dead faint.

LEX AND ALBERTINE tried to tend to Gable as he lay on the ground, but the cane dogs wouldn't allow it. They growled and snapped defensively every time the two humans approached their insensible master.

"I don't think this is the first time they've had to look after him when he's passed out," Lex opined. "It must happen quite a lot. Let's just leave him."

"We can't," said Albertine. "It takes it out of you, being ridden by a loa. And if you're not in the best of health in the first place..."

"He'll recover. We can't afford to wait around, though, not if we're going to go and fetch Wilberforce and then collect Team Thirteen from the Cape Azure on schedule."

"There must be some way of dealing with the dogs."

"There is, but it would involve me killing them, and I doubt you want that."

Albertine conceded the point. "We'll check on him when we get back from Anger Reef."

"*If* we get back."

She darted him a look. "What are you saying?"

"Nothing. Grim joke, that's all. I mean, you heard Gable, or Legba. The way he put it, we're marching straight into the jaws of death."

"Legba can't always be relied on for an accurate summary of the situation."

"Okay, but it still doesn't sound like it's going to be a picnic. I'm just thinking we ought to be realistic about our prospects. Come on. Back to the car."

"Lex?" said Albertine as they retraced their steps through the thickets to the road.

"Yes?"

"What did he say to you?"

"Who? When?"

"Don't be childish. Legba. When he whispered to you just now."

"Nothing. Nothing important."

"Really? Because you seemed pretty shaken by it."

"No."

"You're not going to tell me."

"It's not worth sharing. Really. It might as well have been gibberish for all the sense it made."

"Okay." Her tone suggested not only that she didn't believe him but that she would winkle the truth out of him at some point in the foreseeable future. She had no doubts on that score.

But what was Lex supposed to do? Give it to her straight? Quote Gable verbatim?

How could he?

Dead men won' lie an' liars won' die. That's the truth, Leonard Duncan, and the truth always hurts.

Never mind that the message itself was pretty much unfathomable.

How the hell did Gable know his real name?

NINETEEN
ZODIACS

LIEUTENANT BUCKLER WAS in a tetchy mood. As Team Thirteen loaded their duffel bags into the cars, he refused to meet Lex's eye and answered his enquiries in monosyllables.

Lex put it down to pre-op nerves. Everyone reacted differently to stress. Some masked their tension with talk; others, like Buckler, went the other way, turning surly and uncommunicative.

Once they pulled away from the hotel, Buckler turned to him and said, "We're going to make a detour."

"Where to?"

"I'll tell you when we get there."

"Shouldn't I know in advance? If there's been a change of plan..."

Buckler wasn't interested in providing any further detail. Lex now had the impression that the American's frostiness was targeted—personal. He, Lex, had somehow offended, had affronted him in some way. He didn't much care. It wasn't his goal in life to win approval or ingratiate himself with others.

He drove on, leaving Buckler to simmer quietly beside him.

"Left here," the SEAL commander said eventually.

Lex made the turn. Albertine, in her Suzuki, followed suit.

"Now right."

"Manzanilla Defence Force HQ," Lex said, when it became clear there was only one place they could be headed.

"Got to pick up a couple of items," said Buckler. "Won't take long."

The couple of items turned out to be a pair of Zodiacs. They were, as far as Lex was aware, the Manzanilla Defence Force's entire fleet of seagoing craft: two rigid-hulled inflatables with amateurishly applied camouflage paint jobs. In fact, these boats and a couple of tatty ex-British-Army Land Rovers represented the sum total of the MDF's mobile hardware. But then Manzanilla's standing army was hardly a crack fighting unit, consisting as it did of no more than twenty volunteers, part-timers who held down day jobs but put on fatigues and carried out drills and manoeuvres as and when their work schedules permitted. It was unlikely the island would ever be invaded, and if it was the MDF would doubtless offer only a token resistance before surrendering. The government, though, was pleased to think that it had military capability, however paltry, and the soldiers could if nothing else be counted on to put on a parade in Port Sebastian's Liberation Square every time some foreign dignitary came visiting.

Four MDF soldiers wheeled the Zodiacs out into the main compound on trailers. Lex saw money slip from Buckler's fingers into the hands of the senior-ranking soldier and from there into the breast pocket of the man's blouse. So, this was not entirely an above-board procedure. Then again, nothing on Manzanilla was. Graft was just part of the national economy.

While the boat trailers were being hitched to the cars, Lex received a text message from Seraphina.

Just to wish you luck, sweetheart. You'll be fine. Old pro like you—it's like riding a bike. You never forget how. Hugs and kisses. S xxx

Lex texted back:

So you know I'm fully active again.

Seraphina's reply:

Darling, I know EVERYTHING. Haven't you learned that by now? ;-) You just couldn't help it, could you? Once an operative, always an operative. Bodes well for the future.

Lex:

It's a one-off. Don't get your hopes up.

Seraphina:

We'll see, won't we? It would be soooo nice to have you back in harness, darling. With me cracking the whip again, like before. Mmmm. How naughty that sounds.

Lex:

Cold shower time for you.

Seraphina:

I prefer my showers hot, soapy... and accompanied.

"Who's that you're talking to?" It was Albertine, peering over his shoulder.

Lex flicked the phone out of text mode. "No one. My boss."

"I thought you were self-employed."

"Freelance, yes. She's more agent than boss."

"She?" Albertine arched an eyebrow as high as it could go.

"Something wrong with that?"

"Not a thing. But I could have sworn I read something about hot, soapy showers."

"Jealous?"

"Do I need to be?"

"No."

"Then that's fine," she said, sidling away. "Good enough for me."

Lex watched her go, admiring the rollicking, insolent sway of her hips. The same hips that had gripped him so urgently, so deliciously last night.

All at once, Gable's—Legba's—words recurred, elbowing their way back into his thoughts.

Dead men won' lie an' liars won' die. That's the truth, Leonard Duncan, and the truth always hurts.

Maybe he had misheard. Maybe Gable had actually said his adopted name, and he had mistaken it for his true name. They sounded similar enough, and Gable's accent was thick and he had a tendency to mumble.

In that case, setting aside the matter of a compromised identity, what did the remark actually mean? Dead men? Liars? What was all that about?

Lex knew he could keep worrying at it like a bone for hours and get nowhere. With some effort, he thrust it to the back of his mind.

BACK ON THE road, beneath the surging orange brilliance of a Caribbean dawn, with the inflatable boats bumping along behind them.

"Just come out and say it," Lex said to Buckler. "Get it off your chest. Let's clear the air now, before the op begins in earnest."

"Okay," said Buckler. "Okay. I'm all in favour of air-clearing." He glanced round at Tartaglione and Sampson in the backseat, both of whom looked as disgruntled as their CO did. "Those boats, see, that was kind of a last-minute thing. I didn't think we'd need them... not until I went and took a gander at your buddy's airplane. De Havilland Turbo Beaver. Not in the best of condition."

"It'll fly."

"Yeah, I'm sure it will. I'm sure it'll get us to Anger Reef just fine, probably get us back too, nice and safe and all in one piece. I've been up in rattletraps far worse. The issue here isn't so much the journey as the landing. We're timing it so as we insert at high tide, but even then that isn't going to afford us much clearance in the water. Turbo Beaver's pretty hefty for its size, especially with a full complement of passengers and a load of equipment too. I reckon there's a chance she could lose a float. Coral could rip it right off. We can't have that."

"Hence the Zodiacs."

"Nice shallow draught. Virtually flat-bottomed. We'll skim across just fine."

"So you're pissed off at me because I didn't anticipate this little problem and you've had to resolve it yourself," said Lex. "Well, excuse me, lieutenant, but why didn't you tell me? I could have done something about it if I'd had a heads-up. Shouldn't there be more to-and-fro here?" He waved a hand in the air between himself and Buckler. "A free and frank exchange of data?"

"That's not why I'm pissed off," said Buckler. "Why I'm pissed off is, I went and had a look at the seaplane, like I said."

"So?"

"So, I go to this boatyard where it's being kept, this out-of-the-way place a few miles up the coast. I make the trip there after dark, me and Petty Officer Sampson, we do it together, hire a taxi and go visit, 'cause I felt it should be done, on account of I like to double-check things and sometimes I get a gut feeling, a tingling, my Spidey sense telling me something's off and I need to make sure about it. That's how a guy like me gets to live as long as I have and stay as pretty as I am."

"Debatable," Lex muttered, barely audible even to himself above the Subaru's growling engine.

"And what do we find when we get to the boatyard?"

The question hung over them, and all at once Lex grasped why Buckler might have a legitimate gripe with him.

"I'll tell you," the SEAL commander went on. "A goddamn crime scene. Police tape everywhere. Evidence that there's been a forensics team on the premises—chalk outlines and such. A boat riddled with bullet holes. Bloodstains on the ground. All the signs that there's been an exchange of gunfire and casualties. Sampson and me, we hop the fence and nose around the place, carefully. Nobody there but us chickens. Cops have sealed it off and gone home. We even find blood all over the seaplane, the same fucking seaplane we're supposed to be taking off in today. Now, either all of this is one damn unfortunate fucking coincidence, or you, Mr Dove, have some serious questions to answer."

"I can—"

"You said—I asked you, and you said to me, you said right to my motherfucking face—there'd been no difficulties securing transportation. Was that a lie or was it not?"

"I think my actual words were along the lines of there'd been nothing insurmountable."

"But you're not denying you had something to do with a shootout at the boatyard? Because something makes sense to me now that didn't at the time. When you came to my room yesterday afternoon, I thought I smelled cordite on you. Very faint, but unmistakable. I gave you the benefit of the doubt, decided maybe I was imagining things or else it was just a crappy choice of cologne. I shouldn't have turned a blind eye. I should have called you on it right there and then. Care to tell me why someone would get involved in a small-arms free-for-all in broad daylight on the eve of a covert op? Because any explanation I can think of, it always ends in 'gross stupidity.'

"Come on, Dove," he said, mimicking Lex's gesture of a few moments ago. "You wanted more to-and-fro. A free and frank exchange of data. So exchange, baby."

Lex had to come clean. He couldn't see an alternative.

"Wilberforce has got himself into a spot of bother."

"A spot of bother," Buckler echoed sardonically.

"I've been helping him sort it. He owes money to someone, the type of person you shouldn't owe money to."

"Ah. That'd explain the state of his face."

"Yes. Some of the man's underlings caught up with him the night before last, and he was ambushed again yesterday, along with me and his cousin, at the boatyard. On the bright side, we acquitted ourselves well, all of us. Albertine especially. As civilians go, she's not to be underestimated."

"Well, that makes it all right, then. You won the fricking fight. That's all that matters."

"I'm not apologising for what happened. It wasn't my fault. I didn't plan on any of this. It's shit-awful timing, that's all."

"Do the police know you were there?"

"I think not, or they would have paid me a visit last night."

"And what about this guy Allen's in debt to?"

"What about him?"

"You're sorting it, according to you. So what's his status?"

"Still alive and at large. For now."

"Then it isn't sorted."

"He's not an immediate threat. I've smacked him on the snout with a rolled-up newspaper. He should stay curled up in his basket for a while, feeling sorry for himself."

"This is shoddy, Dove," Buckler groused. "Real messy. Give me one good reason why I shouldn't ditch your ass. And don't say that if I do that, your friends won't co-operate. Your friends are in my charge now, they're committed, and they'll do whatever I goddamn tell them to, even if I have to stick a gun in the back of their skulls to make them."

"My personal situation doesn't affect the mission or my ability to take part in it," Lex said. "We can still take off, put Manzanilla behind us, and nothing will have changed. There'll be no blowback, no fallout, not as far as you're concerned. You're not compromised in any way. The op goes ahead as planned. I can't see what you're complaining about."

"What I'm—?" Buckler thumped the dashboard with a fist. "One, I don't like unexpected developments. Two, Team Thirteen likes to stay on the down low, and you've jeopardised that. Three, and this is the kicker, you're coming across as an incompetent, unreliable asshat, and the guys and me, we hate working with incompetent, unreliable asshats. Ain't that so?"

"Damn straight," said Tartaglione.

"Word," said Sampson.

"So why don't you just fucking shoot me then?" said Lex with an irritation born of exasperation. "If I'm so useless?"

"Don't think I haven't considered it," said Buckler. "But I figure we'd never get anything at all out of your friends if I did. Keeping them sweet means keeping you alive, for better or worse. But you're on probation, that's for damn sure, Dove. Screw up again, in any way, and that'll be it. Third strike and out."

"Some kind of battlefield accident, is that what you mean?"

"Things go wrong during ops all the time," said Tartaglione. "Heat of combat, bullets flying—friendly fire."

"Tragic but true," said Sampson, mock-mournfully.

"Just watch your back, sport, is all I'm saying," said Buckler. "Watch it real close."

TWENTY
EYES ON THE PRIZE

Breaking into the boatyard was a simple matter of clipping through the padlocked chain securing the gates. Team Thirteen had a set of bolt cutters in one of their duffel bags.

"Amazing the cops haven't posted a guard," Buckler remarked as the cars drove in.

"The cops don't have the manpower," Lex replied. "And I'm betting they didn't anticipate anyone coming here today of all days."

"Why not?"

"Sunday, remember?"

"Christ. Is it?" Buckler was genuinely taken aback. "I've lost track. All the travelling..." For a moment his mask of gruff self-assurance slipped and he looked bewildered, even haggard. Team Thirteen relentlessly traversed the planet back and forth, crossing time zones as though they were cracks in the pavement. Lex was familiar with that exhaustion, that sense of perpetual dislocation. He had known it only too well.

"Shee-it," said Sampson, making light of it. "Looks like we'll be missing church, then."

"Grandma's going to kill me," Tartaglione chimed in.

They bundled out of the cars, and Team Thirteen got straight to work unhooking the Zodiacs and letting the air out so that the boats would fit aboard the Turbo Beaver.

"It's going to be a tight squeeze," Wilberforce observed to Buckler. "Eight people, those bags of yours, the boats, and that." He gestured to the large cylinder of compressed CO_2 which the MDF soldiers had supplied to reinflate the Zodiacs.

"So it'll be a little cramped," said the SEAL commander, shrugging. "Plane's got a useful load weight of two thousand pounds. By my reckoning we're under that, which is all that counts. You just worry about flying her, ace. Leave the rest to me."

Wilberforce made his way over to *Puddle Jumper*. Lex accompanied him. They stepped onto the dock, ducking under the strand of police tape cordoning it off from the rest of the boatyard. The planking was dotted with numbered plastic markers denoting the locations of spent shell casings from Lex's gun. The police had done a thorough job here, and Lex wondered whether they had yet linked this incident involving known accomplices of Garfield Finisterre with the incident at Wilberforce's house last night. It was only a matter of time before they did. Virgil Johnson could not be relied on to keep from blabbing, and as for the piratical henchman with the broken leg, he would no doubt clam up to begin with – fear and criminal solidarity would see to that – but if the cops offered to cut him a deal, there was no guarantee he wouldn't start to sing.

The Manzanillan police were as corrupt as any institution on the island, but even they knew the value of justice being seen to be done. Garfield Finisterre was beyond their reach. Any attempt to indict him, with all his political connections, was doomed to failure. Going after an *un*connected British expat, on the other hand, stood a fair chance of success. The wrong man would end up on the wrong side of the law, while the Garfish would be left free as a bird and laughing.

Seraphina had said she had the power to make it all go away, but that would work only as far as officialdom was concerned.

It wouldn't keep Finisterre himself off Lex's back. Lex was coming to the conclusion that the only practical solution to this mess was Finisterre's death. Sooner rather than later, the gangster would have to suffer a fatal and inexplicable mishap. An unsanctioned Code Crimson. One more name added to the list of pariahs and parasites whom Lex Dove had deleted from the world.

Wilberforce stiffened appreciably as he neared the seaplane. The propeller blades were striped with dried blood, like sinister barbershop poles. Blood also dotted the windshield, droplets so dark red they were almost black.

"I didn't mean to..." he began, then stopped.

Lex waited for him to continue, letting him work through it.

"I was just trying to rattle the man," Wilberforce said. "I expected him to dive out of the way, not—not the opposite."

"Don't give it another thought," Lex said. "You saved my neck, Wilb. Things might have gone very differently, for all of us, if you hadn't done what you did. It was a horrible accident, but without it we might not even be alive to have this conversation."

"I can still see him, up here." He tapped his temple. "Getting sliced apart. I don't know if I'm ever not going to. How do you manage it?"

"Manage what?"

"Yesterday I watched you kill people. I'm pretty sure they're not the only people you've killed in your life. I'm responsible for just one man's death—"

"No, you're not."

"—and I feel sick to my stomach just thinking about it. How do you cope with this stuff? The memory of taking a life? The knowledge?"

Lex looked his friend in the eye. "I'm going to level with you. The truth is you don't. You carry on as best you can, and try to console yourself that you did what you had to, what needed to be done. If it's a them-or-you situation—and no question, yesterday afternoon qualifies as that—you have to be thankful that you're the one who survived it and just get on with living the rest of your life. You can't change what happened, but you mustn't let it change you."

"I don't know, man. Not sure I'll ever be able to do that."

"I'm not saying it's easy. But if you don't make the effort, there's a chance you'll wind up dead yourself. Guilt's a killer."

"That why you quit what you used to do and moved here?" Wilberforce asked.

"You mean was it all getting on top of me? Oh, yes. I wasn't handling it well any more. I had no peace of mind. Couldn't sleep. Questions just kept going round and round in my brain, relentlessly, like a hamster on a wheel. It got the point where..." He had begun; might as well finish. "Where I was close to this, you know?" He put two fingers in his mouth, aiming upward into his soft palate. "Just a trigger pull away from ending it all."

"Seriously? But you're so... *together*. I've never known anyone as cool, calm and collected as you."

"On the outside, maybe," said Lex. "But coming to terms with what I'd done, with my past—it's been hard. Damn hard. Getting any kind of equilibrium back. A struggle. Seven years in Manzanilla has helped. Just being removed from where I used to be. Having you for a friend—that's been good for me, too."

"Stop it. You'll make me blush."

"I'm rarely tempted to put my gun in my mouth these days. Most mornings I wake up and I'm feeling pretty optimistic about the day ahead. I'm in a good place, by my standards. I'm as happy as I think I can reasonably ever be. A long, hard road, but I made it. You will, too."

"And you're not worried that all this"—Wilberforce waved to indicate Team Thirteen, bloodied *Puddle Jumper*, the boatyard, the mission—"is going to ruin things? Set you back to where you don't want to be again?"

Lex weighed it up. "None of this has been my choice. *Force majeure*. That's French for 'tough shit,' more or less. It's a hand that's been dealt me, not one I asked for, but one I'm having to play nonetheless. And it's going to be worth it, in the long run. I suppose now's as good a time as any to tell you that I'm in this for the money."

"Me too. Buckler's named a fee. It's enough to pay off the Garfish and more."

"Yeah, but in my case we're talking enough for me to buy us a Sealine F-series."

Wilberforce gaped. "No, man. Don't do this. Don't be bullshitting me. Don't you dare."

"I'm not kidding. Second-hand, not brand new, but still. We can do it, set up that fishing business. You won't need to be in hock to anyone. We'll own a boat, free and clear, and all the gear we need."

Wilberforce's eyes sparkled. His dream, suddenly, tantalisingly achievable. "I don't believe it. For real?"

"A couple of weeks from now you could be captaining a sports cruiser out to sea, with First Mate Dove on deck setting up the rods and handing out the cold beers."

Before Wilberforce could say anything else, Buckler's voice rang out across the boatyard. "Yo, ladies! I appreciate you're having a lovely time gossiping, but we're on the clock and high tide waits for no one. Allen, you should be running pre-flight checks, and Dove, you should be getting your ass out of the way and letting him do that."

"Yes, sir, lieutenant," Lex shouted back, firing off a snappy salute. "Getting my arse out of the way, sir."

Buckler's glare, even over a distance of a hundred yards, could have melted a hole through plate steel.

"Eyes on the prize," Lex confided to Wilberforce. "Mine are. Let yours be, too."

MOST OF TEAM THIRTEEN'S bags went into the Turbo Beaver's freight hold, although two were stowed in the extra cargo space in the floats. The Zodiacs were laid lengthways along the aisle of the cabin, dismantled into their component parts: wooden transoms and thrustboards, aluminium deckplates, deflated neoprene sacs squashed as flat as they could go. Their outboard motors were lodged in the rearmost two seats, belted in place.

"We all set?" said Wilberforce.

Buckler untied the mooring ropes, kick-shoved the plane away from the dock, clambered inside and yanked the door shut. He slid into the seat at the front beside Wilberforce's. Lex and Albertine occupied the two seats immediately behind. The Team Thirteen shooters filled the remaining four rows.

Lex looked across the aisle at Albertine. She was staring out of the window, gripping the armrests.

"Not a good flyer?" he asked.

"Jumbo jets, no problem," she replied. "My cousin's rust-bucket of a seaplane, on the other hand..."

"You think this is bad, you should try taking an internal commercial flight in Russia," Tartaglione said, leaning forward to talk over her seat headrest. "Those planes are so shit, not even the pilots are sure they're going to make it to their destination."

"It would help if they didn't drink so much vodka while at the controls," Sampson chipped in. "That'd bring the crash rate right down."

"Yeah, but it's a catch-twenty-two. If they didn't drink, they'd never have the courage to fly."

"Is this supposed to be helping me?" Albertine asked curtly.

"Just saying things could be a whole lot worse," said Tartaglione. "Trying to put your mind at ease."

"Well, thank you, but don't."

The engine started up, filling the cabin with noise and vibration.

"Welcome aboard, everyone," Wilberforce called out. "This is your pilot, wishing you a pleasant trip. Our journey time is approximately one and a half hours, and we'll be cruising at an altitude of—"

"Cut the crap," Buckler interrupted. "Just fly."

Wilberforce glanced round at Lex, who simply gave a nod that said: *Eyes on the prize.*

"Whatever you say," said Wilberforce to Buckler. "You're the boss."

He let *Puddle Jumper* continue to drift away from the dock with the propeller turning at a low rate. The river current caught and turned the plane. When its nose was facing downstream, Wilberforce upped the revs and began taxiing along the inlet.

As the inlet widened into an estuary, the going got rougher. The clash between waves surging in from the ocean and the river's outward flow created a field of spiky whitecaps. Wilberforce eased the throttle forwards, and soon *Puddle Jumper* was bounding and juddering along, past the inlet's mouth and out onto the open sea. Everyone in the cabin rocked in their seats. The airframe creaked loudly with every impact of the surf chop, and the wings wobbled disconcertingly. Sea spray spattered the windows. Albertine was intoning words under her breath, and if it wasn't a prayer to the loa, Lex had no idea what else it could be.

Wilberforce poured on more speed, and the buffeting started to lessen. *Puddle Jumper* was beginning to skim the waves rather than butting headlong through them. He nudged the yoke back, and all at once the plane was aloft, released from the water's grasp and up into its proper element.

TWENTY-ONE
CALL SIGNS

ONCE *PUDDLE JUMPER* had gained cruising altitude and levelled out, Team Thirteen changed out of their civvies into black jumpsuits and Kevlar vests. Small, lightweight VHF comms headsets were distributed and donned. Both Lex and Albertine were given one.

"Piece of cake to use," Buckler told Albertine. "Channel's pre-selected. Tap the earpiece to speak. Think of it as glorified Bluetooth."

"Testing," said Albertine.

"There you go. Coming through loud and clear. Team Thirteen, sound off."

"Penetrator," said Sampson.

"Warmone," said Morgenstern.

"Jersey Shore," said Tartaglione.

"Whisper," said Pearce.

"Big Chief Dirty," said Buckler. "You, Miz Montase, are Guardian Angel. You'll be known by no other name when we're on comms. As for you, Dove, you get White Feather."

"Don't I get to choose my own call sign?"

"You get what you're given."

"But White Feather? It's kind of insulting."

"Don't read too much into it. It's purely surname-related."

"So you say."

"Take it or leave it, ace."

"White Feather," Lex muttered into the headset mike.

Buckler gave a thumbs-up. All comms were functioning.

Puddle Jumper flew on. A trade wind was nudging in from the side, and Wilberforce worked the rudder pedals repeatedly to counteract it and maintain course. Quarter of an hour after takeoff he was contacted by ground control at Manzanilla International, requesting confirmation of aircraft registration and purpose of journey. He responded by saying that he was on a pleasure trip and hadn't filed a flight plan beforehand since he was flying VFR in low-altitude airways and not intending to cross any national borders.

He listened over his headphones as Manzanilla ground control spoke again. Then he covered the mike with one hand and said to Buckler, "They're demanding a destination. What should I tell them?"

"Tell them there isn't one. You're on a loop, taking sightseers around the coasts of Cuba and Great Inagua then coming home."

Wilberforce relayed this, got an answer, and shook his head at Buckler. "No dice. They're getting very pushy; we're over water, harder to locate if we go down. Which," he added loudly, for Albertine's benefit, "we're not going to."

"All right," said Buckler. "Tell them to call this number." He reeled off a phone number with a US international dialling code and a 202 Washington DC prefix. "When someone picks up, they should quote the following: 'Priority Delta Seven One Niner.'"

A few minutes later, Manzanilla International was back in touch. Wilberforce could only grin.

"They say thank you for that, not a problem, have a nice flight."

Puddle Jumper threaded the strait between Cuba and Hispaniola, the Windward Passage, at 5,000 feet. Turbulence was almost constant at this height. The plane sagged and seesawed in the air.

Albertine's knuckles showed grey through her skin as she clung to the armrests, and her mouth was a tight lipless line. Pearce, by contrast, was dozing, and Morgenstern was doing Sudoku puzzles on a Nintendo DS. As for Sampson and Tartaglione, they were busy swapping combat reminiscences. They switched back and forth between tales of conventional ops from their days as regular SEALs and their more recent exploits as Thirteeners, so that one moment they would be discussing a hostage rescue or a night-time antiterrorist raid, the next recalling how they had helped roust a devil-worshipping apocalypse cult who were attempting to summon some nameless nether-being from beyond with a view to unleashing it upon the world. They didn't appear to discriminate between the two types of mission, as if a band of Mujahideen armed with AK-47s was little different from a winged snake-woman lurking in an abandoned casbah in a southern province of Morocco, as if nobbling a Nicaraguan cocaine baron was on a par with investigating the site of a reported UFO crash in the Peruvian jungle.

Even the strangest things, it seemed, could become mundane if you were exposed to them often enough.

The flow of anecdotes was broken by Wilberforce announcing that GPS now put them within twenty kilometres of Anger Reef. The island should be visible on the horizon shortly.

Everyone craned their necks to look. Buckler spotted it first.

"Objective at one o'clock," he said, and there, amid the jewelled glitter of the ocean, it sat—green and yellow, tiny and lonely, a fleck of dry land in a wilderness of water, like a desert oasis in reverse.

"It's like God hawked up a loogie and spat," was Tartaglione's view.

"Seen bigger pimples," was Sampson's.

Wilberforce banked to starboard and commenced descent.

As the island loomed, the reefs surrounding it showed as a ragged pale halo. Clear sea turned milky where it washed over the coral banks.

Lower still, it became possible to distinguish the crescents of beach between the island's promontories and the scrubby greenery encrusting the shoreline and the lusher, taller greenery growing inland. The remains of manmade structures were visible: a couple of half-collapsed jetties and several huge blocks of concrete which at one time had been the bases for radio masts and radar arrays. The latter put Lex in mind of lost temples to forgotten gods, relics of some ancient civilisation.

Wilberforce turned into the wind to facilitate a smoother landing. *Puddle Jumper* swooped towards the ocean, flaps lowered. The floats touched down once, and again, and then the Turbo Beaver was rumbling and bucking across the water. It eventually levelled, then sank slightly forwards as it came to a dead stop.

The plane had set down a few hundred metres from the coral barrier, and at this angle it became apparent just how low-lying Anger Reef was. The island was a thin green line above the water, even its loftiest palm trees no higher than a two-storey building. If, as climatologists predicted, sea levels were set to rise, they would only have to go up by a metre or so for Anger Reef to be swamped from end to end, its scant acreage completely inundated.

Wilberforce was first out of the door. He had rigged up an anchor from a length of rope and a piece of iron rebar hammered into a hook shape; he tossed it overboard into the crystalline water and watched it snag on the seabed some twenty feet below. *Puddle Jumper* was already drifting, a victim of current and wind, but once the anchor line went taut the plane stayed put, penduluming gently from side to side on the end of its tether.

Then came the task of reassembling the Zodiacs—inflating the air chambers, installing the transoms, thrustboards and deckplates, lodging the outboards onto the sterns. All while balancing on the Turbo Beaver's floats, which made the process more protracted and precarious than it would normally have been. A leatherback turtle came nosing up to the seaplane to check out what was going on. Deeper in the water, sinister slim silhouettes circled: barracuda. The nearby reefs formed a perfect hunting ground for the predators, with huge shoals of small fry milling about, ready to be picked off. Lex watched the big silvery fish glide by. They were unhurried, confident in their top-of-the-food-chain status. At one time, he had felt like that himself—untouchable, a force of nature, dead-eyed, inhuman. He did not welcome the idea of a return to that state of mind. It had served him well as a wetwork specialist, but that was another time, another self, another world. He preferred who he was now, by far. This mission might require him to draw on his old skill set, but not, he hoped, he prayed, on his old persona. He wasn't going back there again, not if he could possibly avoid it.

The Zodiacs were ready. Team Thirteen transferred their bags, and themselves, into the boats.

Albertine gave Wilberforce a parting hug and stepped smartly off the plane. As Lex made to follow her, Wilberforce stopped him.

"Take care of my cousin, man."

"Of course, Wilb."

"I mean it. We fight like cat and dog, her and me, but we're family. And take care of yourself, too."

"Always. See you after."

The first Zodiac chugged away from *Puddle Jumper* with Lex, Albertine, Morgenstern and Pearce on board. Pearce was at the helm, gripping the outboard's tiller arm.

Buckler's Zodiac set off after Pearce's. When it caught up, the two boats accelerated away in tandem.

Looking back, Lex watched *Puddle Jumper* and its pilot recede into the distance. He couldn't help envying his friend. Wilberforce got to sit in his plane twiddling his thumbs, while the rest of them...

Well, whatever the rest of them had to face in the coming hours, it was unlikely there would be much thumb twiddling involved.

TWENTY-TWO
ISLANDFALL

"Whisper, this is Big Chief Dirty." Buckler, on the comms. "We'll skim the coral. Go for flank speed and ship the outboard at the last second. Momentum should do the rest. Copy?"

"Copy," said Pearce.

"Everyone, you might want to hold on to something," Buckler said. "This could get bumpy."

There was nylon safety rope strung along the Zodiac's gunwales. Lex twisted a loop around his wrist and motioned Albertine to do likewise.

Pearce gunned the motor to maximum, and the Zodiac's bow lifted, hydroplaning. Ahead, the sea seethed across the coral. Lex estimated a clearance of six to nine inches. It was going to be tight.

The instant they hit the strip of boiling white, Pearce canted the outboard forwards so that the propeller sprang clear of the water, and twisted the throttle down to zero. The Zodiac scudded forwards, rudderless. Lex glimpsed coral fronds and spars rushing by below, branching extrusions and brain-like lumps, all colours, all textures. So fragile-looking, yet it could ground the boat and tear it to shreds.

They had nearly made it to the other side when something snagged on the hull and all at once the Zodiac was sent spinning, pivoting violently round and round and slewing across the sea at the same time. The boat yawed and the bow started to rise alarmingly, catching the air like a kite. The Zodiac was in peril of capsizing and pitching its occupants out.

Almost instinctively, Lex loosened his hand from the safety rope and lunged forwards, hurling himself into the front of the boat. The sudden shift brought the bow back down flat with a *thump*. The rate of spin slowed, allowing Pearce to reinsert the propeller and regain control. A burst of reverse thrust halted the boat in its tracks.

"Everyone all right?" Buckler asked as his Zodiac drew alongside.

"Still afloat," said Morgenstern. "No damage to any of the main chambers as far as I can see. Think we may have lost a speed skag, though."

Speed skags were narrow tubes running lengthwise along the underside of the hull, aiding stability.

"We can manage without," Morgenstern went on. "It's just going to be a little less smooth of a ride. But props to the English guy. That was some quick thinking there. If it wasn't for him, we'd all be swimming right now."

Pearce touched an index finger to his forehead, then pointed it at Lex.

Albertine shot him a look of gratitude, which was heartfelt.

"Onward," said Buckler.

His Zodiac zoomed off, and the other trailed in its wake.

The seabed shelved upwards, an incline of ribbed sand dotted with clumps of softly waving turtle grass. Within metres of the shore, Buckler ordered Pearce to hold back.

"We'll put ashore first, establish a perimeter. You come in when I give the okay."

Buckler rammed the Zodiac up onto the beach, and before it had even stopped moving Sampson and Tartaglione were out and sprinting left and right through the shallows. Each was carrying a CAR-15 carbine, fitted with an underslung M-203 grenade launcher. At the promontories the two SEALs turned inland and performed a converging sweep along the top of the beach, meeting each other midway.

"Jersey Shore, clear."

"Penetrator, clear."

Buckler waved to Pearce, who engaged the idling motor and beached the Zodiac prow-first as his CO had done. He and Morgenstern piled out and started unloading bags. Buckler was already doing the same.

"I'd love to say that's the worst part over," Lex remarked to Albertine, "but it undoubtedly isn't."

Team Thirteen lugged the duffel bags up to the vegetation line, where marram grass, inkberry and sea lavender grew in shaggy clumps. Undoing the zips, they produced a fine array of ordnance: more CAR-15s, M-60 machine guns, Heckler and Koch MP-5 machine pistols and MK23 semiautomatics, and plenty of ammo. In addition there were KA-BAR fighting knives, hand grenades, flashbangs, and socks of C-4 explosive. The guns and explosives were shared out among the SEALs, holstered, sheathed, clipped to webbing belts and bandoliers, until the five of them were festooned with weaponry. Lex, armed with only his SIG Sauer, felt underdressed for the occasion, like someone who had turned up in jeans for a black tie party.

But that wasn't all. From out of one of the bags came phials of clear liquid, with crucifixes etched onto the glass. Flashlights fitted with what appeared to be ultraviolet bulbs. Stubby wooden stakes. Silver pendants in the shape of ankhs and other arcane sigils, which the Thirteeners hung around their necks. A tub containing some kind of herby-smelling unguent, which they smeared on their faces like insect repellent. Assorted amulets and talismans—clay, wood, metal—which they strapped to their wrists and arms.

"What are you staring at?" Tartaglione demanded.

"You," said Lex, "and all your weirdo bling."

Tartaglione shook his head wonderingly. "Anyone would think you'd never seen guys tooling themselves up with mystical protection before."

Sampson smirked. "I swear, the ignorance of some people..."

"True dat."

"Tartag?"

"Yeah?"

"What have I said about using phrases like 'true dat'?"

"You said I should always use them."

"I said the exact opposite."

"But we have this whole two-tone, brother-from-another-mother thing going on between us, don't we?"

"We do," said Sampson. "But you take it too far."

"Aw man, you know I'm just a white guy who wants to be black."

"And that's a one-way street right there."

"Enough," Buckler barked. "Fun time's over, people. From here on in we are icicles. Installation entrance lies three hundred metres inland. Penetrator, Jersey Shore, you're on point. Whisper, you're our tail-end Charlie. Chatter to a minimum. Let's roll, crew."

TWENTY-THREE
AN AVATAR OF DEATH

IT WAS A low cinderblock structure, not much larger than a double-wide trailer home, situated smack dab in the middle of the island. It had a single tiny window on each side—lookout apertures—and a broad, sturdy door made of galvanised steel. The palm trees encircling it cast a rippling, dappled shade. A balmy, pleasant spot, it seemed. Nothing to be afraid of here. No reason to be on edge.

Except that the door hung ajar and askew. The lock bore a starburst pattern of scorch marks.

"Signs of forced entry," Tartaglione said. He and Sampson were closest to the building.

"That'd be the Marines," said Buckler. "They knocked, no one answered, they busted a hole. Jersey Shore, you and Penetrator move in. Be careful."

At the doorway Sampson went down on one knee, carbine to his shoulder. He nosed the barrel between door and jamb and used it to widen the gap gently. Tartaglione slipped through. Sampson covered his teammate as he checked out every corner of the building's interior.

"Empty, Big Chief Dirty," Tartaglione said. "But there's something you ought to see."

Buckler padded across the strip of open ground between the trees and the building and disappeared inside. Moments later, his voice came over the comms: "White Feather? Bring Guardian Angel over. We need to consult her on this."

Lex ushered Albertine to the building. Inside, the air was oppressively thick and smelled of sea damp and machine oil. As Lex's eyes adapted to the gloom, he made out a caged-off section containing a heavy-duty diesel-powered generator, a hulking great device that surely dated back to the installation's original construction. Judging by the amount of dust and corrosion on it, it hadn't been operational in decades. Opposite lay the entrance to a freight elevator. The sliding doors were stuck part-way open, revealing a profound, impenetrable blackness beyond.

Beside the doors was a symbol. It had been finger-daubed on the wall in some kind of dark sticky substance, and it took the shape of a crude headstone—a cross perched on a pedestal, with diamond patterns adorning its upright and arms. On one side of the headstone the artist had added a miniature coffin and an uncapped bottle, on the other a skull-and-crossbones and a shovel.

"A *vévé*," said Albertine, her voice hushed and containing the faintest of tremors.

"Yeah, thought as much," said Buckler. "And I've sniffed up close and it's painted in blood, just like it looks. The question is: which loa's *vévé* is it?"

"His. The Baron's."

"Had a bad feeling you might say that."

"This is Baron Samedi's realm," Albertine said. "It has been claimed in his name."

"'Abandon hope all ye who enter here.'"

"That and more. You might expect to find a *vévé* like this marking the gatepost of a graveyard. This one is telling us that if we go any further, we're as good as corpses."

There was a moment's silence while that sank in.

"Ho-kaaay," said Tartaglione. "So who's for calling it a day and heading back home?"

The quip didn't raise so much as a chuckle.

"Anything we can do to fix it?" Buckler asked Albertine.

"How do you mean?"

"I mean, could we just rub the *vévé* out? Would that maybe erase its influence?"

"We've seen it now. Rubbing it out won't rub out our memories of it. We're already intimidated by it, as we have every right to be. And whoever put the *vévé* there used blood—and most likely not chicken or goat blood either."

"Human blood?" said Sampson, wrinkling his nose in disgust.

Albertine nodded. "Maybe their own, maybe someone else's. There's only one reason a *vodouisant* would do such a thing, and that's to demonstrate unswerving loyalty to the loa of death. Down below us there's a bokor who has given himself entirely over to the Baron. He has become an agent of death, an avatar of death. He has no fear of the Baron and therefore no fear of the consequences of any of his actions. That suggests he is a very dangerous man, and probably quite mad."

"No shit," said Tartaglione.

"That accepted, is it safe to just go past it and carry on?" said Buckler.

"It would be prudent to adopt some form of protection first," said Albertine. "A *garde*. If only to bolster our mental defences. The *vévé* has spooked us, and fear increases one's susceptibility to magical attack. A *garde* can reverse its malign influence, but I should warn you that it won't be pleasant. You can't ward off a blood *vévé* the way you can most ordinary *wanga* spells, with prayers and song and a dash of eucalyptus oil."

"You saw us putting on an ointment of angelica root and caraway just now. A Wiccan I know brewed it up for us and incanted a charm over it. Won't that be enough to do the trick?"

"Only *vodou* can resist *vodou*. Bring the other two in—Morgenstern and Pearce. And I'll need to borrow your knife..."

*   *   *

THE SEVEN OF them stood in a circle, their sleeves rolled up, left arms bared. Albertine had prepared a concoction in a small china bowl—a grey-brown paste made of rum, garlic powder, flakes of dried cinchona bark, ground-up mandrake root, and a pinch of dust from the floor.

"Brick dust is preferable," she said, "but concrete dust will do."

Using Buckler's KA-BAR knife she made a small incision in her skin, just below the shoulder. She rubbed some of the paste into the wound, at the same time invoking the aid of the *garde* loa, the minor spirits whose role it was to watch over souls in peril.

"I bind you into me," she said, tying a scrap of fabric round her arm. "I seal you inside where you will be able to look out for me."

She went round the circle repeating the ritual for each of the Thirteeners, wiping the knife blade on a rum-soaked rag in between to sterilise it. The SEALs bore the discomfort of the cut with varying degrees of stoicism. Only Tartaglione made any noise, a comic "Ouch." Buckler scowled at him.

Lex, last in line, grimaced as the knife was drawn across his arm but nothing more. Pain was in the mind. Pain was only ever in the mind.

And—it was very peculiar—the instant Albertine finished binding the wound, he felt a huge, overwhelming sense of relief. He looked at the *vévé* on the wall and he saw only a crude, scrawled picture. Not a forbidding emblem of doom but merely a design, something almost abstract, like a graffiti tag. Meaningless to the objective viewer. Even the nature of the substance used to draw it no longer bothered him.

The expressions on Team Thirteen's faces matched what he was feeling. Where they had been tense before, now they were nonchalant. Where there had been concern, now there was indifference.

Tartaglione went up to the *vévé* and gave it the finger. "Superstitious fucking bullshit." Then he crossed himself and spat on the floor.

Buckler tried pressing the call button next to the elevator. Nothing happened.

"Electricity's out?" Lex suggested.

"Shouldn't be," Buckler replied. "When the installation was recommissioned, they sank a geothermal vent. There's a binary cycle power plant feeding this place a constant five kilowatt-hours of free energy per day. Chances are the elevator's been purposely put out of action."

"Why?"

"Probably to keep people like us out." Buckler shone a conventional flashlight down the shaft. "I can see the roof of the elevator car. It's about thirty feet down. There's a pile of what looks like rappelling gear there. And..." He directed the flashlight beam upwards. "Yep. Rope was secured at the top of the shaft. And cut by someone. Take a gander."

Lex leaned in and peered up. There was an iron joist a few inches below the ceiling of the shaft. From it a short piece of rope dangled, the loose end neatly severed.

"Adds weight to the 'intruders not welcome' theory," he said. "No cables or hoist mechanism, so I presume the elevator's hydraulic."

"You presume correctly," said Buckler. "Keeps the profile of this building low. Also, better from a security standpoint. Makes the elevator easier to disable from downstairs, not so easy to sabotage from up here."

"No chance of getting it going from up here, either. Is there any other way in? An external air vent of some kind?"

"None you can fit a body through."

"No backdoor emergency exit?"

"Nothing. This elevator's it, sole point of access and egress. So we've no alternative but to rappel, like the Marines did."

Pearce tossed a rope over the joist and hitched it tight. He tested the knot with a tug, then let the remaining length drop to the elevator car roof. He wound the rope around one thigh and swung out into the shaft.

"Careful now, Whisper," said Buckler.

Pearce just gave his CO a look and dropped out of sight.

Moments later, he supplied a sitrep. "Peachy."

Tartaglione descended next, followed by Buckler, then Sampson.

"Your turn," Morganstern said to Albertine. "Ever done anything like this before?"

Albertine shook her head.

"Then don't copy those guys, sliding down like that. That's just showing off. Loop the slack once around your waist, like so, then walk yourself down backwards, feet against the side, paying out the rope as you go. Don't worry about falling. You won't, and even if you do, it's not far and someone's bound to catch you. Are you listening, team?"

"Roger that," said Buckler. "I'll be keeping the rope steady at this end, Guardian Angel. You can do this. Walk in the park."

Albertine eased herself down the elevator shaft, heeding Morgenstern's advice to the letter. It was slow and painstaking, and Lex was on tenterhooks throughout, until he heard confirmation from Buckler that she'd made it safe and sound to the bottom.

He indicated to Morgenstern that she should go next. "Lady SEALs first."

"Honorary SEAL," she corrected. "It's still the only branch of the US Armed Services that doesn't accept women. I used to be in the Navy's Hospital Corps, a medic, but I've been with Thirteen long enough that the others hardly remember that any more. They treat me like just another shooter, just one of the guys."

"Bet there's an interesting story attached to how you came to join."

"You bet right. There is for all of us. But we don't have time for that right now."

"Not even the abridged version?"

"Okay then. The Cliffs Notes guide to Team Thirteen. For one reason or another, we've all got a reputation for bad luck. You know how it is with people in the military. Things go south for you on a few missions in a row, rightly or wrongly you get singled out, earn a rep as a Jonah, and it sticks."

"So they bundle you all together in the same unit..."

"Figuring, 'What the hell, least they can do is screw things up for each other and not for the rest of us.'"

"Nice."

"Isn't it just?"

With that, Morgenstern leapt into the shaft and slithered down.

Lex took a last look around the cinderblock building. The raw masonry of the walls, the defunct museum-piece generator with its bulky dials and gauges, the bars of dusty sunshine slanting in through the windows. He had a hunch he wasn't going to be above ground again for a good long while. He savoured this final glimpse of daylight, this final breath of fresh air.

"White Feather, something keeping you?" Buckler demanded over the comms.

"Coming."

Lex grabbed the rope and scissored his legs around it like a firefighter descending a pole. He began to lower himself hand over hand. Simply sliding would have shredded his palms to pieces. He didn't have gloves on like the Thirteeners did.

Above him he heard a faint but distinct *creak*. The rope gave a sudden sharp lurch. He froze. There was a pattering sound, granules of something crumbling and falling.

"Hey. What was that?" Buckler said. "What's going on up there?"

A flashlight beam probed upwards. Lex shut his eyes as it passed over his face, and opened them again as it continued above his head.

He heard a second *creak*, this one louder, and in the beam of light he saw the joist shift downwards a fraction. The rope lurched again.

"It's coming loose," he said. "It's going to—"

And it did.

And so did Lex.

TWENTY-FOUR
COLONEL GONZALEZ

PLUNGING THROUGH BLACKNESS.

He didn't have far to drop. Ten, maybe twelve feet.

But he had no means of gauging exactly where the elevator car roof lay. He let himself go limp, but the impact, when it came, was still a bludgeoning, painful shock.

The joist was plummeting after him. He rolled blindly out of its path, and it pounded, end first, into the elevator car. A tremendous, thunderous *clang*. The car shuddered. Someone screamed.

Lex had felt the joist whistle past his foot, missing by millimetres.

There was a second *clang*, duller than the first, as the joist keeled over, fetching up at an angle, its upper end coming to rest against the side of the shaft.

Dust and debris rained down in its wake. People choked and spluttered.

Buckler: "Are we all okay? Who's hurt? Anybody hurt?"

His flashlight swept a hazy glow over everyone's faces. He got nods, grim grins. Lex's shouted warning had at least given Team Thirteen and Albertine time to leap to the edges of the elevator car, so that neither he nor the joist crash-landed on any of them.

The flashlight beam finally found Lex, crouched in a corner.

"What the hell did you just do?" Buckler demanded.

"I'm fine, thanks for asking." Lex picked himself up, dusted himself off. His back and shoulders ached. "No bones broken. Haven't got a bloody great piece of iron sticking out of me."

"You pulled half the building down on top of us."

"Don't exaggerate. The joist must have been loosened from its setting, what with the weight of all of you hanging off it one after another. I was the final straw. That or..." He snatched the flashlight from Buckler and trained it upwards. "Those look like chisel marks to anyone?" Two rectangular slots could be made out where the ends of the joist had been lodged. The concrete around each bore signs of having been chipped away at, especially underneath. "Booby-trapped. Rigged to give way if anybody tried to do what we did. They knew a second team might be coming in after the Marines. They were prepared for us."

"How do we know it's not just natural erosion?" said Buckler. "That hunk of metal's been stuck up there for decades. Sea air eats concrete and cement for breakfast, and maintenance and upkeep hasn't been a high priority around here."

"Scared to admit you might have screwed up? Face facts, great and mighty Lieutenant Buckler. You should have inspected the joist more carefully before Pearce attached the rope."

"This isn't on me."

"Well, who else is it on?" Lex said hotly. "Definitely not me, Yet you instantly tried to blame me for it. You've been ragging on me from the start. According to you I can't do anything right. I'm just a millstone to the whole mission, a stupid Limey blundering around getting in everyone's way."

"Hey, if the shoe fits..."

"You smug git. I could have been crippled just now, or worse. Any one of us could. All you had to do was be a little less gung-ho, a little more cautious. And afterwards your first reaction was to find a scapegoat to deflect the guilt onto. Call yourself a leader? A leader leads, he doesn't pass the buck."

"That's enough, now."

"Is it? Is it, Buckler?"

"Get out of my face, Dove."

Lex did the opposite, thrusting himself up closer to the SEAL commander. "Make me."

"You're pissed, I get it," Buckler said. "Near-death experience, yadda yadda. But if you do not back the fuck down on the count of three, this is going to get ugly."

"Ugly?" Lex retorted. "You've never *seen* ugly."

"Please. Both of you." Albertine interposed herself between them, one hand on Lex's chest, the other on Buckler's. "For one thing, indoor voices. Shouting at each other isn't doing anything except possibly giving away the fact that we're here. Keep it down. And for another thing, while I'm sure all this posturing is good for your egos, it's not helping. An accident happened. We're alive, we're unhurt. Let's just be grateful for that and move on."

The flashlight, shining up from below between the two men, lent their features a wild, hectic air. They glared at each other, sweaty, dusty, nostrils flared. It could easily have degenerated into a brawl. Lex was conscious of his responsibility to the mission, his duty of care to Albertine. At the same time, the urge—the need—to plant a punch in Buckler's face was almost too great to overcome. There was only so much crap a man could put up with, only so much provocation he could take.

Lex was, however, above all else a professional. He reined in his temper. Bit back down the anger and the injured pride.

"This isn't over," he said. "But it can wait."

"Too right it isn't over," Buckler replied. "I'm watching you." He forked an index and middle finger at his own eyes, then at Lex. "Like a goddamn hawk. Try anything dumb, put my or my shooters' lives at risk again, and I will come down on you so hard you'll think Armageddon itself has arrived."

He pushed himself away from the shaft wall, shoulder-butting Lex aside.

"We can still get back up using ropes if we have to," he said briskly. "Someone'll have to climb, but with all those cross braces and guide rails lining the shaft, it's doable. What would be better is if we can get the elevator restarted, which we should be able to do once we're in the installation. There's an access hatch in the top of this thing. Marines must have used it, and that's our way down too."

"See those?" Morgenstern pointed to the inner edges of the hatch, where there were scorch marks and shiny nodules of metal that had melted and solidified again. "It's been sealed up with a blowtorch."

"Sampson?" said Buckler. "You're our Incredible Hulk. You do the honours."

"I prefer to think of myself as our Luke Cage, sir," said Sampson.

"If you say so. I'm not a comic geek like you. Just kick the fucking hatch in."

SAMPSON STAMPED ON the hatch until it was hanging from its mounting, bent in the middle and ready to drop. He reached down, prised it free, and laid it aside on the elevator roof. A dim light gleamed up from below. Sampson poked his head through the aperture for a recon.

"Zilch," he said.

He lowered his bulk down through the hatchway and landed on the floor, surprisingly softly.

Soon everyone else was with him. Buckler tried the Open Doors button, but to no avail.

"Now there's a surprise," he said. "Lights are at quarter power, so I'd say the whole installation's gone into automatic shutdown. The system's designed to do that to conserve energy if demand drops below a certain level. There's a manual reset in the maintenance room on the lowest level. Trip that and we can get the elevator running again. Meantime, these doors need forcing. Sampson, you're up. Pearce, Tartag."

Buckler dug his fingertips into the sliver of a gap between the doors. The other three SEALs joined him, and together they began pulling, two one way, two the other.

"Put your backs into it," Buckler said. Faces contorted with effort; knuckles popped. "Harder. My eight-year-old could do better, and she has asthma."

The doors parted a hair's breadth. Then an inch. A couple of inches. Morgenstern jammed the butt of her CAR-15 in between them and began using the carbine like a crowbar. Sampson braced his foot against the door opposite for additional purchase and leverage.

All at once the doors' mechanism abandoned its resistance and Team Thirteen wrenched them apart almost the whole way. Morgenstern was outside in a flash, swinging her gun left then right.

"Clear."

The others exited the elevator. Overhead emergency striplights provided a low level of illumination, tingeing everything sulphur-yellow. The passage ran twenty yards in one direction and about twice that in the other, turning a corner at both ends. There were a couple of doors, one marked Janitorial Supplies. Otherwise it was just beige walls and durable linoleum flooring, pure military-grade functionality.

Stencilled opposite the elevator were the characters SL1— Sublevel One. Beside the sign was a single bloody handprint, smearing downwards.

"Where our *vévé* artist cleaned his brush," said Buckler.

"Please God, that's all it is," said Sampson.

Buckler consulted a 3D schematic of the installation floorplan on his smartphone. "That way's living quarters and refectory," he said, pointing left. "That way"—right—"leads to test laboratories, communications hub, installation control room, and stairwell. We need to make a sweep of the entire premises, from the top down, in order to check for survivors... and hostiles. Quickest way is if we split up into two groups. You two, with me." Tartaglione and Sampson. "We take left. The rest of you, right. Got that?"

Nods of assent all round.

"Just so's we're clear on this," said Tartaglione, "are we Freddy, Daphne and Velma, or Shaggy and Scooby? I only ask 'cause Shaggy and Scooby always find the monster first."

"Whichever one we are," said Buckler, "you're the dog."

"Ruh-roh," said Tartaglione.

PEARCE TOOK THE lead with Lex's group, heel-to-toeing along the passage with his M-60 at eye level. He rounded the corner, quadranted for targets with the machine gun, then beckoned the other three to follow.

The first room they came to was the refectory. Half-finished meals sat on trays on the tables, food congealing on plates, cans of carbonated drink long gone flat. A few of the tubular steel chairs were overturned. Flies buzzed around the self-service canteen, where desiccated burger patties lay in stacks and French fries in cold soggy clumps.

"The *Mary Celeste*," said Lex. "Only with fast food."

"Kind of reminds me of the day at school when someone found a rat's tail in the meatloaf," said Morgenstern.

Pearce went through into the kitchen, searched, found no one.

They moved on to the living quarters. There were cramped dormitories with three sets of double bunk beds and there were single-occupancy rooms with slightly smarter decor and more lavish furnishings. Ancillary staff and executive. Most of the beds were made. Clothes lay in drawers, folded. Laptops and tablets lay on dressing tables, waiting for their owners to return.

"Where is everybody?" Lex wondered.

Pearce shrugged. "Elsewhere."

The comms clicked. "Whisper? This is Big Chief Dirty. Anything?"

"Nada."

"Bring your people this way, then. RV at the communications hub."

"Roger."

"Three sentences in a row," Lex said aside to Morgenstern, nodding at Pearce. "That's chatty for him."

"But only ever a single word at a time. Pearce is one-eighth Cherokee. Says his 'nation' aren't big on small talk. Or any kind of talk."

Pearce, aware they were discussing him, fixed them with an imperturbable dark-eyed stare. He twirled a finger, helicopter style—*moving out*—and all four of them set off back the way they had come.

Abruptly, Pearce halted. He clenched a fist in the air. Morgenstern stepped past Lex and Albertine to join him.

Pearce pointed to his eyes, then forwards.

Morgenstern looked a query at him.

Pearce held up a single finger.

Morgenstern nodded. She motioned to Lex and Albertine to stay put, and mimed shushing.

Lex drew his SIG and chambered a round as quietly as he knew how.

The two Thirteeners advanced slowly, silently, Pearce in front, Morgenstern covering him from behind.

Albertine nestled close to Lex. He could feel her trembling. He placed his free hand on her forearm, hoping his steadiness would steady her. It seemed to, somewhat.

Reaching a door, Pearce pressed his back to the wall beside it. He jerked his thumb. Someone, the individual he'd caught a glimpse of, had gone in there.

The door led to one of the six-man dormitories. It stood halfway open. Carelessness? Invitation? Trap?

Pearce pointed to himself, then upward, then to Morgenstern, then downward. A high-low entry to maximise the spread of gunfire coverage.

He counted down on his fingers. Three. Two. One.

He swung in through the doorway, sighting along his M-60. Morgenstern matched him at a crouch, CAR-15 levelled.

Both took aim, zeroing in on the same target.

"Who's that?" Morgenstern barked. "By the bunk! Turn round and identify yourself!"

Whoever she was addressing did not reply.

"You have three seconds to comply, or face aggressive action."

Three long seconds passed.

Morgenstern shouldered her carbine and unclipped something from her belt. She held the object up so that Lex could see. A dark green cylinder with holes drilled in it.

Flashbang.

Lex turned to Albertine. "Shut your eyes and cover your ears."

Morgenstern yanked out the pull ring and tossed the flashbang into the room. She and Pearce twisted aside, shielding their heads.

An enormous sunburst of brilliance.

An ear-splitting percussive *crack*.

Smoke drifted out from the dormitory doorway. Pearce and Morgenstern stood back, weapons at the ready.

Someone emerged.

He came slowly through the dispersing smoke. Lex assumed he was stunned by the flashbang, dazzled by a million candela of light and deafened by 180 decibels of sound, disorientated, made meek. He was giving himself up.

He stumbled into the corridor. He was dressed in camouflage fatigues and combat boots, with a Glock 19 pistol snugged in a shoulder rig. His features had a Hispanic cast. A silver eagle, the insignia of a US army colonel, adorned his shoulder.

The surname sewn on his chest pocket read Gonzalez.

Colonel Gonzalez looked around, and what Lex had taken to be dazedness seemed in fact to be something else. A kind of deep-seated perplexity, as though the entire world was a puzzle to him.

His eyes were strange. The irises were unnaturally pale, especially for someone with his complexion. The retinas reflected the sulphurous light queerly, flashing a deeper yellow.

His gaze fell on Pearce and Morgenstern.

Instantly he went on the attack.

TWENTY-FIVE
A WALKING SHAMBLES

IT WAS SO swift, so unexpected, that neither Pearce nor Morgenstern was prepared for it. From a standing start, without a sound, Colonel Gonzalez sprang into action like a tiger pouncing. He swatted Pearce's machine gun out of his grasp and went for his throat. One grubby hand clamped around the Thirteener's neck and started to squeeze. The other lashed out and caught Morgenstern with a savage backhand blow. Her head snapped sideways and she reeled.

Pearce grabbed Gonzalez's wrist and tried to pry himself free, but the colonel bore down with startling strength. His fingers dug into Pearce's flesh as though it were bread dough. Pearce's face turned a terrible shade of red and his mouth worked effortly as he tried to suck in air through his constricted windpipe.

He abandoned the attempt to dislodge Gonzalez's hand and went for the colonel's eyeballs instead, jabbing with his thumbs. Gonzalez seemed unperturbed. His expression was impassive, no ferocity, no aggression, just the calm mask of someone doing their job. He gathered up both of Pearce's wrists with his free hand and levered them aside, out of harm's way. The throttling continued.

Morgenstern had by now recovered her wits. She drew her sidearm, a MK23 semiauto, and lined it up with Gonzalez's temple. Point blank. In a moment's time the top of Gonzalez's skull would be blown clean off.

But the colonel, spying the danger, swung Pearce bodily around and slammed him into his teammate like a living baseball bat. Morgenstern was sent skittering across the linoleum. She managed to get off a shot but it went wild, bullet embedding in the ceiling. She caromed head first into the wall and the gun was jettisoned from her hand.

Pearce's face was now purple and he was starting to spasm uncontrollably. There was no fight left in him. He was on the brink of passing out.

Lex stepped forward, SIG raised. Finally he had a clear line of fire. Before, Morgenstern had been in the way. He hadn't dared take a shot for fear of hitting her by mistake.

He squeezed the trigger and planted a bullet in Gonzalez's shoulder.

The force of the impact alone should have knocked Gonzalez off his feet. Shock and pain should have incapacitated him.

Gonzalez was unfazed. A huge chunk had been taken out of his upper arm, blood was flowing freely, yet he still stood, still strangling Pearce. It was almost as though Lex hadn't shot him at all.

"The head," Morgenstern said, dazed and bleary. "In the fucking head."

Lex recalled Sampson describing how to bring down a zombie. *Head shot. Destroy the brain stem. It's the only way.*

Was that what this was? Gonzalez was a zombie? This was what one looked like?

It really didn't matter. A head shot was a head shot, after all. No one, be they man or monster, could withstand having half their cerebellum punched out by a Parabellum round.

The SIG boomed. Gonzalez's head recoiled like a coconut hit dead-on at a shy. Stuff from it spattered the wall behind.

He ought to have toppled instantly. Dropped like a stone.

How come he didn't? How come he remained upright, remorselessly clutching Pearce's throat in a death grip?

Slowly Gonzalez swivelled his head to look at Lex. A whole portion of his cranium had been removed, as though someone had dug a trowel into his brow and scooped upwards. Grey matter glistened. Blood oozed down his face, carrying shards of skull bone with it.

Yet his eyes still stared, befuddled but bright. Something continued to live inside him, even with half his brain gone.

"Zuvembie," Albertine whispered.

Lex could not make sense of it. He tried to analyse how a bullet in the shoulder at a range of ten yards could fail to stop an opponent in his tracks, let alone a head shot. Gonzalez had survived the unsurvivable. The laws of ballistics had been rescinded. No, the laws of *nature*.

Pearce was in dire straits. His eyes rolled up. He was twitching, his legs kicking like those of a hanged man in his final throes.

Lex tamped down his astonishment. Pearce's life was at stake. That consideration overrode all others.

He advanced on Gonzalez, SIG held out, pumping 9mm bullet after 9mm bullet into the colonel. He aimed for joints, weak spots in the human physiology, anywhere crucial to the movement of the body. Gonzalez might be unkillable, but if his basic biomechanics were messed with, he could surely be crippled, rendered inert.

One shot blasted through the elbow of the arm with which Gonzalez was holding Pearce. The arm was virtually severed in two and, unable to bear the Thirteener's weight any more, tore apart. Pearce fell with the hand still around his neck, although its crushing grip had relaxed. He and the gristle-ended stump of forearm hit the floor together.

Another bullet took out Gonzalez's left knee, and he staggered but shifted his weight to the right leg. He shuffled towards Lex, at the same time reaching for his Glock with his one good arm. The SIG obliterated most of that hand, leaving just the thumb and some of the meat of the palm.

A bullet shattered Gonzalez's pelvis. A bullet gouged through his neck, splintering the cervical vertebrae. His half-missing head flopped, and what was left of his brain spilled out like porridge from an overturned bowl.

Even then, he continued on the offensive. He lumbered forwards, head lolling, yellowy gaze locked sideways on Lex. As long as Lex posed a threat to his existence, Gonzalez would not give up. Indeed *could* not, it appeared. He had to kill Lex, while his body was still able to. Long after the point where he should have been lying on the ground in a lifeless, mangled heap, something drove him murderously on.

The SIG clicked dry. Lex swapped out the spent magazine for a fresh one, and as he did so called out, "Someone! Anyone! What do I need to do here? The bugger won't take the hint and die."

"Just keep firing," said Morgenstern. She had shoved herself up into a sitting position and her MK23 semiauto was back in her hand. "That's what I'm going to do."

Together they pumped a score of bullets into Gonzalez, and more. Gobbets of him flew away like the wreckage from a piñata. He skipped and shook in a grisly St Vitus dance. At last his body could no longer physically support itself. The damage to muscle and bone was too extensive, too catastrophic. He was a walking shambles, more of him injured than intact. His fatigues hung off him in tatters. He teetered on the spot, some three paces from Lex, close enough that the abattoir reek of blood and ruptured organ coming off him was sickeningly strong. He fumbled one last time for his Glock, trying vainly to hook his thumb into the trigger guard to draw it, even though he lacked the fingers to use it. Then he collapsed.

Almost literally collapsed.

Bits of him breaking apart and tumbling off as he fell.

Like a bombed skyscraper disintegrating.

A man became a gory jumble of body parts.

Silence reigned.

BUCKER HAD BEEN yelling over the comms for some time.

"Who's firing? Answer me, dammit! Do you have enemy contact? Have you engaged?"

Lex had been aware of the voice in his earpiece but only distantly, as background noise. He had been too preoccupied with killing Gonzalez to give it much attention.

Now he said, "This is White Feather. We have engaged with one enemy. Enemy is down. No fatalities on our side, but Whisper is hurt."

"How badly?"

"No idea. I'm going to check."

"Do not move from your position. We're on our way."

"Roger, Big Chief Dirty."

Lex knelt beside Pearce. He felt for a pulse and found one. Strong. The Thirteener stirred at his touch. His eyelids fluttered open. He let out a sound that could have been a word or simply a groan. Finger-mark bruises patterned his neck like livid leopard spots. The whites of his eyes were crazed with burst capillaries. His face, at least, was returning to its normal colour.

"Fuck," he croaked.

"Succinctly put," said Lex.

"Morgenstern?"

"Here, Pearce." Morgenstern crawled over to his side. "Let's take a look at you." She palpated his neck gently, then with equal gentleness clasped his jaw and rolled his head from side to side. She inspected his pupils and asked him a few simple questions with yes-or-no answers.

"You'll live," was her expert prognosis. "Contusions. Some trauma to the trachea. You're going to have a hell of a sore throat for the next few days and probably a nasty headache too. But nothing's broken. No nerve damage. Try to keep from talking too much, if you can. That'll aid the healing process."

"Difficult," he said with a partial smile.

"Yeah, I realise it's a big ask."

Footfalls echoed along the passage. The rest of Team Thirteen raced into view.

"Pearce," Buckler barked. "What's your status?"

Pearce raised a shaky but resolute thumb.

"And what in the name of fuck," Buckler said, turning his attention to the mess on the floor, "is that?"

"That is—*was*—someone called Colonel Gonzalez," said Lex.

"Jesus. The site military supervisor. What'd the guy do to deserve being shot to shreds?"

"Refused to die."

Buckler cocked his head. "You being a wiseass?"

"Dove's right, LT," said Morgenstern. "Gonzalez would not go down—not until we'd put the best part of forty rounds in him."

"But why shoot him in the first place?"

"Self-preservation. Gonzalez was attempting to terminate Pearce. With his bare hands."

"Come again?"

"He was a zuvembie," said Albertine. "His mind was not its own. He was under the sway of a bokor."

"You're sure of that?"

Albertine was badly shaken by the carnage she had just witnessed. She struggled to maintain her composure. "As sure as I can be. I've never personally seen a zuvembie before today, but this one matched all the criteria. Tremendous strength. Incapable of speech. Vacant expression. Also, impervious to pain and able to carry on functioning in spite of physical damage. More so than I would have thought possible. Lex and Morgenstern had to virtually demolish him before he would stop."

"But why did he attack?" said Buckler. "What was he doing here?"

"My guess is he was on guard duty. Patrolling this floor. Morgenstern and Pearce challenged him. He viewed them as aggressors and acted accordingly."

"I thought you said he was mindless."

"In one sense, yes. In another sense, no. A zuvembie retains a very primitive understanding of the world. It is capable of basic thought—survival responses and suchlike—and can be put to work performing menial tasks. Somewhat like a human robot. Gonzalez, being a soldier, would have been trained to fight, and would have still known how to while a zuvembie, even if he had no clear idea of who he was fighting, or why. His motor skills remained unaffected, even if his higher cognitive functions didn't."

"He was left here deliberately, then, as a kind of watchdog?"

"That's it. To intercept and confront intruders."

"Shit. Shit, shit, shit." Buckler ran a hand through his hair. "Okay. At least now we know for sure what we're up against. There are going to be more of these things lurking around. But they can be stopped, that's the lesson we can draw from this. It takes firepower but it can be done."

"Might I ask a question?" said Lex.

"Sure. If you must."

"Two questions, actually. The first to Albertine. You said Gonzalez was under the sway of a bokor. Papa Couleuvre, in this instance. Is Couleuvre like a puppet master, pulling the zuvembie's strings?"

"Not as such. He isn't commanding it with mental powers, if that's what you're getting at. Nor is he 'seeing' through its eyes, in case that's worrying you too. Think of it more as the bokor exerting his authority over the zuvembie. He directs it to do something, then leaves it to get on with it. Rather like you hiring someone to wash your car for you. You don't need to stand over the person, showing them where to wipe with the cloth and telling them not to forget the hubcaps. You just expect they'll do the job as required. The only difference is that a zuvembie will keep at whatever task it's set, tirelessly, relentlessly, until you instruct it to do something else."

"Right. I see. So it's not as if killing Papa Couleuvre will somehow halt all the zuvembies in their tracks?"

"No. That's not how this sort of sorcery works."

"Okay." Lex turned back to Buckler. "Then my question to you, lieutenant, is how many people were there originally at Anger Reef? What were the staffing levels here?"

"Round about fifty personnel in total," Buckler said. "Technicians and such."

"That'd be my estimate, based on the extent of the living quarters. And I reckon it would be fair to assume that most if not all of them have been turned into zuvembies."

"How do you figure that?" asked Sampson.

"At the risk of sounding like Sherlock Holmes, it's elementary. There's the combat footage for starters. I counted a good dozen silhouettes moving across the camera's field of vision. Those were just the ones I could see. The Marines were met by an overwhelming force. Logic dictates that the zuvembies outnumbered them by a factor of at least four to one. That suggests that almost everyone here has been, if you will, zuvembified. On top of which, Colonel Gonzalez was a military officer. He had a gun, probably the only firearm on the premises under normal circumstances. It was his responsibility to maintain order and ensure the welfare of the civilians on site. If he was co-opted into the zuvembie ranks—the one person who might have been able to prevent things getting out of hand—then what chance would the others have stood? Then there are the Marines themselves."

"I don't like where you're going with this," said Morgenstern.

"Me neither," said Lex. "Do we have confirmation that they're dead? We don't. What is 'dead' in this context anyway?"

"It was a ten-man unit," said Buckler.

"So potentially we could be looking at sixty zuvembies in all. Ten of them with advanced combat skills and weapons."

"Which they can still utilise even as zuvembies," said Morgenstern. "Gonzalez fought like a motherfucker, and you and I both saw him going for his gun."

"I'm liking the whole situation less and less," said Tartaglione. "Anyone else in favour of a tactical get-the-fuck-out-of-here?"

"Can the Cowardly Lion bullshit, Tartag," Buckler snapped. "We've faced worse odds."

"Have we? Where?"

"Sarajevo, for one."

"I wasn't at Sarajevo. Before my time. In fact, wasn't Sarajevo where...?" Tartaglione trailed off.

A darkness seemed to settle over Buckler. Something bleak and lost flitted behind his eyes. "Yeah," he said hollowly. "It was. And it was way worse than this shit, believe you me. I made it through that. You all will make it through this. Now." Some of his habitual swagger reasserted itself. "In the light of Dove's deductions, which I happen to think are valid, we stick together from now on. Safety in numbers. Pearce? You recovered? Feel able to go on?"

"Spiffy."

"Then let's up and at 'em. We still haven't checked out the communications hub. That was next on the agenda when the shooting started. We'll give it the once-over, then head down to Level Two."

As THEY VENTURED along the passage in a line, single file, Lex tapped Morgenstern's shoulder.

"Sarajevo?" he said, softly so that Buckler wouldn't overhear.

"Don't," she said. "Don't go there."

"But what happened?"

"I mean it. Subject's off-limits."

"Were you there?"

"No. None of us was. Only the lieutenant. And the previous Team Thirteen."

"You mean there was one before this one."

"Did you not get that from 'previous'? Some Sherlock Holmes you are."

"And he's the only one left from that team."

"That brain of yours is really working overtime, Dove."

"The only survivor. What did it? What wiped the rest of them out?"

"We don't talk about it," said Morgenstern. "We don't talk about it because the lieutenant doesn't talk about it. Ask him and he'll probably punch your lights out. Let's just say he went through hell, and leave it at that."

"And by hell you mean..."

"Literally that. Hell."

TWENTY-SIX
SUPPLY CLOSET

THE COMMUNICATIONS HUB was a large chamber crammed with top-spec hardware: computers, plasma screens, phone units, and the rack-mounted amplifiers, antenna controllers and power control system units needed to sustain a high-bandwidth satellite uplink.

None of it remained intact.

Everything had been shattered, smashed, crushed, eviscerated. Even the functional tables and chairs had been broken up, reduced to smithereens. The damage was so extensive, so thorough, that it seemed orchestrated. The room had been systematically vandalised. Whoever was responsible had wanted to make sure there was no way any of the equipment could be reassembled and used again. To that end, circuit boards had been wrenched from their busses and snapped in two. Monitors had been stamped on repeatedly until their front glass plates were white like ice. Cables hadn't simply been torn out of their sockets but shredded to pieces, so that the floor was a snake's nest of rubber insulation and bare copper wire and fibre-optic filament.

"Anyone else think it's not supposed to look like this?" said Sampson.

"Ah, it's not so bad," said Tartaglione. "Bit of duct tape, some superglue, we could have it up and running again in no time, good as new."

"I'm guessing Papa Couleuvre's behind this," said Buckler. "What's been happening here is nothing less than a *coup d'état*. Once he got started with his takeover of the installation, severing communications links would have been his first priority, so that no one could send out a distress signal."

"Surely he'd have known the Pentagon would fly troops in as soon as Anger Reef went off the grid," said Morgenstern.

"But he bought himself some time. And since there was no way anybody in Washington could gain a clear idea of what was going on, the initial response from there would be low-key at best. Which it was. Ten Marines, when, if they'd had intel from someone on site, they'd have known that what was really needed was an army."

"So why's it just the five of us now?" said Tartaglione. "Couldn't we have brought an army as backup?"

"The difference is we're pros," replied Buckler. "We know what we're doing. This sort of shit is our meat and drink."

"Couleuvre strikes me as a shrewd bastard," Sampson observed.

"That'd be my assessment too. What's still unclear is what part Professor Seidelmann has played in the whole deal. He's the big unknown in the equation. He and Couleuvre started out collaborating. It was his show. Are they still in cahoots? Or did Couleuvre turn on him? Enquiring minds need to know."

"Creepy scientist tries to make voodoo super-soldiers and it blows up in his face," said Tartaglione. "Who saw *that* coming?"

"That's the trouble with scientists," said Sampson. "They think just because you can't lab-test to prove the existence of karma, it doesn't—"

"Sshhh!" said Lex.

"Huh?"

"All of you. Pipe down."

Team Thirteen and Albertine looked at him.

"I heard something."

Immediately weapons were raised, cocking levers pulled, fingers curled around triggers.

Lex padded across the floor, doing his best to avoid treading on the piles of high-tech debris. The sound had been muffled, coming from the far side of the room. He checked every place someone might hide, until at least he reached the door to a supply closet. If there *had* been a sound—if it wasn't a stray echo, or just his ears playing tricks—then it could only have originated here. He had eliminated all other possible locations.

He listened hard. Nothing. Not a peep.

He was beginning to think it had been a false alarm, when—there. He heard it again. A faint, choked sob.

He looked back at the others and pointed at the door.

Buckler made a *go* gesture, and Sampson and Tartaglione moved stealthily into position beside Lex.

Lex reached out and tried the door handle. It turned but the door did not give. Locked, or the catch mechanism had been disabled from the inside.

Now there was only silence from the closet—but it was the silence of someone keeping utterly still, not daring to move or even breathe. Lex could almost sense the person's presence by the absoluteness of the hush on the other side of the door.

Another zuvembie, lying in wait? Hoping to sucker them the way Gonzalez had?

Sampson produced a sock of C-4 and broke off a small lump of the plastic explosive. He kneaded it into a thin sausage and tamped it around the handle plate in a C-shape. Then he invited everyone to take a few steps back, drew his MK23, took aim, shielded his face, and fired.

The *bang* was immense. The door whipped inwards, missing a large chunk where the handle had been. Some of the frame had been blown out too.

Lex leapt in front of the doorway, SIG at the ready. There was smoke, and darkness. But he glimpsed a figure near the back of the closet, lurching forwards. A pre-emptive shot to the knee seemed like a good plan.

"No! Please! Don't!"

The figure staggered out into the light, hands raised in submission.

"Don't shoot! I'm not one of them! I'm normal! I'm me!"

The face was familiar. It just took Lex a moment to place it.

"Professor Seidelmann?" he said.

PROFFESOR GULLIVER SEIDELMANN was not the dignified, distinguished academic Lex had seen on the screen of Buckler's laptop, smoothly delivering his pitch for project funding to a group of Washington bigwigs. The man in front of him now was a dishevelled, ravaged version of that Seidelmann, and looked malnourished and completely terrified. His clothes were soiled and he reeked of body odour and human waste. The interior of the closet was commensurately squalid. Empty food packaging lay scattered about, and one corner bore evidence of having been used as a toilet.

As Seidelmann staggered into the room, he blinked around himself, dazzled by the lighting, for all that it was dim. His disorientation was such that he collided with Tartaglione, who caught and steadied him. Seidelmann gave the SEAL a look that was almost pathetically grateful. It seemed to be dawning on him, gradually, that he had not fallen into enemy hands. Whoever these people were, they weren't here to kill him. They might even be his salvation.

"Oh God," he moaned. "Oh God, tell me you're a rescue party. Tell me the nightmare's over."

Buckler stepped forward. "Professor Seidelmann? Lieutenant Tom Buckler, SEAL Team Thirteen. I have to know, sir, are you in full command of your faculties?"

"Am I sane, you mean?" A brittle laugh. "After the wretched time I've had, it's debatable."

"No, I mean are you a zuvembie? I realise it's an absurd question but I have to ask."

Seidelmann straightened up a little. He smoothed his ruffled hair flat and resettled his rimless glasses on his nose. "No, I am most definitely not. But only by the skin of my teeth."

"You're in no way infected, or transmogrified, or whatever the hell the verb is for a person getting turned into one of those things?"

"Artificially augmented," Seidelmann said. "And of course I'm not. I wouldn't be talking like this if I was. I wouldn't be able to converse with you at all. In fact, I'd most likely be trying to kill you."

The professor spoke with some asperity. All the signs pointed to him having undergone an ordeal, a prolonged period of terror and deprivation. Yet he was already recovering from it and regaining his confidence. Not just confidence, either. The man in the video clip had shown a sleek self-assurance that verged on arrogance. Lex could see that trait returning to him now at a rapidly accelerating rate, rising as his levels of relief rose. The more Seidelmann understood that he might just be making it out of Anger Reef alive after all, the more like himself he became.

"I'm famished," he announced. "I managed to scrounge a few scraps of food before I shut myself away in there, but not as much as I would have liked, or needed. I don't suppose any of you has got something to eat."

"Tartag?" said Buckler. "Give the man a candy bar and an MRE."

Seidelmann fell on the chocolate as though it was manna from heaven. He tore off the wrapper and gulped and guzzled with shameless abandon. Then he turned to the Meal Ready-to-Eat, ripping the pack open and separating the items that didn't need to be heated for consumption from the ones that did. He squeezed cheese spread onto crackers, chasing this down with a raspberry-flavour HOOAH! energy bar.

Buckler waited patiently until he was finished, then resumed his interrogation.

"How long have you been in the closet?"

Tartaglione sniggered. "In the closet. That's funny."

Buckler glared at him. Professor Seidelmann just ignored him.

"I'm not sure. What's today?"

"Sunday."

"Six days, then. Since Monday. It feels far longer. Every moment in there was torture, an agony of darkness and despair, but I couldn't think of what else to do. It was the only place I could be safe. I didn't dare venture out, not once. I didn't even dare open the door to look out. In case one of *them* was lurking, waiting for me."

"A zuvembie."

"Yes," said Seidelmann. "That's what Deslorges likes to call them, so I suppose, for want of a better word, that's what they are. But they're a travesty of my work. Not what I intended at all."

So saying, the professor strode briskly towards the door, where Pearce stood guard, keeping an eye on the passage outside.

"Hey! Where are you off to?" Buckler demanded.

Seidelmann halted. "Well, I presume you haven't come here to sit around and chat. Let's get cracking. Commence extraction, or whatever the phrase is."

"Hold your horses. This isn't a rescue mission."

Seidelmann's face fell.

"Not wholly," Buckler amended. "We're here to find out what's been going on and put an end to it."

"You?" The professor looked around at the assembled company. "Us."

"It's just the seven of you?"

Buckler nodded.

Seidelmann barked a laugh. "You have got to be joking."

"You'll be getting out of here soon enough, professor. But not until you've made yourself useful."

Seidelmann snorted. "Useful?"

"Yes, useful. If me and my crew are to do any good, what we require from you is information and co-operation."

"Nothing I can tell you is going to make a jot of difference, Lieutenant Buckler. If this is the full extent of your forces, then our best hope—our only hope—is to leave straight away, while we can. Otherwise we are all going to die—and, if we are very lucky, be allowed to stay dead, permanently."

"The alternative being that we wind up as zuvembies. Like Colonel Gonzalez."

"Just so," said Seidelmann. "Do you relish the prospect of that? Because believe me, I do not."

Again Seidelmann made for the door, simply assuming that everyone else would take their lead from him and follow. When no one did, he was perplexed.

"Pearce?" said Buckler. "If Poindexter here tries that one more time, put a bullet in him. You choose where."

"Affirmative."

"Do you not appreciate the gravity of the situation?" Seidelmann said, rounding on Buckler. "François Deslorges is dug in downstairs, and he's hatching some scheme, I have no idea what, but knowing him it can't be anything good. He has amassed a small army of zuvembies, and with them at his beck and call there is no way you can get to him and no way you can hinder him. If you value your safety, lieutenant, and that of your troops, you would be wise to depart *right now*, taking me with you. Go back out the way you came in, and leave Deslorges to his own devices."

"No can do, prof. I have my orders."

Seidelmann sighed at his obstinacy. "You would rather die?"

"In an ideal world, no. But this isn't an ideal world. It's the world of the US military, where you have two options: do as you're told, or do as you're told. I have been told to put a lid on the problem at this installation, so that is my primary objective. And it will be a damn sight easier to achieve if you, sport, pull your head out your fucking ass and supply me with some background detail."

"In other words, fill you in on Deslorges and his zuvembies, the whole sorry saga?"

"That is exactly it. Maybe if I know more about those things, I'll have a better chance of ending them."

Seidelmann's shoulders slumped. He seemed to realise there was no point in arguing. Buckler had the whip hand. Seidelmann might not like it but there was nothing he could do about it.

"Very well," he said. "Give me a drink of water, some more food, and I'll tell you all I can."

TWENTY-SEVEN
V.I.V.E.M.O.R.T.

"It was a good idea," Professor Seidelmann said. "Correction, a *great* idea. In this era of asymmetrical warfare, when entire battalions can be undermined by the efforts of a handful of determined guerrillas, when terrorists armed with box cutters can cause widespread devastation and the best-funded military and intelligence service in the world are helpless to prevent it, the concept of a standing army is becoming increasingly redundant. The strategy of sending men and women into pitched battle, to overwhelm enemy positions and gain territory, is antiquated. Outmoded. Something for the history books. What's called for these days is not huge numbers of troops—cannon fodder—but rather, far fewer of them. Soldiers of the highest calibre who can be deployed in small units in hostile zones to secure high-value targets and deliver surgical counterstrikes—"

"Please, professor," Buckler butted in. "This sounds like the beginning of a lovely long speech, and it's beautifully put and all, but you're not telling me anything I don't already know. Cut to the chase."

Seidelmann took a swig of water from Buckler's canteen, a move designed to mask his annoyance at being interrupted mid-flow. "I was merely building up to saying that the way forward, the future for the military, is a harder, more durable, more resilient breed of soldier. One who can take the kind of punishment that would hobble an ordinary man and keep going. One who can last longer behind enemy lines, go without rest longer, fight longer, withstand torture longer, survive longer in harsh, unforgiving conditions..."

"Sounds to me like you just described a SEAL," said Tartaglione. "Twenty-six weeks of Basic Underwater Demolition at Coronado—you live through that, you're not a man any more, you're a goddamn war machine."

Sampson cheered in agreement, and the two of them bumped knuckles. Pearce, for his part, nodded sagely.

"Acknowledged," said Seidelmann. "But even a SEAL will succumb to a sniper's bullet or an improvised explosive device. Even a SEAL is vulnerable to the frailties that flesh is heir to. My goal—my dream—was to discover a method whereby soldiers could be made immune to exhaustion and hardened to injury. My researches in this field led me towards Haiti and the *vodou* tradition, specifically with relation to the zuvembie. I learned that the zuvembie was more than just folklore, that there was actually a sound empirical basis for the myth of the walking dead man, and that it was to be found in the application of certain pharmacological substances."

"This we already know too," said Buckler. "Tetrodotoxin, datura, all of that."

"If you're so *au fait* with the subject, lieutenant, is there any need for me to carry on?"

Buckler decided to strike a conciliatory note. "There is, and I'd be much obliged if you would."

"At any rate, I visited Port-au-Prince, and after enquiring around was put in touch with François Deslorges, also known as Papa Couleuvre, a bokor who claimed to be able to create zuvembies. We struck up a working partnership—I shan't bore you with the details, you'd no doubt consider them extraneous—and with his aid I came to an understanding of what a zuvembie is and by what means it is possible to induce a person to become one. Thereafter it was a case of working out how to apply the process practically and in such a way that it could be of use to my employers at the Pentagon—how to take an ordinary general infantryman and turn him into a fearless, inexhaustible, unstoppable killer commando. Deslorges agreed to continue to assist me here, at Anger Reef, in return for a handsome retainer. He seemed, at the time, to be motivated solely by profit, for which reason I felt I could trust him. There's nothing purer or more reliable than sheer greed, is there? I knew he was an unsavoury character with a very shady reputation but I believed he would be biddable as long as he was getting paid. His love of money would keep him honest."

"A *vodouisant* should not love money," said Albertine. "The loa do not approve of acquisitiveness, especially when it's someone exploiting *vodou* for their own gain."

"Yes, thank you, my dear," said Seidelmann. "I take it you're a practitioner of the art yourself? Then you would know as well as I do that there are two sides to *vodou*. Like any other belief system, it attracts its fair share of charlatans and conmen, fakers and frauds, people who are in it only for what they can get out of it. I was under no illusion about Deslorges. From the start I knew he would require careful handling, a certain amount of finessing. Yet, despite his *outré* physical appearance and his quite prodigious intake of marijuana, I felt he was sincere, in his way, and committed to his calling. He seemed—*is*—highly accomplished when it comes to *vodou*, an advanced *kanzo* initiate. Take, for instance, his prowess as a thaumaturge. In Port-au-Prince, as a guest at his peristyle, I watched him perform acts of healing that were quite remarkable, one might even say miraculous. He removed a disfiguring birthmark from a baby's face. He shrank a benign growth on an old woman's neck until it disappeared altogether. In a country like Haiti, with its already negligible health care system made worse by the recent earthquake, a man like Deslorges is a powerful force for good, or perhaps a necessary evil. A witch doctor who's as much doctor as witch. He also could be very charming—charismatic—when he wished to be. I decided that, on balance, it would be safe to extend my association with him."

"But you were wrong."

"Indeed, dear, I was wrong. Very wrong." Seidelmann looked rueful, the snake wrangler who had been bitten by one of his pets. "For our first few weeks at Anger Reef we collaborated peaceably and proficiently enough, Deslorges and I. He assisted me with gauging dosages and adjusting formulae. We were seeking to develop the perfect mixture of herbs and toxins to achieve the zuvembie effect while still allowing the element of self-determination in the subject. We wanted to be able to bring someone to the point where fatigue and discomfort are minimal, almost immaterial, while not being zombie-like in the conventional sense—retaining their sentience and independence of thought. A tricky balance, but the results, in rhesus monkeys, were encouraging. We had animals that could go for days on end without food or water and show no ill effects. Animals that could undergo vivisection procedures happily without anaesthetic, all the while carrying out simple puzzle-solving problems. Animals that could cling to heating filaments with no evident distress even as their paws were slowly scorched..."

"Nice," said Morgenstern.

"Don't think I don't have a conscience about these things, young lady. I'm no unfeeling monster. But if science is to advance, some unpleasant steps must be taken. And unless you've never worn any cosmetics or shampooed your hair with any products that haven't been safety-tested on God's lesser creatures first, don't be so quick to judge." Another swig of water. "Eventually we reached the stage where we were ready to graduate to the next level—humans. Through rigorous experimentation on monkeys we had a product we felt was suitable for use on people with few if any side effects. We elected to call it V.I.V.E.M.O.R.T. I say 'we', but it was Deslorges who came up with the name and then expected me to construct an acronym to suit."

"Which you did."

Seidelmann allowed himself a small smile of pride. "I did. Venously Injected Vitality Elixir Magnifying Ordinary Resilience Twentyfold. The name V.I.V.E.M.O.R.T., and the fact that Deslorges refused to consider any of the alternatives I suggested, ought to have tipped me off to his ulterior motives. Perhaps if I'd been less bound up in my work, less thrilled by the advances I was making... I was, after all, on the brink of that long-sought-after, much-desired breakthrough: the creation of super-soldiers."

"And then, at some point, Deslorges turned you over and butt-fucked you," said Buckler. "Without lubricant."

Seidelmann winced. "With hindsight I should have noticed sooner that he had begun to behave erratically, and should have nipped it in the bud. His timekeeping lapsed. He wasn't down at the labs punctually every morning, as he had been. He seemed to be losing interest in what we were doing, his enthusiasm waning. Sometimes I had to roust him out of his room or the refectory to come and help me. On occasion I would have to go topside to find him, and there he'd be, on the beach, gazing out to sea or else dancing and chanting, communing with the loa. He complained that being underground all the time was making him claustrophobic. His marijuana usage went up. He seemed to have brought along an endless supply of the stuff, and I tolerated the habit in him as I would have in no other work colleague since it relaxed him and made him more amenable. Plus, it's a cultural thing, isn't it?" He addressed this remark to Albertine. "Part and parcel of the West Indian lifestyle, and the *vodou* tradition too. Isn't that right, dear?"

Albertine didn't answer. Her only response was to mutter darkly under her breath, a string of words of which Lex caught just one: "patronising".

"So I disapproved," said Seidelmann, "but couldn't forbid it. In general I could have been firmer with him, but he continued to be helpful, if only intermittently, and he had already contributed so much to the project that I couldn't begrudge him slacking off a little now. To be honest, I hadn't even expected him to demonstrate anything like as much of a work ethic as he did in the initial days, given—again—certain cultural dispensations."

Now Albertine actively bristled. "I could shrivel his balls to the size of raisins," she hissed.

"I think they already are," said Lex.

Seidelmann continued his narrative, blithe to any offence he might be causing. "At the same time Deslorges appeared to be developing an obsession."

"With what?" asked Buckler.

Seidelmann waved a hand. "With here. This installation. Anger Reef. He kept asking people about it: when was it built, how, why. He badgered everyone, even menials like the kitchen staff, but in particular Colonel Gonzalez. He wanted to know the structural specifications of the place, to see plans and blueprints if there were any. No one could help him there. I thought he was just bored and needed something to occupy his mind, a hobby. In a way I was gratified he was showing such an intellectual curiosity about his surroundings. So I suggested he go online, do some searches, see if he could unearth anything. I even let him use my own computer workstation for the purpose. Meanwhile I was busy prepping the first group of human volunteers to try out V.I.V.E.M.O.R.T. on."

"Volunteers," said Buckler. "Don't tell me—convicts and such. Death row inmates looking to get their sentences commuted. People with nothing to lose."

"No, lieutenant. An interesting supposition, but in fact I drew on a pool of your own brethren." Seidelmann said this with such a smug, sly air that Lex, already inclined to dislike the man, felt a spike of actual loathing for him.

"Forces guys?"

"Why not? The Pentagon sourced me a half-dozen individuals who were willing to do more for their mother country than strap on a rifle and march in line. To be fair, they were also a half-dozen individuals each of whom was facing a court-martial and the very real possibility of a stint in the stockade at Fort Leavenworth."

"Ah. Scumbags, then."

"I prefer to think of them as those not temperamentally cut out for a life of military discipline," said Seidelmann. "Among them was a young private who had left another so badly injured and traumatised after a hazing ritual that the second private is now on antidepressants and cannot walk unaided. There was also an MPC specialist who conducted cruel and unusual abuse of terrorist suspects in captivity—guilty not so much for what he did as for being photographed doing it. Once the pictures were leaked onto the internet, his superiors realised they had no alternative but to make an example of him. All in all, these were six of the less pleasant members of your profession, who were given the choice of being guinea pigs for me, and receiving an other-than-honourable discharge and full pension, or jail time and a dishonourable discharge, with no subsequent veterans' benefits at all. In their own interest and that of their dependants, they elected to take the former. Who can fault them for that?"

"Yeah," grumbled Tartaglione. "Goody for them."

"Regular saints," Sampson added.

"Shortly before we were due to begin the human trials, I came across Deslorges prowling the corridors of Sublevel Three, the lowest floor here, where most of the labs are. He was searching for something, it seemed. He kept pausing and listening out. He placed a hand on the walls, on the floor, as though trying to feel through them to detect something on the other side. I watched him a while, puzzled, until finally he became aware of me. First thing he said was, 'Hear that?' I couldn't hear anything apart from the hum of the striplights. 'He's calling,' Deslorges said. 'Who is?' I asked, but he wouldn't specify. He just said, 'He's calling to me. Taunting me. Challenging me.' Again I asked him who and he didn't answer. All I got was this look—this look of wild-eyed anger that I still can't account for. The whites of Deslorges's eyes were glassy and pink. His pupils were markedly dilated. He reeked of marijuana smoke. I wondered if he was having some kind of psychotic episode, the kind that can be triggered by cannabinoids, especially when ingested in excessive quantities. However, he didn't appear altered or maladaptive in any way. On the contrary, he looked and sounded perfectly cogent and normal. Sane. And that, I'm not afraid to admit, alarmed me somewhat."

"You're saying you were scared?" said Lex.

"Is that an English accent I detect?" said Seidelmann. "My, what a motley assortment you lot are."

"Just get on with it, prof," said Buckler.

"To answer your question, me old china," Seidelmann said to Lex, "I think it did scare me. Gave me a chill, at least. I was forced to ask myself what sort of man I'd allied myself with, whether I'd misjudged him, been a little optimistic in my assessment of him. But I was preoccupied. My work was coming to a head. I couldn't let myself be distracted by relatively minor concerns. Tomorrow was D-day, crunch time, the moment when I found out whether nearly a year's worth of effort was going to bear fruit or be in vain. That was my principal focus."

Seidelmann heaved a deep, bleak sigh.

"And that was when the horrors began."

AFTER A SHORT break to compose himself, Professor Seidelmann carried on.

"They filed into the main lab, our six volunteers," he said.

"They looked anxious, and who can blame them? They knew nothing about what they were letting themselves in for. They joked and joshed with one another, but beneath the bravado you could sense the trepidation. We lay them down on gurneys, my assistants and I. We strapped them in. We inserted cannulas. We got everything ready. I went to the refrigerator to retrieve the phials of V.I.V.E.M.O.R.T. I'd prepared a goodly number of doses of the formula. I knew something was awry the moment I took out the tray. A phial was missing.

"Immediately I quizzed all the assistants. They denied guilt. They swore, to a man, that they hadn't been in the lab since yesterday evening, when I'd last checked the trays. Knowing them as I did, I believed them. None of them had stolen the phial. Who, then? Who was the culprit? The only other person who had unfettered access to the lab, who owned a pass card and knew the entry code, was Deslorges.

"He hadn't turned up at the lab that morning, which had surprised me, as I'd thought he would be keen to see V.I.V.E.M.O.R.T. used on humans for the first time—the payoff, as it were, for our months of collaborative effort. My suspicions were aroused. Deslorges had taken the phial. It had to be him. Why, though?

"I sent someone off to fetch him. When that person didn't return after twenty minutes, I sent someone else off. Meanwhile the volunteers were getting restive, starting to grumble and fret. I went ahead and administered each of them with twenty-five millilitres per hour of Propofol via a volumetric IV pump to induce conscious sedation, as I'd been planning to do anyway. That shut them up. Soon they were drifting off, happy in their own headspace.

"Finally, after nearly an hour had passed, I went looking for Deslorges myself.

"I was about to take the elevator up to Sublevel One when I heard a commotion. I turned to see one of my assistants, the second one I'd sent off, a graduate of the Indian Institute of Science at Bangalore, man by the name of Vijay Kanetkar, haring along the corridor towards me. From the flop sweat and panic on his face I could tell he was running for his life. Then a shot rang out. Dr Kanetkar fell at my feet, stone dead.

"I was in complete shock. I could only stare down at poor Kanetkar, uncomprehending. Then I saw Colonel Gonzalez heading my way, arm outstretched, gun in hand.

"I spluttered, asking him what the matter was, what had Dr Kanetkar done, why had he had to die. Gonzalez didn't answer. Gonzalez didn't look like Gonzalez any more. His face was expressionless, blank in a way I had never seen before, as though all the life had departed from it. Which, though I didn't know it at the time, it had.

"Gonzalez stopped in front of me and aimed his gun at me. I now know what it means when people say they were paralysed with terror. I was. I couldn't for the life of me move. I stared down at the barrel of that pistol and heard some small, stupid voice in my mind insisting that it was okay to stand stock still because this wasn't happening, it couldn't be, I must be hallucinating or the victim of a practical joke or something, I simply couldn't be about to die.

"Then a voice—a real voice—cried out, 'Stop!' It was Deslorges. 'Don't shoot. I need him.'

"Gonzalez froze. He didn't lower the gun. He just became a statue. I think that was the moment when I realised he wasn't breathing. His immobility was absolute, as though he were cast in bronze.

"Deslorges strode up. 'Change of plan, professor,' he said. 'Change of boss. I'm in charge now. There's something that needs to be done, and I'm the man to do it. With some help from you.'

"I didn't quibble or cavil. When you have a gun pointing at you and have just witnessed the cold-blooded murder of a colleague, you simply nod and do as asked."

"And what did Deslorges ask?" Buckler wanted to know.

"He demanded my full and unstinting co-operation. He said he had a use for V.I.V.E.M.O.R.T.—a personal project he wished to see through. It was half his formula, he said. He had a right to it. It was as much his property as mine or the US government's.

"'And I'm ahead of you,' he told me. 'I've already tried it out on a human being, and you know what? It works. Brilliantly. Only difference is, I tried it out not on someone who's alive but someone who's already dead.'

"He could only have been referring to Colonel Gonzalez.

"'This here is my zuvembie,' he said, patting Gonzalez the way you'd pat a sports car or a new set of golf clubs. 'My servant. Loyal to me like no living person could ever be. I poisoned him last night.

"It turned out that they had been upstairs, outdoors, sharing a smoke. Gonzalez had a taste for the weed, which I didn't know. Deslorges said they had been indulging together every now and then. Gonzalez was busy taking a good long drag, distracted, and Deslorges puffed some of his Triple Cross Powder into his face, and he was, in Deslorges's own words, gone, gone, gone. Dead in seconds. And then Deslorges gave him a shot of V.I.V.E.M.O.R.T., straight in the neck, and a couple of minutes later he was back.

"'But... how?' I asked. Alarmed as I was, I couldn't contain my curiosity, my ardour for accuracy. 'How can the formula work after death? There's no heartbeat to propel it around the bloodstream. It won't perfuse into the tissues.'

"Deslorges just smiled. '*Vodou*,' he said. 'Of course.'

"I couldn't believe what I was hearing. At the same time, I couldn't deny the evidence of my own eyes. What else would explain the bizarre, unliving condition Gonzalez was in? Not only that, I *wanted* to believe it. The scientist in me wanted to believe that I had helped create a biochemical substance so potent, so fit for purpose, it could actually raise the dead.

"'And now,' said Delsorges, 'you and me, *mon ami*, we're going to do the same to many more people. Everyone in this installation, in fact. Starting with those fellows in the lab.'"

"AND YOU DID?" Buckler prompted.

Seidelmann gave a nod that spoke of a despair so abject, it hurt to recall it. "I did. What choice was there? I had a gun to my head, literally. I—I went along with everything Deslorges told me to."

"You could have resisted," said Tartaglione. "Or maybe run away."

"And go where?" Seidelmann snapped back. "How far do you think I would have got? I'm a scientist, a civilian. I don't fight. I don't *resist*. I'm as keen to live as the next man. So don't give me any of your hairy-chested, damn-the-torpedoes bullshit. It won't wash."

"Deslorges killed everyone in the lab?" said Buckler. "Was that how it went down?"

"Not all of them himself. Gonzalez killed some too, at his master's behest. The assistants first. It was awful. Them running around, screaming. Gonzalez picking them off, shot after shot, emotionlessly, unerringly. Then Deslorges dealt with the sedated volunteers. That powder of his."

"Triple Cross," said Albertine coldly. "A lethal *poudre*. Brewed at midnight with the foulest of ingredients, and infused with the power of Baron Samedi."

"They choked, writhed, strained at their restraints, perished," said Seidelmann. "And then Deslorges started resurrecting them, one by one, with shots of V.I.V.E.M.O.R.T. Chanting over them as they re-emerged from the sleep of death. Wafting incense sticks up and down their bodies. Telling them he was their master now, his the only voice they could hear, his the will they must obey. He, Papa Couleuvre, was their new father.

"I was beyond terror by this point. I was in a place inside myself that felt like the eye of a hurricane. What Deslorges was doing was impossible—unnatural in every sense. And somehow I was responsible for it too. My formula. My work. My science. Deslorges had perverted it but had also unlocked its true potential.

"Only then did something occur to me. I had thought I was the one leading the way, making all the decisions, the senior partner in our working relationship. But what if I'd got that wrong? Perhaps, after all, I hadn't been exploiting Deslorges for what I could get from him. He had been exploiting *me*. Science and the occult had met and wrestled, and the occult, through chicanery and sleight of hand, had come out on top.

"I can't say this revelation made me feel any better about my plight. But it did at least exonerate me from blame. I had done nothing wrong other than not be quite sufficiently vigilant. Deslorges had tricked me. Blindsided me. Played me for a fool.

"How he crowed as those zuvembies came to life in the lab. He even had the nerve to congratulate me. 'Normally a zuvembie takes days to raise,' he said. 'Days of work, and concentration, and devotion, and ritual. Now we can do it in minutes, with no effort at all. *Monsieur le professeur*, you are a genius, and so am I. This is magic and technology blended together in perfect harmony. The next level. *Vodou* two-point-oh!'

"He put me to work, under guard by Gonzalez, mixing up a fresh batch of the formula. He warned me to do it properly. The consequences, if I tried to palm him off with a faulty or inactive product, would be dire. Then he sent his zuvembies out into the installation with orders to kill anyone they saw. He stipulated that they should keep the fatal injuries as non-violent as possible. 'Strangle,' he said. 'Suffocate. Try not to break bones or maim.'"

"He wanted the bodies intact," said Buckler. "Fully functioning."

"What good is a slave whose arm doesn't work or who's lame in one leg?" said Seidelmann. "Soon the zuvembies were hauling freshly killed corpses back to the lab, and Deslorges was reanimating them, and I was supplying him with the wherewithal to do so, and the whole thing was like some fever dream, a delirium I couldn't wake up from, a horror movie I couldn't walk out of."

The professor shivered.

"I fully anticipated that I would be next, after Deslorges was done with everyone else. I would be the last to be slaughtered and artificially augmented, having served my purpose and become extraneous. But once Deslorges had completed his grisly programme of extermination and revivification—he even checked the register to make sure everyone on site had been accounted for—he seemed to forget about me. He was so thrilled with his new zuvembie army that nothing else mattered. Spying an opportunity, I escaped. I slipped through the throng of ambulatory cadavers and hurried up two floors to here, the communications hub, hoping to get an alert out to our Washington contacts. Alas, Deslorges was one step ahead. The place had been trashed, as you see."

"And nobody owns a cellphone here?" said Buckler. "A satphone, even?"

"Not allowed. We've been operating under conditions of the strictest secrecy, which extends to a complete clampdown on personal communications. Internet access is permitted but no email or social networking sites. Those are all blocked externally by a system of firewalls, with no way round. Given that and the destruction of the satellite uplink, I couldn't see what else to do but hide in the supply closet and hope—hope that help would arrive, that some sort of automatic response protocol would be triggered."

"It did. Marines were airdropped in."

"Ah yes. I dimly heard gunfire while I was in my dark little sanctuary. That was how long ago?"

"Three days."

"And now you've come. This magnificent seven. To follow in their footsteps and doubtless fail as they did."

Buckler batted aside the jibe. "During all this time you've been squirreled away, Deslorges—Couleuvre—never came looking for you? He just left you as a loose end? Seems kind of odd."

"I've wondered about that myself. I can only assume he didn't care enough to bother. What kind of threat would I be to him, after all? Or perhaps, in some strange way, he feels I've earned the right to live. Whatever dark fantasy this is that he's playing out, I was instrumental in helping him realise it. He's thanking me by letting me carry on breathing. A professional courtesy, you could call it."

Seidelmann lapsed into silence. Talking so much, after nearly a week of enforced muteness, had tired him out. He scratched the scrubby beard covering his chin and contemplated the high-tech rubble all around, as though seeing in it a reflection of the state of his own achievements and aspirations.

"Well," said Buckler, "that fills in most of the blanks. What we still don't know is what the fuck Couleuvre is up to. What's he want all those zuvembies for?"

"Company?" Tartaglione offered. "Maybe he hasn't got enough Twitter followers."

"Albertine? You have any suggestions? Better than Tartag's, please. Not that that would be difficult."

"None," Albertine said. "Bokors tend to seek power— personal advantage. Couleuvre, as far as I can tell, is no exception. But how he can find it stuck here on this tiny island, in this dungeon of a place, beats me."

"Professor Seidelmann," said Lex, "you told us Couleuvre did searches on your computer. About Anger Reef."

"Yes."

"Any idea what he found?"

Seidelmann shook his head. "He didn't mention anything."

"Why don't we have a look ourselves? It might provide a clue."

Buckler shot Lex a sidelong glance. The SEAL commander clearly resented him taking the initiative, the more so because Lex's proposal was a good one.

"I was thinking the same thing," he said, grudgingly. "Where's your workstation, prof?"

"My office. One floor down."

"Then let's ship out. Dove? You're our go-to guy for babysitting civilians. The prof's yours. Keep him chipper and don't let him out of your sight."

TWENTY-EIGHT
FAILSAFE

Seidelmann was not keen on the idea of going anywhere but up and out of the installation.

"Isn't this a rescue?" he bleated to Lex as the group filed towards the staircase. "How can dragging me further into the lion's den be in any way construed as rescuing?"

"Take it up with Lieutenant Buckler," Lex replied. "I'm just the hired help."

"I have no intention of dying today—not after all I've been through."

"Good for you. Neither do I."

"This is madness."

"And whingeing about it makes it so much more bearable."

Seidelmann could see he was going to get no sympathy from the Englishman, so gave up trying.

Sampson nudged open the door marked STAIRS and peered down. "No bogeys, far as I can tell," he said, "but visibility's for shit. Too damn many shadows."

"Proceed with caution," Buckler advised.

"Yeah. I was going to do that."

They descended at a snail's pace, into gloom. The concrete steps bore dark brown smears and streaks, and Lex pictured Papa Couleuvre's zuvembie minions heaving bloody, freshly killed corpses down the stairs, leaving gory stains behind. There was no sound except the whisper of their own footfalls and the rustle of clothing.

Sublevel 2 was much the same as the floor above, although the lighting seemed marginally dimmer, as if to remind them they were that bit deeper down, that bit further from the sun. The air felt chillier, too, and clammier.

Sampson and Tartaglione peeled off left and right to check the junctions at either end of the passage. They pronounced the coast clear in both directions.

"You do the honours, prof," Buckler said, and Seidelmann, with a show of great reluctance, led the way to his office.

It was a small room furnished with a simple metal desk and an uncomfortable-looking typist's chair on castors. Seidelmann had personalised it by hanging up the framed diplomas Lex had seen on the video clip, along with the photo of him shaking hands with the former president. These decorations were incongruous in such a sparse, modest space, like a duchess's jewels loaned to a pauper. They added nothing but the impression that Seidelmann was an insecure man who needed constant validation of his own status.

Seidelmann booted up the desktop PC, typed in his password, and called up the internet browser history. He scrolled through, looking for sites Papa Couleuvre had visited. Everyone clustered round him, Buckler and Lex at either shoulder.

"Here we are," Seidelmann said. "Searches on early Cold War history, US military construction projects around that time, the Cuban situation, geography of the Caribbean, Anger Reef itself... The dates of the searches tally with when Deslorges started getting curious about this place. I had no idea how extensively he pursued the topic. There are reams and reams of pages listed. It would take hours to go through them all."

"Narrow it down to sites he visited more than once," Lex said. "If he hit on something particularly juicy, chances are he'd have gone back for a second look."

Seidelmann squinted at the screen. "That's logical. It'd likely be towards the end of his online sessions as well. If he was after a specific item of information, once he'd found it there'd be no need to go on."

After a few more mouse clicks, he said, "Here's a potential candidate. Visited three times in two days, less than a fortnight ago. I'll just pull it up." He examined the result. "Oh dear. Doesn't look very authoritative, does it?"

The screen showed an amateurishly designed website. The layout was clumsy. Yellow text blared against a black background, the font too large as though someone was shouting rather than talking.

"Some kind of conspiracy theory forum, it looks like," said Seidelmann. "See the list of subject headings? CIA Mind Control Projects. Reverse-Engineered Alien Spacecraft Technology. Sedatives In The Water Supply. The Illuminati Killed JFK. God knows what Deslorges dug up from here, but doubtless it wasn't good. Or accurate."

"Do a keyword search for Anger Reef," said Buckler.

Seidelmann tried. "Nothing."

"Worth a shot. How about listening post? Radar monitoring? Underground installation?"

"Nothing, nothing and nothing. Just by speed-reading, I can tell this is a site run by oddballs for oddballs. It's all outlandish claims backed up by not a scintilla of credible evidence. And the grammar and spelling are atrocious. Here's someone who's managed to get Hitler's name wrong. Two 't's. And the abortion he's made of 'Führer'... That's the level of intellect on display. The internet, one of the greatest cultural and scientific achievements of all time, and it's become the haunt of illiterates and hopelessly gullible—A-ha."

"What?" said Buckler.

"Well, that's why we didn't find it using keywords. Installation has more than one 'l', you idiot." He was talking to the screen. "This is a comment posted on a thread about military bases, secret ones and not so secret ones. Someone's saying that all major underground US military installations carry a failsafe in case they're overrun by enemy forces. The person claims he used to work in the command centre at NORAD, monitoring the attack detection systems for incoming intercontinental ballistic missiles and, in the wake of nine-eleven, for rogue commercial aircraft as well. He says, and I quote, 'If the Russkies or whoever stormed Cheyenne Mountain, no way were they gonna be allowed to keep it to themselves.'" Seidelmann's lip curled over the word *gonna*. "'There's a purge protocol in place that'd leave them with nothing but a smoking ruin and a handful of ashes, if activated.' Someone else then asks him to elaborate. 'You mean like a ton of napalm or something?' And our friend replies, 'Like that only bigger and a lot more radioactive.'"

"The next poster calls bullshit on that," Buckler said. "Whole thing degenerates into a slanging match."

"Yes," said Seidelmann with mild amusement. "Squabbling, name-calling—all terribly productive. There ought to be some kind of minimum educational requirement before an individual is allowed to post anything online. A university degree at least."

"Smart doesn't always equal wise," said Tartaglione.

"Yeah," said Sampson. "I've heard of professors who've done really dumbass things. Like let their science projects get hijacked by psycho voodoo priests."

Seidelmann huffed. "Point taken. I just hate to see wilful ignorance paraded so openly."

"Radioactive," said Pearce. He was suggesting that everyone seemed to be overlooking this salient word.

"My thoughts exactly," said Buckler. "The guy is implying that NORAD has some sort of last-ditch nuclear failsafe built in. It blows itself up from the inside if there's a fatal security compromise."

"Is that true?" Lex asked.

"It's way above my pay grade to know the answer to that. It's possible, I guess. Main thing is, Deslorges read it and it must've struck a chord. He figures if NORAD has a nuclear device hidden somewhere inside, mightn't Anger Reef too?"

"But Anger Reef doesn't," said Seidelmann. "I'd know if it did. I'd have been told, surely."

"Would you, prof? The place spent ages out of action. It's been sitting here doing nothing for a generation or more. I doubt there's many people alive who were present when it was built, and in any case only a select few would have known there was a nuclear device on the premises. It would have been installed under conditions of utmost secrecy, and it wouldn't be on any of the official blueprints. Somewhere buried in some archive there'll be a record of its existence, but I'd be surprised if anyone in the current administration even knows about it. It's an old secret, and old secrets get forgotten."

"You're saying you think this bomb thing might be true, chief?" said Morgenstern.

"It's just conceivable." Beneath his moustache, Buckler's mouth was set in a grim line. "Anger Reef was, in its day, a highly sensitive site. It was slap bang in the middle of a Cold War flashpoint zone. They were paranoid times. Nobody'd want somewhere like this to fall into enemy hands if it could possibly be avoided. If that looked like happening, simplest course of action would be nuke the place, give the Soviets a pile of glowing rubble to sift through."

"Be that as it may," said Seidelmann, "even supposing there *was* a bomb once, it wouldn't still be here. It would have been dismantled and removed as part of the decommissioning process."

"Couleuvre seems to believe otherwise."

"And he's such a reliable source."

"You worked with him, prof. You had a high opinion of him, 'til he turned you over and fucked you in the ass. You think he's the type to go chasing after something that doesn't exist?"

Seidelmann blustered but didn't have an adequate answer.

"But what does he want with a nuke?" Morgenstern asked.

"What does anyone?" said Lex. "Terrorism. Blackmail. Something to sell on the black market. Delete where applicable."

"Power," said Albertine.

"Yes, that pretty much sums it up: power. With a nuke, Couleuvre's no longer just any old bokor. He's the biggest, baddest bokor of all time."

"The sorcerer supreme," said Sampson.

"He would have death in his hands, too," said Albertine. "The ability to kill on a widespread scale. That would curry great favour with Baron Samedi. He could offer the Baron thousands and thousands of souls. The ultimate act of worship, a mass sacrifice."

Everyone exchanged looks. The temperature in the room, already low, seemed to drop a few degrees more.

"He really has to be stopped," Lex said. "Now, before it can go any further."

"You heard the man, Thirteeners," said Buckler. "Lock and load. Mission just hit critical. There's a madman with his eye on a thermonuclear prize. Let's go ruin his day."

TWENTY-NINE
COLD WAR LEGACY NIGHTMARE

Professor Siedelmann had described seeing Papa Couleuvre searching for something on Sublevel 3. It stood to reason that the nuclear device, if there was one, would be located there. The purpose of any bomb would be to obliterate Anger Reef entirely, and that could be best achieved by detonating it at the deepest point available. The force of the explosion would be channelled upwards through the installation, undermining even as it was cremated. A sun-hot fireball would erupt below ground but little if any of the blast would escape to the surface. The entire island would collapse neatly in on itself, sinking beneath the waves. Anger Reef would vanish in an instant, as if it had never been, like a poor man's Atlantis.

The more Lex considered it, the more plausible the presence of a bomb on site seemed. It was a scorched earth policy typical of the Cold War era, when both power blocs on either side of the Iron Curtain were desperate not to give their opponent an inch. Should the Russians have rumbled the presence of a listening post on Anger Reef, and perhaps made an aggressive move against it, the Americans were in a position to dispose of it literally at the touch of a button. All personnel would evacuated, and then ka-boom. *Ha ha, Ivan. Installation? What installation?* Gone would be all that high-tech radar and sonar equipment, far more sophisticated than anything the Russians possessed and therefore of great interest to their scientists and engineers. Gone without a trace. Every last scrap of evidence flushed away. A Pyrrhic victory maybe, but a victory nonetheless. In Cold War logic a loss could still be counted as a win, so long as it meant the other superpower did not win either.

It had been an insane age, geopolitically. Was the world any saner now? Not much, Lex thought. Nor much safer.

And if Couleuvre was on the money and Anger Reef did come fitted with a nuclear failsafe, the levels of global danger were in no way going to be diminished. This was yet another of those Cold War legacy nightmares, like the nukes that disappeared on a regular basis from airbases and naval yards belonging to the former Soviet Union and wound up in the hands of very insalubrious regimes and organisations. Lex had personal experience on that front, having once gatecrashed just such a transaction in a mountain pass in the higher reaches of the Hindu Kush, on the Afghanistan-Pakistan border. A renegade Ukrainian colonel had been attempting to sell a single eighteen-megaton warhead from an R-36 missile to a jihadist group. Before the briefcase containing five million dollars in bearer bonds could change hands, however, a rocket-propelled grenade landed in the middle of the gathering and put paid to their dreams, whether ideological or financial. Clean shots from an L115A3 sniper rifle picked off the injured and dying, after which Lex called in a covert US Explosive Ordnance Disposal Team to retrieve the warhead, render it safe and whisk it off to the Pantex facility in Amarillo, Texas, for disassembly. He wouldn't forget in a hurry the looks on the faces of all the participants, seen through the reticle crosshairs of the RPG launcher: the sheer avarice in everyone's eyes, while a weapon of mass destruction lay snug in the back of a nearby Land Cruiser, poised to become an atrocity.

That had been a job he would have done for free, if asked. And he was beginning to feel the same way about the present mission. All at once, there was more at stake than the threat posed by a regiment of zuvembies. Far more. Papa Couleuvre had morphed from bogeyman to potential mass-murdering monster, and Lex had dealt with enough of those to know that they deserved no mercy, no quarter, nothing but the same primal revulsion and loathing you felt for a hornet or a scorpion. They needed to be swatted, stamped on, crushed, before they could do more harm.

The door to the staircase beckoned. Tartaglione, at the head of the group, was just a few metres from it.

Then Lex heard shuffling. The sound of feet clumsily dragging. From behind him.

He turned. They all turned.

Zuvembies.

A good dozen of them.

They were marching down the passage, three abreast. Their pale dull eyes were fixed on the group of living beings. Interlopers, as they saw them. The enemy. They moved with deadly purpose, stiff-jointed but determined, their menace unmistakable.

The merest moment of panic. An involuntary pause for shock, for taking stock.

Then Buckler cried, "Hostiles! Move! Move!"

Lex, Albertine, Seidelmann and the Thirteeners scrambled away from the oncoming zuvembies, making for the door.

Which opened.

To reveal more zuvembies.

THIRTY

TRIPLE-PRONGED ASSAULT

IT WAS ALMOST, but not quite, a pincer movement. Had the staircase zuvembies emerged a couple of seconds sooner, they and their passage counterparts would have successfully trapped their quarry between them. Lex and company would have been bookended by the two contingents, boxed in with no room for manoeuvre, and would have been besieged on two fronts at once.

As it was, Tartaglione had drawn level with the door when it opened, and his reactions were quick. He shot the frontmost zuvembie in the chest with his CAR-15. The zuvembie staggered backwards under the impact, colliding with another zuvembie behind. Without hesitating, Tartaglione grabbed the door and slammed it shut. He grasped the handle and held it level, at the same time shouting, "Go! Go! Go!"

Everyone else hurried past while Tartaglione kept a tight grip on the handle. The zuvembie on the other side was pushing down on it. The undead creature was visible through the window slit inset into the door, straining and thrusting, teeth bared. Blood oozed from a neat hole in its sternum.

"Fucker's strong!" Tartaglione said, grimacing with effort.

It was all he could do to keep the handle horizontal. "Can't hold it... much..."

Then a fist smashed through the safety glass. The hand, belonging to another zuvembie, grabbed Tartaglione's collar. It yanked him towards the door. His head jammed into the broken window slit.

Sampson ran to his side and began pulling his free arm. Tartaglione, yelling, frantic, was the rope in a bizarre tug of war.

Meanwhile the first set of zuvembies was closing in.

Morgenstern shouldered her carbine and started firing at them. Hunks of flesh flew away, but the zuvembies didn't falter. They lumbered on, remorseless. One of Morgenstern's bullets severed a spinal column. The zuvembie collapsed on the spot, but its comrades just booted it aside and carried on. The semi-paralysed zuvembie didn't give up either but clawed its way along the floor, useless legs trailing.

Sampson and Tartaglione were both doing their utmost to resist the zuvembie's grip on Tartaglione's collar, but even their combined strength was no match for its unholy might. They were losing the battle. Tartaglione was being dragged head-first through the window, even as he still struggled to keep the door shut.

"Give me a second," Sampson said. "I'm letting go."

"You're what now?" Tartaglione exclaimed. "Don't you do that. Don't you fucking dare."

"Chill. I've got a plan."

"It better be a fucking good one."

Sampson unhitched the KA-BAR knife from his belt and brandished it point down. "Get your stinking paws off my buddy, asshole," he roared, and plunged the blade into the zuvembie's wrist. Sawing and levering, he swiftly separated hand from arm. Blood glugged from the stump in sticky rivulets. Tartaglione sprang free, the zuvembie's fist still clamped to his clothing. His head was bleeding freely from gashes inflicted by the broken window glass.

"Fall back!" Buckler yelled to both men, and Tartaglione and Sampson reeled away from the door just as the first set of zuvembies reached them. They bundled down the passage, ducking under the suppressing fire that Morgenstern was continuing to lay down. Tartaglione was dazed and bleeding. Sampson was supporting him, half-carrying him.

"But those are people," Albertine protested as they ran. "We shouldn't be shooting them."

"*Were* people," Buckler corrected her. "They're dead. They just don't act like it. And as long as they're going balls-out to kill us, yes, we should be shooting at them."

Pearce, ahead, skidded to a halt. "Motherfucking..."

Yet more zuvembies had come into view. They tramped along the passage, an assortment of civilians, some in casual dress, a couple in lab coats, one in a chef's uniform, another in a janitor's coveralls. The chef was carrying a meat cleaver, the janitor a broken-off broom handle with a sheared, splintered tip. Their mouths hung slack but their eyes had the same yellow cast and the same bleak fixity as those of the zuvembies at the other end of the passage.

The pincer movement had just graduated to a triple-pronged assault.

"Fire at will," Buckler ordered, and he and Pearce opened up. Buckler's M-60 clattered. Pearce's MP-5 barked. Lex joined in with his SIG. Morgenstern was still blasting away in the opposite direction with her CAR-15, a one-woman rearguard action. Albertine, Seidelmann, Sampson and Tartaglione were sandwiched in between.

The air was torn by the cacophony of gunfire. Bullets pounded into the zuvembies in torrents, but had pitifully little effect. They weren't stopping them. They were barely even slowing them. The zuvembies slogged onward, relentlessly narrowing the gap at either end. Some of them were whittled away to rags and ribbons, but whatever unnatural force animated them refused to let them lie down. It propelled them stubbornly on. A shattered leg? The zuvembie would hop. Both legs ruined? Crawl. Even when rendered headless, the creatures were undeterred. A cockroach would have envied their imperviousness to damage.

As Buckler paused to reload, Sampson stepped up to take his place.

"I'm thinking grenade," he said.

"And I'm thinking that's a no-go," said Buckler. "At this range? Passage would channel the blast as blowback. Every chance we'd frag ourselves too."

"Then what's the plan, boss?"

"The plan is we keep firing 'til there's either none of them left or none of us."

"Guess that'll have to do."

The group was bunched tight, shoulder to shoulder, back to back, and now the zuvembies were just a few paces away, a mere metre or so. The nearest ones sprang, hurling their bullet-ripped bodies at the living humans.

Pearce found himself grappling with the chef, fending off blows from the meat cleaver. In life, the chef had been a corpulent man. Much of his blubber had been flayed off by the volleys of bullets, but he still wobbled massively as he swung the cleaver at Pearce. His flabby arm worked like a piston, descending again and again. Pearce blocked with one arm, all the while pumping rounds from his machine pistol into the zuvembie's belly. Viscera slithered out, but the chef neither noticed nor cared. He hacked mechanically, methodically, bit by bit wearing Pearce down, hammering away at his defences.

Finally he got through. The cleaver bit into Pearce's shoulder, and the laconic Thirteener let out a jagged cry of pain.

The chef withdrew the cleaver and pulled back his arm to deliver a fresh blow.

Incensed, as if he couldn't believe what the chef had just done, Pearce launched himself at him. He grabbed the cleaver and wrested it out of the zuvembie's grasp. Then he returned the favour by whacking the chef with the cleaver seven or eight times, sinking the blade deep into the zuvembie's ample flesh. He would have carried on until the chef was just so much chopped mince, had the janitor not attacked too. Suddenly Pearce was looking down at his own stomach and at the snapped-off broom handle that had been thrust into him to a depth of several inches.

"Sneaky," he mumbled, then fell.

At the other side of the group, Morgenstern was swamped by zuvembies. They were too close for the carbine to be of practical use any more, so she resorted to her handgun. She shot the zuvembies in the centre of their body mass, as she'd been trained, but more in hope than expectation of a positive result. The semiauto's clip was rapidly expended, and then the zuvembies were all over her, clawing, clutching, hauling her down.

Sampson leapt to her assistance. He wrenched zuvembies off her, to the accompaniment of some highly creative swearing. But with each zuvembie he sent flying, another rose to take its place. They swarmed in, their numbers overwhelming. Soon Sampson was as beleaguered as Morgenstern was. Lex watched him struggling valiantly to stay upright, sinking beneath a tide of ravaged limbs, contorted hands and silently impassive faces.

"Lex, oh God, it's hopeless," said Albertine.

"There must be something we can do. Your *vodou.* Can you use it on these things?"

"Yes, if there weren't so many of them, if I had the time..."

Time, Lex had to admit, was the one thing they did not have. "Then we'll just have to make do with guns," he said.

Pearce, Sampson and Morgenstern seemed lost, as good as dead. Only Lex, Buckler, Albertine, Seidelmann and Tartaglione remained standing, and Tartaglione was in bad shape. Half his face was masked with blood, and he was weakened and on the brink of lapsing into shock. That he was still with the group at all was thanks to Sampson. As for Seidelmann, he was cowering behind Buckler, wringing his hands. "I knew it," he intoned. "I knew we should never have come down here. It was madness. I said so. I *said*."

"Prof," snarled Buckler, "if you don't shut the fuck up, so help me I'll kill you myself."

"Go ahead. Do it. Put me out of my misery. At least it'll be quick."

"Don't tempt me. If I didn't need every last round of ammo..."

A zuvembie broke past Buckler and made a lunge for Lex. Lex whipped his SIG up, lodged the barrel against the creature's mouth, and gave it some radical root canal surgery.

The slide on the gun locked back. Clip empty. And the zuvembie, jaw hanging by just a few shreds of skin and tendon, clamped both hands onto Lex's head and began twisting. Lex felt the unearthly power radiating through the thing's cold, dank skin. Its touch was repugnant. The zuvembie was attempting to break his neck. He could hear—feel—his own vertebrae creaking. He fought back, jabbing a thumb into the creature's eyeball; smashing its nose; tearing its ear. But those were standard defensive moves, effective against men, not monsters. They meant nothing to a zuvembie.

Eventually, in desperation, he kicked its legs out from under it. The zuvembie crashed to the floor, taking him down too. Lex contrived to land on top. The hands remained fastened in place. The zuvembie wrenched clockwise and anticlockwise. It was doing its best to decapitate him, twist his head off like a champagne cork. He tried prising its fingers away, but its grip was vicelike, unshakeable.

The blood roared in his ears. His vision blurred.

His hands found the zuvembie's dangling jaw. He dug below, into the slippery mass of exposed meat that had been its buccal cavity. A tongue slithered over his probing fingers. He sank his nails into raw flesh and started scrabbling, burrowing, rending. He delved between muscles. He tore through sinews. He felt the elastic resistance of veins and snapped them. He was pulling the creature apart from the neck downwards, dissecting it with his bare hands. He was rummaging in the engine of its anatomy, in the hope that if he destroyed enough working parts he could shut the whole machine down.

It was a race to see which of them, Lex or the zuvembie, could annihilate the other first.

Now Lex had penetrated through to somewhere inside the zuvembie's shoulders, behind the collarbone, and all at once he felt its hands slacken their hold a little. He must have hit some crucial seam of connective tissue. He redoubled his efforts, pulling pieces of the zuvembie up, out, sideways, filleting madly. Finally it let go. One of its arms slumped limply to the floor; then the other.

Lex recoiled, leaping away from the creature, away from the ragged mess he had made of its upper torso. He shook his hands wildly to rid them of the blood and the wet clots of flesh that clung to them. He experienced a revulsion— of himself, of the butchery he had performed—that was so visceral he nearly vomited. He wanted to scream. He had committed appalling deeds in his time, he was no innocent when it came to acts of slaughter, but this—this was a whole new level of horror.

The sound of someone shouting his name broke his trance of disgust.

Albertine.

A zuvembie had her in its clutches. The creature was snapping its teeth at her neck, hell-bent on chewing out her throat. She was managing to ward it off but her forearms were already bleeding from several bite wounds.

Lex lunged at the zuvembie, dimly registering that it was female, a lab technician, no doubt one of Seidelmann's assistants. His fingers slotted into the corners of her mouth and he yanked backwards as though pulling on the reins of a horse. He and the zuvembie staggered together, away from Albertine, until his shoulders struck a wall.

Out of the corner of his eye he spied a fire extinguisher, mounted on a bracket. He snatched it free and clubbed the zuvembie with it. The zuvembie went down after several heavy blows, and Lex continued to slam the fire extinguisher onto her, breaking bone after bone. Arms, spine, pelvis, legs— none of her skeleton was spared. Lex shattered the creature internally, section by section. Her efforts to resist, to retaliate, grew progressively feebler and more spastic. Whenever she tried to rise, her limbs bent rubberily and would not support her. Soon all she could do was flop about and writhe uselessly like a landed eel.

Lex straightened, heaving for breath. Another zuvembie incapacitated. He searched round for the next target.

He saw Buckler overrun but bellowing defiance...

Albertine pinned between two zuvembies...

Seidelmann curled into a ball, head buried in hands, sobbing...

He knew then that it was a lost cause. There were too many of the enemy and they were too strong. The battle was almost over, the outcome decided.

A voice rang out.

"*Ça suffit.*"

It echoed down the passage, deep and clear.

As though a switch had been thrown, the zuvembies froze.

"We have made our point. They have been shown who's boss."

The zuvembies had become like statues. They held their poses, utterly motionless.

Threading through the tableau of the undead came a thickset man dressed in Nike high-tops, baggy tracksuit bottoms, and a weightlifter's singlet that showed off a stocky, well-muscled torso and liberally tattooed arms. He strode like a king, assured of his domain and his authority. His hair was styled in a curly, bleached Mohawk.

Papa Couleuvre.

THIRTY-ONE
THE ERROR OF HIS WAYS

IF LEX'S SIG had been loaded, he would have planted a round in Couleuvre's skull then and there. In the event, all he had was the fire extinguisher. He charged at the bokor, brandishing the heavy red cylinder.

With a hand that was gauntleted in gold and silver rings, Couleuvre made a casual gesture. He had arrived with an escort of two zuvembies, both of them in US Marine battledress. At his unspoken command the zuvembies moved in front of him, forming a barricade. Lex pounded one in the chest with the fire extinguisher, to little effect. The other caught him in a bear hug and felled him. The extinguisher flew from his grasp. His arms were wrenched behind him. A knee ground between his shoulderblades. He was pinned down, face crushed to the linoleum.

"Ah-ah-ah!" Couleuvre bent over him, wagging a finger. "Naughty boy. You do not get to do that. That is not how this is going to go."

He issued an instruction to the other zuvembies. In no time, the Thirteeners, Albertine and Professor Seidelmann were up on their feet, all held fast by the creatures. Tartaglione and Pearce were both being supported rather than standing. The former was semiconscious. The latter was bent double over the broom handle that impaled him, breathing hard against the pain.

"Better," said Couleuvre. His accent was a blend of lyrical French and syrupy Caribbean, each word delivered with a wry languidness. He struck Lex as supremely self-assured, a man who knew exactly what he was and didn't give a shit what anyone else thought. "So what do we have here? Some more American troops, come to see what became of the lost patrol. And dear old Professor Seidelmann. How have you been keeping, *mon ami*? I knew you were hiding somewhere. If you had had any sense, you would have built yourself a raft and got off the island. At the very least you might have lit a fire on the beach, hoping to attract some passing ship. But then you are not that resourceful, eh? You know I could have found you any time, had I looked. But the truth is, I could not be bothered. You were no threat to me."

"Deslorges," said Seidelmann. "François. Please. Listen. I brought these people down here. It was a trick. I knew full well we'd run into some of your zuvembies and most likely you too. I laid a trap, and they fell for it."

"Backstabbing weasel-ass piece of shit," Buckler hissed.

"I'm giving them to you as a peace offering," Seidelmann continued, disregarding him. "They're yours, and all I ask in return is that you let me go. You don't have any argument with me. I just want to leave this place alive. Come on, we're colleagues, aren't we? I've treated you with respect. I gave you everything you needed to execute this... *coup* of yours. Fair's fair, eh? Do me this favour, in return for the many favours I've done you."

Lex couldn't decide whether Seidelmann had genuinely played them for fools or he was desperately, cravenly concocting a story in order to save his own skin. Either way, the sheer shamelessness of it was breathtaking.

"As I recall, Gulliver," said Couleuvre, "you never acted like I was your equal. To you I was just some dumb Third Worlder with some handy bits of knowledge you could use. Now I'm the one calling the shots. The shoe is on the other foot. How does that feel? Not so nice, I imagine."

"François, I'm begging you..."

Couleuvre cut him off with a slash of the hand. "I will deal with you later. Hmm, now what is this?" He had turned his attention to Albertine. "I am liking what I see. I am liking it very much."

Albertine said nothing, just met his scrutiny with a hostile, imperious glare.

"But wait. There is the smell of mambo on you." Couleuvre put his face close to hers and took a lengthy, theatrical sniff. "Oh yeah, *ma cherie*. You reek of the *sevis loa* and the Rada *nachon*, the slow, cool spirits. Nice and safe, that is how you like it. Who are your husbands? Damballah maybe? Yeah, I think so." He snorted in derision. "A loa who cannot even stand the sight of blood. You have to take the sacrificial animals to another room before cutting them up. Cannot do it in front of him. How pathetic is that? A snake loa, but a snake without venom or fangs. You would be better off being married to a mouse!"

He chortled long and hard at his joke. Albertine simply said, "Compassion and wisdom are not weaknesses. Mock Papa Damballah at your peril."

Couleuvre found this amusing too. "I mock who I want, when I want. There is nothing I fear. I have power like you wouldn't believe. And *you*." He swung round, bringing himself back to Lex. "Pick him up," he said to the two zuvembie Marines.

They dragged Lex upright.

"Who *are* you?" Couleuvre sounded quizzical, intrigued. "I sense the Baron all over you. These soldiers from America, they have killed, of course, but not as much as you have and not in the way that you have. Yes, you have been the Baron's ambassador for many years. You may not realise it but it is true. You are unique in that it is all you have done—brought death to others. Death has been your living."

Lex acted nonchalant. Legba, after all, had said much the same to him that very morning.

"The Baron smiles on men like you," Couleuvre went on. "You venerate him with every trigger you pull, every knife you slide in, every bomb you detonate. Oh, I do like you."

"The feeling," Lex said, "is not mutual."

"It does not have to be. But is it not pleasing to know that someone appreciates your talents? I doubt you have ever been thanked or congratulated for your work. *Au contraire*. You are a grubby little secret, *n'est-ce pas*? Your country would never admit to knowing you, let alone giving you your orders. And what is worse is, you are so good at it. Murder. If you had not been able to do it for a living, legitimately, how would you have coped, I wonder? What would you have done with yourself? Where would you have channelled that ability to switch off your conscience and kill?"

"You don't know what you're talking about. You don't know me."

"I know *me*," said Couleuvre, "and I know the Baron, and I know that the three of us have much in common, *monsieur*. That is enough."

"Well then, since we're so alike," said Lex, "you surely won't have a problem with me telling you that I will find a way of making you next on my list of victims."

Couleuvre opened and closed his hand in the air like a yapping mouth: *big talk*. "You cannot lay a finger on me. Your fate is in my hands. Same goes for all of you. I can snuff you out, all of you, easy as a candle flame. Want proof?"

He swivelled back round to Professor Seidelmann.

"This man."

Seidelmann cringed.

"This scientist." He spat the word like a curse.

"François, please..." Sweat had popped out on Seidelmann's brow.

"Who believed I was working for him when actually he was working for me. A user who got used. A man who thought his test tubes and microscopes were somehow superior to my spells and potions."

Couleuvre pointed to one of the pair of zuvembies who were holding Seidelmann between them.

"Show *monsieur le professeur* the parts of him he never expected to see. Show him how complacent and blinkered he has been. Show him the error of his ways."

"François, I helped you. I gave you the opportunity to achieve something you'd never have been able to alone— V.I.V.E.M.O.R.T. And I paid you well, goddammit. Don't do this, I implore you. I'll—"

The zuvembie plunged a hand into Seidelmann's abdomen like a blunt sword. Seidelmann's eyes bulged. The zuvembie's arm disappeared into him, halfway to the elbow. Seidelmann's mouth gaped soundlessly. The zuvembie twisted hard and drew its arm out, clutching a fistful of glistening innards. It held them up to Seidelmann's face, obeying Couleuvre's orders to the letter. Then it dumped them on the floor and delved into the professor's belly again.

Albertine choked in horror. Buckler, Morgenstern and Sampson looked on pale-faced and aghast.

Seidelmann didn't even scream. It was as though this obscene intrusion went beyond pain. The torment overloaded his nerve endings. His mind was unable to process the magnitude of the signals it was receiving. He gazed down at himself in disbelief as the zuvembie fetched out more and more of his soft slippery vitals. The creature, which was in part his own creation, was ferreting around inside him as though he were a lucky dip, a bran tub full of prizes.

Because he did not scream, it was not clear at what point during the process Seidelmann died. It was over within a minute. There was at least that.

Throughout, Papa Couleuvre simply smiled.

And kept his eyes fixed, not on Seidelmann, but on Lex.

THIRTY-TWO
THE PERFECT WORKERS

"IMPRISON THEM," SAID Couleuvre to his zuvembies. "I can always do with more workers but I do not have time to perform the transformation ritual right now. Take all of their weapons away, put them in a room, and guard them well. I will come for them later."

The zuvembies started relieving the Thirteeners of their guns, knives and grenades. They did it brusquely, as though stripping fruit from trees. The weapons formed a sizeable heap on the floor beside the sprawled, hollowed-out remains of Professor Seidelmann.

The zuvembies then herded the SEALs and Albertine into a knot. Lex was shoved forward to join them.

"Not him," said Couleuvre. "The Baron's man interests me. I would like to have a little chitchat with him." He beckoned to Lex. "This way."

Lex threw a quick glance at Albertine: *It isn't over. Don't give up. While I'm alive, there's always something I can do.* Albertine nodded, understanding, though not believing. He noted that she still had her shoulder bag. Good. Not all of their weapons had been confiscated, then.

The zuvembie Marines frogmarched him off.

"So, you have a name, Baron's man?" Couleuvre asked as their little procession descended the stairs.

"Dove."

"A first name?"

"Not for you."

Couleuvre chuckled. "Okay, Monsieur Not For You Dove. If that is how you prefer it. There is no need to be unfriendly. I believe you and I have much more uniting us than dividing us. You just have to be shown."

"Having seen how you treat your friends," Lex said, "you'll forgive me if I keep my distance."

"Seidelmann, you mean? A fool and a failure. So arrogant, so convinced of his own greatness."

"And you're not?"

"I have reason to be arrogant," said Couleuvre matter-of-factly. "You only have to consider what I have accomplished, not just at Anger Reef but in my entire life. I was born in Cité Soleil, the largest slum in Port-au-Prince, not to mention the largest slum in the western hemisphere. My mother was a prostitute and my father a petty criminal. She succumbed to AIDS and he to the Tonton Macoutes, both when I was small. I grew up with what they call 'battery acid insides'—the perpetual gnawing hunger that comes from having never enough food to eat. I foraged and fought. I had nothing, nothing at all, except rage and a will to better myself, to become feared and powerful, able to command respect. And that I have achieved, through my determination, my inner strength, and my *engagement*— my pact of loyalty—with Baron Samedi."

"A self-made madman."

"*Peut-être*." Couleuvre sounded genial, but Lex caught a flash of malevolence in his eyes. He should, he realised, be careful not to goad the bokor too far. Not if he wished to survive this encounter. "Within my community, I am regarded as a force for good. People come to me when the authorities fail them—and the authorities always fail them. They know I can get things done. If you are being hassled by some thug, if your daughter has been raped or your son shot, if thieves have broken into your home and stolen everything, who do you turn to? Not the police. Not the courts. They are worse than useless. The police are in the gangsters' pockets. They are fat, lazy and corrupt. And the courts serve no one, except maybe the lawyers and their wallets and their egos. All over Haiti it is the same. Only someone like me can right wrongs. Only someone with real power like me can get you the justice you crave."

"And in return you take people's money."

"Of course. Of course. Who works for free? Certainly not you, Monsieur Dove. It is no disgrace that I get paid for my services. It does not diminish what I do. The loa themselves demand tribute—gifts, food, trinkets. Why should not I? It is the same when I heal the sick. Believe me, I charge less than some doctors, and I am more likely to get results. If you have talked to Professor Seidelmann, you probably have an image of me as a wicked creature, a hyena in human form. This is far from the truth."

"What are you, then?" Lex asked.

"A dreamer. A schemer. An idealist. A man who intends to hold to account those who should be held to account."

"Meaning...?"

They had reached Sublevel 3, identical to the two sublevels above but dingier and noisier. Sounds of thumping and crunching reverberated along the passage from far away, and the air was tinged with a fine, powdery dust that tasted and smelled like concrete.

"Meaning I am prepared to confront and challenge someone whose acts of violence have blighted the world," said Couleuvre.

"I hate to break it to you, but Osama bin Laden's dead."

"I am not talking about any mere terrorist. Not someone who has snuffed out a few hundred lives here, a few hundred there. No, my target is the greatest source of injustice there has ever been."

Jigsaw pieces started to slot into place in Lex's mind. A vague outline of an idea was taking shape. He could almost grasp what Couleuvre was getting at, and it seemed as absurd as it was appalling.

They passed doors marked LAB 1 and LAB 2. No doubt it had been in one of those rooms that Seidelmann had brewed up his V.I.V.E.M.O.R.T. and Couleuvre had hijacked the formula for his own esoteric purposes. The taste and smell of concrete was growing stronger, the pall of dust thicker.

"I heard him calling out to me," said Couleuvre, almost dreamily. "Every time I was down on this level, the voice came to me, louder, clearer. It was not simply in my mind. It was an actual sound, in my ears. As real as anything. How could I not listen? How could I ignore it?"

And now they rounded a corner, and before Lex's eyes there appeared a scene that was both industrious and hellish.

Zuvembies, dozens of them, moved to and fro. Some were carrying armfuls of rubble—chunks of concrete ranging from pebble-sized to football-sized—which they transported into rooms on either side of the passage, emerging moments later unburdened. Others were ascending from a huge hole at the end of the passage, a cavelike entrance that had been hewn out of the floor and one wall. They came up with more of the rubble, which they passed to their comrades before turning and descending back into the pit. It was a zuvembie chain gang, a machine of the living dead, labouring repetitively and monotonously. Clothes hung off emaciated frames in tatters. Hands were bloodied and raw from hefting all that debris. In the hazy half-light Lex saw faces that seemed utterly resigned, as though the zuvembies knew they would have to keep at these tasks until their bodies broke down or doomsday arrived, which happened sooner.

From the pit itself rose a remorseless pounding and clanking. Couleuvre motioned to the zuvembie Marines to release Lex. He invited him to go closer to the pit and inspect. "No need to be cautious," he said. "None of them will bother you. They have a task, and that is all they are focused on."

Lex peered over the lip of a tunnel that went down at a shallow incline, over thirty feet deep. Yet more zuvembies were crammed together at its base, toiling away with hammers, fire axes, chisels, crowbars, any and every sort of metal tool. They hacked, chipped, bashed and scraped, eating through solid concrete inch by inch. The other zuvembies scooped up the biggest pieces and brought them up and out. The rest of it, the stuff that was too small to carry, littered the tunnel floor, a shin-deep drift of gravel and shaley flakes.

Mute, uncomplaining, uncaring, the zuvembified personnel of Anger Reef were doing Couleuvre's bidding. They dug and fetched and dumped, burrowing into the installation's very foundations, moles, miners, mules, slaves.

"The perfect workers," Couleuvre said, gloating. "They do not take breaks. They do not need to rest. They have been hard at it twenty-four hours a day for nearly a week, and they are so close now, so close. A breakthrough is at hand. And he is singing high and loud, a hymn of fear and agony because he knows I have almost reached him. Perhaps you hear it too...?"

Lex shook his head. "Nothing but the racket your victims—your innocent victims—are making. What's down there, Couleuvre? What are you after? Who is this 'he'?"

"I think you know, Monsieur Dove."

"Assume I don't. Tell me."

"Bondye," said Couleuvre.

This was more or less the answer Lex had anticipated. "God."

"None other."

"And not, maybe, a thermonuclear bomb?"

"You say that as though there is a difference."

"I believe there's a very great difference," said Lex.

Couleuvre looked grave. "And you would be incorrect. They are intertwined. The one is an aspect of the other. Bondye. Bomb. Both are judgement. Both are slaughter. Both bring death to millions. Both cannot be argued with or appeased."

"And this particular bomb, if it's even there, if it's even still operational, which I doubt..."

"Oh, it is there. Trust me."

"What are you planning on doing with it?"

"What else does one do when one gets an opportunity to meet God face to face? Tell Him a few home truths. Remonstrate with Him. Teach Him a lesson."

"I don't follow."

"You want me to spell it out? Very well." Couleuvre ran a hand over his rooster strip of blond hair, a casual act of preening. "When I find the bomb I will set it off. I will stand in front of it and defy it to destroy me. My power against Bondye's—and we shall see who wins."

THIRTY-THREE
A DEITY OF MASS DESTRUCTION

LEX FOUGHT THE urge to laugh.

"I can tell you right now who's going to win," he said. "Not you."

"You underestimate me."

"Human being versus nuclear fission? Sorry but that's not even a contest."

Couleuvre blinked calmly, saying nothing. Around them the zuvembies carried on their task, deepening the pit little by little.

"For fuck's sake, why?" Lex demanded. "Why do such a crazy thing?"

"I told you. To challenge Bondye. To teach Him a lesson."

"But what's God ever done to you?"

Couleuvre's face creased, as though a bolt of lightning were zigzagging across it. "What has Bondye done? Hmmm. To the world, over the centuries? Brought endless suffering and ruin. All those wars, those massacres, those inquisitions, carried out in His name. Countless millions have died. But to me personally? Perhaps I can remind you of a tragedy that hit my country quite recently."

"The earthquake."

"Just so. One January evening, out of a clear blue sky, comes a seven-point-zero magnitude earthquake. A quarter of a million buildings are demolished, just like that. Three hundred thousand people are killed, the highest casualty rate of any single earthquake ever. A million more are left homeless. Overnight, most of Haiti becomes a holocaust zone. Bodies pile up in the streets. Relief supplies take forever to come through and are poorly distributed. Aftershocks ripple across the country and nobody knows what is going on. Communications are down. The government is in disarray. There's looting, chaos, widespread panic."

"Sounds to me like every earthquake there's ever been," said Lex. "It was a terrible event, no question. On Manzanilla, no one could talk about anything else. There were charity drives. We sent a load of rice, flour and medicine over. We did everything we could to help. As did other countries. I don't see what you're driving at."

"You were not there," said Couleuvre. "To feel the ground shaking under you, as though being kicked from below by a giant... To see houses that have collapsed with whole families inside... To hear the cries of those trapped in the ruins with no hope of rescue... And then the corpses. We were stacking them up on the sidewalks and in alleys. Nowhere else to put them. And in the heat, as they began to decompose—the stench! I saw a stray dog biting at one, gnawing off a hand and running away with it. I saw crows flying off with human eyeballs in their beaks. I saw an infant squatting beside its dead mother, huddled against her bloated belly, because it had nowhere else to go and no one else to look after it. What had Haiti done to deserve this? Nothing. Nothing."

"It wasn't some kind of punishment. You make it sound like one but it wasn't. It was a random natural disaster. Just something that happens. An act of—" Lex faltered.

"Go on, say it."

"All right then. An act of God."

"*Précisément*! The very words. An act of God. Bondye. Bondye Himself did it to us. He flapped His mighty hand, tectonic plates moved, and my country suffered. It suffered as no other country has done. Some of our most prized historic landmarks were flattened, including the Cathédrale Notre-Dame de L'Assomption. Some of our most prominent citizens were killed, including the Archbishop of Port-au-Prince. What kind of deity does that to one of His own places of worship and one of His own Christian representatives on earth? I will tell you. A deity who does not care, that is who. A deity who is so indifferent to His creation that He can smash parts of it without thinking, perhaps with even realising. A deity who needs to be reminded of the responsibilities a god should have."

"Okay, look," said Lex. "I'm not getting into a whole theology debate, because it's a subject I know nothing about. But I am confused. Not so long ago you were telling me about Baron Samedi, how he's the loa of death, how I'm his right-hand man, his ambassador, because I've killed people."

"*Mais oui*. And?"

"Well, you worship him and serve him. He's your husband, your master. If he's all about death, then what's your problem with Bondye being all about death too? There's a basic contradiction there. Surely Bondye and Samedi are on the same page. If Bondye kills three hundred thousand people, doesn't Samedi revel in that? Doesn't it make your loa rub his hands and cackle with glee?"

Couleuvre looked pleased, as though Lex was posing exactly the questions he wanted him to. "No contradiction. There is more to the Baron than simply death. He loves life as well. It is knowledge of one's own inevitable end that makes living more valuable, more exciting. We dance in the shadow of death, we eat, we fuck, and enjoy these things all the more because we know they cannot last. Without death, life is meaningless, and without life, death is too. The Baron and his wife Maman Brigitte look forward to receiving our souls in due course, but before then they wish us to make the most of our brief time as flesh-and-blood beings. They see death as a climax, the final great party. To them it is a special occasion, a cause for celebration. They are not casual about it. They are not indiscriminate or callous."

"And Bondye is."

"As the Haitian earthquake proved. I cried to the Baron afterwards. Weeping, on my knees, I begged him to explain to me how Bondye could do such a thing. But he just shook his head in sorrow and shrugged his shoulders. He could not understand either. Bondye is as mysterious to the loa as He is to us mortals. They struggle to make sense of His behaviour no less than we do."

"Is triggering a bomb really going to grant you a personal tête-à-tête with the Almighty?"

Couleuvre shrugged his shoulders: *why not?* "It is a weapon of mass destruction. Bondye is a deity of mass destruction. The bomb, you could say, is just another of His loa. And it is not as if I have a choice. Bondye Himself has laid down the challenge, through the bomb. I must respond. I cannot back away. I am no coward. What I'm hoping is that you will agree to help me."

"Me?" Lex's eyebrows shot up.

"The Baron's man. An assassin of acute skill and prowess. The Baron tells me he visited you last night. He joined the army of your victims. He followed their souls, hitching a ride with them as they made their pilgrimage to you in your sleep. He was drawn by their hunger for you, their hatred, their desire. He saw you, and what he saw impressed him. He very much wanted you to travel to Anger Reef and meet me. He felt we would make a good team."

A weird, horrible feeling stole over Lex. His nightmares about being mobbed and mauled by his Code Crimsons were deeply unpleasant but they were, nonetheless, *his* nightmares. They were private. No one had a right to know about them but him.

And here was Couleuvre, whom he had met barely twenty minutes ago, revealing a familiarity with these innermost secrets of his psyche. It was cruelly intimate. A violation.

"Don't think that's going to happen," he growled, letting rancour leak through into his voice. "Not a fucking chance."

"The Baron has assured me that my magic will be increased by your presence beside me."

"If there's a nuclear bomb going off on this island, I aim not to be around when it happens."

"You will not be escaping. Do not be under any illusion as to that. Why not stand with me instead as I tame the bomb with my *wanga*? Together we can show Bondye that we mortals are no mere ants to be trodden on and crushed without care or consequence. We are worthy of His respect."

"Where is this bomb anyway?" Lex shifted one foot, a subtle sidestep that brought him a few inches closer to the bokor. "Your zuvembies have dug all that way and you still haven't found it."

"It was buried," said Couleuvre, studying the pit. "When Anger Reef was mothballed, it seems the Americans could not be bothered to go to the trouble of dismantling the bomb. They left it where it was, in a hidden chamber at the foot of a vertical shaft leading down from this sublevel. They poured tons of concrete down the shaft, filling it in, and walked away."

While Couleuvre was talking, Lex edged another few inches closer still. His whole body was tensed, ready. This was his best chance and probably the only one he would get. Couleuvre was musing, distracted. The bokor had a thick, strong neck. The jugular stood proud. A half Nelson chokehold would soon stop the flow of blood through that, causing transient cerebral ischemia. In thirty seconds he would be out cold. Maintaining the pressure for a further two minutes would result in irreversible hypoxic brain damage.

"Did you find that out online?" he asked.

"The loa have knowledge you can't get even from the internet," Couleuvre replied. "And Monsieur Dove?"

The fist seemed to come out of nowhere. The punch was powerful and well aimed, a backhander with plenty of weight and force behind it. The gold and silver rings acted like knuckledusters.

Lex lay on his back, head ringing. His jaw was numb, thick, swollen.

"The loa can also alert you to a man's intentions," said Couleuvre. He snapped his fingers, and the zuvembie Marines jerked into life, seizing Lex once again. Undead fingers dug painfully into his arms, all the way to the bone it seemed.

"Such a pity," Couleuvre sighed. "I felt I could count on you. So did the Baron. We are both disappointed." To the zuvembie Marines: "Take Monsieur Dove to join the others. He can be dosed with V.I.V.E.M.O.R.T. like the rest of them. If he will not help me one way, he can help me another."

THIRTY-FOUR
PRISON BREAK

THE ZUVEMBIE MARINES hauled Lex back up to Sublevel 2. He didn't even try to resist. He was still stunned from Couleuvre's blow. He couldn't recall ever having been hit so hard. His thoughts were scattered, pinging about in his brain like pachinko balls. His vision kept drifting out of focus.

He was hurled unceremoniously into a storeroom of some kind. A door slammed. Around him, voices rumbled like bubbles bursting underwater. Gradually they began to make sense.

"...Lex? Lex?" Albertine. "Speak to me."

"Ugh. Shit." He sat up shakily, feeling as though he were on a boat in rough seas.

"Easy now. Are you okay?"

"Just."

"I take it your little chitchat with Couleuvre was a free and frank exchange of opinions," said Buckler.

"He bent my ear. Tried to recruit me. Belted me a good one." Lex worked his bruised, tender jaw. Unbroken, but not for want of trying. A molar wobbled in its socket when he probed it with his tongue. "Suppose I asked for it. I *was* moving in to kill him."

"You had a shot?" said Morgenstern.

"Yeah, but the bugger saw it coming. Like he had some kind of sixth sense. The loa warned him, he said." Lex peered around the room, seeing shelf upon shelf laden with folded linen, supplies for the entire installation. Some had been pressed into service as makeshift bandages for Tartaglione and Pearce. "Field dressing. Your handiwork?" he asked Morgenstern, who nodded. "How are they doing?"

"Tartag's been bitching and whining, so we know he's all right."

"I'm right here," Tartaglione protested. His head was partially mummified with torn-up strips of hand towel. "Don't talk about me like I'm not."

"We always try and act like you're not here," Sampson said. "It's wishful thinking."

Tartaglione lofted a middle finger. "Your mother."

"And Pearce?" asked Lex.

Morgenstern's expression said it all: *not good*. Pearce lay on the floor with a bound-up shoulder and a blood-drenched bedsheet fastened round his waist like a cummerbund. He had passed out.

"I worked the broom handle out and managed to stem the bleeding, but there's no way of telling what's been pierced inside him. If it's any part of his intestine, we're looking at peritonitis and, well, you know where that leads. He needs proper medical attention urgently."

"So we're all about the good news," said Buckler. "What's Couleuvre's game anyway? Any clues?"

Lex gave a summary of what he had seen down on Sublevel 3. His account was met with a dark silence, which Tartaglione broke. "So let's get this straight. We have no guns. We're going to be killed and turned into brainless minions. And Couleuvre's got a date with a nuclear weapon which he's going to set off just to make some whack-job religious point. Oh man, this is perfect, just perfect. We are the dictionary definition of screwed."

"Tartag," said Sampson, "I love you like a brother, but if you do not nut up and be a man, right now, I will unwrap that Indian-ass turban of yours and use it to strangle you."

"Thanks, pal. Good to know I can count on you for support."

"Any time."

"But I mean it. What the hell can we do? Lieutenant? Anyone?"

Albertine raised a tentative hand. "I think I know how to stop the zuvembies."

"What, seriously?"

"Go on," said Buckler.

"Couleuvre has used strong sorcery, and there's also Seidelmann's formula to take into account," said Albertine. "That's an unknown factor. I've never dealt with anything like this before. But a zuvembie is basically an unwilling slave. There's a soul inside, still tethered to the body when it ought to be free—a soul cowed into obeying Couleuvre, enabling the body to do as he asks. I can use my own *vodou* to attempt to release that soul, and therefore incapacitate the zuvembie it belongs to, like removing the hard disk from a computer. But it has to be on a one-to-one basis. Individually, not en masse. I will need to prepare a *poudre* for the task."

"And it'll work?"

"I'm not sure. I have the necessary ingredients and I know what I'm doing, but..."

"Never mind. It's a plan. Our only plan. We have to try *something*. What are you waiting for, Miz Montase? Get busy."

ALBERTINE BEGAN WITH a *lave tet*, a ritual washing designed to strengthen her resolve, dispel bad energy and bring her into closer rapport with her personal loa. She sprinkled her head with water in which herbs had been steeped. At the same time she chanted and made obeisance.

Next she invoked her loa directly by inscribing a cabalistic diagram on the floor in marker pen. It was a crossword-like symbol made up of the names of her three *vodou* husbands:

```
                    D
     ERZULIE FREDA
                    M
                    B
                    A
                    L
                    LOKO
                    A
                    H
```

She gazed at it for a while in a deep meditative trance.

Lastly she mixed together a selection of powders from her bag, adding them to a bowl and stirring with an index finger. She murmured the names and qualities of each one as she poured it from its little stoppered bottle. "Bend Over Powder—it breaks hexes. Myrrh Powder—it breaks curses. Compelling Powder—it forces obedience. Conquering Glory Powder—it overcomes obstacles to achieving one's goals." In all a dozen powders went into the mix, which she then decanted into a velvet pouch. She secured the neck of the pouch with its drawstring.

"Done," she said. "I'm not promising anything, but..."

"But nothing," said Buckler. "We've got zuvembie knockout dust and we're going to use it. The question is *how* we're going to use it. Facing off against the whole of Couleuvre's little army isn't going to fly. We're down by two and we don't have even a pocket knife between us. Our best play isn't a stand-up fight, it's a tactical withdrawal. Some of us get the hell out and summon reinforcements."

"Some of us?" said Lex.

"Specifically, you, Albertine and Sampson. Just the three of you guys. You move quick, keep low, steer clear of trouble, and hit the surface running. Get on the plane and hightail it. Once you're in the air, Sampson can get himself patched through the right people on the shortwave and call in help."

"But what about you?"

"We have injured, and I'm not leaving anyone behind," Buckler stated firmly.

"But boss—" Tartaglione began.

"Not even a dipshit like you, Tartag."

"You say the sweetest things."

"And Hospitalman Morgenstern has to stay to keep Pearce stable."

Morgenstern didn't even blink, just nodded. Lex couldn't help marvelling at the unflinching loyalty Buckler commanded from his team. The Thirteeners were a misfit bunch, and their lieutenant was the biggest misfit of them all. Perhaps that was why they respected him so much.

"Now, that door isn't locked," Buckler said. "But there's four zuvembies stationed outside. Couleuvre seems to think that's all the security he needs. He reckons we're licked and we're just going to hunker down here and wait to die. What say we show the *faux*-hawk motherfucker how wrong he is?"

THE ZUVEMBIES WERE arranged in a semicircle in the passage, poised to intercept anyone who emerged from the storeroom. The breakout was going to have to be fast, hard and timed perfectly. Buckler and Morgenstern would run interference, enabling Lex, Albertine and Sampson to make their bid for freedom.

"I've got these undead sons of bitches figured out," Buckler said. "They're autistic about their master's orders. Long as we don't step foot outside this room, they don't react. Moment we do, *bam*, they're onto us. We can use that to our advantage."

They got ready, lining up at the door, Buckler and Morgenstern in front.

"Dove?" said Buckler.

"Yes?"

"We all get through this, you and I need to sit down and talk. There's things you don't know that I think you ought to."

"I'll look forward to that."

"I wouldn't if I were you, sport. It's not going to be happy-clappy fireside stuff. And Sampson?"

"LT?"

"We *don't* all get through this, you're elected to head up the next Team Thirteen."

"Aw shit."

"Yeah, poisoned chalice. Choose your recruits well. I know I did."

Buckler grasped the door handle and tugged it open. Outside, in the passage, the zuvembies stirred like sleepers awakening. They bunched together around the doorway, forming a sturdy wall.

"Hey, you ugly fucks," Buckler taunted. "This here's a prison break. Just so's you know."

The zuvembies stared.

"In a moment we're going to cross the threshold. Want to stop us? Do your worst."

Morgenstern had a bedsheet in her hands, the ends twisted around her fists, a loop dangling between.

"On my mark," said Buckler. "Three. Two. One. Go!"

He and Morgenstern propelled themselves out of the doorway. Buckler shoulder-barged one of the zuvembies, creating a gap in the wall. Morgenstern ducked low, turning her momentum into a skid, like a baseball player sliding home. She slipped the sheet around another zuvembie's ankles and yanked the creature off its feet, all in one clean motion.

Lex and Albertine raced out next. Albertine had tipped a small amount of her *poudre* from the pouch into her cupped hand. As a zuvembie shifted to block her path, she puffed the powder straight at it.

"Leave!" she commanded. "You are free. Damballah compels you. Leave this body and go to your rest."

The zuvembie staggered, clawing at its dust-streaked face. Its eyes roved wildly. All at once the dull implacability that characterised it and its brethren was gone. The zuvembie seemed uncertain, riven by inner conflict.

Then its baleful yellow gaze altered. Comprehension dawned. For a moment, barely a split second, the thing seemed recognisably human, no longer a hollow shell but a sentient being. Lex could have sworn it looked relieved, even grateful.

Then the zuvembie crumpled like a sack of meat. It lay flat out, devoid of animation, utterly inert. Dead. Not undead. Not living dead. *Dead* dead.

There was no time to celebrate Albertine's success. Sampson caught her and Lex from behind and hustled them along the passage, yelling, "No gawking. Let's move!"

Two of the three remaining zuvembies swivelled and gave chase. The third, the one Morgenstern had toppled, was locked in a struggle with the female Thirteener. The pair of them writhed on the floor, the zuvembie pinning Morgenstern's legs, Morgenstern scrabbling to extricate herself.

"Hey, assholes!" Buckler shouted, waving his arms. "What about me? Don't forget me."

One zuvembie continued on after the three fugitives. The other spun round and made for Buckler. He danced backwards, evading its outstretched arms.

Lex poured on speed, hauling Albertine with him. Behind them a shrill scream cut the air. He looked back and saw that Morgenstern was now smothered by the zuvembie. It lay on top of her in a grotesque parody of the missionary position. Morgenstern beat at it with her fists. The zuvembie took hold of her forearms and, with no discernible effort, bent them sideways, snapping them both just above the wrist.

Morgenstern's scream turned into a long, drawn-out guttural grunt of fury and agony. She headbutted the zuvembie three times in swift succession, smashing its nose with her brow. The zuvembie retaliated in kind, hammering its forehead down onto her face. The force of the blow was such that it popped one of Morgenstern's eyeballs clean out of its socket.

Still she fought, battering the zuvembie with her knees, even her elbows, despite the pain this undoubtedly sent down both sets of shattered radius and ulna. Buckler was trying to reach her, but he had his own zuvembie to contend with. It kept charging and he kept having to dodge.

Sampson halted. He was torn. He wanted to go back help his teammate, but he had pre-existing orders. Besides, the third zuvembie, one of the Marines, was closing in. It had almost caught up.

"Jesus fucking Christ," he hissed through gritted teeth. "This ain't fair." He hurried off again after Lex and Albertine, casting one last despairing glance over his shoulder.

Morgenstern let out a final, horrendous howl of pain and defiance, which her zuvembie assailant cut short with a punch that landed like a meteor, stoving in her entire face. The crunch of bones was like an axe splitting wood.

As Lex and Albertine rounded the corner, Buckler's voice echoed after them down the passage. It was a cry that came from the gut, an appalled, abysmal "Nooooo!!!"

THEY RAN ON, Sampson huffing along behind them, the zuvembie Marine behind *him*, maintaining its dogged pursuit. They skirted around the body of Professor Seidelmann. The pile of confiscated weapons had been cleared away, nowhere to be seen. Briefly Lex wished there was time to go searching for them. He had never yearned to have a gun in his hands quite as much as he did right then.

They reached the door to the stairs. Sampson was lagging. Like many a big man he was not a fast runner. The zuvembie was now within touching distance of him. Its fingertips found his collar and snagged it, jerking him to a halt. Sampson spun to face the creature.

"Oh no you don't! This is for Morgenstern." He smacked the zuvembie several times, hard as a heavyweight boxer. He might as well have been flicking it with a feather duster.

Albertine broke away from Lex, emptying more of her *poudre* into her palm. She flung it in a cloud at the zuvembie, repeating her incantation from before.

Again, an instant of confusion followed by an instant of clarity.

Again, a sudden, total collapse as the Grim Reaper reclaimed what was overdue and rightfully his.

Sampson peered down at the zuvembie's body, panting hard, then turned to Albertine.

"You," he said, "are a miracle worker as well as the goddamn sexiest woman I have ever met. Please tell me you're single. I want you to have my babies."

Albertine cast a look in Lex's direction.

Sampson nodded. "Thought as much. Can't blame a guy for trying, though."

THEY MOUNTED THE stairs. Sublevel 1 seemed to be all clear. They proceeded with caution anyway. Too much had gone wrong on this mission to allow for complacency.

The elevator loomed ahead.

"How's your climbing?" Lex asked Sampson.

"For shit. Look at me. I ain't built for agility. Yours?"

"The elevator shaft's lined all the way up with struts and braces. They'll do for handholds and footholds. It's no cakewalk but I think I can manage. I'll carry a rope up with me and secure it at the top for you and Albertine to use."

"Cool. Then we're golden." But Sampson's expression was bitter.

"For what it's worth, I'm sorry about Morgenstern."

"Not as sorry as I am. Morgenstern was good people."

"She gave her life so that we could get away."

"Yeah, so let's not blow our chance."

No sooner had Sampson said this than a figure stepped out through the elevator's open doors.

"Wilberforce?" said Albertine.

"Wilb?" said Lex. "Why are you—?"

Wilberforce hung his head. His shoulders slumped in shame. "I'm sorry," he said. "This isn't my fault."

Two men followed him out.

They were Garfield 'the Garfish' Finisterre—sunglasses propped on bald-shaven head, as ever—and one of his seemingly neverending supply of henchmen.

Both were carrying handguns, and the guns were pointed at Wilberforce's back.

The Garfish grinned at Lex.

"Well, well, well," he said. "That was easy. I come lookin' for the white guy who keeps fuckin' up my shit, an' what do I find first thing? Him an' his voodoo witch bitch, along with some fat-ass scumbag I never met. Hey hey, this is my lucky day."

He turned the gun on Lex.

"An' it's about to be your *un*lucky day."

THIRTY-FIVE
TEN SECONDS TO DECIDE

"WILB?" SAID LEX. "Please tell me you didn't bring them here. You haven't sold us out."

"No!" Wilberforce replied hotly. "No way, man. I'd never."

"Then how...?"

Finisterre's grin broadened, becoming a gloat. "One word, spook. Transceiver. The LoJack from my own car. Last night I had Virgil remove it from the Jeep and plant it on Wilberforce's plane, right down inside one of the floats where you'd never think to look. It was obvious you were plannin' on goin' somewhere. Virgil couldn't tell me where, but I didn't need to know, long as I had a way of trackin' you. I hired another seaplane, fired up the GPS, an' lo an' behold, here we all are havin' a joyous reunion on some piece-of-shit little island I never knew even existed." He cast a quick glance at his surroundings. "What the hell is this place anyway? Some kind of prison?"

"It's somewhere you really do not want to be," said Lex.

"With you in my gunsights? I think it is."

"Dove, who is this pimp motherfucker?" Sampson demanded. "'Cause if he thinks pointing a Desert Eagle at me is going to stop me from pounding his sorry ass into the floor..."

"Let me handle him," Lex said. "Listen, Finisterre. You have a beef with me, that's fine, I understand. What you don't realise is that we're in serious trouble. All of us. If we don't get off the island immediately, we run the risk of being attacked by something very nasty. Worse: we could all be vaporised in a nuclear explosion."

"Something nasty? Nuclear explosion?" The Garfish roared with laughter. His henchman joined in, dutifully, sycophantically. "Yeah, right. I'm supposed to believe that?"

"Man's not lying," said Sampson.

Finisterre's face narrowed in anger. "Bullshit. I'm not fallin' for any of that garbage. You'd say any old shit to save your skin, Dove."

"Okay. Don't believe me. That's your prerogative. But I'm going up that elevator shaft whether you like it or not."

"Oh yeah?" Finisterre fired. The bullet whipped past Lex's ear. He heard it buzz by like a wasp and then the whine of a ricochet as it deflected off a wall further along the passage. "Next one's in your head. Or his. Leroy?" The henchman, taking his cue from his boss, pressed his own gun up against Wilberforce's temple. "Maybe you're not scared for yourself, Englishman, but your friend? That's another matter."

"Lex," said Wilberforce. It was both apology and plea.

"You just don't understand the situation," Lex said to the Garfish.

"Yeah I do. I've got you by the balls, that's the situation."

Lex decided to try a different tack. "Then—money. I can pay you a decent sum. Half a million Manzanillan, how about that? If you'll just let Wilberforce go and allow us past."

"You negotiating with this dick now?" said Sampson.

"I don't see that I have a choice."

"Money," said Finisterre. "That's one thing I already got plenty-plenty of. Besides, how're you goin' to pay me, boy? I don't take no cheques, an' I doubt you're carryin' that much in cash on you."

"I can guarantee to give it to you. The moment we're back on Manzanilla."

"So it's a promise, huh?" Finisterre let rip with another of his booming laughs. "Know what my mama used to say about promises? They're worth less than piss in the wind. That applies especially to ones comin' from you, Dove. You'd as soon spit on me as cough up what you owe. The point is, we're past the money thing, you an' me. Way past. This ain't about debts or interest on loans or any of that any more. This is about you puttin' men of mine in the hospital an' the morgue an' generally interferin' with the smooth runnin' of my day-to-day business affairs. This is a blood feud." He waved the gun back and forth, sketching an imaginary line between himself and Lex. "There's only one kind of payment that'll balance these books."

"Let's rush him," Sampson muttered.

"No," Lex shot back. "Wilberforce will be dead before we're even halfway there."

"Of course, I'm not averse to takin' a bonus on top," the Garfish added. He was eyeing up Albertine. "Treatin' myself to that little honey over yonder. Wilberforce's cousin, right? You're fine, girl. It'd be a pleasure introducin' you to my pal Little Garfield. Only, he's not so little, if you get my meanin'."

"You lay a finger on me," Albertine warned, "you'll never see your Little Garfield again."

"That supposed to intimidate me? I know you're some big-shot voodoo mambo. My man whose leg you broke, he swears you've got supernatural powers. An' maybe you have, maybe you have. But I ain't met the woman yet who can do a thing about it when she's flat on her front an' there's ten inches of cock up her batty hole. Then she's got two choices, either moan or scream, and frankly I don't care which it is. Makes no difference to me. In many ways screamin's better. Means I get more of a ride."

"Oh you are one classy individual," said Sampson. "It's going to be a delight beating that eight-ball head of yours against a wall 'til it breaks."

"I have no argument with you, American," said Finisterre, all at once sounding reasonable and personable. "You, my friend, are more than welcome to leave. You'll find a rope hangin' down in the elevator. Climb up, go, it's all good. My business is with Dove an' Wilberforce an' his cousin, an' frankly I'd prefer there not to be any witnesses."

"You must have me mistaken for some kind of moron. You'd shoot me in the back soon as I got past you."

"You have my word I won't."

"Maybe you should take him up on the offer, Sampson," said Lex. "Only one of us has to get to the surface. Might as well be you. Especially as you're the one who knows exactly who to send a mayday to."

"You don't honestly believe this asshole? I don't even know the guy, and already I can tell he's as slippery as rattlesnake shit. I wouldn't trust him to let me go free any more'n I'd trust him to babysit my thirteen-year-old niece."

"If a girl's old enough to bleed, she's old enough to butcher," said Finisterre, and Leroy tittered.

"Not helping your case, dickwad," growled Sampson.

"No, that's true, Mr American. But my offer stands. What if I give you a time limit to decide? A deadline always helps focus the mind. Ten seconds, startin'"—he glanced at his watch, a Patek Philippe Nautilus—"now."

"Go," Lex urged Sampson. "Morgenstern bought us this opportunity, remember? You yourself said we mustn't waste it. Finisterre's even supplied the rope for you to climb."

"And if he shoots me?"

"Five seconds," said Finisterre.

"The crazy thing is, I don't think he will. He's not honest but he is honourable, in his way. And let's face it, if he doesn't shoot you when you go, he might well if you stay."

"In other words, what have I got to lose?"

"Two," said Finisterre. "One. Time's up. Okay, what'll it be?"

"All right," said Sampson. "Dammit, all right. Topside it is."

"There. That wasn't so hard, was it?"

"But I swear, you try anything funny, asswipe, and you're dog meat."

"As God is my witness," said Finisterre, and underlined his sincerity by crossing himself.

"And by the way, for the record, I ain't fat. This is all muscle."

"I apologise. The insult was uncalled for."

Sampson turned and looked gravely at Lex. "You'll find a way of clearing up this mess, right? Albertine, Wilberforce, they're civilians. This isn't their world, it's ours, and they've no place in it. Promise me you'll make sure they're okay."

"Absolutely. And in turn, you promise me you'll get on the radio in *Puddle Jumper* and bring down a hundred tons of hell on Anger Reef."

"Done."

Finisterre waggled a hand impatiently. "Come on, let's hurry it up. I'm itchin' to get started on Dove. Not to get finished with you, though, Englishman. Oh no. It's goin' to be a long, bad death for you, an' I'm goin' to savour every second."

Sampson steeled himself. Shoulders squared, he set off towards the elevator, keeping his gaze firmly fixed on Finisterre and specifically Finisterre's gun. The least sign of the Garfish reneging, the merest twitch of a trigger finger, and Sampson would dive for cover. And if the bullet missed its mark, would come up fighting.

"No."

This came from the far end of the passage, and it was as much a resigned sigh as an objection.

Papa Couleuvre appeared, flanked by zuvembies. More zuvembies filed up behind him.

"Who the fuck are—?" Finisterre began, but Couleuvre didn't let him complete the sentence.

"Hmmm, another Baron's man," he said, giving him the once-over. "Quite the fellowship we have now."

Finisterre swung the gun, training it on the bokor. "Don't move."

"Or what?" said Couleuvre serenely. "You will shoot?"

"Don't make me."

Couleuvre gestured. The zuvembies hastened forward.

"The escape is over," he said, speaking now to Lex and the other fugitives. "A valiant effort, bought at a high price, but doomed to failure. I really have lost patience with all this resistance and disruption. It is using up precious time."

"What *are* those things?" Finisterre demanded. As the zuvembies approached, he, Leroy and Wilberforce were getting a better look at the creatures, and what they saw filled them with bafflement and an instinctive dread.

"What you are going to be," replied Couleuvre, "just a few minutes from now."

The events that followed unfolded with wearying predictability. Finisterre fired. Leroy fired. The zuvembies strode on, wounded but unfazed. Within moments they had overpowered the two crooks. Finisterre and Leroy were in their custody; Wilberforce as well.

Lex surrendered, as did Albertine. Sampson, so close to the elevator, just yards from the route to freedom, could see no alternative but to do so too.

"*D'accord*," said a satisfied Couleuvre. "There is a wisdom in recognising when you are outclassed and beaten. Don't fight fate."

Lex could scarcely believe their bad luck. Had the Garfish not arrived when he did, the escape party might even now be up on the surface, crossing the beach to the Zodiacs. Their goal had been tantalisingly within their grasp. And now...

Now there really did seem to be no hope.

THIRTY-SIX
IN LAB 1 AND LAB 2

THEY WERE TAKEN down to the laboratories. Lab 1 and Lab 2 were, it transpired, a single large room divided unequally into two chambers, with a half-glassed partition between. Lab 1 was stuffed with biotech equipment—centrifuge, electron microscope, incubator, modular liquid handler, PCR protective chamber—while 2, the smaller space, contained a half-dozen steel gurneys lined up in a row.

One of the partition's windowpanes was starred with a bullet hole. Much of the equipment lay strewn, broken. Dried black bloodstains crisscrossed the floor and scabbed the walls.

Here was where V.I.V.E.M.O.R.T. had first been used and where Couleuvre's slaughter of the installation's personnel had begun.

The group of captives was separated up. Albertine, Wilberforce, Finisterre and Leroy were consigned to Lab 1. Couleuvre had the zuvembies tie their wrists and ankles with electrical flex and then attach these restraints with more electrical flex to various immoveable fixtures around the room. Albertine was deprived of her shoulder bag.

"Not making that mistake twice," said Couleuvre, placing the bag on a high shelf—contraband. "No more sneaky little mambo tricks from you, lady."

Lex and Sampson were shoved through the connecting doorway into Lab 2. Four of the gurneys were already occupied. Buckler and Tartaglione had two. The unconscious Pearce lay on another. The fourth was a bier for the body of Morgenstern, whose face was so mutilated as to be all but unrecognisable. The three still-living Thirteeners had been bound tightly by leather cuffs and straps connected to the gurneys' frames.

"And this is where we put the dangerous ones," Couleuvre said.

The zuvembies forced Lex and Sampson down onto the spare gurneys. Both men resisted but, against the superior preternatural strength of zuvembies, it was futile. In no time they had been buckled in. Lex strained against the cuffs and straps but there was no slack, no leverage, not an inch of give. He was held fast.

The sense of helplessness was agonising. He felt vulnerable, emasculated. He fought down a growing panic, ordering himself to stay calm, keep a clear head, be in control. It wasn't over yet. The outlook was bleak, but while he lived, while his mind still functioned, there was always a chance of turning the situation around.

"Now stay there and be good," Couleuvre instructed Lex and the Thirteeners. "It will not be long. I will deal with the others first, then come round to you."

"No!" Lex yelled. "Leave them alone!" His concern, of course, was for Albertine and Wilberforce. Finisterre and Leroy he couldn't have cared less about.

Couleuvre, anyway, ignored him, exiting Lab 2 with a dismissive wave. Back in Lab 1, the bokor fetched phial trays out of a refrigerator and began unpacking sterilised hypodermics from their wrappers.

By craning his neck Lex could just see through the partition windows. The fear etched on the faces of Albertine and Wilberforce sent a surge of adrenaline through him. He writhed wildly and blindly against his bonds, every sinew stretched, every muscle straining. The blood roared in his ears. He was aware of an animalistic wail coming from his own throat, a wordless ululation of rage that didn't sound human even to him. Soon enough he was exhausted. He sank back against the gurney's cold, unyielding metal, panting like a dog. All he had to show for his efforts was a sore wrist, which he had chafed until it bled.

"It's no use, sport," said Buckler from the gurney adjacent. "We're going nowhere."

In Lab 1, Finisterre was attempting to ingratiate himself with Couleuvre. His low voice resonated through the windows.

"Listen, man, I can make you rich. Super rich. Name your price. I'll give you anything you want. Girls? I can get you girls. Car? I'll buy you a fuckin' Ferrari. Just—just don't do this, okay? Whatever you've got in mind, you don't have to do it to me. I can be your friend, the best friend you ever had." Around his sunglasses his bald pate glistened with sweat.

"I do not need any of that stuff," Couleuvre replied. "I have a higher calling, brother."

Finisterre switched to threats. "For God's sake, I'm the Garfish. You do not fuck with the Garfish."

"But I am not fucking with you," said an unperturbed Couleuvre. "I am just making you into more than you could ever dream of being."

Finisterre's bravado collapsed. "Don't kill me," he said, his voice clogged by a sob.

"It is not killing. Do not look at it like that. It is granting you new life. You are a Baron's man, so you should appreciate what is coming. The death that you have brought to so many others is not going to stake a claim on you. You are going to surpass death. Not everyone gets the chance to die and still live."

"Take him." Finisterre nodded strenuously at Leroy. "Him instead of me."

Leroy mouthed off indignantly in response. His allegiance to his employer had just found its limits.

"Why, when I can have you both?" Couleuvre summoned the nearest zuvembie, then paused over Finisterre and Leroy. An index finger hopped from side to side. He appeared to be performing an eenie-meenie-minie-mo method of elimination.

His finger alighted on Leroy. He gave the zuvembie the go-ahead, and the undead creature clamped a hand over the henchman's face, covering his mouth and pinching his nostrils shut.

Leroy took a minute and a half to suffocate. His eyes bulged. His whole face seemed to swell up. His heels rattled a tattoo on the floor. Finally his eyes rolled upwards, the irises disappearing from view, leaving just the capillary-crazed whites showing. His head lolled.

Couleuvre administered a dose of V.I.V.E.M.O.R.T. into Leroy's arm and carried out a perfunctory *vodou* ritual over the corpse—incense and chanting.

"Soon be ready," he said, and moved on to Finisterre.

The drug lord was hyperventilating with alarm and terror. He moaned, swaying his head to and fro. Lex could not help feeling a small twinge of satisfaction. The Garfish was getting no more than he deserved. He was also, in extremis, showing his true colours. He wasn't facing death bravely. Like any bully, he was, when the tables were turned, nothing but a coward. He babbled, begged, cajoled, prayed, wept.

Couleuvre remained unmoved. A quiet instruction to the zuvembie, and Finisterre was subjected to the same treatment as his henchman. He took longer to die. He was taller, with a greater lung capacity. Two minutes passed, three, before asphyxiation was complete. He slumped sideways, and the sunglasses slipped from his head onto the floor.

Again, Couleuvre injected and incanted.

Leroy was beginning to revive. A groan of horror escaped Wilberforce's lips. The dead henchman's neck and shoulders spasmed, as though little jolts of electricity were being shot through him. His jaw started to work round and round in a cud-chewing motion. His eyeballs rolled back down, revealing his irises again, which now bore a pale yellow tinge like all the other zuvembies'. He tried to rise but was prevented by the lengths of flex securing him. Couleuvre took a scalpel and sliced through the bonds. Leroy tottered to his feet and stood, stoop-shouldered and obedient, ready to serve his new master.

Finisterre was soon upright too. The great gangly drug lord cut a humbled figure. His expensive clothing and accoutrements hung limply off him, now just so much gaudy, hollow finery. No longer did he seem arrogant and untouchable. He had become merely another member of Couleuvre's zuvembie horde, an undead underling. A man who had ruled Manzanilla through fear and brute force had become a creature with no needs or desires of his own and no will save Couleuvre's.

The bokor, by this time, was all set to create a third new zuvembie. He gaze turned on Wilberforce, who himself couldn't tear his eyes from Finisterre and Leroy. The dark miracle that had just occurred was beyond Wilberforce's comprehension. Lex could see an edge of madness in his eyes. Death might actually come as a blessing, sparing Wilberforce a plummet into out-and-out insanity.

Couleuvre was poised to give his zuvembie assassin the kill command. Abruptly, he raised his head. He turned this way and that, questing, quizzical. Something had caught his attention. Some sound?

A broad smile buttered its way across his features.

"They have found it," he exclaimed. "They have breached through. Bondye stands revealed. Bondye in all his glory."

Without another word he hurried out of the laboratory, leaving several stationary zuvembies, including the two recent additions to their ranks, along with a perplexed Wilberforce and a relieved Albertine.

The two cousins had been granted a reprieve.

But for how long?

LEX LAY BACK on the gurney, numb with despair. Events in Lab 1 had cast a pall over the people in Lab 2. The atmosphere, already grim, now verged on desolate. Nobody met anyone else's eye. Nobody seemed to want to speak.

"Man's got his bomb," Sampson finally said. "I guess it really is game over."

"It may not work," said Buckler. "Jeez, how long's the damn thing been sitting there? Thirty years? Wires and contacts could be corroded. The trigger mechanism could have seized up. The plutonium core's probably decayed beyond viability. Odds are it'll go off with a fizzle and a fart instead of an almighty bang."

"You think, LT?" said Tartaglione.

"I don't know. I'm trying to look on the bright side. It's what I do."

"Yeah, chief," said Sampson, "you're always a regular ray of sunshine. Famous for it. All the bars we hang out at, the guys all say, 'You know that Tom Buckler? He's just one big bottle of happy juice, he is.'"

"Damn straight," said Buckler. "But I've got to tell you, all of you..."

"Hell no, please don't get schmaltzy on us."

"Not intending to, Tartag. All's I was going to say was, don't be afraid."

"Kind of late for that, don't you reckon? I think I already peed myself a little tiny bit."

"I mean of dying. Because I believe—no, I know—there's something on the other side. There's more."

"You know?" said Lex.

"Sure I do. I've been there."

Lex recalled a conversation he had had earlier in the day. "Sarajevo."

"Who told you?"

It wasn't betraying a confidence. She was dead, after all. "Morgenstern. She said something happened to you a few years back, in Sarajevo."

"Something did," said Buckler.

"But you prefer not to talk about it."

"I do. But I guess, in the situation we're in, it might be, I don't know, instructive?"

"Go on, then. If it'll help."

"You really want to hear it?"

Lex did his best to shrug. "Why not? Isn't as if I've got much else to do at present—apart from wait to die."

THIRTY-SEVEN
SARAJEVO

TEAM THIRTEEN FLEW into Butmir International Airport on a freezing, fogbound winter morning. This was about five years ago, maybe nearer six. Heading up the squad was Master Chief Eugene Exton, an ROTC graduate who had racked up hundreds of hours of mission time in some of the hairiest combat zones on the planet. A stand-up guy who took shit from no one and gave you shit only if you deserved it.

Buckler was the junior member of the team, the FNG—Fucking New Guy—having been a Thirteener for just three months. The very first operation he'd gone on had involved a nest of vampires, and that had been a goddamn eye-opener all right. Baptism by fire. He was still finding his feet in the crazy, fucked-up, Stephen-King-meets-James-Bond world of Team Thirteen.

Their objective was an industrial park in Sarajevo's Novi Grad municipality, specifically a warehouse unit that had been turned into a nightclub. A decade after peace had come to post-Yugoslavia, the kids were dancing again, deafening themselves with dubstep or techno or some other such moron music while necking down the kind of pharmaceuticals that made that type of racket bearable.

Only, at this particular venue the happy vibes had turned to screams one night. The warehouse had become a slaughterhouse.

Casualties had topped a hundred and fifty. The survivors, few that they were, claimed to have seen ghosts whisking through the crowd of ravers, slitting throats, gutting bellies, ripping out hearts and spines.

The Bosnia-Herzegovina authorities publicly dismissed these accounts as nonsense. A bunch of kids off their faces, tripping balls on ketamine and ecstasy? Amid lasers and flashing lights and clouds of dry ice? Of course they hadn't seen ghosts. The official line was that gangsters, Russian mafia most likely, had rampaged through the place with machetes and samurai swords, settling some grudge or debt they had with the nightclub's owners.

The unofficial line was somewhat different. Somebody somewhere in the national government knew there was more to the incident than met the eye and knew, too, about Team Thirteen. Calls were made, and while, on the face of it, it wasn't an American problem, there had been American boots on the ground during the Balkan crisis, so the US had some sort of moral obligation in the region. It was, it seemed, a kind of legacy issue.

Because, see, in that selfsame warehouse, back in 1995, there was a massacre of Bosniaks—Bosnian Muslims. On the orders of General Ratko Mladić a couple of hundred of them had been rounded up by the Serbian paramilitary unit known as the Scorpions, marched into the warehouse, and scythed down by machinegun fire. UN peacekeepers had found the bodies the next morning, led to them by an informant.

And now the very pissed-off spirits of these victims were back and had exacted bloody vengeance on a bunch of civilians no less innocent and undeserving than they themselves had been.

After the incident, a Catholic priest went in to bless the nightclub and cleanse it with holy water. He was torn to pieces by unseen forces.

An imam tried to do much the same, and wound up just as dead.

Now it was Team Thirteen's turn, and Master Chief Exton led the squad into the cavernous building with a plan to, in his words, "lay some motherfucking ghosts with extreme prejudice".

The ghosts attacked, but Team Thirteen were armed with guns loaded with special ammo—fragmentation rounds containing a bead of iron-mercury suspension at their core. That shit was like hydrochloric acid to spooks and spectres. Fucked them up big time. And as if that wasn't enough, the Thirteeners had EMP-burst projectors that played havoc with the electrical fields that ghosts used to manifest themselves tangibly. The ghosts needed to adopt solid forms in order to cause physical harm. An EMP-burst projector disrupted them, like throwing a stone into a pond. It dispersed them into ineffectual ripples.

Trouble was, these ghosts were an unusually strong variety. Master Chief Exton was startled by how much telluric energy they were sucking up from their surroundings. They were taking hits but kept on coming. And there were so many of them, so goddamn many.

What Exton didn't realise—what no one realised until later—was that the warehouse was sited on a Thin Patch. That was the name for places where the membrane between the earthly realm and others was, well, thin. Thinner than normal. Porous, even. Shit from other worlds and dimensions could leak through at a Thin Patch, and the other way round. The Bosniak ghosts were being fuelled by power from elsewhere, serious netherworldly power, demonic power. Something on the other side of the Thin Patch was giving them extra juice, meaning the Thirteeners' dedicated weaponry was not having the impact it ought to.

Put simply, the squad were getting their asses handed to them.

Master Chief Exton sounded the retreat. Team Thirteen made for the main entrance, only to find the door shut fast, sealed by the ghosts, unbudgeable. Great big steel thing. Even a grenade couldn't make a dent.

Trapped. But Exton kept a cool head. The ghosts were swarming around, ragged phantom shapes swooping from the roof beams, hurtling past the DJ's station and the bar and the dance floor. Gaping jagged mouths. Outstretched ectoplasmic talons. A fucking nightmare. But Exton kept the orders coming: "Enfilading fire. Watch your six. Cover the man next to you. Maintain pressure on these sons of bitches. They can't keep going forever."

Unfortunately it felt as though they could.

Team Thirteen started taking casualties. One man down. Then two more.

Buckler couldn't remember much about what happened next. His last sight of Exton was the master chief with a dozen ghosts swirling around him in an angry opalescent blizzard, slashing and rending. Exton went down with guns blazing.

Buckler was aware that he was the last team member standing. Then everything seemed to melt and crumble. Reality shifted.

It appeared that, with Exton's death, some kind of quota had been met. The Bosniak ghosts had caused the requisite number of fatalities. The crimes against them had been cosmically cancelled out. What was owed had been repaid, corpse for corpse. The force that powered them was now summoning them back. The ghosts were sucked through some kind of portal, spinning in a downward spiral as though caught in an eldritch Coriolis effect.

Buckler was pulled along with them. He was ensnared in their slipstream. He struggled but couldn't fight it. He clung to anything he could, but the vortex was as irresistible as a whirlpool at sea. He went flailing through the Thin Patch. It felt, weirdly, like passing through a layer of cold, damp silk.

What lay beyond?

Hell.

Rocks. Boiling lakes. Streams of lava. Some of the foulest, most grotesque demons the mind could conjure up. Everywhere, the sounds of torment and agony, resounding up to a sky that looked like a stormy sunset. The stench of sulphur and barbecued meat. It was just how Buckler used to picture hell during religious instruction classes at grade school, particularly the ones with Mrs Flinders presiding, a pinch-faced old biddy who seemed to exult in the Old Testament tales of revenge and suffering and the Book of Revelation's apocalyptic scourges.

Maybe Buckler's own imaginings and prejudices created this version of hell. Maybe it conformed to what he expected he was going to find. Maybe hell would appear different to different people. Maybe hell was personally designed, tailor-made for each of us.

Anyway, Buckler took one moment to panic, then segued straight into evade-and-survive mode. He was a Navy SEAL, goddamit. A SEAL stuck behind enemy lines. Wherever he might be, however hostile the terrain and the natives, he had the training to cope. Even in hell itself.

He kept on the go. He steered well clear of the horned, hooved, batwinged demons whenever they were on the march. He found high ground from which to observe the lie of the land and plot his next move. He stayed safe and alive.

He had no idea how long he scurried and skulked in that place. There was no night and day. The sky remained perpetually the same, always orange and brown, seething and boiling. His watch did not work. His circadian rhythm was shot to pieces. Oddly enough, he did not feel hunger or thirst. He seemed to be in a kind of stasis, one long continuum of now. He slept occasionally—catnapped, more like—but never really felt tired. He would just stop for a bit, hole up, rest, close his eyes, then wake up and carry on. Time was obviously passing, but passing in no way he had ever known or could fathom.

Often he came close to being discovered and caught. The demons had sensitive noses. They would scent him, and form packs, and hunt him, and he would flee and just somehow managed to outrun them or hide from them.

And then there were the souls he saw, naked human figures being subjected to the worst kinds of old-school torture: torn, maimed, mutilated, eviscerated, stretched, racked, broken, burned, pierced, impaled, flayed. Punished for wrongs they had committed while alive. Raped and sodomised and brutalised and humiliated in a constant orgy of retribution and purgatorial justice.

Vaguely he hoped to find a way out, an exit, perhaps another Thin Patch he could force himself through. That was the objective that kept Buckler going when all he really wanted to do was collapse and curl up into a ball, howling in madness and despair. He vowed to break free. He would escape hell. He shouldn't be here. He had fallen in by mistake. Surely, under the circumstances, there ought to be a loophole that allowed accidental visitors like him to leave.

And then one day—or night—or twilight—he got careless, or perhaps the demons finally got their shit together. He found himself surrounded by the things. They were closing in from all sides. Whichever way he turned, whichever direction he ran in, demons, demons and more demons. A whole horde of the fuckers. His luck, or whatever else had been keeping him out of their clutches, providence perhaps, had run out.

He wouldn't let them capture him. He drew his sidearm and stuck the barrel beneath his chin. Could you kill yourself in hell? If you died here, where did you end up? Only one way to find out. Wherever he was about to go, at least it couldn't be worse than where he was.

Then, salvation.

They weren't angels. They were just men.

They came raging down to cut a swathe through the demons, blasting with rifles and machineguns, leaping and shooting and mowing down.

They were Team Thirteen, and Master Chief Exton was in command.

"Sorry we're late!" Exton called out to Buckler. He was looking remarkably spry for someone last seen being torn to shreds by vengeful ghosts. "Been searching high and low for you. Your sorry ass was damn hard to find."

It rapidly dawned on the demons that they were licked. They turned and scurried off with those pointy tails of theirs between their legs.

"Yeah, that's right!" Buckler's dead teammates yelled at their retreating backs. Demon corpses littered the ground around them. "You better run, you scuzzbuckets. Go back home to your butt-ugly mommas."

"Come on," said Exton, extending a hand to Buckler. "You've been here long enough. This is no place for you."

Buckler wasn't lying on the ground. Nevertheless he felt as though he was being helped up. Exton pulled him back onto his feet, lent him a shoulder to lean on, walked him out of there, out of the infernal pit, into the light of day...

"THEN I TOOK another look," said Buckler, "a closer look, and it wasn't Eugene Exton at all. It was just some straggly-haired old geezer, a bum or something. He was babbling at me in Serbo-Croatian. Couldn't understand a word but I figured he was telling me I was okay. That or he was pissed at me because I'd just tripped over him or something. We were outdoors. It was raining. That shitty industrial park in shitty Sarajevo. Most of the buildings still with the pockmarks left by bullets and mortar shells. The tramp got me as far as the main road and left me there. Took my wallet, boots and gun, and I was too dazed to stop him. Sweet guy. A while later some women came along. A while after that, cops and an ambulance. It had been three days since Team Thirteen entered the nightclub. Took me some time to get to grips with that. Only three days. I lay in hospital, and the American consul was trying to debrief me and get to the bottom of what happened, and all I could think was,

'Three days? Not possible.' Where I'd just been, it had felt a damn sight longer. Three months at least. If not three years."

He paused, then resumed: "So that's it. Happy little bedtime story, huh? And I don't have to look at you, Dove, to tell that you're not buying a word of it. Frankly, I couldn't give a shit. I know it's true, right down to the last detail. That's all that matters."

"Actually, you'd be surprised," said Lex. "Yesterday I'd have said you hallucinated the whole thing. You were out cold for three days. Your mind went wandering. You dreamed about hell. Had a vision, perhaps. Nothing more than that. Today, though..."

"Today your world's different."

"Back to front and inside out. More things in heaven and earth, et cetera."

"To me, what I experienced tells me one thing for sure," said Buckler. "We don't die. Death isn't a period, it's a comma. There's more to come afterwards. That's not hippy-dippy New Age bullshit. It's not religious dogma either. It's fact. I'm the proof. I've been there, come back, got the T-shirt."

"Trick is," said Sampson, "you got to make sure you don't end up same place the lieutenant went. Play your cards right, and what's waiting for you is like Daytona Beach during spring break—topless coeds and endless beer."

"I don't recall reading about that in the Bible," said Tartaglione.

"Hey. The LT said hell was how he imagined it. I'm picturing heaven as being how I imagine it. You get what you expect, right?"

There was melancholy beneath the bravado. Lex could hear it. He felt it himself. They were condemned men, joking in their final minutes of life, fighting down their dread. A last battle. A last victory.

Footfalls in the passage outside announced Couleuvre's return.

Lex had made up his mind. He would demand to be next to receive a dose of V.I.V.E.M.O.R.T. His motives were purely selfish. That way he wouldn't have to watch Wilberforce and Albertine get turned into zuvembies. He wouldn't have to bear the guilt for failing to save them from a fate that was almost literally worse than death.

THIRTY-EIGHT
THE PERKS OF RANK

Buckler, however, beat him to it.

"Yo! Papa Hors d'Oeuvres!"

Couleuvre strode over to the gurney Buckler was stretched out on. "You mock me? You make fun of my *kanzo* name?"

"That's the general idea, yeah."

The bokor side-swiped him with a vicious punch. "Never do that."

Buckler spat blood. "You got your nuke now. You don't have to convert the rest of us into your zuvembie monkeys, surely. The job's done."

"The ceiling of the bomb chamber has been breached," said Couleuvre, "but the hole is not large enough yet. I can look through but not get through. I need access to the bomb itself, and for that more zuvembies are required. Besides, it is better to have my enemies docile and under my control than not."

"Then start with me."

Couleuvre considered it. "If it will silence your insolent tongue, why not?"

"LT, no," said Tartaglione.

"Ah, might as well get it over with, Tartag," said Buckler.

"One of the perks of rank—jumping the queue."

Couleuvre beckoned over the zuvembie who had murdered Finisterre and Leroy.

"Any last words, Ogun's man?"

Buckler just grinned. "Better do it right, voodoo child. That's all. I'm not forgiving of mistakes."

"Oh, there'll be no mistakes," Couleuvre assured him.

The zuvembie laid hands on Buckler's face.

Lex averted his gaze and tried not to listen. He and Lieutenant Tom Buckler had not seen eye to eye on many things but he had nonetheless developed a grudging admiration for the man. Buckler's gruffness and irascibility were a front, masking someone who cared deeply for his team and who led the best way: by example. He might be a bastard but he was a bastard on the side of the angels. The world would be a poorer place without him.

Tartaglione let out a soft, low wail.

Buckler died quietly, in itself an act of defiance.

PAPA COULEUVRE TOOK his time over Buckler's resurrection. For all his blitheness, he seemed to have taken the lieutenant's warning to heart. He performed the rite slowly and carefully, keen to ensure that nothing went awry. No mistakes.

When the dead SEAL's eyes snapped open, Couleuvre pursed his lips in satisfaction. "*Voilà.* You are back and you are mine. My voice is like a drug to you now. You crave it. You need it. You wish for nothing but to hear me and do my bidding. Rise." He unbuckled the gurney's restraints. "Rise and obey."

The zuvembified Buckler heaved himself off the gurney.

"Prove to me your loyalty," said Couleuvre. "Kill these other soldiers. Start with him." He pointed at Sampson.

Buckler crossed over to Sampson's side.

"Hell no," said Sampson. "This ain't right. Couleuvre, you're a stone-cold bastard, you know that? I hope that bomb flash-fries you. No, I don't. I hope you get to die of something long and lingering and painful like rectal cancer, you big Frenchified sack of shit."

Couleuvre smirked. "How I die is of no consequence to you, just as how you die is of no consequence to me."

"You smug—"

A whimper from Lab 1 cut Sampson off.

Couleuvre whirled. "What now?" he snapped imperiously. Then his jaw dropped. "*C'est impossible*," he breathed. "I never told him to..."

On the other side of the glass, Albertine looked frantic. It was she who had whimpered. She was shying away from Finisterre, head bent, as if trying to escape his attention. Lex couldn't fathom why she was suddenly intimidated by him more than she was by any of the other zuvembies, until he noticed that Finisterre had put his sunglasses back on. One of the lenses was missing. Presumably it had been knocked out when the glasses had fallen off his head onto the floor.

The detail snagged in Lex's mind, reminding him of something. Of someone.

Couleuvre, meanwhile, had sunk to his knees.

"My lord," he said in a quavering sigh. "You have come. You have chosen a *chwal* and ridden down from heaven to grace us with your presence." He clapped both hands onto his head three times.

The atmosphere in the laboratories seemed suddenly charged, electrified, filled with power and a terrible, heavy sense of oppression, like the air before a thunderstorm.

Finisterre flicked his fingers, inviting Couleuvre to come to him. The bokor went to Lab 1 with his head bowed, and that was when the penny dropped for Lex. He recalled the figure he had seen in his nightmare, the character who adorned many a wall in the form of graffiti art and many a forearm as a tattoo.

Baron Samedi.

The Baron was here.

The loa now inhabited the frame of Garfield Finisterre, who once again looked imposing and dangerous. Just as the tramp Gable had played host to Legba, so Finisterre had been commandeered by Baron Samedi.

No wonder Albertine was so petrified.

Death incarnate was in the room.

THIRTY-NINE
LIMPET SOUL

BARON SAMEDI, THROUGH Finisterre, spoke.

"I like this horse," he said. "I like how he feels. I am comfortable inside him. His clothing, his physique, even the sound of his voice suits me."

"My Baron, my lord, my husband..." said Couleuvre in hushed tones.

"Yes, yes." Finisterre adjusted the sunglasses on the bridge of his nose. One eye looked down through the lens-less aperture with stern amusement. "You're mountin' a challenge against Bondye."

"Yes, my lord. Yes! Have you come to give me your blessing?"

"That depends."

"Bondye is cruel and merciless. He should be made to answer for all that He has done."

"I know, and I sympathise," said Finisterre. "We loa have long recognised that Bondye does not always meet His responsibilities or answer all prayers. We struggle to find a balance between what appears to be His will and what is right for you mortals. That is our role as intercessors, and our burden. Often we are no less baffled by Bondye's ways than you are. It pains us, all the strife and sufferin' He visits on the world. We can't always interpret the divine plan. Sometimes it almost seems that there isn't one."

"So you'll help me? Say you will."

"My faithful servant, I will observe and if required will become involved. I must admit I'm curious to find out whether your bid to confront Bondye will bear fruit and, if so, what will come of it. You may, perhaps, change everythin'. Equally you may change nothin'."

"With you by my side, I cannot fail."

"Don't count on me, Couleuvre. I am notoriously fickle."

"Of course, Baron." But Couleuvre's voice, so awed and eager, gave the lie to his words.

MEANWHILE, BUCKLER SEEMED to be taking an unusually long time over killing Sampson. Lex realised he wasn't hearing any of the expected noises. No splintery cracking of bones. No frantic back-of-the-throat gulping and gagging. No drumbeat of heels.

He twisted his head round, and what he saw astonished him.

The zuvembified Team Thirteen leader was surreptitiously releasing Sampson from the restraints.

Sampson looked no less startled than Lex felt. He leapt off the gurney the moment the last cuff was undone. He stared at Buckler, scowling hard.

"LT? You still in there? Jesus, you are, aren't you?"

"Go," said Buckler in a slow, creaky voice that sounded as though it was coming from somewhere deep and far away, some inner cavern. "Tartag. Pearce. Free."

Sampson, in spite of everything, didn't hesitate. An order was an order.

Buckler turned and began untying Lex.

Lex scanned the SEAL's face. To all appearances, Buckler was no different from any of the other zuvembies. Yellowed irises. Frozen, statue-like features. Vacant expression. And yet...

"How?" Lex said.

"Don't... know," said Buckler, the words hissing out of him like steam. "Don't... care."

"You're resisting Couleuvre's commands."

"Somehow... I'm still... in charge of... me. Hard. Like wading... through mud... up to my armpits."

"But I don't understand. How come you can do this and no one else?"

"No use... asking. Gift horse. Mouth."

Unstrapped, Lex pounced to his feet. In Lab 1, Couleuvre was still prostrated before his loa. There were three other zuvembies in there, guarding Wilberforce and Albertine. Lex and the Thirteeners were weaponless. Still, they had to go on the offensive, no question. They at least had the element of surprise on their side.

Buckler led the charge. Lex and Sampson were close on his heels. Tartaglione remained in Lab 2, doing his best to bring Pearce round.

Finisterre was the biggest target in the room and potentially the most dangerous. Buckler barrelled straight into the loa zuvembie, knocking him off his feet. Sampson charged another of the zuvembies, while Lex took a slightly different tack. He snatched up the scalpel Couleuvre had used earlier, than dived over to the cousins and began sawing through their bonds.

A cry from Wilberforce alerted him to a zuvembie—Leroy—rushing towards him. Lex slithered around Leroy's legs and whipped the scalpel through one of his Achilles tendons then the other. Leroy flipped forwards under his own momentum, his feet staying flat on the floor, sundered at the ankle. He fell prone and Lex scrambled onto his back and dug the scalpel through the very jazzy beach shirt he was wearing, down in between two of his thoracic vertebrae. He levered the blade around. Blood and spinal fluid spurted.

Leroy was in effect quadriplegic now, but to make sure he was fully immobilised Lex tipped a heavy workbench over onto him. Then he finished freeing his friends.

Albertine sprang up and snatched her shoulder bag from the shelf where Couleuvre had placed it.

Lex ran to help Sampson, who was in difficulties. The Thirteener had managed to ram a retort stand part-way down the gullet of the zuvembie he was fighting, but the creature, undaunted, was clawing at his face, pushing his head away with tremendous force. Two of its fingers were inside Sampson's mouth and tearing at the corner of his lips. Its thumb was perilously close to gouging out an eye.

Lex hacked at one of its hands with the scalpel, slashing tendons. The hand went limp. Sampson, for his part, bit down on the two fingers, clamping his jaws together as hard as he could. His teeth severed the fingers at the first knuckle. He spat the tips out disgustedly and kept working with the retort stand, thrusting it even further inside the zuvembie like a plumber trying to unclog a blocked drain.

Buckler and Finisterre were going at it hammer and tongs, throwing each other back and forth across the laboratory, whaling on each other with whatever implements came to hand. Equipment crashed. Shelves were shattered. Broken glass flew. Finisterre—or was it Baron Samedi?—laughed uproariously, revelling in every second of this.

"Your soul is still your own," Samedi said in Finisterre's bassy tones. "Couleuvre failed to drive it down so far inside you that it was lost from sight. You must be strong in spirit. Or... is it somethin' else?"

Buckler's only response was to drive his fists into Finisterre's solar plexus. The big man flew backwards as though struck by a car, but he recovered and was back in the fray in a flash.

"Yeah," he said, clobbering Buckler with a computer keyboard. Plastic keys sprayed like handfuls of dice. "You've been places, haven't you? Your soul has travelled and returned, and that's given it strength—made it harder to shift. It was dislodged once, and it's learned to cling like a limpet to prevent a repeat of that. You're a lucky boy, soldier."

"Always... thought so," said Buckler, retaliating with an enamel kidney dish, which bent like tinfoil against Finisterre's skull.

Finisterre kneed him in the thigh, buckling his leg. "Doesn't make you immortal, though. I destroy this body of yours, you're done. But you destroy the one I'm usin', and what do I care? I'm a loa, just hitchin' a ride. This is rented accommodation, not my own house."

"You talk... too fucking... much." Buckler hurled a small trolley at Finisterre. "Giving me... earache."

Finisterre only laughed again. His exposed eye was lit up with a manic glee. "This is fun. You poundin' me, me poundin' you. Shame neither of us can really hurt the other."

"Won't... stop me from... trying."

"That's what I love about mortals. They don't give up, no matter how futile it seems. They're little sparks, burnin' briefly yet oh-so-brightly."

Both Lex and Sampson were still attempting to bring down the zuvembie they were grappling with. The last remaining zuvembie in the room had been prevented from reaching them by the savage fight between Buckler and Finisterre. It was stuck in a corner, unable to get past.

But now a gap appeared, and it lunged through...

...only to be confronted by Albertine, who tossed her *poudre* at it.

The zuvembie reeled and fell.

Albertine swung round and delivered another handful of *poudre*, this time at the zuvembie who was giving Lex and Sampson so much grief. It, too, fell.

A third handful went Finisterre's way, but he shrugged it off.

"I'm a loa, Damballah's girl!" he jeered. "You don't drive *me* out with a few herbs and a couple of lines of fancy prayer."

Panting hard, Lex scanned the room.

Someone was missing.

"Couleuvre," he said. "Where the hell's Couleuvre?"

"Bastard sneaked off," said Wilberforce. "Used the fighting as cover and scrammed."

"Where to?" asked Sampson.

Lex had a feeling he knew. "Where else? He's gone for his beloved bomb, hasn't he?"

"Then go... after him," said Buckler, injecting as much urgency as he could into his constricted, papery voice. "I'll... handle... this guy."

"Oh, you will, will you?" said Finisterre.

"I'll give it... my best fucking... shot."

"Wilb," said Lex. "See those two over there?" He was pointing at Tartaglione and Pearce. The former had managed to rouse the latter from unconsciousness. "Go with them. Pearce'll need help walking. Get to *Puddle Jumper* and start her up."

"What about you, man?"

"Duty calls."

Lex made for the door, along with Sampson. Albertine joined them, and it didn't even occur to either man to object or protest. The time when they had regarded her as a mere civilian noncombatant was long past.

The three of them ran along the passage, heading for Couleuvre's dig site, where the nuclear bomb lay and where the bokor's horde of undead slaves was at its densest and most numerous.

FORTY
THE BONDYE BOMB

ALBERTINE'S *POUDRE* TOOK care of the first two zuvembie guards they encountered, but her supply was almost exhausted.

"Only enough for one more," she said.

"Then make it him," said Lex, meaning a zuvembie Marine who was posted at the lip of the pit.

Albertine ran at the creature, ducking under his arm as he raised his gun to fire. A delicate hail of powder and a few muttered words felled him like a lumberjack's axe.

Lex relieved the Marine of his gun. He launched himself down into the pit, skidding around the worker zuvembies. He was of no interest to them. They had been programmed for a specific purpose. Nothing else mattered.

At the bottom, Couleuvre was squeezing himself legs first into a rough-hewn hole in the concrete. It was a tight fit. His shoulders barely got through.

Lex fired, but Couleuvre vanished into the aperture at the same moment. The bullet missed by a whisker.

Lex halted at the hole.

"Couleuvre! Listen to me. You don't have to do this. You have nothing to prove."

Below him, dimly, he made out a chamber the size of an upended cargo container. Somewhere at the base of it were two dark silhouettes. One was moving—Couleuvre. The other was static, an object with the dimensions of a refrigerator or a coffin—the nuke.

Lex loosed off two more shots. The reports were deafening in the confines of the chamber, the muzzle flashes blinding. He had no idea if he'd hit Couleuvre.

"That isn't God," he shouted down. "It's something left over from long ago that nobody wants."

"You have just described Bondye," Couleuvre replied. His voice sounded taut, with a pained, rasping edge to it. Had Lex winged him? Maybe even, with luck, wounded him fatally? "And what if He does not want us either? What if we are just a joke to Him? Bondye made us, then got bored, and now He just kicks us around. That is, when he can be bothered to remember us."

"Couleuvre." Albertine had slithered down to join Lex. "I speak with the authority of Damballah, the compassion of Erzulie Freda and the reason of Loko. As one *kanzo* initiate to another, I beg you, stop this now. Those who question Bondye's will always come off worst."

"I am questioning nothing, mambo. I am standing here daring Bondye to show Himself. If He is stronger than me, if He is so perfect and wonderful, He can prove it by manifesting His power. We will soon see if He really is God or just a weakling and a bully. I am not doing this for myself. Do you not see? It is on behalf of all of us, all mankind."

Lex's eyesight was adjusting to the gloom in the chamber. Couleuvre was bent over, fiddling with the bomb. Lex took aim, then realised that the gun was empty.

He tossed it aside. "Right, I'm going down in after him."

"Lex, you can't."

Just then an array of tiny lights winked on below. Their glow illuminated a control panel with a row of switches and knobs.

"*Bien,*" said Couleuvre. "There you are. I knew it. I knew you would not back away."

The bokor was limned by the panel lights. His face shone with sweat, avid, mad. A rivulet of blood glistened as it trickled from a wound in his arm.

"Couleuvre, it's not too late," said Lex. "Just think for a moment. Think it through. Mightn't this be what Bondye wants—you calling him out so that He can swat you like a fly? What's would be the point of it all then? You won't have achieved anything."

Couleuvre wasn't listening. He was busy with the control panel, trying switches, experimenting, figuring out.

All at once a humming filled the chamber—a high-pitched whine that sent a thrill of horror through Lex.

He heard a steady, inexorable ticking that emanated from the bomb. The sound of plastic numerals flipping over. A readout charting the time until detonation. Second after second, passing heavily, remorselessly.

Couleuvre took a step back. He flexed his fingers, limbering up. He began to pray, calling on Baron Samedi, Maman Brigitte, all of the loa, asking them for succour and power. "For Haiti," he said. "For your people. For justice. I will prevail."

Lex levered himself away from the hole. "Countdown's begun. No idea how long we've got."

"Can you shut it down?" Albertine asked.

"How? Nobody ever taught me defusing nukes. This one shouldn't even be working."

"Then we have to run."

"I don't know what difference it'll make, but hell yes."

THEY SCRAMBLED UP out of the pit on all fours. Lex didn't need to pause and explain to Sampson. One look at their faces and the Thirteener knew the worst.

They made for the stairs, full tilt. On the way they came across Finisterre's body. It lay half in, half out of the entrance to the laboratories. Finisterre's head was twisted round on his neck. His tongue bulged between his lips.

"The LT beat his ass," said Sampson. "Hot damn."

Then the overhead lights flickered and brightened. The installation seemed to buzz with sudden new life around them. Air conditioning units started up. Static sizzled over a PA system. The low, steady pulse of the geothermal plant could be felt through the soles of their feet.

"And he's got the power going again. Meaning..."

Lex finished the thought. "The elevator."

Buckler was waiting for them there. On his zuvembie-blank face there was just a perceptible hint of triumph.

"So we... win."

"Not quite," said Lex. "Couleuvre's about to get his private audience with the Almighty. Couldn't stop him."

"Shit. That's not... going to be... pretty."

They piled into the elevator and Sampson stabbed the button marked S for Surface. The doors rolled shut, but slowly, so slowly.

Too slowly.

A large hand shot through the opening. It clamped against the rim of one of the doors and began pushing it back. Another hand did the same with the other door.

Finisterre loomed through the gap. His head hung askew, ear touching shoulder. He said nothing—his kinked larynx prevented it—but his intent was clear. No one was escaping, not if he had anything to do with it.

Buckler applied himself to the left-hand door, providing a counterforce. Lex, Sampson and Albertine copied him with the right-hand door. Grunting, shoving, they resisted Finisterre's efforts. Finisterre silently strained. His head flopped forwards, lolling like a tulip on a broken stem.

Inch by inch, the doors began to creep back together.

Now Finisterre's knuckles were pressed against his temples. He slid his hands up over his head in an attempt to gain a better purchase.

"Harder," said Buckler.

One last desperate effort, and...

The doors squeezed Finisterre's neck. Buckler gave a final, full-zuvembie-strength thrust. They slammed together, decapitating Finisterre.

The head rolled onto the floor of the elevator, landing face up. Blood leaked from its pinched-off stump.

Somehow the sunglasses had stayed fixed in place throughout all of this, and Finisterre's visible eye glared balefully up at the four passengers as the elevator rose, shuddering and grinding, towards the surface. His mouth moved, as though there was much that he—or Baron Samedi—had to say.

Buckler stamped on the head, smashing it like a Halloween pumpkin.

"That's quite enough... of that," he said. "Sport."

FORTY-ONE
MYSTERIOUS WAYS

THEY RACED ACROSS the beach. Lex and Buckler were bent double, lugging a Zodiac behind them, Buckler doing most of the work. The other Zodiac bobbed out at sea, close to *Puddle Jumper*. A second seaplane sat an anchor a quarter-mile to the west. It was the one Finisterre had charted, a Grumman Albatross, larger than the Turbo Beaver, with a broad flat belly and floats attached to struts beneath the wings.

Everyone scrambled aboard the Zodiac in the shallows. Sampson pulled the starter cord on the outboard. The motor spluttered, died. Sampson tried again. Again no joy.

For Lex, the agony lay in not knowing how long the countdown timer on the nuke was set for. Five minutes? Ten? It would be better if they had a fixed deadline. At least then he might have some idea if they were going to make it. As things stood, the bomb could detonate at any moment. He assumed it had been fitted with a delay fuse long enough to allow for complete evacuation of the installation. But perhaps not. It was possible that, in the days of the Cold War, personnel at Anger Reef were expected to make the ultimate sacrifice if need be— all hands going down as the ship was scuttled.

Sampson cursed the motor after it failed to fire a third time.

Albertine snatched the starter cord out of his hand. "Damballah," she said, "be with us. Hear my plea."

She pulled, deftly.

The motor grumbled and then roared.

"All right!" said Sampson, beaming brightly. "Halle-goddamn-luiah."

He grabbed the tiller and gunned the throttle.

Puddle Jumper's turboprops were already turning.

"Can't be finessing this," Sampson said as the boat neared Anger Reef's protective ring of coral. "Just going to have to grit our teeth and go for it."

The tide had ebbed. The coral was closer to the surface. The Zodiac sped across the effervescent white water, scraping, bumping, bouncing. Rending sounds came from the hull as the speed skags were ripped to shreds.

Then a jutting spike of coral snagged one of the main chambers. There was a hiss of escaping air, and the Zodiac began listing precariously to one side.

Sampson's response was to pour on more speed.

The boat rode lower in the water. The outboard's blades screeched as they dug into the coral, churning it to bits.

"We're not going to—" Sampson began, and then the Zodiac slewed violently and capsized, flinging everyone out.

Bubbles thundered in Lex's ears. For several moments he had no idea which way was up. He thrashed, fighting turbulence. Abruptly he surfaced. He gasped in a breath, then peered around.

Heads popped up. Buckler. Sampson. Thank God, Albertine. They were all of them safe, treading water. The Zodiac, by contrast, was sinking, a saggy deflated wreck subsiding beneath the waves. As luck would have it, the boat had overturned just at the outer edge of the coral ring, depositing its passengers in open water. Had they been thrown onto the coral, none of them would be in one piece.

Lex turned to see *Puddle Jumper* chugging towards them. Tartaglione was leaning out from the door, one hand extended.

"Swim!" Lex yelled, and they did.

IN THE SEAPLANE, dripping wet, Buckler told Wilberforce to fly and not look back. Then he hailed the Albatross on the radio and gave its pilot similar advice.

When the pilot asked why, Buckler simply said that if he didn't he would die.

Out of the window, Lex saw the seaplane's propellers whir into life.

Puddle Jumper jockeyed across the water and finally soared free.

Anger Reef disappeared to the rear, quickly growing small. It looked serene, innocent, the sea lapping its fringes, the palms waving idly in the breeze. Lex found the island's superficial tranquillity hard to reconcile with the mayhem and murder that had gone on underground. Beneath paradise, hell.

Perhaps the nuke would not detonate. Fifty years old. After all this time, there was every reason to think it had become impotent.

And yet the control panel had lit up, the timer mechanism was still functional...

Anger Reef receded further into the distance. It seemed almost certain the bomb was a dud.

Then the island seemed to give a leap, as though thumped from below.

A heartbeat later, it crumbled into a bowl-shaped depression, imploding in on itself.

A heartbeat after that, the sea erupted in a perfect white dome, engulfing Anger Reef entirely.

It took several seconds for the shockwave from the explosion to reach *Puddle Jumper*. The airframe shook and rattled from end to end. Wilberforce fought with the yoke and pedals to keep the plane stable. *Puddle Jumper* dipped, yawed, then steadied.

"Jesus," breathed Sampson. "Shit. We're okay. I thought at the very least the nuke might frazzle the avionics."

"Underground nuclear explosions... don't give off... an electromagnetic pulse," said Buckler. "Only airburst ones... do. Something to do with... triggering changes... in the ionosphere."

"I'll remember that for next time," said Tartaglione.

The dome of water collapsed gracefully, flattening, smoothing. Soon it was just a circular blister in the sea, flecked with roiling debris and glittering dead fish.

A voice came over the radio—the Albatross's pilot. "Man, what in hell's name was that?"

"Don't ask," said Wilberforce. "Just be glad you got clear in time."

PUDDLE JUMPER SAILED on, and Lex looked across the aisle at Albertine. She smiled wanly. He smiled back. Neither of them spoke. Nothing needed to be said. They were alive. They had survived.

Silence reigned throughout *Puddle Jumper*. Buckler finally broke it.

"Couleuvre... got his wish. He and God... went toe-to-toe. God got in... the knockout punch."

"Sounds like you mean it, LT," said Sampson. "Like you're saying it really was God back there."

Buckler did a stiff approximation of a shrug. "How else... could a nuke that old... have worked? The Lord moves... in mysterious ways... but He *does* move."

"Sure does," said Tartaglione. "He brought you back from the dead, didn't he? Just when we needed you. Honest-to-gosh miracle."

Buckler nodded noncommittally. "Still not... sure how I'm... feeling about that," he said. "Might take a while... to adjust to... how I am now. I'm not what I... used to be... that's for damn sure. But I may just be... a little bit better. Anyways, don't... worry your pretty little heads... about me. I can... deal. Pearce? What's your... status?"

At the back of the plane, an ashen-faced Pearce lofted his hand feebly. "Laughing."

"Hang in... there. When we're closer to land... we'll radio ahead... for an ambulance. Get you seen to... ASAP."

"Aces."

"And you, Dove." Buckler turned his dead, yellow gaze on Lex. "I said... we had to talk. Now's the... time."

"What's there to say?" said Lex.

"Plenty."

"Can't the debriefing wait? I'd rather just enjoy the fact that I'm still breathing."

"This isn't... a debriefing. So shut up... and listen. You're not going to... like what you hear... but you need to... hear it."

FORTY-TWO
HOME

PUDDLE JUMPER HAD taken off from Anger Reef with seven people on board.

It landed at Manzanilla with six.

Pearce and Tartaglione were whisked straight off to hospital.

Sampson accompanied them.

Buckler returned to the Cape Azure Hotel to file his mission report to his bosses in Washington.

Wilberforce and Albertine both drove to their respective homes for a shower, a meal, and a good long rest.

FOR THE NEXT several days, Rikki the mongoose hung around outside Lex's house. He snuffled about in the garden and along the verandah, perpetually on the lookout for food. There was always plenty for an omnivore like him to eat—grubs, rats, small birds, fruit, the odd snake—but he especially enjoyed the tasty scraps the human gave him. That was the extent to which he missed Lex, unsentimental beast that he was.

Rikki wasn't actively waiting for the human to return. The house felt strange without its owner there, however. Too quiet. As the days passed, the mongoose began to think about moving on elsewhere, finding a new burrow, new hunting grounds, a new home...

EPILOGUE

CAROLINE HARTINGTON SWITCHED on the house's security system, as she did every night at roughly the same hour, 10PM. A series of bleeps and flashing LEDs indicated that the entire building was in lockdown mode. Every door and window was now electronically bolted and wired to sound the alarm at the least sign of forced entry. The CCTV cameras that covered porch, driveway and back garden were all fully active. The panic buttons were live. The Hartington family's large Victorian semi-detached villa in Holland Park had become effectively a fortress.

She went upstairs to check on the kids in their rooms. Saskia was Skyping with her best friend Emily. Teddy was doing his homework, nodding along to the music in his earbuds while he sourced facts for a history essay online.

Caroline then popped her head round the door of Peter's study. He too was at his computer, going over the closing figures on Wall Street with a glass of brandy to hand. She tiptoed in and planted a kiss on the bald crown of his head. Peter patted her rump with absentminded affection.

All was well. All was as it should be. Her home was quiet and peaceful. Her family were all safe and sound under one roof.

A feeling of inexpressible contentment washed over Caroline.

She went to the kitchen for a glass of Chablis. This, too, was part of her evening routine, an indulgence at the end of the day, a signal to herself that she could finally begin to unwind and relax. She would sip the wine while checking her phone for any last messages that needed attending to, and then maybe draw herself a nice hot bath laced with lavender oil.

She opened the door of the huge Smeg refrigerator and fetched out a bottle.

When she closed the door, a man was standing beside her.

An intruder.

The chilled, condensation-slick bottle slipped from Caroline's grasp.

The man caught it before it hit the floor.

"Mustn't waste that," he said. "Looks like a decent tipple. Oh, and a loud crash might bring hubby running, and we wouldn't want that, would we, Caroline?"

He smiled.

"Or should I say Seraphina?"

"Leonard," Caroline managed to stammer out.

"No. Lex. Remember?"

"Lex. But—but you're..."

"Dead?" The smile widened. "So Lieutenant Buckler said in his report. So you were meant to believe."

Caroline whipped round and lunged for the knife block on the countertop nearby. She drew a huge Sabatier carver and brandished it in front of her defensively.

Lex shook his head, pitying. "Come on, Caroline. We both know I can have that off you before you ever get a chance to use it."

"Don't come any closer." Caroline began edging away from him. The microwave was just a metre away, almost within arm's reach. "Don't even think about it."

"And you," said Lex, "stay absolutely still. Don't move another inch. I know there's a panic button inbuilt into that microwave. You tap in a four-digit code, and a car full of MI5 operatives will be here in under three minutes. How on earth is that going to help you? In three minutes I can kill you, both your children and the very wealthy Peter, and be long gone before the security detail arrives."

Caroline halted. The logic in Lex's statement was irrefutable. Hitting the panic button would achieve nothing apart from hastening her death and the deaths of her family.

"Kill me then," she said, "but for pity's sake leave my husband and kids alone. They've done nothing." Her voice dropped an octave, becoming the husky, seductress tones of Seraphina. "Please, Lex. At least do that for me. After all we've been through together, all we've shared..."

"I have questions," Lex said. "Here." He handed her the wine. "Sit. Have a drink."

Caroline was puzzled, but she sensed she was being granted a stay of execution—a chance to state her case—and she took it. She uncorked the Chablis and glugged some of it into a glass with a trembling hand. She sat at the island in the middle of the kitchen, placing the knife next to her on the marble work surface. Lex perched on a stool on the opposite side. Caroline took a long swig of the wine. The knot in her stomach loosened a little.

"Well now, where do I start?" Lex said. "It was all a set-up, wasn't it? Me going to Anger Reef. I was never meant to be just a liaison for Team Thirteen in Manzanilla. The plan all along was that I would have to participate in the actual mission."

Caroline nodded. "Why else do you think we offered you silly money?"

"That was you? Not the Americans?"

"Us. I faked that whole business of checking to see if they would agree to raising the offer. We were prepared to go up as far as five hundred thousand if you'd kept haggling. The whole point was to make the financial carrot irresistible. A sum you couldn't turn down."

"And getting Wilberforce involved—another essential component of the plan."

"Absolutely. Team Thirteen could have inserted into that installation in any number of ways. But since you happened to have a close friend who happened to be a seaplane pilot... Well, it was perfect. We predicted you would never let Allen go on his own. You'd tag along to make sure that he was okay. And then his cousin got drawn into it as well, that girl, what's her name? Augustine?"

"Albertine."

The way he said it confirmed Lieutenant Buckler's hints in his report. The girl and Lex were an item. "Albertine," Caroline said. "We had to make sure that you had plenty invested in the mission, a significant personal as well as practical stake. Did you work all of this out for yourself or did somebody tell you?"

"It should have been the former but in fact it was the latter."

"Who?"

"Buckler. He wanted a clean slate with me."

"How indiscreet of him."

"Maybe. But the Tom Buckler who went into Anger Reef was not the Tom Buckler who came out. He's a changed man in so many ways."

"I'll say," said Caroline. "Medics at Walter Reed Naval Hospital in Bethesda, Maryland, have been poking and prodding him like mad."

"Bet he's loving that."

"They can barely account for what's happened to him, but they're very excited. He's become almost superhuman, I hear. Increased strength, enhanced endurance..."

"At the expense of being clinically dead. Hardly a fair deal, I'd say. What I want to know—need to know—is why? Why do this to me? Why drag me into a mission long after I'd officially retired?"

Caroline took a fresh sip of wine, this one calmer and more measured than before. "Why do *you* think, Lex?"

"I assume to get rid of me," he said. "You suckered me into going on a high-risk op in the expectation that I wouldn't return."

"And what benefit would that be to us?"

"Old wetwork pros aren't meant to live out the rest of their days in peace. They know too much. They know—literally— where the bodies are buried. You yourself told me that you were still keeping tabs on me in case I was bribed or captured by people from the other side. Simpler, cleaner, to do away with me. Snip the thread rather than let it unravel."

"So you faked your death. You had Lieutenant Buckler claim in his report that you'd been killed at Anger Reef, another mission casualty like Hospitalman Morgenstern."

"Wilberforce dropped me off close to Manzanilla. I swam ashore at a quiet cove and I've been lying low ever since."

"Except here you are," said Caroline. "Suddenly back in the land of the living."

"I had to stay off the grid so that I could travel to London and have this chat. It was the only way I could get answers."

"You could just have phoned. Far less effort than crossing the Atlantic, locating me, staking out my house, breaking in..."

"Face-to-face is better."

"You wanted to see me, Lex. Admit it. After all this time, you were curious to get a glimpse of the real Seraphina."

"That was a factor," Lex acknowledged.

"And?"

"You're not what I imagined. But then I didn't think you were going to be."

Caroline pouted, but she knew it was true. The persona she projected as Seraphina did not reflect the real her. The real her was an average-looking fortysomething wife and mother with a bit of a turkey neck and boobs that were nowhere near as pert as they had been before childbirth. She ate sensibly, did Pilates, tried as hard as she could to keep in trim. Expensive auburn highlights masked the ineluctable onset of grey hair.

Ultimately, though, she was waging a losing war against age and cellulite.

Seraphina was an idealised version of herself, a role she played, a slim, gorgeous, commanding figure who flirted outrageously, never grew old and always had fun. This was one reason she was glad none of the operatives she controlled was ever likely to meet her in person. The woman she wanted them to picture was a far cry from the woman she was.

"Also," Lex said, "on the phone you could tell me anything, any old rubbish. This way I'm guaranteed to get at the truth."

"You'd like the truth?"

"I'll be annoyed if you try to fob me off with anything else."

"Then here it is. We didn't want you dead."

"Really?"

"No. It would be a shame, a great loss. We do still trust you, Lex. You were a loyal knight for so long. All the psychiatric evaluations have you down as someone who would never betray his country. We wanted you back in the game. That's all."

Lex was startled.

"Oh yes," Caroline went on. "You're too valuable an asset to be languishing out there kicking your heels in some Caribbean nowhere. You still have plenty of years of usefulness in you. When the Yanks contacted us about hiring you, we saw a chance to lure you back. We thought, 'Give him a taste of action again, remind him what it was like, he'll come crawling on hands and knees begging for more.' We've never regarded the past few years as retirement. You may have, but we've always thought of it as a sabbatical."

Lex was silent, digesting the news. The kitchen clock ticked softly.

He said, "Part of me thinks you're lying. Just trying to save your own skin. But another part of me..." He trailed off.

"Do you want to be back in, Leonard?" This time, her use of his former forename was deliberate. "The door is wide open.

We'd welcome you like a shot. I've got at least three Code Crimsons I could send you on right now. How does South Africa sound? I'm told Cape Town is lovely this time of year."

She could see he was debating it inwardly.

But not for long.

"No," he said. Firmly. With finality. "I have a new life. I like it. I have friends. A woman—an amazing woman. It's all waiting for me back on Manzanilla. That's where I belong. That's the future. Me and Wilberforce out on our boat. Me and Albertine, getting to know each other better. I'm... I'm happy, Seraphina. Happy in a way I've never known before. So thanks, but no."

He stood. He looked as though he was going to depart. Or perhaps not.

"Are you...?" said Caroline.

"Am I what?"

"Going to kill me now?" Her voice was small and meek, mouse-like.

Lex leaned close to her, his reflection appearing in the well-sharpened blade of the carver.

"Not so long ago," he said, "someone gave me some advice. Someone who deserves paying attention to. He said, 'Dead men won't lie and liars won't die.' I thought it was a prediction but it seems it was a recommendation as well."

"What does it mean?"

"In this context, I'm the dead man who won't lie down, and you're the professional liar who isn't going to die. At least not today. I promise you that."

Caroline's shoulders sagged with relief.

"But," said Lex, "call me again, ever, about anything, and—"

He faked grabbing for the carver.

Caroline almost fainted. Her heart clattered like a toy rattle. "Clear?"

She just about managed to compose herself. "Crystal."

"Good. I'll see myself out."

For a long time after Lex was gone, Caroline Hartington sat nerveless, numb, scarcely able to move.

Finally she took out her phone and scrolled through the directory to the name Leonard Duncan. She selected Delete from the options menu.

The onscreen prompt said:

Delete contact.
Are you sure?

Caroline, never surer, hit the Yes icon.

END CREDITS

Author . . . . James Lovegrove
Solaris Editor in Chief . . . . Jon Oliver
Solaris Desk Editor . . . . David Moore
Solaris Publishing Manager . . . . Ben Smith
Publicity . . . . Michael Molcher
Technical Assistance . . . . Jonathan Morgantini
Cheerleading . . . . Kit Reed
Essential Maintenance Staff . . . . . . Lou Lovegrove

TEAM THIRTEEN MAY RETURN...